Bobby March
Will Live Forever

Bobby March
Will Live Forever

Alan Parks

W F HOWES LTD

This large print edition published in 2020 by
W F Howes Ltd
Unit 5, St George's House, Rearsby Business Park,
Gaddesby Lane, Rearsby, Leicester LE7 4YH

1 3 5 7 9 10 8 6 4 2

First published in the United Kingdom in 2020
by Canongate Books Ltd

A CIP catalogue record for this book is available
from the British Library

ISBN 978 1 00400 347 1

Typeset by Palimpsest Book Production Limited,

For Pamela Hunter
and for Dale Barclay

'Control thy passions lest they take vengeance on thee'
　　　　　　　　　　　　– Epictetus

'So you want to be a rock 'n' roll star'
　　　　　　　　　　　　– The Byrds

It's Billy the desk sergeant that takes the call. A woman on the phone, breathless, scared, half crying. She says, 'I'd like to report a missing child.' And suddenly everything changes.

When news of a call like that comes in, everyone sits up at their desks, stops filling in their pools coupon, puts down their half-eaten rolls. The ones with kids open their wallets under their desks, look at the pictures of Colin or Anne or wee Jane and thank God it's not theirs that have gone. The young ones look serious, try not to imagine pulling some weeping toddler from a cellar or from under a bed, being congratulated by the boss, thanked by a tearful mother.

Those that are religious cross themselves or say a silent prayer to keep the kid safe. And those that have lived through a case like this before say hello to the familiar dread and fear in their stomach, the knowledge that there is no end of bad things that men can do to children, that the missing child might be better off dead already.

And like a pebble dropped in the water, the ripples start to spread throughout the city. No matter the lockdown, news of a missing child always gets out. Cops come home, tell their wives and girlfriends not to tell anyone but they do. A shilling drops in a phone box across the road from the station, a reporter at the **Daily Record** answers and a beat cop earns a tenner for his trouble. Isn't long until the boys selling the papers outside Central Station are shouting 'Final edition! Missing girl!'

And before you know it the missing girl is all the city is talking about. It's all the cops talk about when they assemble in church halls to get instructions for the search, all the reporters talk about – how they can get to the parents, taking bets on when she'll be found. It's all the kids in the back courts talk about, whispered rumours and stories about being dragged into a car.

And as the night falls and the chatter dies down there's still one person who doesn't know what Glasgow is talking about. Alice Kelly. She's the one person who doesn't know that all of Glasgow is talking about her. All she knows is that she's got a cloth bag over her head, that her hands are tied and that she's wet her pants. And there's one other thing Alice knows. It doesn't matter how hard she cries for her mum, her mum can't hear her. Nobody can.

16th February 1964

Glasgow

The train was freezing but he didn't care. The 6.15 to King's Cross. He was really going. Tom had brought a bag of cans with him, handed them out as they left Central. They were drinking them now. Him, Scott, Barry and Jamie. All of them feet up on the seats, full of chips, smoking away. Telling jokes. Pretending they weren't nervous.

Bobby sat forward and checked his pocket again. It was there, just like every other time he'd checked. The contract he'd had to beg his dad to sign. Couldn't sign it himself, too young, only seventeen. His dad said he should become an apprentice, steady money, but no way was he doing that. Two weeks of sulking and begging and eventually his dad gave in.

He couldn't believe it when he saw it. Parlophone written at the top of it. Just like The Beatles. Exclusive rights to the music of The Beatkickers. Wee Bobby March from Arden, him, in a train going to London to do a recording session for the same

3

label as The Beatles. Tom said it would be fine, told him not to worry about it, that he was the only one of them that could actually bloody play.

He looked round the carriage. Tom wasn't wrong. Jamie was a half-decent drummer when he tried. Scott couldn't play the bass to save his life and Barry could hold a tune. Just. But that wasn't all that mattered, Tom said. What mattered was that Barry was good-looking, very good-looking. And he knew it. Steel comb was never out his hand, fixing his hair, wee backcomb to give it height, then a perfect blond fringe. Clothes always right, whitest teeth Bobby had ever seen.

The carriage door slid back and Tom was standing there. Polo neck and a pair of denims. Was a big guy, Tom, six foot odds, strong. Used to work on the furniture vans. Now he was the Beatkickers' manager, had bought them the suits and everything. And they were going places. He clapped his hands.

'All good, boys?' he asked.

They nodded, held up the cans in cheers.

Scott dropped his chin to his chest, burped loudly. They all started laughing.

'Dirty bugger,' said Tom, pretended to give him a clout over the ear. Scott swerved, almost fell off the seat.

'That'll teach you,' said Tom. Then he pointed at Barry. 'You, son, you come wi' me for a minute.'

Bobby took a swig of his warm beer, wondered why it was always Barry Tom needed to talk to. Maybe he was giving him tips about tomorrow, microphones, that sort of stuff. Barry stood up, followed Tom out the door. Scott burped again. They laughed again.

13TH JULY 1973

CHAPTER 1

McCoy looked at his watch. Quarter past eight. The call had come in just before six last night, so fifteen hours or so she had been missing. The time for her to have got lost or stayed at a pal's was long gone. A thirteen-year-old girl doesn't go missing for fifteen hours, overnight, without something being very, very wrong.

He turned into Napiershall Street and swore. Any hope he'd had of having a quiet look around was gone. The circus had already come to town. Concerned-looking mums with weans in their arms talking to each other in hushed voices, kids attracted by the police cars, a few press blokes he recognised from the dailies sitting on the wall smoking, waiting for any new developments. *Evening Times* photographer wiping the lens of his camera with his tie. Four or five panda cars parked outside the pub and an incident van set up across the road. Was even some nutter with a sandwich board with a biblical quote on it walking up and down, handing out tracts. He swore under his breath, crossed the road and headed for the entrance.

7

The doors of the Woodside Inn had been wedged open to try and let some air in. He stepped in and realised it wasn't doing much good, was even hotter inside. A few shafts of light from the closed-over shutters pierced the fog of dust and cigarette smoke, making the place feel more like a church than a Maryhill pub. Took his eyes a few seconds to adjust to the gloom, to see how much the Woodside had changed.

Wasn't really a pub any more, was now a temporary Police HQ. Twenty or so uniforms, hats off, sleeves rolled, were sitting on the benches at the back being handed door-to-door assignments by Thomson. A big map of the surrounding area – Maryhill, North Woodside, Firhill – was laid out on one of the tables, corners held down by Johnnie Walker water jugs. Map was marked into sections, some of them scored off already. A young police-woman was wandering round with a tray of pint glasses full of water, handing them out to everyone. Two blokes in boiler suits were trying to connect three navy-blue telephones sitting on the bar, while the landlord sat on a stool at the side looking like he didn't know what had hit him, fag in one hand, pint in the other.

The door to the Gents opened and the one person McCoy didn't want to see came out, wiping his hands on a paper towel. Bernie Raeburn in all his portly glory. Raeburn was one of those men that took a bit too much care over what they looked like. Brylcreemed hair, neat moustache,

8

silver tie pin, shoes shined. Probably thought he looked quite the thing. To McCoy, he just looked like what he was: a wide boy. Raeburn dropped the paper towel into a bin by one of the tables and peered over at McCoy. Didn't look happy to see him. Didn't look happy at all.

'What you doing here?' he asked.

'Was at a call round the corner. Just came to see if there was anything I could do?' said McCoy.

'Did you now?' said Raeburn, looking amused. 'Think we'll manage. Plenty of us boys here already.'

'Okay.' McCoy resisted the urge to tell Raeburn exactly where to shove his boys. 'Any news?'

'Getting there,' said Raeburn. 'Getting there . . .'

He held his finger up. Wait. Took his suit jacket off, smoothed down his pale blue shirt. Decided he was ready to speak.

'Actually, McCoy, there is something you can do to help. Need you to go back to the shop, tell Billy on the front desk to start calling round. Want anyone who hasn't already gone on their holidays back in, soon as. Need the manpower for the door-to-doors.'

McCoy nodded, kept his temper. Tried not to look at the row of new telephones on the bar.

'So the sooner the better, eh?' added Raeburn, looking at the door.

McCoy stood there for a minute, trying to decide what to do. The pub had suddenly gone silent, could even hear the big black flies buzzing against the windows. Knew everyone was

9

watching, waiting to see what would happen. Round twenty-odds in the continuing fight between Raeburn and McCoy. They'd even opened a book back at the shop: how long will it take before one lamps the other? Current best bet was about a week.

McCoy took a breath, smiled. Being talked to like that was almost more than he could take but he knew that unless he did exactly what Raeburn told him, he'd be on report soon as Raeburn's fat fingers could fill out the form. Raeburn's plan was simple. Just keep pushing and pushing in the hope McCoy'd react and then he would have an excuse to get rid of him. McCoy wasn't going to give the bastard the satisfaction. Not today anyway.

'Will do,' he said cheerily.

He was outside the pub before his fists uncurled. He got his cigarettes out his pocket, was lighting up, thinking of the various and many ways he'd like to hurt Raeburn, when he looked up and Wattie was standing there.

'Heard you were here, sir,' he said.

'Was at a call. Offered to help but seems Raeburn's fine as he is. Wants me to get back to the shop.'

Wattie's blond hair was stuck to his head with sweat. Dark rings spread around the underarms of his short-sleeved shirt. He wiped a hanky across his forehead, noticed McCoy looking.

'Been doing door-to-doors, up and down the bloody stairs of these closes,' he said. 'I'm sweating like a glassblower's arse.'

McCoy laughed. 'Christ, Wattie, where'd you get that one?'

Wattie grinned. 'My dad used to say it.' He opened his top button, loosened his tie. 'First time I've actually known what he meant.'

'So that's the bold Raeburn's great idea, is it?' asked McCoy. 'Interview a load of people who've seen and heard bugger all so he can tick that off on his list? He's even stupider than I thought.'

'Harry, come on, It's no my fault that Raeburn is—'

'I know, I know,' said McCoy. 'Just joking.'

Wattie was right. It really wasn't his fault. Poor guy, caught between the devil and the deep blue sea and he knew it. Had to take his hat off to the bastard for that one. What better way to wind McCoy up than by keeping him away from what was going to be the biggest case of the year and bringing Wattie in as his right-hand man. Rubbing salt in the wound didn't come into it.

Wattie held up a list of addresses. 'Got to ring a few more bells. Want to come with me?'

McCoy nodded and they set off up Maryhill Road, sticking to the shady side of the street.

'Any news?' he asked.

Wattie shook his head. 'Nothing we didn't know last night. Alice Kelly's still missing and half the Glasgow force are running around like blue-arsed flies trying to find her.'

'What's the mum saying?' asked McCoy, as they

11

walked round a queue of people waiting at the bus stop outside McGovern's.

'Not much. If the poor cow's no crying, she's almost catatonic. Her sister's come from Linlithgow, she's up there with her now. Next-door neighbour's taken the baby in.' Wattie got his hanky out his pocket, wiped the sweat from his forehead again. 'You should see the house, it's mental. Like a bloody shrine. Celtic, the Pope and John F. Bloody Kennedy.'

McCoy smiled. 'Sounds like every other good Catholic household. Half the houses in Glasgow are like that.'

'Maybe,' said Wattie. 'But the whole bloody place was covered. I even got a tea in a mug with the bloody Lisbon Lions on it.'

'Surprised you managed to swallow it through your gritted teeth,' said McCoy. 'She give a statement?'

Wattie nodded. 'Seems the wee girl was cracking on all morning, asking her mum for money for a cone. The baby was playing up and her moaning wasn't helping, so she gives in and says the girl can have five pence.'

McCoy looked back down the street. 'She go into Cocozza's?'

Wattie shook his head. 'She met the neighbour that's taken the baby when she came out the close, told her she was going up to Jaconelli's.'

They looked up the hill, could see the familiar awning of Jaconelli's in the distance.

'Cone's only four pence up there, it's five in

Cocozza's. If she went to Jaconelli's she'd have a penny left for the penny tray, was going to get a bazooka joe. Mum thought she was just coming down to Cocozza's across the street. Only reason she let her go.'

'So?' asked McCoy, getting his cigarettes out his pocket. 'Let me guess. Seen in Jaconelli's then?'

Wattie shook his head. 'Nope. The last sighting was the neighbour. Saw her walking up Maryhill Road before she went back in the close. She disappeared into thin air somewhere between her flat and Jaconelli's.'

'And what's Raeburn saying to that?' said McCoy, stopping to light up.

Wattie checked his list of addresses, looked up the street and they started walking again.

'He's saying someone must have seen her. He's got every bugger he can get a hold of, including me, doing door-to-doors. Forty-six is up here, no answer last night or earlier this morning.'

'He's from Govan, Raeburn. Glasgow born and bred,' said McCoy, shaking his head. 'You'd think he'd realise these door-to-doors are a waste of time.'

Wattie looked at him. 'How come?'

'There's a reason no one's answering. Today's Fair Friday. Most of the people that were around yesterday will have left today for their holidays. You're going to be knocking on a lot of empty doors. Even if somebody did see her, they'll no be back for a fortnight.'

Wattie looked pained. 'Shite. Never thought of that.'

'Aye well, you're from Greenock, that's an excuse. Raeburn should have, though. Whole bloody city is on holiday for the next two weeks.'

Wattie checked his bit of paper, stopped outside a close. 'This is us. They knocked the door last night, no answer. Trying again.'

'Great,' said McCoy. 'Please don't tell me it's the top flat.'

'You're in luck,' said Wattie, stepping into the dark of the close. 'First floor.'

They tramped up the stairs. Inside of the close was cool and dark, with just the noise of a radio from one of the flats. Sounded like Lulu, of all people.

'Where's the dad?' asked McCoy, as Wattie knocked on the door.

'Belfast, apparently. Working. Been away for a week or so.'

No reply. Tried again.

'Mother got a boyfriend?' asked McCoy.

'Don't know,' said Wattie.

'Should find out. You know as well as me, nine times out of ten it's the dad or the stepdad.'

Knocked again. They waited.

'Told you,' said McCoy. 'Be away on their holidays.'

Wattie nodded, looked at his bit of paper.

'How many more? asked McCoy.

A quick totting-up. 'Another twelve.'

They walked back down the stairs, could hear the radio better now. Definitely Lulu. 'I'm A

Tiger'. They stepped out the close, back into the heat and the glare of the sun.

'Well, much as I'd like to accompany you on your travels, Wattie, I have my orders. Have to get back to the shop.'

Wattie looked pained. 'Harry, you know working with Raeburn isn't up to me. I didn't even want—'

McCoy held his hand up. 'I know, I know. Don't worry about it, it's between me and Raeburn. And I'm not that bothered. Quite enjoying the peace and quiet. But you stick in there. This is a big case, see what you can learn.'

Wattie grinned. 'Then report back to you?'

'Did I say that? Now, beat it before Raeburn sends out the search party.'

Wattie nodded, started walking up the road, stopped and turned. 'Forgot to say. Think Raeburn might be putting you on they bank robberies.'

'What?' said McCoy, dismayed. 'You're joking, aren't you?'

Wattie grinned. 'Thought you'd be happy. Got to be better than twiddling your thumbs, though.'

'Not for me, it's not. I like twiddling my thumbs.' Dawned on him. 'And this would be the robberies you and Raeburn have been on for two months and still haven't got anywhere? Great. Tell him thanks but no thanks.'

'Not sure you've got much of a choice,' said Wattie. 'What you going to say to him?'

McCoy sighed. Knew Wattie was right. Just when things couldn't get any worse, they had.

15

'Please tell Detective Sergeant Raeburn I would be delighted to help with the investigation in any way I can.'

Wattie smiled. 'I'll maybe not say it exactly like that. Files are on my desk. Have a look.'

Wattie waved, walked up the road looking back down at his bit of paper. McCoy watched him go, couldn't believe how hot it was already. Might get a taxi to the shop, wasn't sure he could face walking there, not in this weather. Anyway, wasn't like he was going to get a hold of anyone. Anyone who had holidays would have gone by now, and even if they hadn't, they weren't stupid enough to answer the phone and get pulled back in. He opened his packet of fags and realised he'd only one left. Crossed the street to the newsagent. There was a board leaning against the wall outside. Crossed wire covering the headline.

'SEARCH CONTINUES FOR MISSING GIRL'.

Raeburn had his work cut out for him. This was the kind of case that sells papers, gets people talking, wanting to know all the grisly details. The kind that gets a braying crowd outside the court. Pitt Street would be on him too. Longer the girl was missing, the more incompetent the polis would look and the big boys couldn't have that. They'd want her found, soon as. And if she was dead by the time Raeburn found her? Then he'd better get the guy who did it. And quick.

CHAPTER 2

McCoy recognised the shirt. Was made of some sort of black see-through material with wee silver stars on it. He recognised it because he'd had the same one on last night, only then he was onstage at the Electric Garden, not lying in an unmade bed with a syringe sticking out his arm. Rest of the outfit was the same, too. Jeans, pointed cowboy boots, some thin silver chains around his neck and some cloth bands tied round his wrists. Hair was remarkably intact. That spiky blond feather cut you would recognise at a hundred yards. That, the hooked nose and the wide grin that made up Bobby March. Rock star.

He'd only been back in the shop five minutes, had just got the phone list from Billy on the front desk and was about to call Sammy Howe to tell him his trip to Aviemore was off when the phone started ringing. Was the manager of the Royal Stuart Hotel. Suspicious death. And, being the only bugger left in the shop, he had to deal with it. He'd been expecting to see some businessman lying dead with a heart attack, wallet cleaned out by whichever girl he'd picked up on the Green. Really wasn't expecting this, not at all.

He was trying to breathe through his mouth, but it wasn't doing much good. There was no way around it: the hotel room stank. Incense sticks, sweat, whatever Bobby March had eaten the night before. He walked over and opened the window: immediately, the noise of the trains on the bridge, glare of the sun on the Clyde below. He stood there for a minute looking out, trying to let the room fill up with less fetid air. Was helping a bit.

He turned. 'They know yet?' he asked the hotel manager.

'Who?'

'The hardcore downstairs,' said McCoy.

He'd had to walk through them to get in the hotel entrance. Four or five teenage girls and one boy with glitter all over his face. All of them had the cloth bangles, most had an approximation of the crop. Couple of them in Bobby March T-shirts. The boy's had looked homemade. Fuck knows what they would be like when the news broke.

'Don't imagine so,' said the hotel manager.

McCoy looked at him. Tweed jacket, toothbrush moustache, ramrod straight back. Didn't look like he'd be very familiar with rock stars or drug over- doses. More likely parade grounds and shouting at scared National Service boys.

'Rest of the band?' asked McCoy.

'Billeted in deluxe rooms downstairs,' said the manager. 'All still asleep, apparently.' Look on his

18

face demonstrating exactly what he thought about that kind of behaviour.

'And the maid discovered him when?' asked McCoy.

'About ten thirty. She knocked a few times, called out, but there was no response. Thought the guest had checked out. Most do by that hour. No response from his room so she used the master key to get in.'

'And he was . . .'

The manager pointed at the bed. 'Exactly like that.'

McCoy looked over at Bobby March again. Remembered what he'd been like last night, up on the stage. Shit, if he was honest. He'd looked out of it, forgetting words, half playing the songs. McCoy was about to leave, call it a night, when March turned to the band and nodded.

First notes of 'Sunday Morning Symphony' rang out and suddenly Bobby March moved up a gear, became what he had once been, the best guitarist of his generation. He grabbed the mic, grinned, sang the first line and the crowd, including McCoy, went mental. This was what they had all come to hear. He powered through all twelve minutes of the song, played out his skin, made you remember why The Rolling Stones had asked him to join, and ended on a dime.

The hall went wild, standing, clapping, shouting. March stood there sweating, looked wrung out, whatever power he'd summoned had run out.

'This is from our new album, *Starshine*!' he announced, and that's when McCoy left. He'd had the misfortune to hear it.

The stuff about The Rolling Stones had haunted Bobby March ever since it happened. They'd asked him to audition after Brian Jones got chucked out. He came down to Barnes, did a couple rehearsals at Olympic. Keith Richards told some reporter waiting outside that it was 'the best version of the Stones there ever was' and they asked him to join.

Bobby did the one thing nobody, including Keith Richards, expected. He said thanks but no thanks. Had decided he had his own career to follow. By the look of the hotel room, the half-empty takeaway boxes, and the fact he was staying in the Royal Stuart and not the Albany, playing the Electric Garden not the Apollo, it might not have been the best decision Bobby March ever made.

'Twenty-seven,' said McCoy. 'Another one.'

The manager looked blank.

'Jimi Hendrix, Janis Joplin, Jim Morrison. All twenty-seven when they died.'

The manager nodded, still no real idea what he was talking about.

McCoy sat down on one of the chairs in the wee seating area. There was an acoustic guitar leaning against the coffee table, leather jacket on the other chair, copy of *Melody Maker* and an overflowing ashtray by the side of the bed. Not exactly private jets and TVs out the window. Just a room in the

20

kind of hotel that made its money from weddings and Masonic dinners.

If Bobby March had to die, he'd probably done it at the right time. Probably be more famous dead than he was alive. Two great albums, *Sunday Morning Symphony* in 1970 and *Postcard From Muscle Shoals* in '71. Still, two great albums were better than loads of rotten ones. McCoy bent forward. A couple of the cigarette ends had lipstick on them.

'No girlfriend?' he asked the manager.

He shook his head. 'Just Mr March.'

McCoy walked over by the bed, had another look around. Wasn't quite sure what he was looking for. Lipstick on the pillow? A forgotten earring? Whatever it was, it wasn't there. Seemed odd for a rock star to be sleeping alone. Or maybe McCoy just believed all the sex, drugs and rock and roll stories. He walked through to the bathroom. Didn't know what he was looking for there either. A message on the mirror in red lipstick? All he found was a shaving kit, a bottle of hay fever tablets and a plectrum on the edge of the sink. He put that in his pocket. Souvenir. Walked back through to the bedroom.

The stink of the room hit him again. In this heat, it was impossible to avoid. Not much he could do here and the sight of the lifeless body on the bed was getting to him. McCoy told the manager he'd wait for the medical examiner downstairs and left him staring at the body. He stepped out the room into the long corridor. Only smelt marginally better. A bucket of floor cleaner and a half-eaten hamburger sat on a tray outside one of the rooms.

He should really have told the manager not to let any press or photographers in, but he forgot. If truth be told, he wasn't really focused on Bobby March and his untimely demise. Mind more concentrated on the fact he was down to acting as a duty officer at a suspicious death. Much as he'd liked Bobby March's music, the last thing he wanted to do was fill out forms about his time of death and start phoning his next of kin.

The lift pinged and he got in, pressed G, and looked at himself in the mirror on the back wall. He needed a haircut. Needed a holiday. Needed to be anywhere but in a boiling hot lift, the stink of Bobby March's last curry on him, suit jacket over his arm, dark rings under the arms of his shirt, a sheen of sweat on his face.

Things had to change. And soon.

CHAPTER 3

The lift door opened and revealed the hotel restaurant in all its glory. McCoy remembered reading about it in the paper when the place opened. Owner had been on holiday to Fiji or somewhere so decided to name the place the Tiki Bar and do it up like a South Sea hideaway. That was the idea. The reality was more like an amateur dramatics production of *South Pacific*. Wee bamboo roofs over the booths, mural of a white sandy beach, plastic flowers and coconuts everywhere.

McCoy grimaced and sat down. The waitress eased her way out from behind the bar, sticking her chewing gum under it as she did. She was dressed in some sort of raffia fringe skirt and bikini top, a flower garland round her neck. Effect might not have been so bad if she was Polynesian, or even had a tan; didn't work quite so well when you were a peely-wally Scottish girl with freckles and a half grown-out curly perm.

'Aloha. Welcome to the South Seas. Can I get you a cocktail, sir?' she recited in a bored Glasgow accent.

'Pint,' said McCoy. The thought of a cocktail at that time in the morning was more than even he could cope with.

She nodded and wandered off. Big navy-blue kickers flashing through the raffia every so often. He had a look at the menu while he waited for his drink. The specialty of the house seemed to be chicken breast in a banana and sherry sauce. No wonder the place was empty.

Pint arrived and he took a long draught.

'Mr McCoy, I wasn't expecting to see you here.'

He looked up and Phyllis Gilroy was standing in front of him. In a concession to the heat, the medical examiner's usual tweeds had been replaced by light-blue trousers and a flowery, patterned shirt. The battered brown leather briefcase was still in place. She was looking round the restaurant with a mixture of wonder and horror.

'I wasn't aware the South Seas was famed for its cuisine,' she said.

'I've had a look at the menu. Believe me, it's not.'

'This isn't one for the likes of you, is it? An overdose?' And then it dawned. 'Don't tell me. Raeburn?'

McCoy nodded and she sat down across from him. The waitress appeared and Gilroy ordered a Coke, waited until she'd left before she began.

'Have you spoken to Murray about it?' she asked.

McCoy nodded. 'Nothing he can do. He's in Central for the next six months, or until they find someone else to do it.'

24

'Yes, he finally had to give in. They kept on and on at him. Still, another six months isn't the end of the world.'

'You sure? In Perth?' he asked. 'I went there for the day once. That was enough.'

'Fair point.' She hesitated. 'I know it's not really my place to say, but my – thankfully limited – experience of Bernard Raeburn wouldn't lead me to believe he's an ideal replacement. Especially with this little girl missing. How on earth did that happen?'

McCoy shrugged. 'I don't have enough experience, Thomson's not good enough, Reid's about three months from his pension. They needed to bring someone in to replace Murray and Raeburn's been waiting for a promotion for years. Looks like all the handshakes and the arse-licking at the lodge dinners finally paid off.'

The waitress appeared again and put the Coke down with a grunted 'Aloha'. McCoy dug in his pocket for change. 'My treat.'

Gilroy took a long drink, watched the raffia skirt head back towards the bar. 'In Glasgow, of all places. Extraordinary.'

McCoy took another drink, watched the waitress get the gum from under the bar and stick it back into her mouth. 'Well, that's one word for it.'

'Having said that, this is probably the first time that outfit's ever been suitable attire,' said Gilroy. 'It was sixty-eight degrees at nine a.m. this morning. Unbelievable.'

McCoy smiled. 'Thought you'd be used to it.'

She smiled. 'Hardly. We left India when I was three. All I can really remember is the sunshine coming through green leaves and some figs on the path in the garden.' She pointed upwards. 'Famous, I believe?'

McCoy nodded. 'Bobby March. Guitarist. Let's just say his glory days were behind him. Good in his day, though. Really good. Been a junkie for years, if you believe what you hear. Looks like his luck just ran out.'

She nodded. 'As it so often does in those cases. Any news?'

She didn't have to say any more. The whole city seemed to be waiting for news of Alice Kelly, good or bad.

McCoy shook his head. 'Nothing new. Mind you, way it's going I'd be the last to know.'

She shifted in her seat, looked annoyed. 'Well, I think it's ridiculous. A case like that and you're sitting here while that fool Raeburn is in charge . . .'

McCoy shrugged, tried to sound less annoyed than he really was. 'Nothing I can do. He's made it very plain he thinks I'm less than the shit beneath his shoe. Seems I'm best employed writing up reports about dead junkies. Could be worse, I suppose. He could have put me on public liaison.'

'Why the enmity?' she asked. 'I never quite understood.'

McCoy sighed, told the story. 'I did three months

26

at Eastern when I started, partnered with Raeburn. He was like the rest of that shop. Backhanders, fit-ups and the path of least resistance. Not my idea of being a polis. Raeburn took it personally when I asked for a transfer. And now that's come back to bite me right on the bum.'

She nodded. 'I see. Unfortunately that account of Mr Raeburn doesn't surprise me in the least.'

There was also the small matter of Raeburn harassing Stevie Cooper for more and more 'look the other way' money for his sauna in Tollcross, but McCoy wasn't going to let Gilroy in on that one. Raeburn pushed and pushed, raids every week, then Cooper got so pissed off he just closed the place down, moved away. Least when it was open Raeburn was getting his twenty quid a week. Now he was getting bugger all, courtesy of McCoy's big pal Cooper. No wonder he didn't like him.

Gilroy smiled, had thought of something. 'What are you doing tonight?'

McCoy looked up. 'Tonight? Nothing. Only plus about all this is I'm on regular hours.'

'Excellent. I'm having a dinner tonight and I'd like you to come. Never know, a night out might cheer you up a bit. Half seven for eight?'

McCoy nodded, heart sinking. He'd walked straight into that one. No chance to make up an excuse now. A night out might well have cheered him up, but a night at Phyllis Gilroy's wasn't the kind of night he was thinking about. Not by a long shot.

Gilroy stood up, picked up her bag. 'Mr March, here I come. See you later.'

McCoy said goodbye, watched as she walked towards the lift, pressed the button. How had he managed to get himself into this?

The dinners were famous. She had one every week, a gathering of the Great and the Good of Glasgow. All of them, no doubt, making small talk about stuff he'd never heard of, looking at him and wondering what he was doing there. And he'd have to wear a bloody suit and tie in this heat. He drained his pint, got up to go. Just five minutes earlier he'd thought he couldn't feel any sorrier for himself. Showed how wrong you could be.

The group of four or five fans outside the front door had sat down on the pavement, were holding hands, singing 'Sunday Morning Symphony'. Didn't look like they'd heard the news yet, but it wouldn't be long. News like that leaks fast: chambermaids, barmen, porters. Best get out of here before the wailing starts and the press turn up.

The boy with the glitter on his face looked up. 'Is he still in there, mister?'

McCoy nodded, started walking up Jamaica Street. Someone else could break the news.

CHAPTER 4

After a whisky, a bath and a shave, McCoy was wandering around the flat in his skivvies drinking a big glass of tap water. The windows were wide open but he didn't care. If anyone was interested in looking at him in his underwear then God help them. Was still about seventy degrees, no sign of a breeze, so he was avoiding putting his clothes on until the last minute. Then he had a sudden thought. Was he supposed to bring something? That seemed familiar from posh West End dinner parties. If so, what? Chocolates? Flowers? A bottle of the type of rotten wine he could afford?

Thought of asking Susan, even picked up the phone, but put it back. Things hadn't been going that well since she'd got the place at Manchester uni. Her phone calls were getting less and less frequent, weekend trip down there had been more awkward than anything else. New uni pals not sure what to make of a Glasgow polis. Her and him trying to fill up the silences, pretend everything was hunky-dory, same as it had been up here. Both of them knew it was pretty much over,

29

bar the shouting. Turned out he'd been a bit of a holiday romance, right place right time, no more no less. He just needed to take it on the chin and get on with it.

He put his shirt on, buttoned it up and stepped into his trousers. He'd looked around but couldn't find anything in the house he could take anyway. The half bottle of Grant's sitting on the mantel-piece didn't seem quite right and the shops would be shut by now. He'd just have to show up empty-handed. Looked at himself in the mirror as he tied his tie. His face was red from the sun, freckles on his nose coming out. He put his shoes and his jacket on, picked up his keys from the bookcase and pulled the front door shut behind him.

Wasn't that far a walk to Phyllis Gilroy's house, just up his street and over. Noticed the change as soon as he topped the hill. Suddenly the kids in the streets weren't wearing their big brother's or sister's hand-me-downs. The bikes they had were new-looking, shiny. Even their accents were different, softer, posher. The line for the ice-cream van was a neat crocodile shuffling forwards, not the free-for-all it was in the schemes. He was in Hyndland now, right enough.

Six Beaumont Gate was a tall, red-sandstone townhouse. The kind of place that reeked of old money and privilege. Four floors and a basement, a garden in the front full of spiky bushes, front door with a stained-glass panel of a Highland landscape. He pressed the bell and waited. Figured if he got out by half nine he could be back at the Victoria in time for the usual Friday night lock-in. Heard footsteps and the door opened.

'Harry! Excellent. Glad you could make it,' said Phyllis, beaming at him.

Trousers and blouse had been replaced by some sort of white dress with big red flowers on it. Thought for a minute she'd hurt her head, then realised it was a turban thing of the same material.

'Sorry, I didn't bring anything . . .'

'Don't be ridiculous, we've enough wine to sink a battleship!' She held the door wide. 'Come in!'

He followed Phyllis through the hall and down the stairs, the noise of chatting and laughing drifting up, and found himself in a basement kitchen about twice the size of his whole flat. A large wooden table in the middle was covered with a patchwork cloth, candles dotted on it, some sort of metal rack above it with copper pans hanging down. The wall at the opposite end was almost covered with an enormous painting of two wee kids, red hair and freckles, words and bits of newspaper stuck all over them. A raised panel to the side of the picture had bells and the name of the rooms above them. Summon the servants without getting off your arse.

A record was playing in the background. *Sunday Morning Symphony* of all things. Six people were sitting at the table, glasses of wine in front of them, all of them looking up as he appeared.

31

Phyllis put her hands on his shoulders. 'Everyone? This is a colleague, and hopefully a friend of mine, Harry McCoy. Was at a bit of a loose end tonight, so he was kind enough to join us.'

Phyllis pointed at the table.

'Harry, this is Jack and Eden Coia.' A tiny elderly couple smiled up at him. 'Edwin and John on the left,' she went on. An older man with specs and a younger one. She continued, pointing at the furthest seat from where they stood, 'Professor Hobbs at the top.' Bald, fat, flushed. Phyllis nodded at an empty seat. 'And next to you is Mila de Ligt.' Young, blonde, jeans and a collarless man's shirt. She looked up and waved.

'Now,' said Phyllis, sitting him down, 'as you can see, we are in the kitchen this evening, bit cooler and a bit less formal, so enjoy yourself. White or red?'

He'd only been sitting down for a few minutes, just managed to swallow a half glass of red, when the inevitable question came up.

'So, Harry, Phyllis tells us you are a policeman?' Hobbs pronounced 'policeman' as if it was something he'd never heard of.

Harry nodded.

Hobbs pointed to the record player with his cigarette. 'Phyllis said you were there today.'

'We both were,' said Phyllis. 'I thought I better give his music a go, least I can do. I bought it on the way home. I rather like it, you know,' she said, putting a big platter of bread, cheese and olives on the table. 'Was the last copy left in Woolworths.'

32

'Dead rock stars one day, bank robbers the next. Your life must be rather fascinating, I would imagine,' said Hobbs, spearing a bit of brie with his knife.

McCoy was just lifting a bit of cheddar to his mouth when he realised the whole table had turned to look at him. He put it down.

'Can be,' he said. 'But it's the same as most jobs. Some bits of it are interesting, some as dull as ditchwater.'

'The little girl?' continued Hobbs.

McCoy nodded, didn't have to ask what he was talking about.

'I can't even imagine what the poor mother is going through,' said Eden, shaking her head. 'Whole thing is tragic.'

Hobbs was looking at him in expectation. 'You must know something.'

'No more than you,' said McCoy evenly.

'I find that hard to believe,' said Hobbs, looking round the table for support. 'What is the theory you are working on?'

'I'm not working on a theory,' said McCoy. He was starting to get annoyed. Even if he did know anything about Alice Kelly, he wouldn't be telling this fat arsehole, no matter how much he felt entitled to know.

Hobbs laughed. 'Well, that's not very reassuring! May I ask why not?'

'Police business is confidential, Phillip, as you should well know,' said Phyllis, rescuing him. 'So

33

stop hectoring our guest. This is a dinner, not an interrogation. Now, who fancies the gazpacho? I couldn't face making hot soup in this heat.'

McCoy sat there for a bit, eating – drinking? – his gazpacho and trying not to get any angrier. Should have known better than to come. He was just putting his spoon down when Edwin the poet leant across the table, spoke quietly.

'Don't worry. Phillip Hobbs is an arse. Always has been. Always will be.' Then he grinned.

After that, the evening started to look up a bit. Edwin the poet turned out to be a bit of a laugh. Cheeky wee guy, dirty sense of humour. His friend constantly rolling his eyes as he described the trouble they'd got into on some trip they'd been on to Greece.

Mila didn't say much. He supposed Glasgow accents were difficult enough, never mind if you're Dutch, but she smiled, tried to join in. He was half listening to some argument between Mrs Coia and Edwin about the value of public space in city planning, whatever that was, when Mila leant into him and whispered.

'God, this is boring.'

He laughed, hadn't expected it. He turned and she was smiling at him.

'I love Phyllis but she does have some very dull friends,' she said.

'Me included?' asked McCoy.

She wrinkled her nose. 'Not sure yet. Phyllis said you might be able to help me.'

34

'How's that, then?' asked McCoy.

She lit up, blew the smoke away, held up an expensive-looking camera.

'I'm a photographer. A charity called Shelter have asked me to document the lives of people living in poverty in Glasgow. Bad housing, people who are living on the roads . . .'

'The streets,' said McCoy. 'We say the streets.'

She smiled. 'Sorry, the streets. Phyllis thought you might be able to introduce me to some of these people.'

McCoy sighed. He was getting a bit sick of being Glasgow's official representative for the downtrodden. He couldn't face wandering about Glasgow trying to find Charlie the Pram with Mila in this heat, no matter how good-looking she was.

'I can't just now,' he said. 'Have to work, short-staffed at the moment, but I know someone who can. Friend called Liam. Just the man you need. I'll introduce you.'

'Is he a social worker?' Mila asked. 'A charity worker?'

'Not exactly,' said McCoy, not wanting to tell her last time he'd seen him he was passed out on a grate at the back of the St Enoch Hotel. 'He's more someone who knows Glasgow, knows everyone. He's your man, believe me.'

'Thank you,' she said. 'That would be most helpful.'

He was just about to ask her why they'd got a Dutch woman to take photos in Glasgow when

35

he heard heavy footsteps on the stairs. He looked up and the last person he expected to see was walking down them. Chief Inspector Murray. He'd a new suit on, and a new haircut, was carrying a holdall, smiling. Looking very much at home.

'Still bloody boiling out there,' he said, taking his jacket off and hanging it over the last empty chair. 'Have I missed the food?'

He sat down and Phyllis got him a plate, put it in front of him. 'I think you know everyone, don't you, Hector? Oh, this is Mila – a photographer friend, here from Rotterdam. I bought some of her pictures last year when I was on holiday.'

They nodded at each other and Murray started putting food on his plate as Phyllis poured him a large glass of red wine.

All McCoy could do was watch in amazement. Murray didn't like wine. He didn't like wearing a suit unless he had to. And last McCoy knew, attending a dinner party was a fate worse than death for him. Yet here he was, chomping away, asking Edwin how his holiday to Greece had been. Sharing a laugh with Mrs Coia. There was only one explanation McCoy could think of: him and Phyllis must be seeing each other. He knew they were friends, but he thought it was just that. Shows how much he knew. Must have been written on his face.

'What are you grinning at?' asked Murray, pointing his fork at him.

'Nothing,' said McCoy. 'Nothing at all.'

Wasn't until after the coffee that Murray stood up. 'Phyllis, will you excuse us for ten minutes? Work calls.'

He nodded at McCoy, and McCoy got up and followed him upstairs. They ended up in the big front room, grand piano, lots of dark wood panelling, a smell of beeswax polish. A huge portrait of a serious-looking middle-aged man with an Edwardian moustache looked down at them from over the fireplace. Little title on the frame: 'Sir Phillip Gilroy'.

Murray pushed a sleeping ginger cat off the cushion, settled down on a leather armchair and pointed at the one opposite.

'How long's this been going on?' asked McCoy, sitting down and trying not to grin.

'If that was any of your bloody business I'd tell you,' said Murray.

Suddenly struck him. 'Does Janet know?' he asked.

Murray nodded. Face giving nothing away.

'And?' asked McCoy.

'And Janet's fine about it. She's living in Peebles now. With her friend.'

McCoy was about to ask about the friend but thought better of it.

'And that's that,' said Murray. He started looking for his pipe. Seemed that part of the conversation was over.

'How's that arsehole Raeburn getting on?'

McCoy shrugged.

'He still giving you the bum's rush, is he?'

'Yep. Not allowed anywhere near anything,' said McCoy.

'Raeburn's bloody loss. He better find that wee girl and quick. Stupid bugger should take any help he can get.' He pulled his pipe out his pocket, banged it on the heel of his shoe and a shower of ash fell into the grate.

'Not much I can do about it,' said McCoy. 'How you getting on in Perth?'

'I'm surviving. Counting the days until I leave.' Murray sat back in his chair, looked at him. 'There's another reason I'm here. Wanted to talk to you.'

'Oh aye. What about?' said McCoy warily.

'You remember John?' Murray was padding his trouser pockets. The hunt for his matches was on.

'Your brother John?' McCoy asked.

Murray nodded, gave up the search and reached for a bronze lighter on the coffee table. Lit his pipe.

'Yep. What about him? What's he done?' asked McCoy

Murray's face re-emerged from a cloud of bluish smoke. 'John? Not a thing. Pure as the driven snow, our John. It's his daughter Laura. She's run away again.'

McCoy listened, as Murray told him the same old story. She was fifteen, didn't get on with her mum and dad, had come home drunk a couple of times, was seeing boys, dogging school.

'Not sure that's much different from any other fifteen-year-old,' said McCoy.

'It is now. She's been gone for two nights and John and Shelia are climbing the walls.'

He leant forward, reached round and got his wallet out his back pocket, opened it and handed McCoy a photo. Must have been taken at some family celebration. Looked like a restaurant or a hotel. Laura was a good-looking girl, big dark eyes, long brown hair. She was standing a little distance away from the rest of the family, not much but enough to let you know she'd rather be anywhere than standing there with her mum and dad and her wee brother. From the photo, McCoy would have guessed she was eighteen or nineteen rather than fifteen.

'I don't get it,' said McCoy. 'Why all the cloak and dagger? Why's this not going through the shop? She's only fifteen, they'll look for her, especially if she's the boss's niece. Has your brother not reported her missing?'

Murray shrugged, looked a bit guilty. 'Not officially.'

'Why not?' asked McCoy. 'What's the problem?'

Murray sighed. 'John's the deputy head of Glasgow Council. The last thing he wants is his runaway daughter plastered all over the front of the *Evening Times*. And between you and me he's going to run as an MP next year. Glasgow West are going to select him. Deal's done. He doesn't want Laura's behaviour scuppering his chances.'

'What a gent,' said McCoy.

Murray looked resigned. 'He's a prick, always has been. If he wasn't my brother, I wouldn't cross the street to piss on him if he was on fire.' He blew out another cloud of smoke, waved it away. 'Was tempted to tell him to sort out his own bloody mess, but I'm fond of Laura. The last thing I want is anything happening to her.'

'Maybe she's just staying at a pal's, putting the wind up her mum and dad?'

Murray shook his head. 'If only. Seems young Laura has developed an interest in the seamier side of our fair city. She was seen in the Strathmore last night.'

McCoy wasn't expecting that. The Strathmore was only half a mile up the road from where they were sitting, but that half a mile put it right into Maryhill. And the Strathmore was a dive even by Maryhill's less than stellar standards.

'Apparently she was with a guy called Donny MacRae, pissed, making a right arse of herself,' Murray added.

'Donny MacRae? That Donny MacRae?' asked McCoy. Things were looking worse by the minute.

Murray nodded. Rubbed at the reddish stubble coming through on his chin, made a noise like sandpaper. 'Do me a favour, Harry, just find her and deliver her back to her comfy bed in Bearsden. Get my bloody brother off my back.'

McCoy nodded. Wasn't like he could say no. If there was anyone in the world he owed it was

Murray. 'Give me a couple of days. I'll find her. Thanks to Raeburn, I've got bugger all else to do.'

'And Harry? This is between you and me, eh?' said Murray. 'Nothing official.'

McCoy nodded. Looked up as the clock on the mantelpiece struck nine.

'And here was me thinking I'd a night off,' he said. 'Was going to go to the lock-in at the Victoria.'

He stood up to go.

'Janet's not bothered,' said Murray. 'Don't worry about her. She's got her own life now.'

McCoy nodded. Wasn't sure if he believed him or not.

They went back downstairs and McCoy said his goodbyes to Phyllis and the rest of the guests. Thought he'd give it a go, nothing to lose.

'Actually,' he said to Mila, 'I've got to go and have a look at a pub up the road. Fancy coming? Might be a good place to take photos, if you fancy it?'

She smiled gratefully. 'Yes, I would, let me get some more film.' She disappeared upstairs.

He left Murray down there, sitting beside Phyllis, a glass of red wine in his hand, tie undone. What age was Murray? Late fifties? Suppose he still had a life to lead. Still a shock, though. Stood in the hall waiting for Mila to come down. Took the photo out his pocket and had another look. Laura Murray looked out at him. Fifteen going on eighteen. Trouble. Heard Mila on the stairs, put it back in his wallet.

41

They stepped out the door and into the warmth of the night. Streetlights had just come on, moths flickering round the yellow lights. Mila put her arm in his and they started walking up Byres Road towards the Strathmore. Streets were busy, weather and the holidays getting everyone out for the night. Stopped while Mila took some pictures of three drunk women at the taxi rank. They were swaying, holding hands, singing 'Delilah' at the top their voices.

McCoy didn't know anything about photography, but Mila looked like she knew what she was doing. Let them pose and grin for a few shots, then dropped her camera to waist level, kept talking to them, still pressing the shutter without them knowing. They finished the song and she gave them a kiss each, hurried up the road towards McCoy.

'Sneaky,' he said.

She grinned. 'Oldest trick in the book, but not many people notice. You must be very observant, Harry McCoy.'

'Comes with the job,' he said. 'Strathmore's up this way.'

CHAPTER 5

From the outside it might have been the same old Strathmore but inside everything had changed. Now it was more like a student union. The whole pub was dim, only illumination was green and red light playing over the walls, lighting up the posters of bands and record sleeves stapled to them. The loudest jukebox McCoy had ever heard was blasting out 'All Right Now'. Even the smell of the place was different. Patchouli oil and sweat as opposed to the usual spilled beer and stale cigarette smoke. It was stifling too, heat hitting you as you walked in.

Clientele had changed as well. The Strathmore had been a drinkers' pub, men with pints barely talking to each other, watching the clock so's not to miss last orders. Only young person in there had been the bookie's boy, who came in to collect the lines from the regulars. McCoy had thought the general atmosphere of misery would fit in with Mila's project. Not now.

Now everyone was under twenty-five. Boys with long hair and beards in a uniform of denim flares and T-shirts or vest tops, a gloss of sweat on their

43

faces. Girls all had long straight hair, dungarees or hot pants, platform shoes. Couple of them even had wee stars stuck to their cheeks. And every one of them, boy or girl, seemed to be smoking a roll-up.

He managed to get a wee table as far from the jukebox as possible and Mila sat down, took her jacket off immediately and asked for a vodka and tonic. McCoy took his jacket off too, rolled up his sleeves, took his tie off, scrunched it into his pocket and undid the top buttons of his shirt. Felt a bit less like a cop.

'You be all right?' he asked. 'Be back in a minute.'

'She'll be fine,' said a girl sitting at the next table. 'We'll look after her. Come and sit with us. Come on, hen!'

Mila tried to say she was okay but the girl wasn't taking no for an answer. She cleared a space on the bench beside her and patted it.

'Here. Here's a space. C'mon!'

Mila gave up, got up, and sat down beside her. Tried to put her bag on the table but couldn't find any space amongst the empty glasses and ashtrays. The girls at the table looked like they'd been at it for a while, all looked pleasantly stoned or drunk. All of them shouted hello, started to chat. One of them asked her where she got her top. Another one offered her a slug of her pint.

McCoy left them to it, walked up to the bar, taking a good look around as he did so. No Laura or Donny MacRae to be seen anywhere. Stood

44

aside as two girls helping another one to the toilets barged past. The one they were rescuing had obviously taken something that didn't agree with her: her eyes were wide, she was mumbling about 'the eyes in the wallpaper', half crying, half giggling, feet dragging along the floor.

The jukebox whirred again, clunked as the record fell and 'Drive-In Saturday' started blasting out. McCoy pushed his way through the crush of sweaty bodies at the bar and got in by the far end. At least some things at the Strathmore hadn't changed. Tam Dixon was still behind the bar, scars, scowl and buzz-cut intact.

They shook hands. 'Harry McCoy,' said Tam. 'Long time no see, what brings you up here?'

'What's going on, Tam?' asked McCoy, looking round at the crowd of youngsters, some of them even dancing in the space where the dominoes tables used to be. 'When did all this happen?'

Tam leant forward to make himself heard above the jukebox.

'Year or so ago. Was Wee Tam that did it. Got the jukebox in, got all the young ones coming. You're lucky there's no a band on tonight, the place'd be even busier then.' A girl along the bar shouted 'yoo-hoo' and waved a pound note at him. Tam glowered at her, and the pound note and smile disappeared.

'Tell you something, Harry, it's bloody chronic, noise and spewing lassies everywhere, but fuck me do they young ones drink – never made so much bloody money in my life.'

A boy squeezed in beside McCoy at the bar, Mickey Mouse T-shirt, flared cords and sand-shoes. Must have been dancing earlier, long hair plastered to his head with sweat. Tam served him, handed over two pints.

'You not bothering about age any more, Tam?' asked McCoy, watching the boy weave his way back to the dancers and hand one of the pints over to a girl that looked like Marianne Faithfull's younger sister. 'He can't have been more than sixteen, it's like a bloody youth club in here.'

'That what you're here for, Harry?' Tam said, defensively. 'Check up on my customers?'

McCoy shook his head. 'Nope. Habit. Can't help myself.'

He took the picture of Laura Murray out his pocket and handed it over. 'You see her in here the past couple of nights?'

Tam dug a pair of black-framed specs out his trouser pocket, put them on and looked hard at the picture, moving it closer in to focus. He shook his head. 'Naw, never seen her before.'

'You been going to acting classes, Tam?' asked McCoy. 'That what the specs are for? Trying to look convincing? She was in here the other night, Donny MacRae's hands all over her arse. She's fifteen. I'm a big polis now. A detective. I could have this place shut down in twenty minutes, so stop taking the piss.'

Tam sighed. He nodded at a young barman with frizzy ginger hair and a Led Zeppelin T-shirt to

46

take over, lifted up the counter hatch and beckoned McCoy through. McCoy followed him past the payphone on the wall, the crates of empty bottles, the big metal barrels, into the living room.

He pulled the door shut behind him and the shouts and David Bowie cut off immediately. McCoy looked around. Swirly blue carpet, black-and-white telly with the sound down, Robin Day mouthing away, painting of a Highland glen above the mantelpiece. Home Sweet Home.

Tam poured him a whisky from the bottle on the sideboard, the good stuff, not the stuff he served at the bar, and lowered his bulk onto the couch.

'You're right enough. She was in here the other night, pissed she was, making an arse of herself. She left with him, Donny MacRae.' He licked his lips nervously. 'You know him, do you?'

McCoy nodded. 'One of Alec Page's boys, isn't he?'

Tam whistled through his teeth. 'Not any more, he's not. Alec Page's in the hospital. No be getting out for a long while.'

'He's what?' asked McCoy. 'What happened?'

Tam wound the gold tape off a new packet of Kensitas and lit up.

'Happened a couple of weeks ago, they found him in a flat in Barlornock. Two big slashes across his face, nose was damn near off. Top of his ears cut off too.'

'Jesus . . .'

'And that's no even the worst of it. Somebody told me they'd broken each of his fingers as well, bones all shattered.'

'Did they get someone for it?' McCoy asked.

Tam snorted a laugh. 'What you asking me for? You're the bloody polis!'

'Aye well, Balornock's no my patch. Would have been through Northern. They get anyone? Mind you, it'd be a first for those clowns if they did.'

Tam shook his head, took a swallow of his whisky. 'Naw, and I don't think they ever will. Nobody's talking, but let's just say it's Donny MacRae that runs Page's boys now. Take from that what you will.'

'Is the girl with him?' asked McCoy.

Tam shrugged. 'I don't know. She was the other night. Hope it's no permanent, for her sake as well as yours. Don't get to be a top boy like MacRae without being a right bastard.'

McCoy swallowed over the rest of his whisky and put the glass down on the tile-topped coffee table. 'I need to find her, Tam.'

Tam looked reluctant, fiddled with the butts in the ashtray on the arm of his chair. Finally decided to speak. Sounded serious, scared even. 'I never told you this, Harry, I mean it. I don't want MacRae coming anywhere near me. Don't even want him to know my name. Promise?'

McCoy nodded.

'He's a bad bastard right enough, stories I could tell—'

McCoy held his hands up. 'Okay, okay! I get the picture, Tam. You're shiteing yourself. Nobody'll hear anything from me. Deal?'

Tam went to nod and started coughing instead. Proper deep smoker's cough. Spat some phlegm into a cloth hanky, had a look, then folded it away.

'MacRae's got a flat over in Dennistoun. Whitehill Street. Last close before the factory. If he's no in here or in the Lamplight with his boys, he'll be there.'

McCoy left Tam sitting in the wee sitting room and made his way back to the bar. Got the vodka and tonic for Mila and a pint for himself. Weaved his way back to the table. Was about to say sorry for taking so long when he realised the table was empty. Mila and the girls had gone.

'You the polis?'

He turned and a boy with long brown hair and a beard was standing there holding a pint.

McCoy nodded.

'Mila said to tell you she's gone to a party, not to worry about her.' He held out McCoy's jacket. 'Said she'll see you another time.'

McCoy stood there, drink in one hand, suit jacket in the other, feeling like a right arse – an *old* right arse at that. Red wine at dinner must have got to him, making him think he was all that, impressing Mila. Seemed obvious now. Why would a girl like Mila, ten years younger, beautiful, talented, be interested in him? A thirty-year-old polis in a John Collier suit, hair starting to go grey, sweat stains on his shirt.

He knocked back the vodka and tonic, left the pint on the table. If he was quick he could make the lock-in at the Victoria. Sit there setting the world to rights along with all the other sad lonely bastards looking for one more drink on a Friday night.

Jukebox started again. T. Rex. Definitely time to go. He took one last look round for Laura Murray, but she was nowhere to be seen. There were lots of girls like her, though. Too young to be here, too much make-up, too drunk to look after themselves. The only difference was they didn't come from Bearsden or have fathers that were councillors or uncles that were police chiefs. Didn't have people like him looking for them.

McCoy squeezed past a winching couple, pushed the door open and stepped out onto Maryhill Road. Breathed in the fresh air, then lit up. Threw his match into the gutter and started walking.

Someone else would have to worry about them.

8th August 1965

Richmond

The Beatkickers were over before they began. Single didn't get played on the radio, didn't get in the charts, and Parlophone suddenly didn't want to know. That was that. Everyone went home except him. No way was he going back to Arden, to his dad telling him he was right and he should have been an apprentice joiner after all.

So he stayed in London, pawned his suit, got a room in some house in Kensal Rise. Him and a crowd of Irish navvies. They saw his guitar, told him he could make money playing in the pubs around Kilburn, so he did. Ended up playing with a band that had a residency at the Galtymore. They played whatever was in the charts that week, Irish ballads for the older guys, 'Happy Birthday'. He didn't mind it, made some money, started buying dope from the West Indian guys on Bonchurch Road. Had a good time. But he knew he was just treading water.

Started looking in **Melody Maker**, found out

where the good bands were playing. Eel Pie Island, the Marquee. Started taking a night a week off from the Irish pubs, going to see people, trying to make friends. Trying to get closer to what he wanted. A real band.

Was at the Marquee one night watching The Who and got talking to some guy who said he was their manager, funny-looking posh guy with wavy hair, said his name was Kit. Bobby told him he was a guitarist and the guy told him Long John Baldry was starting a new group and was looking for someone. Then he told him if he played his cards right he'd get him an audition. So he did.

Sun was up, getting hot. Bobby finished the last of the joint, flicked it in the river and started walking back towards the Athletic Grounds. Had to weave his way through all the people sitting on the grass. All of them stoned or pretending to be, passing bottles of cheap red wine. Finally made it to where the stage had been set up and wandered round the back. Saw John, couldn't miss him really, all six foot seven of him. He started to walk towards him and realised he was surrounded by Eric Burdon, Julie Driscoll, young Stevie Winwood. He turned and started walking the other way.

Just what he needed for his first gig. He was nervous enough with knowing all those guys would be there. John had told him there might be a few guests, he seemed to know everyone, but he wasn't expecting that. He sat down near a couple with a puppy and the girl leant over, offered him a drink from their bottle of wine. He took a deep slug, said thank you. He knew he could play, he never worried about that. Finding something to say to those kinds of guys, that was the bit he worried about.

'Oi! Wanker!' A cockney voice from across the way.

He looked up and Rod was walking towards him. He smiled. Rod the Mod. Hair backcombed and pushed forward, white jeans, black turtleneck, striped blazer. Only one of them that paid attention to him, that he could talk to, liked the fact he was from Glasgow.

'What you sitting here for?' asked Rod, eyeing the girl with the puppy.

Bobby shook his head. 'Just having a think.'

'Yeah, well, forget that. We're on in twenty minutes. Just enough time to get pissed.'

Bobby nodded, stood up. 'Tell me why it is you're Scottish again?' he asked, as they walked towards the backstage area.

'Because I say I am, you prick!' shouted Rod.

Then he clattered him on the back of the head and started running. Turned and shouted, 'Hurry up! Nineteen minutes now!'

14TH JULY 1973

CHAPTER 6

If McCoy needed reminding what a big deal the Glasgow Fair was, he got it as soon as the cab turned into Killermont Street. Thirty or so special buses were lined up outside the bus station, paper destination signs pasted to their front windows. Dunoon, Fairlie, Troon. The drivers all standing outside them, caps on the back of their heads, sleeves rolled up, having a last fag, passing round a bottle of Irn-Bru.

The taxi stopped at the lights and McCoy watched the long line of families waiting to board. Mums and dads, the occasional granny, all of them laden down with bags and cases, trying and failing to calm down excited weans dressed up for the trip. Must have been a couple of hundred of them. All looking forward to a fortnight in some boarding house with cruet extra and nylon sheets. They were welcome to it.

He leant forward in the seat and took his jacket off, rolled up his shirt sleeves. Was only half eight and must have been sixty odds already. The heat-wave was showing no signs of ending. McCoy liked a nice day as much as the next man, but it was starting to get too much. Glasgow wasn't used to this kind of weather either, didn't suit it somehow. The harsh sunlight showed up the reality of the city – no cloudy weather or drizzly rain to soften the picture. The sunlight picked out the decay, the rubbish on the streets, the ruined faces on the group of shaky men outside the off-licence waiting for it to open.

The city had become dusty, dry; it even smelt different, of hot asphalt and drains and bins gone over in the heat. This was the kind of weather that made people edgy, do stupid things, drink too much, start fights. The kind of stuff Glasgow needed more of like a hole in the head.

He started yawning as they drove towards the centre of town, found it hard to stop. He wasn't used to being up this early on a Saturday morning, but needs must. Fact he'd been in the Victoria until after twelve probably wasn't helping much either. Could still picture himself standing in the Strathmore with a pint in one hand, a vodka in the other. Not a pretty picture. Still felt like an arse. He'd called into the shop as soon as he'd woken up. Still no news, according to Billy. Everyone was at it full tilt but they were still working in the dark.

The reason he was up so early was because guys like Donny MacRae normally weren't and he wanted to catch him still half asleep, unawares. And if Laura Murray had stayed the night with him all the better. Would have her home before lunchtime. Might even get a chance to spend the afternoon in the park with the paper and some sandwiches and a few cans.

Ten minutes later the cab pulled up in front of the Wills Factory on Alexandra Parade. He'd always liked the factory for some reason, looked like a thirties palace, big signs saying 'Capstan' on one wing, 'Golden Virginia' on the other. This was the first time he'd seen it shut up, though, chains on the gates, doors locked. The Glasgow Fair: the two weeks when the factories closed and you took your holidays, whether you liked it or not.

He paid the driver, crossed the road and started down Whitehill Street. The line of soot-stained tenements stretched up one side, chemical works the other. One lonely Austin Morris parked half up on the pavement. He found the close Tam had told him about, number 286. 'SPUR YA BASS' in white paint on the wall and a broken window with brown tape over the cracks next to the entrance.

He dropped his fag, stood on it and stepped into the darkness of the close. Had to admit a part of him thought Murray and the girl's parents were going about this the wrong way. Seemed to him the easiest way to get someone like Laura back was to just let her go. Was pretty sure the glamour of staying in a single end in a shite close like this with a boyfriend that could hardly string two words together, no matter how good-looking he was,

59

would wear off pretty soon. No money, no family, just someone like Donny MacRae asking her why she hadn't done his washing and giving her a slap to make sure he did. Still, wasn't up to him, he was just doing what he was told. Better get on with it.

He made it to the top floor, picking his way through the empty beer bottles and newspapers that littered the top landing, stood in front of MacRae's front door and listened.

Nothing.

He knocked.

Nothing.

Knocked again, harder this time, even gave it a boot. Still nothing. Swore, then gave the handle a go. Was amazed when it turned. Luck going his way for once. He pushed the door open, stepped inside and immediately wished he hadn't.

Wasn't difficult to work out why MacRae hadn't answered the door. He was lying on the press bed, very pale and very dead, naked but for a pair of blue underpants and one red football sock. His eyes were wide open, staring up at the ceiling, his chest a mess of cuts and stab wounds. The grubby white sheets he was lying on were soaked with blood – blood that McCoy realised was only just starting to dry.

A wave of dizziness hit and he looked away quickly, counted down from ten, tried to breathe slowly. Could hear flies buzzing against the windows, a lorry going by on Alexandra Parade, the rattle of the bottles on a milk float. There was a Rangers team poster on the wall, looked at that, tried to remember the players' names: Sandy Jardine, John Greig, Alfie Conn? The dizziness began to fade; he started to feel normal again. Experimented with a look over at MacRae. Managed it without his head spinning. Hoped he was going to be okay.

MacRae's flat was a typical single end. A one-room flat at the corner of a tenement. Bed, kitchen, everything, stuffed into a twenty-foot-square room with the wallpaper peeling and a dull stink of damp. There was a steady ticking noise. Took McCoy a minute to realise what it was, thought it was a clock at first. Wasn't. It was the blood dripping off the end of McLeod's hand, dropping into the shiny pool forming on the lino.

He edged over to the bed and looked down at what was left of Laura's boyfriend. Donny MacRae's ginger feather cut was stiff with blood, a couple of knife wounds below his pale blue eyes, blood from them congealing round his nose and mouth. He was, or had been, a good-looking guy. Even with the mess his face was in, you could still see it. Body was like a boxer's, slight but hard with muscle. Tattoo of King Billy on his bicep. Perfect bad boy dream of every rebellious middle-class girl like Laura Murray. No wonder she'd fallen for him. Fallen hard enough to prefer a shithole like this to a big comfy house in Bearsden. A fly landed on MacRae's face, crawled around,

61

made its way into the blood around his eye. McCoy looked away. Enough was enough. Time to clean up.

There wasn't much to get rid of. A paperback on the bed, a Scottie dog brooch sitting on the table. An ashtray full of butts with lipstick on the ends sitting by the bed. He put the brooch and the butts in his pocket, picked up the book. Didn't seem that likely it was Donny MacRae who was halfway through *The Great Gatsby*, so he put that in his pocket as well.

He slid his arm under the pillows. Sat MacRae up like some nurse making a patient comfortable and felt around. Came out with a rolled-up nightie and an earring, then eased him back into position. He wasn't completely cold yet, couldn't have been dead that long. Was hard to tell in this heat, though. McCoy put his jacket back on and jammed the nightie in his pocket with the rest of her stuff.

There was no question Laura Murray had left in a hurry – left so quick the door was still open. The real question was whether she left before or after Donny MacRae got himself ventilated. That wasn't McCoy's problem. Murray could worry about that. As long as he'd done his job and not missed anything, Laura had never been there.

He checked he'd no blood on his shoes to leave footprints, pulled MacRae's door shut behind him, walked down the stairs and out into the street. Whitehill Street was still quiet, no one up and around yet. If he was lucky no one would have seen him, and even if they had it was just another punter, nothing to worry about.

There was a caravan parked along from the factory – 'Jean's Rolls' painted on the side, hatch open, bowls of sugar and a jar of teaspoons on the fold-out counter. Why it was open when there were no workers to buy anything he had no idea, but he wasn't complaining. Hadn't had any breakfast and he was starving. He soon found out. And he'd only asked for a cup of tea and a roll and sausage.

'I've nothing else to do, son. I'm here every day at six for workers from the factory, then I just stay on for the pubs shutting.' She laughed. 'I'm like a permanent bloody fixture.'

The woman behind the counter pointed to a photo in a frame of a shy-looking boy with glasses and a navy uniform, hung by the hob.

'I lost my son in the war. Some German bastard bombed his boat. All hands lost. Only two months before the bastards surrendered as well. Just his luck.' She crossed herself. 'They wanted to give me some posthumous medal. I told them where to stick it. They took my boy. I want him back, no a bloody wee coin on a bit of ribbon. So that's my story. Here, come rain or shine. What am I gonna do at home? Sit in an empty house twiddling my thumbs? I don't think so. Would drive me up the bloody wall. Rather be out here watching the world go by. If I enjoy it, why not?'

'Why not, right enough,' said McCoy, somewhat taken aback by the woman's desire to tell him her entire life story. 'Tell you what, you make good rolls too. I'll take another one.'

While she made herself busy, he decided it was worth a try.

'Mind if I ask you a question?' McCoy pointed at the side of the van. 'Jean, is it?'

She nodded.

He held out the picture of Laura Murray. The woman took it and peered at it.

'You seen her around here?' he asked.

Jean looked at him. 'Why d'you want to know?'

'Her mum and dad are looking for her, she's only fifteen. I'm trying to get her back.'

Jean handed McCoy his roll, took the dowling stick away from the counter and pulled the flap down to reveal a large painting of a bacon roll. Well, more like a brown circle with two stripes of red, but he thought that's what it was meant to be. She reappeared from round the back of the van holding two packets of cigarettes.

'Want one? I've got hundreds – the girls at the factory trade them for rolls.'

McCoy nodded, took one and they crossed the street and leant on the wall overlooking the Monklands canal. The canal wasn't really a canal any more, just a long trench that was starting to get grown over. They'd drained it a couple of years ago, supposed to be building yet another motorway.

Jean took out a box of Swan Vestas and lit up. McCoy had the feeling she needed another push. The white lie.

'That Kelly girl going missing has sent her mum and dad right off the edge. Wondering if that's happened to their daughter too. The mum's in a right state, can't stop crying, the dad's out all hours, all over the city trying to find her. You recognised her, didn't you? You see what goes on around here. Help us, Jean. Please.'

Left it at that and tried to look as sad as possible. Seemed to work. Jean started talking.

'She was here this morning,' she said. 'Crying her bloody eyes out.'

'What about?' asked McCoy, trying to sound innocent.

'God knows. Couldn't get any sense out her, just gave her a cup of tea, tried to get her to calm down. She got in a taxi and that was that.'

'She say where she was going?' he asked.

Jean shook her head. 'Nope. But I heard what she said to the driver.'

'What was it?' asked McCoy.

'Told him to drop her on Queen Margaret Drive. By the swing park.'

McCoy thanked her, walked up the road. Jean hadn't told him much, but it might just be enough to find Laura Murray. He stopped at a phone box outside the Royal. Picked up the handset as an ambulance pulled in, lights on, siren wailing.

'You've got to be bloody kidding me!' Murray said when he got through. 'Dead? You sure?'

'Yep. Dead all right,' said McCoy. He was

holding the door of the phone box open; heat was making the smell of piss overwhelming. 'Body's a right mess, must have been stabbed twenty or so times at least.'

A pause on the line, sound of fumbling. With news like he'd just given him, it had to be Murray fumbling about for his pipe. Came back on the line.

'Christ. What a bloody mess.'

'In more ways than one,' said McCoy. 'But a bloody mess she hopefully won't have anything to do with. Removed all traces of Laura Murray from the premises. I'll call it in to Northern anonymously. Those clowns'll have it down as a gang thing soon as they hear who he is and how he died.'

'And is it?' asked Murray.

'Who knows? There's been a bit of jostling for position lately. Chances are.'

A pause. The inevitable question. The one McCoy didn't even want to ask himself.

'You don't think Laura's got anything to do with it, do you?'

An elderly man with a gas bill in his hand had appeared by the phone box, was peering in, giving him the evil eye. McCoy shifted round the other way. Tried to sound even.

'You tell me, Murray. She's your niece. I don't even know the girl.'

'Not sure I do any more. If she's got anything to do with this, we're going to have to bring her in. Jesus Christ . . .'

'Look,' said McCoy, fanning the door back and forward, wondering exactly how many people had peed in there. 'It won't be her. She's fifteen, nice girl, goes to a private school and probably plays bloody netball. Is she really going to be able to overcome someone like Donny MacRae? Stab the life out him before he does anything about it? MacRae could take care of himself. Not going to be overpowered by a teenage girl, is he?'

Unless he was asleep when she started in on him, he thought, but wasn't going to suggest that to Murray yet. Needed to speak to her, find out what really happened before he gave Murray a heart attack.

'You still there?' asked McCoy. The man had walked round the other side of the phone box, was peering in at him again.

'Yes,' said Murray. 'Just thinking. You're right. Must be one of his bloody gangland pals. You any nearer to finding her?'

'Getting there,' said McCoy. 'I'll let you know.'

He hung up. Was tempted to make another call just to annoy the stupid bugger but he didn't, held the door open.

'All yours, mate. Enjoy the piss.'

The man took the door, muttered 'dirty bugger' under his breath and pulled the door closed behind him.

CHAPTER 7

McCoy could tell by the expression on Billy the desk sergeant's face that he wasn't having a good day. He had one receiver cradled in his neck while the other phone on the desk rang angrily. Holding the fort for all he was worth. He hung up the one under his neck and took the other off the hook, laid it down on the desk, hissed 'Fuck off!' at it.

'Going well, then?' asked McCoy.

'Aye, and you can fuck off too, smart arse,' said Billy.

'Any news?' asked McCoy.

Billy shook his head. 'Still radio silence from the Woodside.' Took a dry roll from a bag on the desk and started chewing. The phone started to ring again. He picked up.

'Stewart Street.'

Listened. Grimaced.

'I can assure you, madam, we are doing all in our power to find Alice. It's not—'

Listened. Grimaced again.

'Yes, I am eating actually. Yesterday's bloody dry roll, if you must know. It's all I've got because

I've been behind this desk all bloody night, so is that all right with you?'

McCoy could hear the woman's angry voice squeaking out the phone from the other side of the desk. Left Billy to it and walked through to the office.

For once the office was just a room full of empty desks. None of the usual chatter and ringing phones; even the usual fug of cigarette smoke had gone. Place looked about the emptiest he'd seen it. Between the holidays and Alice Kelly, he was the only one in. Or so he thought.

'Any news from the Woodside?'

PC Walker emerged from under a desk with a pencil in her hand. 'Dropped it,' she said, smiling at him.

'Not according to Billy,' said McCoy. Struck him. 'Why you not up there?'

'I was,' she said. 'Mr Raeburn sent me back. Guess they had enough people to hand out glasses of water.'

'Long you been here now, Tracey?' asked McCoy, taking his jacket off.

She thought for a second. 'Near enough four months,' she said.

'Enjoying it? he asked.

She looked wary.

'Off the record,' he said.

She looked relieved. 'Not really, not if I'm being honest. Hoped I'd be doing more than making tea and trying to laugh along with the insulting jokes, but so far that's about it. Oh, and dealing with drunk females in the cells who don't have any sanitary protection, which was obviously my life's ambition. I'm making a tea. You want one?'

McCoy nodded, watched her walk over to the wee kitchen. Must have been – what? – mid-twenties? Good-looking girl, seemed smart. Had no idea why anyone like that would want to be a polis. She was on a losing wicket before she started. Hard enough to be taken seriously in a job like this as a woman, never mind a young and good-looking one.

He sat down at his desk. Felt a bit strange, with the office being so quiet. He leant over and put Thomson's wireless on to fill up the empty space. Familiar choppy guitar riff of 'Brown Sugar' faded away and 'Yellow River' started. He leant over again and switched it off. There was only so much a man could take.

He sat back in his chair, listened to Tracey humming away in the kitchen, wondering what was happening up at the Woodside Inn. Alice Kelly had been missing for almost forty hours. Chances were, if they were going to find her alive they would have done by it now. Whether anyone admitted it or not, they were looking for a body now. The phone rang, made him jump. He picked it up.

'McCoy,' he said.

'Need to speak to a detective.' Sounded like an old man. Gruff voice.

'I'm a detective, how can I help you?' said McCoy, getting the pencil out from behind his ear and looking for a bit paper.

'I killed her and I fucked her first and then I fucked her again.'

McCoy sighed, put the pencil down. 'And your name is, sir?'

The phone went dead in his ear. He put it back in the cradle. Shouted through to Billy.

'Billy! Thought you were supposed to be filtering the bloody nutters?'

An exasperated shout came back. 'Give us a break! There's just me here and the bloody phone's going every five minutes! Can't catch every mad bugger!

Billy had a point. Cases like this attracted them like bees round a honey pot.

'I did it.'

'I saw who did it. He was my boss.'

'My neighbour looks shifty. I found porn mags in his bin.'

'I saw a space ship hovering above Maryhill Road.'

'My brother-in-law likes wee girls, he's always hanging about outside school playgrounds.'

It just went on and on, every nutter in Glasgow crawling out the woodwork.

PC Walker appeared with two mugs of tea, put one down on his desk.

'Thanks.'

He sipped it. Rotten. The phone started ringing again. He shouted through. 'Billy!'

A shout came back through. 'It's legit.'

'Bloody better be,' McCoy mumbled under his breath and picked up. Listened.

This time it was.

71

CHAPTER 8

The address was in Thornliebank, right on the edge of Glasgow. So on the edge that McCoy wasn't sure if it still was Glasgow any more. Might be Paisley? East Renfrewshire? What he did know was that it was bloody miles away.

He managed to purloin a uniform who was headed to the Paisley Station for a game of five-a-side to give him a lift, persuaded him it was on the way. Jamie was his name, some big Highlander with sandy hair and hands the size of shovels. There were fewer of them now, those big Highland lads. There were loads when McCoy started in the force: big gruff guys from up north, took no shit. Half the force seemed to have been made up of them. Police force loved recruiting them. They thought if they didn't have connections to anyone in Glasgow they were less likely to be compromised or have some cousin doing housebreaking that they would turn a blind eye to. Thought that they had 'good moral character' too. Wee Frees, half of them. God-fearing men. There was still some detective over in Western, McCormack, something like that, couldn't remember. Lived up the road from him, funnily enough. Came from Ballachulish. Quiet sort, kept himself to himself. Good reputation, mind you.

Jamie drove slowly and didn't say much. Suited McCoy fine. He rolled the window down, let the breeze fill the car. Smell of cut grass, car exhausts, parched earth. Summer.

'You no boiling with that uniform on?' he asked.

Jamie nodded. 'Melting.'

And that was that. Didn't say another word until he dropped him off. Probably realised how much out his way McCoy had taken him.

Like most of the streets in Thornliebank, Arden Avenue was a long road of pebbledash four-in-a-block flats, neat wee gardens at the front, kids on bikes and roller skates zooming round. He walked up past a man watering his garden with a hose-pipe and stopped outside number 23. Wasn't quite sure what he was going to say to Wullie March. Maybe he just wanted to talk to someone who knew exactly what had happened to his son. A courtesy call, really. Kind of thing he used to do when he was a uniform. He sighed, rang the door-bell and waited.

'You looking for Wullie?'

McCoy looked round, realised the voice was coming from the next-door garden. A middle-aged man in a vest, shorts and black socks was sitting in a velvet-covered armchair in the middle of a sun-parched lawn. Wee table beside him with a can of lager and an open paperback copy of *Papillon* on it.

73

He caught McCoy looking at the armchair. 'I dragged it out this morning, couldn't find the key for the bloody hut.'

McCoy nodded, none the wiser.

'Deckchairs are in the hut,' he explained.

'Ah,' said McCoy. 'Wullie March, aye. You seen him? Said he'd be in this afternoon.'

The man smiled. 'Did he? Stupid bugger. He's never in. He'll be where he always is.' He pointed at the back of a large building just across the street.

McCoy walked round onto Barrhead Road and stood there for a minute looking at THE TRADEWINDS HOTEL as it proudly proclaimed itself via a big wrought-iron sign sitting on a big wrought-iron boat. The front of the building was white, clean lines – supposed the idea was that it looked like a yacht club or something, effect somewhat spoiled by the graffiti on the side.

'HOLE IN THE WALL GANG COUNTRY!'

Somebody with a spray can had obviously been watching too many cowboy pictures. There were a lot of places like the Tradewinds around Glasgow. Hotels, not pubs. Didn't think anyone ever stayed in them, but if they had a couple of bedrooms upstairs it meant they could apply for a hotel license and sell drink on a Sunday. And that was the day they made all their money, people coming from everywhere. He pushed the door open and went inside.

The lounge was huge, big booths, rows of seats, rows of one-arm bandits, and a stage at the end, smoke and dust whirling in the light from the big windows along the side. It was more like the kind of place you got at Butlin's or Pontins holiday camp than a pub. The difference was holiday camps tended to be busy, happy places, full of people having a good time. The Tradewinds was anything but. Sheer size made the five or six wee groups dotted around look even more miserable. All of them elderly men, all of them nursing pints, all of them smoking for Scotland.

He walked up to the bar and ordered a Coke and a pint. Drank the Coke over quickly in one slug and handed the glass back to the barman.

'Must have been thirsty,' he said.

'I was,' said McCoy. 'Still bloody boiling out there.' He took a sip of his pint. 'You know Wullie March?'

The barman nodded, pointed over at an elderly man sitting by himself at the window. Even in this heat, he had a bunnet and a cardigan on. And even at this distance, McCoy could see his hand shaking as he raised his pint up to his mouth.

'Give us a double whisky,' said McCoy to the barman. 'What kind does he drink?'

Barman snorted. 'He's no that fussy, believe me. Old bugger stops just short of turps.' He pressed a glass into the Bell's optic twice, handed it over. 'Gie him that. He'll think his ship's come in.'

McCoy took it and walked over to the table. Big picture window behind Wullie March affording a view of a newsagent, a butcher's, a parked Viva and a queue of people waiting at a bus stop. Cowes it was not.

'Mr March? You called the station, spoke to me? Detective McCoy.'

Wullie March's wee rheumy eyes took McCoy in. Then they took in the glass of whisky in his hand.

McCoy held it out. 'For you,' he said. 'Mind if I sit down?'

March nodded, shaking hand reached out for the whisky and he swallowed it over. Instant look of relief on his face.

'Sorry about what's happened,' said McCoy. 'He was a young man. Must have been a shock.'

March nodded. Now the distraction of the whisky was out the way he was looking at McCoy properly. So McCoy did the same. March was probably only fifty odds but the drink had taken its toll, burst blood vessels on his cheeks and nose, eyes red-ringed and watery. Tremor in his hands. Suit trousers shiny, white nylon shirt beneath the cardigan yellowing around the collar.

'It was. You the polis that dealt with my son?' he asked.

'I was,' said McCoy.

'Where's his bag? You got it?' said March.

McCoy looked blank. 'What bag?'

March's face crumpled, looked genuinely upset.

'Sorry, was it a sentimental thing?' asked McCoy. 'Did he have something in it? Photos?'

The upset face turned angry in a second. March

spat out the words. 'I knew it, some bastard's stolen it. I fucking knew it.'

He looked up at McCoy, anger now becoming fury. Pointed a nicotine-stained finger at him. 'Was it you? You take it, did you?'

'Me?' said McCoy. 'No! I'm a polis.'

'Think that makes a difference, do you?' said March. 'I've known more bent polis than you've had hot dinners.'

'Fair enough,' said McCoy. 'Not arguing with you there, but I'm not one and there wasn't a bag in his room. I would have seen it.'

March's hands had formed into fists, face going red. 'Well, someone's had it and I want it, should be mine. I should get it, shouldn't I?'

McCoy nodded. Started to wonder exactly how much of a toll the drink had taken on Wullie March.

'What kind of bag was it?' he asked, trying to get him back on track.

March shook his head in disgust. 'Some bloody hippy-looking thing. Cloth, long strap, wore it over his shoulder. Got it in Greece. Sandy-coloured. Had it for years, never went anywhere without it.'

'And what was in it?' asked McCoy.

March's face lit up. 'Money, there'd be money in it, wouldn't there? My boy did well, should have had money.'

He looked at McCoy, horrible smile on his face. 'And that money's mine now. It's owed. I'm his next of kin.'

McCoy nodded. Thought about Bobby March lying dead on his bed. Thought about how his father hadn't asked anything about him. Just all about the bloody bag and the hope of some easy money for more drink. More than likely the bag was where he kept his drugs and his fags rather than the wads of cash March was imagining.

'He still have pals back here?' asked McCoy. 'Girlfriends? Anyone he would see?'

March shook his head. Looked at the empty whisky glass. McCoy wasn't biting. Yet.

'No. Didnae even come and see me. Hated Glasgow. Couldn't wait to get out of it. Went to London when he was seventeen. Some band he was in. I had to sign his record contract because he was so bloody young. Never came back here, if he could help it. Hated it.'

He seemed to drift off, stared out the window at the queue of people at the bus stop across the street. Snapped back, looked at McCoy. 'Will you find the bastard that's taken it? It's a crime. They've got it and they've got my money. I haven't worked for years. I need it. I'm entitled.'

McCoy held his hands up. 'I'll see what I can do. Okay?'

March nodded, shaking hands took a ready-made roll-up out his baccy tin.

'Why'd he hate Glasgow so much?' asked McCoy.

March shook his head. 'No idea. It was his home.' He looked at him as if something had just

78

dawned. 'You know any newspaper reporters? They'd pay for my story, wouldn't they? Could tell them all about Bobby, everything they want to know. Got pictures from when he was a wee boy. A gold record, too. How much that be worth, you reckon?'

McCoy shook his head. 'I'm a polis. Don't know anything about newspapers or gold records.'

March looked at the empty whisky glass. Tried to look like he was about to cry. 'My poor boy, my poor wee boy.' Took a filthy hanky out his cardigan pocket and blew his nose into it.

McCoy knew he was laying it on thick, had to be daft not to, but he gave in. His son was dead after all, so he bought him another whisky and left him to it. Told him he'd be in touch as soon as he found out anything.

CHAPTER 9

McCoy sat down on the steps of the Sherriff Court and lit up. Across the road, Glasgow Green was full of sunbathers dotted about on the grass. In the distance the tinkle of an ice-cream van somewhere in the park. The mortuary, a low bunker-like building, was next door to the court, but he wasn't going in. Not if he could help it. Gilroy knew him well enough to know she could find him out here, away from the blood and the smell and the running water flushing whatever it flushed down the sinks. He was just going to sit here on the steps, enjoy the sun and wait for her to come out.

He took his jacket off, noticed his shoe was undone and bent over to tie it. When he looked back up, he was standing there, the boy from outside the hotel. The glitter on his face had two clear lines cutting through it where the tears had rolled down his cheek. His lip was trembling.

'You all right, son?' asked McCoy.

'He's dead. Isn't he?' he asked.

McCoy nodded.

Tears grew in the boy's eyes, rolled down his

cheeks. He sat down by McCoy and started to weep, snotty gasps and choking sobs. McCoy was a bit taken aback, wasn't quite sure what to do. Wasn't often he had a sixteen-year-old boy breaking his heart beside him. He reached out his hand, clapped his back, thin cotton wet with sweat, label sticking up. A Woolworths vest he'd decorated himself.

'Come on, son, try and pull yourself together a bit, eh? It's sad, but what's happened's happened, eh?'

A few sniffs, a rub at the eyes and he sat back up. The felt pen 'BOBBY MARCH' he'd written on his vest was smudged from the sweat and the tears. The boy looked down at it.

'My dad threw my real one in the bin. Had to make this one. It's shite. I know it's shite.'

McCoy was about to say no it isn't but didn't think he'd be able to make it sound even halfway convincing.

'Why'd he throw it away?' asked McCoy.

'Because he thinks I'm a poof,' he said. 'Says a T-shirt like that is for lassies.'

He wiped the snot from his nose, rubbed it on the stone stairs.

'Broke my records too. And now he's dead.'

Lip went, looked like he was about to start crying again. McCoy thought quickly, dug in his pocket, brought out the plectrum. Had a wee Bobby March logo on one side. Les Paul logo on the other. He held it out to the boy.

'Here,' he said. 'Take this. Don't tell anyone, but it was one of his.'

The boy just looked at him, eyes wide.

'Take it,' said McCoy.

The boy stretched out his hand and took it. Looked at it like a priest would look at some holy relic and carefully put it in his pocket.

'Now cheer up, eh?'

The boy nodded, smiled at him.

'That's the best thing anyone has ever given me. Thanks, mister.'

'A mortuary's an awful place,' said McCoy. 'It'll no help you.'

'I just want to be near where he is,' he said, with painful honesty.

Wasn't much McCoy could say to that, supposed he wasn't doing any harm.

'You at the concert last night?' he asked the boy.

Shook his head. 'Too young. Wouldn't let me in.'

McCoy looked at him. At the tear-stained glitter on his face, the felt pen T-shirt, the school trousers that were too short for him.

'What's your dad going to say when you get home?' he asked.

'He's not going to say anything,' he said quietly. 'He's just going to beat me to fuck like usual.'

Something about the boy reminded McCoy of himself at that age, wasn't sure what. Maybe the sense that life was shite and it looked like it was always going to be shite for someone like him. McCoy dug in his pocket, looking for change, came out with a fiver. Fuck it.

'Take this,' he said, holding it out. 'Go to Listen

in Renfield Street and buy yourself a proper T-shirt. Then go in the toilets and wash the glitter off. Money left, you should be able to go and get yourself another copy of *Sunday Morning Symphony*. Hide it under the bed. The last thing you need tonight is your dad leathering you.'

The boy took the note, looked stunned. 'Thank you. Thank you very much.'

'One fan to another, eh?' said McCoy

He nodded, then grabbed McCoy in a bear hug. Started crying again. McCoy managed to peel him off, told him to get to Listen before they sold out and he ran off towards Argyle Street.

McCoy watched him go, good deed for the day done. Looked at his watch. Three o'clock. Wondered if the inevitable had happened yet. A panicked phone call from some woman who'd been walking her dog in Ruchill Park or by the canal and had seen a wee leg poking out from the bushes. What would happen then? Press would get worse, the gory details, pictures of the grieving parents. And with that the pressure from Pitt Street would get worse too.

'Penny for them,' said Gilroy, sitting down on the step beside him. 'You're miles away.'

'Sorry,' said McCoy. 'Just having a think.'

She looked at him. 'You appear to have glitter on your cheek.'

McCoy rubbed at his face. 'God knows where that came from. That it gone?'

Gilroy nodded and they sat for a minute looking out over the park. At the kids running round, waiting in the ice-cream queue, playing with their mums and dads. Doing the kind of stuff Alice Kelly wouldn't be doing again.

'I hate to ask, but any news?' asked Gilroy.

McCoy shook his head. 'Not that I've heard. Been in the wild west interviewing the dad.'

'Let's keep hoping then,' said Gilroy. She held up a buff-coloured file. 'The matter in hand. One Robert Thomson March. Born 12th April 1946. Died 13th July 1973. I'm assuming you don't want to see the pictures?'

'Too bloody right,' said McCoy. 'So, what's the story? Is there one?'

'There might well be,' said Gilroy. 'There might well be.'

'Really?' McCoy was surprised.

'Cause of death is an overdose of an opiate. Had small traces of cocaine and Mandrax in his bloodstream also.'

'Didn't do things by half then,' said McCoy.

'Both so small no real effect on his death, but . . .'

'But? You're enjoying this, aren't you?'

Gilroy smiled. 'The life of a medical examiner can be a dull and lonely one. Need to brighten it up somehow. Two interesting things,' she said. 'The amount of heroin in his bloodstream was extremely high. Much more than the usual margin for error – taking in usual strength, quantity and so on. It was three times the normal level in a confirmed drug user.'

'An overdose?' asked McCoy. 'Deliberate, you

mean? Mind you, I might have killed myself if I'd made his last album.'

'That's one option,' said Gilroy. 'Another is what I believe is known as a hotshot, according to my lab technician. A deliberate overdose prepared by someone else.'

'There wasn't anybody else there, I don't think,' said McCoy. 'Just March.'

'Which leads me to my other interesting thing. You might have to rethink that idea,' said Gilroy and smiled. 'Mr March was right-handed, I looked on his album cover.' She mimed him playing guitar. 'That would imply he would inject himself in the crook of his left elbow.'

Dawned on McCoy. 'Fuck, you're right. The syringe was sticking out his right arm.'

'Precisely,' said Gilroy. 'Somewhat of an anatomical impossibility to inject your own right arm with your right hand. Presumably someone else did it for him.'

'He was murdered?' McCoy asked.

Gilroy shook her head. 'Not necessarily. Could be a friend injected him, got the amount wrong. Made themselves scarce when they realised what had happened.'

'Were there any—'

'Fingerprints on the syringe?' She grinned.

'You're way ahead of me,' said McCoy. 'As always.'

'There were some partials, but two sets. March's themselves and one other. Not on file, unfortunately. I got Hester to do a quick check. The chances are they are a woman's prints, though. TRC was 116.'

'TRC?' asked McCoy.

'Sorry. Total Ridge Count. Average for men is 145.'

'So where does that get us?' asked McCoy.

Gilroy stood up, brushed the dust off her trousers. 'It gets me the rest of the afternoon off, as it all went so quickly. Not entirely sure where it gets you.'

She went to go. Turned. 'Ah, I forgot. Mila was asking about some man you mentioned to help with her photography assignment. A Liam, I think?'

McCoy felt his face going red. Flash of him standing there with the drinks in his hand. Had forgotten Mila was staying with Gilroy.

'Speaking to him this weekend,' he said. 'I'll get it fixed up.' Changed the subject as fast as he could. 'By the way, you didn't see a bag when you were in March's room, did you? Some hippy-looking thing, cloth?'

Gilroy shook her head. 'Not that I remember. Why?'

'His dad's asking about it. Seems to think he should have had it with him.'

Gilroy waved, walked back into the shadows of the mortuary. McCoy watched her go, thought about what she'd told him. Bobby March's over-dose was starting to get complicated. Just what he didn't need.

He stood up. Thought about the other thing he didn't need and had to get on with.

Finding Laura bloody Murray.

CHAPTER 10

Jean said Laura Murray had told the cab driver to drop her 'by the swing park'. And that's where he was now, standing on the corner of Queen Margaret Drive and Hotspur Street. There were still kids out playing in the evening sunshine, trying to push the swings over the bar at the top, hanging onto the roundabout for dear life. Mums and dads were sitting on the benches, keeping watch. Didn't blame them, after all. Whoever had taken Alice Kelly was still out there.

He walked along Hotspur Street, noise of the kids getting quieter as he went. All he had to do now was remember which close it was and he was laughing. He plumped for number 45 and started climbing the stairs. The heat had turned whatever was in the rubbish bags lying outside the front doors; the whole stairway stank of rotting food. He got to the top and chapped the door. Noticed someone, a disgruntled customer no doubt, had carved 'IRIS IS A COW' into it.

The door was pulled open and Iris McLean was standing there, seemed less than pleased to see him. She looked him up and down.

'Well, well. Harry bloody McCoy. What brings you up here?' she asked.

For once Iris wasn't in her usual Joan Crawford of Glasgow get-up. Must have been off duty. The tailored suit she normally wore had been replaced by a shapeless dress, flowery pinny over it. Hair bundled under a net, slippers instead of the usual high heels.

'Cooper's no here,' she said, going to close the door.

McCoy stuck his foot in it to stop her. 'No come to see Cooper, Iris, come to see you.'

She looked even less pleased and pulled the door open. 'Better come in, then.'

Was still too early for the shebeen to be in full swing. Pubs were still open, no need to buy Iris's overpriced drink as yet. The living room was empty, record player in the corner quiet for once. Was strange to see the place in the daylight and while he was sober. Normally if he was here it was dark and it was because he was drunk. It looked like an ordinary living room: three-piece suite with antimacassars draped over the back, some dining chairs along the wall. There was a picture of a green lady above the fireplace and a view of Loch Lomond above the couch. Only thing giving the room's real purpose away was the ten or so ashtrays and twenty or so pint glasses lined up on the table.

'Come on in the kitchen, I'm stocktaking,' she said, walking through.

The kitchen was Iris's domain. No one got in here unless she let them, least of all punters. Normally one of Cooper's heavy boys would be sitting on a chair in the doorway to make sure no one got out of order, but it was too early for him as well. Usually turned up about nine. Last time McCoy had been here Jumbo was filling in, the usual guy having got into an argument with some bloke from Carantyne and a Stanley knife.

Crates of beer and whisky were piled everywhere. Hardly any room to move. Pulley hanging from the ceiling draped with bedsheets and towels. A clue to the other service the shebeen offered. Hidden behind an unsteady wall of beer crates was a press bed, picture of a wee girl in a frame on the drawers beside it, and a Sacred Heart on the wall. Bleeding and sorrowful. No doubt with good reason, if poor Jesus had to watch the goings-on in the shebeen.

Iris sat on the bed and McCoy sat down on a pile of Red Hackle boxes – only the cheapest of gut rot for Iris's customers.

Iris lit up a cigarette and started doing her make-up in a wee hand mirror.

'How's business?' McCoy asked amiably.

Iris shrugged. 'Okay. Been better, been worse.' She was outlining her mouth in bright red lipstick while she was talking. 'People always find the money for drink, even if it has to come out the rent money or their weans' mouths.'

She looked round the mirror at him. Looked

amused. 'This what you're here for, is it, McCoy? A wee chat about my future prospects?'

McCoy took the picture of Laura Murray out his wallet and handed it over. Iris barely looked at it and handed it back.

'Laura Murray. She's staying somewhere around here and she shouldn't be. Her mum and dad want her back home, she's only fifteen.'

Iris looked unimpressed. 'What's the big deal? I was only thirteen when I ran away from home.'

McCoy looked round the crowded wee kitchen, at the damp marks on the ceiling, the wallpaper that had seen better days, the dirty window.

'Not sure that was the best decision you ever made, was it?' he said. Immediately wished he hadn't. Was meant to sound funny, just came out sounding cruel.

Iris's face hardened. 'Fuck you, McCoy. You try staying in a house where your da comes knocking on your bedroom door every night after your maw's gone to sleep and see how you like it.'

McCoy held the picture up. 'The girl,' he said. 'Need to know, Iris.'

'And what makes you think I know anything about her?' she asked.

'Because we all know bugger-all happens around here without you knowing about it,' said McCoy. 'And she was a pal of Donny MacRae's. Sure that toerag's been up here a few times.'

'That dead toerag, you mean,' she said. 'Pity, he was a bloody good customer.'

'See what I mean?' said McCoy. 'Nothing passes you by, so I'm damn sure some young posh girl knocking about Hotspur Street hasn't either. I don't have time for this, Iris. I know you think I'm a useless bastard, but I'm still a polis. So answer me.'

Iris managed to look McCoy up and down while still looking down her nose at him. Not an easy feat.

'Polis? Don't bloody kid yourself. No to me, you're no. You're just another drunk banging on my door wanting a drink at one o'clock on a Saturday morning.'

Drew a blue stripe across her eyelid, ramped up the venom. 'You found that wee girl yet?' Didn't wait for him to answer. 'Thought not. Bloody useless, the lot of you. She could be lying dead and you're up here asking me about some bloody teenager. You should be ashamed of yourself, should be out there—'

'Iris, so help me I'll—'

She went back to applying her make-up. 'Donny MacRae used to bring her up here, flashing his wee posh bird around, her thinking she was drinking with Al Capone. Bloody comical, the two of them.'

'Where's she staying?' asked McCoy.

She shrugged. 'No idea, but if it's around here somewhere I could find out.' She raised her eyebrows expectantly.

McCoy took a fiver out his wallet, shook his

head. 'Mercenary as ever. You get her a message, Iris. Tell her to meet me in the Golden Egg at four o'clock tomorrow night. If she's no there, I'm going to take it personally and two big uniforms will be chapping on your door at half nine asking to see your licence to sell intoxicating liquor. Understood?'

She nodded her head, gave him a dirty look and tucked the fiver under the mattress. 'You always did have a nasty streak, McCoy. Better watch it doesn't get you in trouble one day.'

'Thanks for the advice, Iris. I'll keep it in mind.' He stood up. 'You seen Cooper?'

She laughed. 'You're joking, aren't you? No one has, not for weeks. I only deal with Billy Weir now.'

McCoy was surprised. 'Billy? How come? Is Cooper away somewhere, then?' he asked.

Iris put her make-up brush down, smirked at him, triumph on her face. 'Well, well, so you don't know everything after all, do you, smart arse? Some best pal you are. Away and visit him, see for yourself.'

She stood up. 'Now bugger off. I've got stocktaking to finish.'

CHAPTER 11

The cab stopped by the stairs at the bottom of Hillhead Street and McCoy got out, paid the man, crossed the road and turned into Hamilton Park Avenue, started counting the numbers along. Stopped and looked up at number 21. Let out a low whistle. Cooper must be making even more than he thought. The house was very big and very ugly. It stood in its own garden, trees each side, big bay windows on the ground floor, two more storeys above that, the River Kelvin rolling along in the park next door.

He couldn't believe it. Didn't look like the kind of place Cooper would buy in a million years. Normally guys like him stayed where they felt safe, in their home patch, no matter how much money they had. Thousands and thousands in the bank and still staying in a wee council house in Springburn. Then he remembered. The American girlfriend was still around. Maybe she had persuaded him to become a West Ender. Only one way to find out. He walked up the path and pressed the bell.

Waited for a minute, could hear the river flowing,

then the door opened and Billy Weir was standing there, denim shirt, denim jeans and grey socks.

'Harry! How you doing?' He held out his hand to shake, big smile on his face, seemed very pleased to see him for some reason. 'C'mon in. Leave your shoes by the door.'

'What?' asked McCoy. 'You kidding me on?'

'Don't ask,' said Billy, rolling his eyes. 'Ellie. Strict rule.'

McCoy shook his head, took his shoes off, glad to see he had matching socks on, and followed Billy into the house. Had a look around and tried to remember it was Stevie Cooper he had come to see. The hallway was wall to wall white carpet, pile so deep his feet were disappearing in it. Two big vases of white lilies were sitting on a table, huge silver-framed mirror behind them. The walls were half dark-wooden panels and half tartan wallpaper. On the far wall there was a big framed poster for an old Jimmy Cagney film. *Angels with Dirty Faces.*

McCoy nodded at it. 'That supposed to be funny?' he asked.

'She got it for his birthday,' said Billy. 'Cost a bloody fortune, apparently. The kitchen's this way,' he said, disappearing down the steps.

The kitchen could have given Phyllis Gilroy's a run for its money. It was massive. Even had French windows opening out into a walled garden. There was a round white table in the middle, no legs, just a central stalk, orange kitchen units along one wall and some sort of big, red iron stove thing on

94

the other. The floor was old flagstones, pleasantly cool beneath his stocking feet.

Billy gestured to the table. 'Take a seat. Want a can?'

McCoy nodded, still trying to take it all in.

'Sorry about the shoe thing, would drive you bloody mad,' said Billy, opening the fridge and taking out two cans of Tennent's. 'Jumbo forgot one day and she went fucking mental.'

He sat down, put a can in front of McCoy, nodded out at the garden. 'Speaking of which, take a look out there.'

McCoy stood up, walked over to the French doors. Right at the bottom of the garden, a hulking figure was digging weeds out a floral border with a hoe, dumping them in a wicker basket.

'No way . . .' said McCoy. Couldn't believe what he was seeing. 'Is that Jumbo?'

'Aye, that's him,' said Billy, shaking his head. 'Gone mad for the gardening, can hardly get him out the bloody place.'

McCoy sat down, opened his can, took a swig and looked over at Billy. 'Do you want to tell me what's going on here?' he said. 'I feel like I'm dreaming.'

Billy grinned. 'Some place, isn't it? Only got finished last week. Ellie and some decorator bloke have been at it for months. Might be a waste of time, though. Her and Cooper had a big fight and she fucked off back to New York yesterday.'

'Wasn't really talking about the house,' said McCoy. 'Iris tells me she only sees you now, not Cooper. That right?'

Billy nodded, shifted uncomfortably in his seat.

'So what's Cooper up to? Been a while since I've seen him, right enough.'

'You know . . .' said Billy. 'This and that.'

'No, I don't know. What?'

Billy didn't say anything. Just looked at him.

McCoy was starting to get annoyed. 'Billy, what the fuck's going on? Where is he?'

'He's upstairs,' said Billy.

McCoy stood up. Billy grabbed his arm. 'Harry . . .'

McCoy pulled it away. 'What's up with you, Billy?'

Billy shook his head. Looked down at the table.

McCoy left him there, headed back to the front of the house and the stairs. Started climbing. Shouting up as he did, 'Stevie? You up here?'

No reply. He reached the landing, tried again. 'Stevie! It's McCoy.'

Still nothing. There were four or five doors on the landing. He pushed one open. An empty room with a set of ladders, stripped walls and rolls of wallpaper on the floor. Tried the next one.

'Stevie!' he shouted.

Was the bathroom, all avocado suite and taps with chunky clear handles. He was starting to feel uneasy. Something really wasn't right. He pushed the next door open.

'Ste—'

Stopped halfway through and stood there in the doorway, staring down at Stevie Cooper. He was naked, sprawled across the bed, dead to the world, wooden cigar box with a blackened spoon, length of rubber tubing and a syringe in it lying on the covers beside him.

He couldn't believe what he was looking at. Didn't want to. Heard footsteps behind him and Billy was at his shoulder.

'How long has this been going on?' asked McCoy.

'Month or so,' said Billy.

McCoy turned away from Cooper, looked back at Billy. 'Christ, Billy,' he said. 'You should have told me.'

'I know, I know,' said Billy. 'I wanted to, but he told me he'd kill me if I did.'

'Is he okay?' asked McCoy.

Billy nodded. 'Aye, he's fine, just out of it.'

McCoy stepped forward and looked down at him. Cooper had changed, changed a lot. Had lost weight, muscle tone, left arm dotted with wee puncture marks and a big bruise over the inside of his elbow. His eyes were closed, head back, the scars from his past battles looked faded and pale against his deathly white skin. Even had the beginnings of a beard; blond stubble on his chin.

McCoy looked away, almost felt like crying. Was the first time he'd ever seen Cooper look vulnerable. Since they were kids Cooper had always been the strong one, the tough one, hard enough to take anyone or anything on. Not now. He moved to the bed, shook Cooper's arm.

'Stevie, it's Harry. Can you hear me?'

Shook his arm again, harder. Nothing.

'The mornings,' said Billy. 'He's better in the mornings. Come and see him then.'

McCoy nodded. Couldn't be any worse. 'This can't go on,' he said.

Billy nodded. 'I know, I know.'

Scale of it hit him. He turned angrily. 'What the fuck, Billy?'

Billy looked half sad, half guilty. 'I know, I know. Started off a couple of times a week, him and Ellie, then it was most nights, then she tried to get him to stop but you know Stevie. No one can tell him anything. He just kept saying his back was agony, that smack was the only thing that took away the pain.'

Now it made more sense. His back. The back that he always said was fine. McCoy knew it was far from healed but hadn't realised quite how bad it was. He'd been attacked six months or so ago, someone took a sword to it. Minor muscle damage was all Cooper had told him. Real story was obviously different.

McCoy sat down on one of the wee armchairs by the bed and tried to think. Billy was hovering over him, looking like a kid that had been caught doing something he shouldn't.

'Away and get us a whisky, eh?' he said, just to get rid of him.

Billy nodded, hurried off, glad to have something to do.

McCoy sat back in the chair and tried to think. Couldn't take his eyes off Cooper, how different he looked. He moaned and rolled over and McCoy could see the scar on his back properly now. It was a couple of feet long, three or four inches wide. The scar he said didn't hurt, that he said was fine. The scar Cooper had got from a maniac with a sword while he was trying to defend him.

McCoy had relied on Cooper all his life: he'd been there since he was a wee boy, scaring everyone off, keeping him safe. Taking the brunt of anything that threatened them. And now he looked like he couldn't defend himself against a kitten.

Looked like it was his turn to step up now. He lit up, watched the curtains blow in the breeze from the open window and tried to think. Cooper had worked hard to take over the Northside. Planned and schemed and fought. Finally had what he wanted. A business, respect and, going by the look of the house, money – a lot of money. And if he wasn't careful he just might be about to lose it all. If he was in this state most of the time, word was going to get out. It had to. And if it started to be common knowledge, then Cooper was toast. If it got to Ronnie Naismith or any of those guys and they smelt weakness, they would pounce.

Goodbye to the Northside. Goodbye to Cooper, too.

Billy reappeared and handed him a tumbler half full of whisky. He took it. Knocked half back.

'Right,' said McCoy. 'This is what we're going to do.' He pointed to the bed. 'First of all, get that bloody box off the bed and bin it. I mean it.'

Billy looked wary. 'He'll go nut job.'

'Aye well, we'll worry about that in the morning,' said McCoy. 'The girlfriend definitely gone for good?'

Billy nodded. 'Think so. Seemed serious this time. Told him he was a useless junkie and called a cab for the airport.'

'Right. In that case, get Iris round here tomorrow. Tell her she's moving in for a couple of weeks.'

Billy looked horrified. 'You're joking, aren't you? Iris here?'

McCoy was having none of it. 'No, I'm not, Billy. I'm not joking about any of this. You understand?'

Billy looked resigned, shook his head.

'First thing tomorrow you need to do something,' said McCoy.

'What?' asked Billy, looking puzzled. 'Do what?'

'Something that people are going to notice. And you need to make sure and tell everyone it was Cooper's idea. Make sure everyone knows he's still planning things, doing things. Need you to buy something, do someone over . . . just do something that makes people think he's still in charge.'

Billy nodded.

'If he wakes up in the morning and starts calling the odds, call Dr Purdie. Get him to knock him out with something, right?'

'Okay,' said Billy.

'State he's in, I can't see him being able to do much damage, but it's Cooper. You never know. Maybe get Jumbo up here when Purdie arrives. If you can tear him away from his bloody flowers, that is.'

Billy nodded again. Smiled. Looked relieved that things were changing.

McCoy moved closer to him, deliberately got right in his face. Billy's smile faded. 'And, Billy, when this is fixed, you and I are going to have words. You should never have let him get in this state. And I'm not happy about it. Get me?'

'Things just got out of hand, Harry, it all happened quick. And you know what Cooper's like when he's on one. He won't listen.'

'I don't care, Billy. You're his number two. Supposed to be his right-hand bloody man. Supposed to be looking out for him. You better start acting like it or you won't be much longer. Get me? I'll see to it.'

McCoy pushed him out the way and made for the stairs.

Ten minutes later he was in the Pewter Pot sitting at a table at the back, pint and a whisky in front of him, thinking about what he'd just seen. Cooper wasn't Cooper any more. Not the Cooper he knew. That Cooper wouldn't be living in a fancy house with a fancy girlfriend and a bloody smack habit.

He sipped his pint. He needed to buy some time

101

for Cooper to recover before anyone knew what the fuck was going on. Had a horrible feeling it might be too late already. *He* knew. *Billy* knew. *Jumbo* knew, and seemed like Iris had a good idea. Tomorrow Dr Purdie would know and who knew who the fuck else had been in that house. Some one-night stand of Billy's? Some friend of Ellie's who decided to tell the juicy tale to her mates in a crowded bar. Glasgow was a small place and Cooper was big news. If the story was out, they had even less time than he thought.

The pub door opened and a boy came in with tomorrow's *Sunday Mail* under his arm. McCoy waved him over, bought one. Opened it out and looked at the front page.

'SOMEONE MUST KNOW SOMETHING!'

They'd managed to get hold of another picture of Alice Kelly. Paper crown from a Christmas cracker on her head, smiling, bit of Christmas cake in her hand. Looked even younger. Even more innocent. A quick scan of the article revealed they'd nothing new. Just an exercise in keeping the pot boiling until she was found.

He put the paper down, wondered how Wattie was getting on. If he was being honest he didn't much care right now. The state of Cooper had knocked him for six. Felt out of sorts, sorry for himself and sorry for Cooper. Hoped that Billy would go gung-ho tomorrow, that it would buy them time. Nothing else he could do now but sit there in the pub and get pissed. Wasn't going to help in the long run, but it would make him feel better for a few hours. Sometimes that was enough.

Or it would have been, had Raeburn and Thomson not walked into the pub ten minutes later. In all the Cooper drama, he'd forgotten the Pewter Pot was Raeburn's local. He'd just wanted a drink, and quick, and it was the nearest pub.

Raeburn barely nodded at him, headed for the bar, and Thomson came over.

'All right, Harry. What you doing here?'

McCoy shrugged. 'Just passing. What you been up to?'

'Went to see some nonce that lives in they big flats up near Byres Road. See if he had anything to say.'

'Did he?' asked McCoy.

Thomson shook his head. 'Knew nothing, said he hadn't heard anything. And, believe me, that bastard would know. He moves in some right dodgy circles.'

'You believe him?' asked McCoy.

'Aye. Not sure Raeburn did. Tried to get heavy, punched the bloke a few times. Didn't get us anywhere. Just ended up with some middle-aged music teacher with a bleeding nose crying his eyes out.'

McCoy sipped his pint. 'Sounds like Raeburn all right. Always was fond of chucking his weight about.'

On cue the man himself appeared, two pints in his hands. One for him, one for Thomson. Subtle.

McCoy swallowed over the rest of his pint. Stood up. Nodded at Raeburn. 'How's it going?' he asked.

Raeburn looked at him. 'Good. Getting there. You off?'

McCoy nodded. 'Just came in for one.'

Raeburn sat down, lit up. 'Actually, there is something you can do for me, McCoy. For the Kelly investigation.'

'What's that?' asked McCoy.

'You know Dirty Ally, don't you?'

McCoy nodded.

'Go down to his stall tomorrow, ask him if anyone's given him any dodgy films to develop lately. Wee girls. Know what I mean?'

'Will do,' said McCoy and headed for the door. Heard Raeburn say something like 'only thing he's fit for' to Thomson, just loud enough for him to hear. He kept walking, wasn't going to give him the satisfaction. Stepped out into the street and took a few breaths. Raeburn's day would come soon, he was sure of that. Just depended on McCoy keeping himself under control until it did.

He hailed a taxi, told it to head down to the Victoria. Really did need a drink now.

11th February 1967

Cromwell Road

Bobby wasn't quite sure how long he'd been lying on the floor. Wasn't quite sure how long he'd been in the flat. Wasn't quite sure about anything really. He giggled. What he was sure of was that Iggy said she'd be back soon. Gone to see Victor. New stuff. Liquid this time, not blotters. Maybe he should get up. He thought he was hungry but he wasn't sure, couldn't remember the last time he'd eaten anything. Was sure him and Duggie had gone to a cafe, but when was that? Yesterday? Last week? Giggled again.

His vision was almost straight now, just the edges fading away into streamers. Could see the cat sitting on the windowsill, bathing in the sunshine. Could hear a radio somewhere outside. Donovan. He'd played on that one. Played on so many songs now he could hardly keep track. P.J. Proby, Lulu, the Walker Brothers, even played on a Stones track. Couldn't remember which one. His manager's phone going all the time, everyone looking for the best session guitarist in London.

He waved his hand in front of his face, watched the streamers. And here he was lying on a floor waiting for Iggy. Couldn't think of anywhere he'd rather be. Hadn't seen Syd for a while, maybe he'd gone with Iggy. Maybe he was next door. Was pretty sure he'd hear his guitar if he was here. Never put it down. The cat stretched, yawned, jumped down and headed for the kitchen. Donovan finished and 'Heartbreak Hotel' came on. He lay there and listened, music filling his head.

Song finished, he heard the door open and then Iggy and Syd were standing there, grinning. Iggy held out a tiny brown bottle.

'Got it,' she said.

She knelt down beside him, unscrewed the top, held the dropper over his left eye.

'Ready?' she asked.

He nodded.

'Keep still now,' she said. Squeezed the rubber bulb and a drop wobbled on the end of the glass tube, fell, and landed on his eye.

He blinked a couple of times, eye burning a bit. Couple of seconds of Syd and Iggy looking down at him. Nothing much seemed to be happening. Then . . .

'Oh God,' he said, big grin on his face. 'Oh my God . . .'

15TH JULY 1973

CHAPTER 12

Even being half pissed when he got to bed hadn't helped McCoy sleep. Sight of Cooper lying on the bed, gone to the world, had got to him. Felt like the rug had been pulled out under his feet. That wasn't what Cooper was supposed to do. Cooper was supposed to be the same all the time. Strong, confident, scary – not lying there, out for the count with a syringe beside him.

He eventually got fed up of the tossing and turning and put the radio on about half five. Waited for the news. Alice Kelly was still missing, police were overrun with volunteers asking to help in the search. He knew they meant well, but it was the last thing an organised search needed, people running about, trampling over evidence, getting bored and going home when they didn't find her in twenty minutes.

He got dressed, made a cup of tea, watched the sun coming up behind the cranes at the bottom of the hill. Another hot day, by the look of the bright blue sky. He dumped the last of his tea in the sink, picked up his keys and his fags, headed for the door. Up and at them.

Sundays Dirty Ally had a stall at the Barras rather than at Paddy's. Sunday was his day to be legit. None of the under-the-counter photosets or pictures he developed that couldn't go to Boots, or the second-hand porn mags. On Sundays it was cameras, lenses, photo equipment. Just another friendly stallholder.

McCoy used go to the Barras with his dad when he was a boy. All the shouting and crowds and the chance of a poke of chips was the best start to a Sunday he could think of. Now he couldn't think of anything he'd rather do less than battle through the crowds, but he needed to get it out the way, make sure Raeburn didn't have anything on him.

The Barras had been there as long as he could remember. Saturday and Sunday mornings, rain or shine. Was a big market in the East End that sold everything from curtains and carpets to meat trays and old army regalia. Half inside, with rows of stalls in big warehouse buildings, and half outside, with stalls set up in the street. On week-ends, most of the population of Glasgow seemed to be wandering round, looking for a bargain.

McCoy got out by the Squirrel, usual rebel songs blaring out the windows, and made his way along Stevenson Street. Luckily the hot weather and the holidays had lessened the crowds a bit. The market had a listless air today; it was just too hot. The stallholders were sitting beside their goods fanning themselves with newspapers or just sitting with their faces up to the sun, trying to get a tan.

110

He walked past one of the patter merchants doing his routine. Standing on a box behind a stall stacked with curtains, bedclothes, tea sets. McCoy stopped for a minute to listen, was hard to resist – these guys had always been his favourite when he was wee. The bloke had his top off, big tanned belly, swept-back silver hair, five or six gold chains round his neck. Must have been sixty odds. Wasn't letting it stop him. He was holding a fanned-out tea set in his left arm, in the right a broomstick. He was scanning the crowd, catching their eyes.

Started quiet.

'Not twenty pounds.'

'Not fifteen pounds.'

Started to get louder. Crowd getting excited.

'Not even ten pounds!'

Louder still.

'Would you believe me if I said seven pounds?' he shouted. 'Just as well because that would be a lie! Because, hold onto your hats, ladies . . .'

Another scan of the crowd. Big grin on his face, chains flashing in the sunshine.

'Ready?'

Suddenly he battered his broomstick off the counter, loud crack making everyone jump.

'Five pounds for this fine bone china tea set! Only have a couple, so get in quick!'

His plants in the audience held up fivers, shouted they wanted one, and of course some others got caught up in the excitement, handed over their fivers for a boxed-up factory reject tea set with wonky flowers on it. Some things never changed.

McCoy left them to it, wandered into the cool of the dim warehouse, usual smell of damp, candy floss and chips. He walked down past the rows of different stalls, heading for Ally. His stall was at the back. A prime position next to a stall selling broken biscuits and one selling parts and spare bags for hoovers. Ally looked up from fiddling with a camera, saw him coming, smiled, exposing his small, brown tobacco-stained teeth.

'Mr McCoy, how's the boy? You after a camera for your holidays? Got a good deal on a Leica. Fancy that? Bloody good camera, a Leica. Thirty quid to you. What d'you say?'

'I say nope,' said McCoy. 'Need a word.'

Ally sighed, told the guy with the broken biscuits he'd be back in ten minutes and followed McCoy back out into the sunshine. McCoy bought two cones from the ice-cream van and they sat on the wall opposite the pet supplies stall.

Ally licked his cone. 'No had a cone for years,' he said. 'Good shout.'

McCoy nodded, tried to eat his before it melted all over his hands. 'You know this wee girl that's gone missing?' he said.

Ally nodded, looked wary. 'Aye. Up in Maryhill?'

McCoy nodded. 'Anyone brought in any photos to be developed lately? Girls younger than they should be?'

Ally looked at him with great umbrage. 'Excuse

112

me! What kind of person do you think I am exactly?' he said.

'Don't give us it, Ally,' said McCoy, licking the ice cream off his fingers. 'Remember I've read your record sheet, so I know exactly what kind of person you are. The kind that would do anything for money, and for something like developing photos of that young girl I'm guessing you could charge a fair amount.'

Ally sniffed. 'I really wouldn't know.'

'Aye, and I'm playing for Celtic next year. Come on, Ally, this is off the record. I don't care what you've been up to in your wee dark room. I just need to know if anyone has an unusual interest in young girls. This is about getting Alice Kelly back, not about your money-making sidelines.'

Ally finished his cone, wiped his hands on his trousers. Decided to come clean. 'No for a while. Despite what you think, stuff like that doesn't come in that often,' he said.

McCoy nodded, had no real reason to disbelieve him. He stood up, finished the last of his cone. 'You'll let me know if it does,' he said. More of a statement than a question.

Ally nodded, McCoy turned to go, start walking back towards town.

'Although something else came in the other day,' said Ally.

McCoy stopped, turned. Ally was grinning. McCoy walked back and sat on the wall again.

'What?' he asked.

'Wouldn't you like to know,' said Ally. 'It'll cost you.'

McCoy looked at him. Didn't say anything. Ally started to look nervous.

'Some people like this weather,' said McCoy. 'Cheers them up. Me, I don't. I get too hot, sweaty, in a bad mood. So if you don't tell me what you're on about, Ally, I'm going to kick your head in. Right here, right in front of the pet supplies stall.'

Ally tutted. 'Was worth a go, no need to be nasty.'

'Ally . . .' growled McCoy.

'Pictures of your pal,' said Ally. 'I've got some very interesting pictures of your pal.'

'Who's that, then?' asked McCoy.

'You've only got one pal. C'mon, I'll give you a goosey-goosey.'

There were six of them. First three looked like they had been taken without him knowing. Door of the bedroom framing Cooper sitting on the bed bare-chested. First one, he had a rubber tube round his arm. Second one, he had a Zippo lighter under a spoon. The third one, he was injecting himself. Next three were all pretty similar. Cooper must have passed out. Whoever had taken them had come into the bedroom. In all three he was lying back on the bed, dead to the world, empty syringe in his hand.

McCoy sat down on the wee stool behind Ally's stall, felt sick, felt like he couldn't breathe. What he was trying to prevent had happened already. Someone trying to cash in on Cooper's condition.

114

'Good stuff, eh?' said Ally.

'Who brought them in?' asked McCoy.

'Boy. Twelve, thirteen. Handed me the roll of film and twenty quid and said he wanted them developed. Would be back in a couple of days. Said a man had given him a quid to do it.'

'What man?' asked McCoy.

Ally shrugged. 'That was all he said – a man.'

He went to take the photos back. McCoy held onto them.

'I need these and the negatives,' he said.

Ally sucked air through his teeth. 'Not sure I can do that, Mr McCoy. What do I tell the boy when he comes back?'

McCoy got his wallet out. Had forty quid and change. Handed over the two twenties. 'You tell him light got in the camera somehow, the film was blank. Right? Give him some old exposed film.'

Ally took the money, shoved it into his pocket.

'Right?' said McCoy again.

'Aye right, I promise,' said Ally. Shuffled round in one of the trays behind the counter. Handed McCoy a glassine envelope of negatives. 'Happy now?'

McCoy took them, moved in on Ally. 'I swear, Ally, if any of these turn up, or I hear you talking about them, I'll fucking destroy you. Get you charged with everything I can think of, plus I'll make sure everyone thinks you took the photos as well. Barlinnie will be hell on earth. Got me?'

Ally nodded. 'Christ, you need to calm down, Mr McCoy. Deal's done. Forty quid. We're square.'

McCoy walked out the darkness of the warehouse into the heat and sunlight, photos and negatives in his pocket. Trouble was, he didn't trust Ally as far as he could throw him. Chances of him staying quiet were even at best. He walked up to Trongate wondering who had taken the pictures and why. Billy? Ellie? Couldn't be Jumbo, he didn't have the wits about him. Stopped. Couldn't believe it. He crossed over. Big red letters on the wall of Goldbergs department store.

'BOBBY MARCH WILL LIVE FOREVER!!'

He stood and looked at it. Had a fair idea who would have done it and he probably used the T-shirt money he'd given him to buy the spray paint.

CHAPTER 13

McCoy sat down at his desk and dumped Wattie's files in front of him. First instinct was to go to Cooper's with the photos but he didn't think he'd be well enough to make any sense. Besides, he didn't really want to be there when Cooper discovered the box of smack had been binned on his orders. Decided to leave Billy and Dr Purdie to deal with it. Let them earn their money for once. Also, he knew if he went there now he'd blurt something out about the photos and he needed to have a proper think, work out how to approach it first. Needed something in the front of his brain and to let the photo problem wheel away in the back. Hence the files.

He lit up, opened the first one. Was the latest, only last week. Some robbery at the Southern General of all places. Two masked guys with rifles burst into the administration block, threatened the wages clerks – two middle-aged women, by the look of them – told the accountant they would 'shoot his fucking face off' if he didn't open the safe. Sensibly he did and they got away with thirty-six thousand quid of wages. Were seen getting into a blue Cortina and driving off, driver also wearing a balaclava. The Cortina, stolen, was dumped by a warehouse in Hillington.

'We meet again.'

McCoy looked up and PC Walker was standing there.

'You ever leave this place?' he asked.

'Nope,' she said. 'Sleep in a wee nest of paper under my desk.'

'I believe it. You busy?' he asked.

'You joking?' she replied, looking around the empty office. 'I've even started washing the mugs.'

'Good,' said McCoy. 'Away up to the Woodside Inn and tell Raeburn that Dirty Ally was a dead end.'

'I could phone and tell him,' she said. 'Be quicker.'

'You could,' said McCoy, 'but this way you get an hour out this dump and an hour in the sunshine.'

She smiled, recited, 'Detective McCoy said Dirty Ally was a dead end.'

'That's it. He'll know what it means.'

McCoy sat back in his chair, watched her get her hat on and go. He had sent her for his benefit as much as her's. Much as he appreciated her enthusiasm he didn't want to spend the next hour with her eyes burning into his back, desperately hoping he'd ask her to do something. He dropped some ash onto the top file, brushed it off and opened it. Heart sank. Raeburn had done him over, right enough. What he knew about armed robbery you could write on the back of a bloody postage stamp.

Three-quarters of an hour, three fags and a mug of tea later he had made his way through four other files. Five robberies in all. All the same scenario. Two armed guys, a driver, in and out as quick as possible. All over Glasgow as well. A Royal Bank in Townhead, a Savings Bank in Carntyne, a wages office in a factory in Barmulloch

He'd left the best one until last. A post office in Westray Circus. He knew Westray Circus well. A row of shops in the Milton where the buses turned around before they went back into town. Far as he remembered a friend of his mum's used to work in the post office there. He read through the file. Looked like she still did. Margery Royce had been interviewed by Wattie. He skimmed through it, nothing much, basic description of what happened. Security van turned up at nine, unloaded the cash. Soon as the van left, two blokes burst in. McCoy smiled. Apparently 'one was a right wee smout', according to Margery. Threatened the two women with a sawn-off shotgun and a pistol, gave them two sports bags to fill up and were away within two or three minutes. He flicked through the file. As predicted, a stolen Corsair found later, this time abandoned by the train tracks at Whitehill.

The fact that the robbers turned up within a few minutes of the money delivery meant they must have been watching the post office for a while, making sure it came at the same time each week. He flicked back. Wattie had asked the women if they'd noticed anyone suspicious hanging around. They hadn't. Wasn't surprised. The post office was always busy, all the pensioners that came in for their money liked a chat. Christ knows, was probably the only conversation most of them had all week. Looked at his watch. Maybe he would go and see what else Margery might have remembered. Wasn't exactly the best idea he'd ever had, but to be honest it was the only thing he could think of. Besides, the Woodside Inn was on the way back. Sort of.

McCoy got a pool car brought round. Eddie, one of the mechanics, pulled it in front of the shop, got out and gave him the keys.

'Sorry, Harry. It's a pile of shite, but they're all out, up at the Woodside.'

McCoy looked at the car. A Viva on its last legs. Great.

'Should be all right,' said Eddie. 'Might stall a few times, but just pull the choke out if the bugger does. I wound the windows down, but it's still like a bloody oven in there.'

McCoy got in. Eddie wasn't lying. The car was stifling, smelt of sick too. No doubt some jakey had thrown up in it last time it was out. He was just about to drive away when he saw Billy the desk sergeant and a middle-aged man coming out the station doors. Billy pointed over at him and the man nodded. Wasn't hard to work out who he was. Looked exactly like Murray, except about ten years and a good few stone lighter. McCoy sighed, turned the engine off, got out the car.

John Murray walked towards him, looking less than happy. McCoy held his hand out to shake but he didn't take it.

'Are you the one that's supposed to be looking for my daughter?' he asked.

McCoy nodded, back already up.

'Well? How are you getting on?' he asked.

'Getting there,' said McCoy. 'Hopefully have a meeting with her tonight.'

Murray's face clouded over. 'A meeting?' he asked. 'Why do you need to have a meeting? Just get her home. I need her home quick, didn't my brother tell you that?'

McCoy reached into his pocket for his cigarettes, took his time lighting up. Far as he was concerned he was doing John Murray a favour. Didn't like being treated like a bloody errand boy.

'Your brother told me lots of things,' he said. 'You're some sort of councillor, that right?'

Murray correctly took it as the insult it was. Got even less friendly. 'If you mean that my job is deputy head of the Glasgow District Council, then yes, I am some sort of councillor.'

'Good at it, are you?' said McCoy, exhaling a cloud of smoke in Murray's general direction.

Murray looked McCoy up and down. 'I'm not entirely sure what that has to do with you, but yes, I'm very good at it.'

121

'Good,' said McCoy. 'Because you know what? My job is being a polis and I'm very fucking good at it. And instead of doing it I'm working off the books to help you and your brother out. All my time spent just so there are no wee surprises in the paper to scupper your chances of being an MP.' He stopped, dropped his cigarette and stood on it. 'So if you'd like to get back to issuing dog licences, or whatever the fuck it is you think you're good at, and leave me the fuck alone to get on with it, then maybe your daughter'll be home sooner than you think.'

He opened the car door, got in and drove off. Looked in the rear-view mirror. Murray standing there looking like he's had a bucket of cold water thrown over him. Served the wanker right.

The streets were quiet – so quiet he could hear the distant clanging of church bells as he pulled away from Stewart Street and that was about it. No traffic, no one around. Anyone who hadn't gone away would be in one of the parks already or in their back garden lying on a towel reading the Sunday papers.

He drove north up past the Royal and headed for the Milton. Mind you, if Margery heard him calling where she lived the Milton he'd be in big trouble. According to her, she lived in Parkhouse and she made sure everyone knew it. Parkhouse was supposed to be the posh bit of the Milton, posh meaning it was on the other side of Ashgill Road. Apart from that McCoy was at a bit of a loss as to why it was different. Same flats and houses, same empty streets, same council estate as far as he could see.

He stopped at the lights at Atlas Road, looked over. Passenger in the car next to him had her head deep in *The Citizen*. Banner headline: 'ALICE: BIGGEST MANHUNT IN GLASGOW HISTORY'.

To McCoy, it was already looking like a lost cause. Chances are Alice had been dead within a couple of hours after she went missing, murdered by someone she knew. Reminded himself to ask Wattie if he'd asked about the mum having a boyfriend. Much as the idea terrified the public and gave the papers a chance to scare everyone, in reality kids being snatched away by strangers hardly ever happened. Truth was, it was usually a relative, a neighbour, some shopkeeper who served them sweets every day. Someone they trusted. Someone they knew.

Lights changed and he got going. All he could do was the same as everyone else in Glasgow. Just wait for the inevitable.

The Milton was enjoying the sunshine. Kids were out in the streets, girls playing ropes, boys playing kerby, adults sitting in chairs in their gardens, constant noise of ice-cream-van chimes, general air of holidays about the place. Margery lived on Crowhill Street. He turned in and pulled up by her house. The next-door neighbours had a paddling pool in the garden, toddler in a swim-suit, big nappy under it, splashing away as her mum and dad sat on kitchen chairs, both of them eating ice poles. He walked up the path and chapped on Margery's door. Couple of seconds later it opened and Margery was standing there in a flowery dress, hat, holding a shiny handbag the size of a small suitcase.

'Harry!' she said. 'What you doing here? I was just on the way to Mass. They're having a prayer vigil for that wee girl that's missing.'

'No problem,' said McCoy. 'I'll walk you up.'

Margery smiled, closed the door behind her and they set off up the path, Margery waving at the couple next door.

'Least they're no bloody shouting at each other for once,' she said to McCoy under her breath.

They were only a few hundred yards up the street to St Augustine's when Harry remembered what it was about Margery that drove him bonkers. She never shut up. Ever. Talked constantly, didn't even seem to pause for breath. He nodded periodically as she blabbered on, let it wash over him. Thought about the photos. What were they for? To show to someone like Naismith? Persuade them Cooper was an easy target? He'd always trusted Billy, but maybe when he saw Cooper developing a habit he let it happen, saw his chance. He hadn't come and told him about it, after all. Didn't quite believe it, though. Billy was a born right-hand man. Liked the perks and the status but didn't want the danger of being in the firing line.

He tuned back in. Margery was still going strong.

'So, when she died, God rest her soul, Father Martin says to me, "Margery, how would you feel about doing the flowers, now Teresa's gone?" So I says I'd love to, Father, and I could see Agnes McConnel out the corner of my eye as I said it. The face on her! Pure beeling. Looked like she was chewing a wasp. Couldn't help myself, laid it on thick. It's such an honour to be chosen, Father, I says, a real privilege, and Mary McConnel turns and walks away, cheap bloody heels she always wears tapping on the tiles. Stupid cow. So that's me now. I get there two hours earlier, get all the flowers sorted. Have to say, Harry, I really enjoy it. Wasn't sure I would, to be honest. I was just delighted to do it to shove it up Mary McConnel's hole. But I'm loving it now, even thinking of taking it up professionally, you know, weddings and that. How's your maw?'

No space for an answer before she started again.

'I went up to see her the other week, seemed a bit brighter, she was sitting in the garden, got a bit of colour on her face. Only good thing about that bloody place, that garden. I don't know who does it, but they keep it lovely. It's like a—'

McCoy had stopped walking. Margery stopped too, looked at him. Was just about to start again, so he jumped in quick.

'I'm here as a polis, Margery. Need to talk to you about the raid.'

Was like she'd been deflated like a balloon. Suddenly looked scared, like a fragile old woman.

He nodded over at a bench. 'Come and sit down.'

She did, took a packet of Rothmans out her bag, leant in as Harry lit his lighter for her. 'It was horrible, son,' she said. 'Really horrible. I was terrified.'

'I'm not surprised,' said McCoy. 'The two guys. Anything about them you remember?'

She shook her head. 'No really. I already told the other policeman, big lad, blond hair.'

'Wattie.'

'Watson, aye, that was his name. Very polite. Lovely suit too, must have cost a good few bob. I said to him, where would you get a suit like—'

'Margery . . .'

'Sorry,' she said. 'One was big and one was wee. I mean really wee for a man. Five foot maybe. Other one was about the height of you. They had balaclavas on, jeans, blue shirts, nothing special. Sandshoes, both dressed the same.'

'They say anything?' asked McCoy.

She shook her head. 'Not much, and it was only the wee one. He said it was a raid, chucked a holdall thing at me, told me to fill it up. The big one didn't say anything but the wee one kept looking at him like he was the one in charge.'

'He have an accent, the wee one?'

'Naw, just sounded like Glasgow, like you or me.'

McCoy realised her hands were shaking. Took one in his. She smiled.

'The post office said they'd send me and Doris on a holiday. Recover, you know? I said naw, rather be here, got the flowers to do now and I feel safe here, even though it happened here. People I know all around me. I could chap any door, go in for a cup of tea. Know what I mean?'

McCoy nodded.

'You know who they are?' she asked.

'Nope. That's what I'm trying to find out.'

Margery smiled. 'Away up to Liddesdale Street and ask Mr Norton. He was a bank robber, wasn't he?'

McCoy nodded. 'A long time ago he was. A big one. He got done for it, was in for a few years. Think he's a bit old for it now. Haven't heard much about him for ages.'

'Well, he's no short of a bob or two, I'll tell you that. Always turned out smart, picked up in big cars, gives money to the weans in the street. Thinks he's Daddy bloody Warbucks.'

McCoy stood up. 'I'll have a think about it. You take care of yourself, Margery. Remember, anything else, you let me know.'

She nodded. 'Will do. I'll see you, son. I'll tell your maw you were asking for her.'

McCoy left her there on the bench finishing her cigarette. Not sure he'd really heard much that could help. One thing maybe. He'd forgotten all about William Norton. If anyone knew about bank robberies, it was him. Besides, he really didn't want to go back to the office on a day like this. Maybe he'd just take a walk and see if Mr Norton was home.

CHAPTER 14

Liddesdale Drive was in deepest Milton, no illusions of Parkhouse here. He parked the car behind a VW Beetle up on bricks and got out. Had a look around. Like all the streets round here, it was wide and empty, no other cars. Just a few dogs and kids milling about, a smartly dressed elderly couple on their way back from church. Flats were four storeys high, balconies with rusting wrought-iron railings across them. Some people had obviously decided tipping things off them was quicker than carrying them down. Front gardens were dotted with old mattresses, even a gas cooker in one.

'Look after your car, mister?'

He turned and a boy, nine or ten, shorts, stripy T-shirt and scabby knees, was looking up at him, holding his hand out.

'Just ten pence, that's all I ask. If I'm guarding it, stops it getting tanned. Every bugger round here knows not to mess with Georgie Buchan, if you know what I mean.' Winked.

'Problem is it's no my car and it's on its last legs anyway. So I don't care if it gets tanned or not.'

The junior Al Capone's face fell. McCoy dug in his pocket and found a ten pence. Held it out. 'Which close is Mr Norton's?'

Georgie pointed across the street. 'That one.'

He held his hand out again and McCoy dropped the coin into it. 'And that includes looking after the car,' he added.

Georgie nodded, saluted. Climbed up and sat on the car bonnet, scanned the street side to side like a lookout on a tank.

McCoy crossed over, was just about at Norton's close when two things happened. A dark blue Jag pulled up behind him and William Norton appeared in the doorway. Norton was late fifties, dressed in a navy double-breasted blazer with brass buttons, grey slacks, open white shirt, hair slicked back. Like he was en route to his golf club for an afternoon round. He stopped and looked at McCoy, took him a couple of seconds to realise who he was.

'Well, well. McCoy, what you doing here?'

Meanwhile the driver had got out the car, was hovering somewhere behind McCoy's shoulder. McCoy turned, saw who it was. Duncan Stewart. Checked suit and shoulder-length red hair set off by two livid scars on his cheek, cold smile on his face. McCoy had run into him a few times. Was a right bastard. As evil as they came.

'Want to step back a bit, Stewart?' said McCoy. 'Your breath is giving me the boak.'

Duncan's smile got even colder and he stepped back two paces.

McCoy turned back to Norton. 'Came to have a wee word. That okay?'

'Did you now?' said Norton. He looked up at the sky, sun on his face. 'Lovely day,' he said. Looked back at McCoy. 'You going to spoil it for me?'

McCoy shook his head. 'Unofficial. Just need some advice.'

Norton pointed at the car. 'In that case, in you get.'

McCoy had the in with Norton because of his son-in-law Danny, one of the Blue Angels. A driver in a Cortina hadn't seen Danny's bike and had pulled out a side street into Garscube Road. Danny went straight into the side of the car, then went flying over it. McCoy had just come out the tobacconist's across the road and had seen the whole thing. Fact that he told the court it was the driver's fault meant he was 'decent for a copper' in Danny's and hence Norton's eyes. That and a bit of flattery had got him his ride in the car.

He got in the back of the Jag and Norton eased in beside him, nodded at Stewart and they pulled away. Inside, the car was a cool cocoon of dark leather and new car smell. Norton rolled down his window, lit up a Rothmans.

'Need to ask you about some bank robberies,' said McCoy.

Norton laughed. 'Thought you weren't going to spoil my day,' he said.

'Don't worry, I know you're retired. It's not about you,' said McCoy. 'Just need a bit of help.'

'Let me guess . . .' began Norton, looking annoyed. 'Westray Circus? Bloody cheek of it. On my patch as well.'

McCoy nodded. 'That and the Southern General. Couple of others. Any ideas?'

Norton looked at him. Dark eyes narrowed. 'Even if I knew anything about them, which I don't, why would I tell you? Picking Danny up after he's had a smash buys you some common courtesy and a shot in my big motor. Not a grass in your pocket.'

'I'm no asking you to grass,' said McCoy, trying to get him back on an even keel. 'I'm no that stupid. I'm supposed to be investigating these armed robberies and I know bugger all about them or any other ones, come to that. So, any tips?'

Norton laughed. 'I'll say one thing for you, McCoy, you've got some bloody cheek.'

The car pulled up at the lights at the bottom of Bilsland Drive.

Norton tapped the driver on the shoulder. 'Duncan? Away and get me some fags, eh?'

Stewart nodded in the rear-view mirror, turned into Maryhill Road, pulled in by Millie's Motors and got out.

Norton waited until he was in the newsagent's, then turned to McCoy. 'Two pieces of advice for you, son. It's a nice day, the sun's shining and I'm in a good mood, so listen because this is the best advice you're ever going to get. You don't catch bank robbers, they get themselves caught. One of them always feels he's being shortchanged or he can get away with fucking the other ones over. They fight amongst themselves, make noise, buy stupid stuff, get noticed.'

McCoy nodded, made sense. 'And two?'

Norton smiled. 'Two's simple. If you're not out this car by the time Stewart gets back with my fags, I'm going to do something I regret involving the razor in my jacket pocket.' He leant in to McCoy, smell of aftershave and cigarettes. 'A joke's a joke, son, but if you ever treat me like some grass again it'll be the last thing you do. Now get out my car.'

McCoy watched the Jag pull away. Wasn't sure he'd learnt much about bank robberies. Knew one thing, though. Even if Norton was retired, he was still someone not to be messed with.

CHAPTER 15

McCoy walked back to the car, just what he needed in heat like this. To give him his due, the Junior Al Capone was still on duty, sitting on his bonnet scanning the Milton streets. He gave him another ten pence for his diligence and drove back towards town, past Maryhill Road, past Munns Vaults and the undertaker's, past Jaconelli's. Knew where he was going to end up, couldn't help himself.

He had to admit, he quite liked Norton. Had a bit of style about him even if he was a dinosaur, part of an earlier generation. At least you knew where you were with him. McCoy smiled to himself – where he was with Norton was firmly in his bad books.

Thomson was standing outside the Woodside Inn when he got there, directing two uniforms with coloured ropes trying to erect some sort of cordon round the pub. Needed to stop 'every bugger' wandering in, as he described it. The crowd around the pub had got even bigger: even more kids, even more reporters. More people with nothing else to do but sit on the walls or stand around eating cones, smoking cigarettes, hoping that something was going to happen and they were going to be there to see it.

Thomson shook his head, kept his eyes on the lads with the ropes, shouting advice, telling them how much of an arse they were making of it. Ropes finally up to his satisfaction, he turned to McCoy and told him he was in luck. Raeburn was at Pitt Street giving them a progress report.

He went to walk into the pub and Thomson shouted after him, 'Your pal's no in there, by the way.'

McCoy stopped. Turned. 'Where is he?' he asked.

'Up at Ruchill Park organising the fingertip search,' said Thomson. 'And no, before you ask, there's no bloody news, just me stuck here trying to keep this bunch of idiots away from this bloody pub.'

McCoy cursed, realised he'd have to walk back up the hill. He left Thomson to it, took off his jacket and set off. A woman he vaguely recognised from the TV news was interviewing some of the mums with weans in their arms. Must be desperate. He heard her ask 'And what do you think has happened to Alice?' as he walked past. Didn't wait to hear the answer. If the woman had told her the truth, said she was probably lying dead somewhere, they weren't going to show it anyway.

McCoy couldn't remember ever being in Ruchill Park, just knew it was big, hill right in the middle with a flagpole on top of it. He crossed at the lights, stayed on the shady side of the street, wondered what Raeburn was telling Pitt Street. The usual, he imagined. We're expecting a break-through soon, getting close. Whether it was true or not that was what they wanted to hear – the only thing they wanted to hear.

McCoy stopped for a minute; even in the shade it was boiling. He loosened his tie, unbuttoned his shirt. Walked past the old men passing a bottle outside the church at Queen's Cross, up to Murano Street and through the gates to the park.

First thing he saw was a line of uniformed polis stretching across the bottom of the hill, slowly inching their way forward, heads down, trying to find some sort of trace of Alice Kelly in the parched grass. Could see Wattie behind them, another thirty or so uniforms gathered round him listening as he pointed out the route they were to take. They walked off, formed a line over by the trees and started the same head-down walk. McCoy put his fingers in his mouth and whistled. Wattie looked up, waved, walked over.

They found a bench on the path beside a bed of wilting pansies and sat down. Wattie's shirt was damp with sweat, sticking to his back. He took a look round, decided no one would see, pulled it out his trousers, unbuttoned it and started flap-ping the tail around, trying to get some air between the clammy cloth and him.

'Had a quick look at your robbery files,' said McCoy. 'You sure you finished school?

Wattie sighed. 'And to think I was almost missing working with you.'

'Any news?'

Wattie shook his head. 'Think I'd be up here sweating my arse off if there was?'

'Fair point,' said McCoy, lighting up. 'How's the bold Raeburn getting on?'

Wattie looked vaguely guilty, knew he shouldn't really be telling tales out of school, spoke quietly as if Raeburn might hear him. 'Far as I can tell, we're getting nowhere,' he said. 'And Raeburn's getting more and more wound up, shouting the odds, acting like a right arse. Gone up to Pitt Street to give them a report. Trouble is he hasn't got anything to tell them, least of all anything that'll shut the papers up, which is what they really care about.'

'And here was me thinking he was your new best pal,' said McCoy.

Wattie looked exasperated, still flapping his shirt in the wind. 'I didnae chose this, McCoy, you know that fine well. I'm no bloody stupid. I know the only reason he's got me on board is to annoy you.'

'Okay, okay. I know. Sorry.'

McCoy felt a bit guilty. Was too easy to wind Wattie up about his new role as Raeburn's right-hand man. And that was Raeburn's plan, he supposed. Oldest one there was. Divide and rule.

'These bloody bank robberies you've dumped me with . . .' He raised his eyebrows. 'Inside job?'

'You not read the file?' asked Wattie.

'I told you, I tried to, but there's only so much bad grammar and atrocious spelling a man can take.'

Wattie shook his head. 'Don't think so. I interviewed all the staff, checked their backgrounds, seems they're all clean. Plus there were too many different kinds of places, post offices, shops, banks. Can't have had someone in each place. Think that's asking too much.'

'Should have thought of that,' said McCoy glumly.

'It was thirty-two grand from the Southern General alone, Harry. That's a lot,' said Wattie, one eye on the advancing line of uniforms.

'What are Pitt Street saying to it?' he asked.

'They're not happy, not happy at all. Word is they were about to pull Raeburn in for a bollocking about it before this Alice Kelly case came up.'

'Maybe they'll go back after him when the girl turns up,' said McCoy.

Wattie stopped flapping and looked at him. 'You don't get it, do you, Harry? He's dumping it on you deliberately. This Kelly case has given him the excuse. It's not him Pitt Street'll be after. It'll be you.'

McCoy sat back on the bench, reality of the situation dawning on him. 'It's hard to believe, but Raeburn is even more of a sneaky bastard than I thought,' he said in wonder.

Wattie nodded. 'And he's a devious bugger, too. Dumps the robberies no one can get anywhere with and meanwhile solves the Kelly case, highest-profile case of the year, looks like a hero.'

McCoy sighed. 'And I end up fucked.'

'I didn't say that . . .'

'Suppose I better take a proper look at the bloody files, then,' said McCoy.

Wattie grinned, sat down beside him on the bench. 'Might not be that bad an idea.'

'What's Mary saying to Alice Kelly?' asked McCoy. 'She pumping you for all the details?' Realised what he'd said. 'If you'll pardon the expression.'

Wattie shook his head. 'I've hardly seen her, been working so hard I haven't really been home. Besides, she knows I wouldn't be able to tell her anything.'

'Does she?' said McCoy, trying not to sound surprised.

Besides being a senior reporter at the *Record*, Mary wasn't someone that usually took no for an answer, even if she was your girlfriend. *Especially* if she was your girlfriend. Was hard to imagine Wattie laying down the law, but couples were funny things.

They sat for a minute and watched the slow progress of the uniforms advancing up the hill. Both of them hoping that there'd be a shout, one would look up, hold up his hand, say he'd found something. McCoy nodded over to the park stretching out in front of them.

'This bloody park's huge. Then beyond that there's all that scrub ground behind the football stadium.' He pointed over to the left. 'Canal basin's just over there. She couldn't have disappeared in a worse place.'

'Tell me about it,' said Wattie, sounding downhearted. 'They're starting the divers in a couple of hours. He's held off as long as he can but . . .'

McCoy knew what he meant. Soon as the divers were out the press would be right on it, the parents would find out. May as well just ring them up and tell them we think your daughter's floating face down in the Forth and Clyde canal, bear with us while we fish her out.

'Raeburn's getting some police dog delivered from Stirling. Asked the maw for a pair of the girl's socks, see if the dog can get a scent.' Wattie wafted his shirt again. 'So what do you think?'

McCoy decided to be the better man and tell the truth. 'Much as it pains me to say it, I think Raeburn's doing not a bad job.'

Wattie looked surprised. 'Wasn't expecting to hear that.'

McCoy shrugged. 'He's been a polis for twenty years. He's an arse, but he's not completely useless. Knows the mechanics.' He smiled.

Wattie shook his head. 'Can never tell with you, McCoy. Not sure if that's a compliment or a slap in the face.'

'It's a compliment!' he said. 'Always delighted to congratulate a fellow officer on sterling work.'

'Now I know it's not,' said Wattie.

'By the way, how's the mum and dad?' asked McCoy.

'Ah, here we go. Was waiting for that.' He looked round, no one within earshot. 'I was just about to tell you. Between you and me, I think there's something funny going on there.'

'Like what?' asked McCoy.

Wattie lit up, flicked the spent match towards the bin. Missed.

'Well, you speak to the mum and the little girl was an angel. Helped look after her wee brother, played with the kids in the close, did what she was told. Door-to-door uniforms got the same story.'

'But . . .' said McCoy.

'But I talked to the neighbours myself, pressed a bit harder . . .' He sat forward, lowered his voice. 'She's thirteen, but neighbours say they see her out at all hours, hanging about with older kids. Full of cheek, more of a teenager than a wee girl.'

'So she might have had the gumption to go for a wander on her own? Or with a boyfriend?'

Wattie shrugged. 'Don't know, but it could mean she knows whoever's taken her, that it's not just some stranger bundling her into a car out the blue. Might have gone with someone voluntarily, thought she was being all smart and grown up and then found herself in real trouble.'

'Which is a whole different ball game,' said McCoy.

Wattie nodded. 'I'm sure some of this is just gossiping neighbours, but they also said the mum's no much of a mum. Apart from letting Alice run wild, she's had the Cruelty up at the baby a few

140

times. Neglect. Left him alone while she's downstairs in the pub. Neighbour's could hear him crying for hours. And it seems she's no averse to coming home with men pals when the husband's away.'

McCoy shook his head. Never ceased to amaze him how eager people were to put the boot in. Whatever Alice Kelly's mum had or hadn't done, her kid was missing, probably dead, and it was going to be all her fault because she didn't bleach her net curtains often enough.

'How about the dad? What's his name?'

'Finn,' said Wattie, waving at a persistent fly in front of his face.

'Finn? Finn?' said McCoy. 'Last Finn I heard of was a Christian Brother at Nazareth House and he was a right bloody psychopath. Finn Kelly? Sounds like he should be playing at the bloody Shamrock Inn.'

Wattie nodded. 'I told you the bloody house was like a shrine. Up the IRA and all the rest.'

'What's this Finn doing in Ireland anyway?' asked McCoy.

Wattie shrugged. 'Nobody's really sure. Mum said he was working for his cousin. Some building site in Belfast.'

'Got a record?' asked McCoy.

Wattie shook his head. 'Straight. Labouring jobs mostly. Drove a van for Tennent's for a while. He's getting the plane from Alderhay. Should be here this afternoon.'

141

'Make sure you're there when Raeburn talks to him, eh?'

Wattie nodded. Looked at his watch. 'Fido or whatever the bloody dug's called should be here by now. Better get going.'

'Norton gave me the bum's rush. Mostin's in Peterhead. Big Rab's getting on seventy. Can't see it.' McCoy thought again. 'Roddy Curry?'

'What?' asked Wattie, looking puzzled.

'Bank robbers!' said McCoy.

'I thought we were talking about Finn Kelly?' asked Wattie.

'We were. But now, thanks to you and my impending career collapse, I'm thinking about bank robbers.'

'He's in Barlinnie,' said Wattie. 'Roddy Curry.' Tried to look at his watch without McCoy seeing.

'Away you go before Raeburn gets back and catches you with the enemy,' said McCoy.

Wattie nodded, stood up. 'Have a proper read of my files, then I'll go through it with you. Maybe you'll see something nobody else did.'

'Mr Watson!'

They turned and a female in uniform was running towards them. McCoy shaded his eyes, realised it was PC Walker. He nodded at Wattie. 'Better button up your shirt, don't want the poor lassie overcome with desire.'

'Shite,' said Wattie, starting to button quickly.

'All right, Tracey?' said McCoy. She nodded, was breathing hard, tried not to look as Wattie

142

unzipped his trousers, exposing paisley-patterned underpants, and tucked his shirt back in. 'You still up here?'

'Got roped into pint-glass-of-water duty,' she said. 'Feel like a bloody barmaid. Least they'd get some bloody tips.'

She put her hand to her mouth, realised she was being too familiar. Tried to compensate. 'Mr Raeburn sent me up to get you, Mr Watson. He wants you back at the Woodside.'

'Lucky you,' said McCoy. 'Probably wants his arse wiped.'

Wattie shook his head. 'Can't help yourself, can you?' he said, and followed PC Walker down the hill.

McCoy watched Wattie go, hated to admit it but he missed him. Missed his enthusiasm, missed having someone to work with. Couldn't think of anything he'd like to do less on a day like this than sit in the office reading a pile of bank robbery files. Still, knew he had to get on with it and a part of him hoped he would find something in the files they'd all missed. Something he could use to find the robbers, then ram that right up Raeburn's arse.

Stood up, felt the sun on his back. The files could wait. Too nice a day to sit in an empty office trying to work out what Wattie was on about. The mention of Mary had given him an idea.

CHAPTER 16

The new *Daily Record* building, two ugly reddish boxes sitting on top of one another, had been built in the middle of the wasteland that used to be Anderston. Sat there surrounded by mud and half demolished tenements. The cab dropped McCoy off and he walked up the steps, through the glass doors and to the desk, held out his police card.

'Detective McCoy to see Mary Webster.'

The girl behind the desk nodded, picked up the phone and a couple of minutes later the lift door opened, revealing the woman herself in all her glory.

'What you doing here, McCoy?' she asked.

Mary, as always, looked the part. Not that McCoy was quite sure what that part might be. A pair of red velvet hot pants were attached to braces that snaked over a white satin blouse peppered with pictures of Donald Duck. Suede platform boots completed the look.

McCoy nodded over to the row of angular and uncomfortable-looking seats by the window.

'Just saw your other half,' he said, sitting down.

'Did you now?' said Mary, lighting up. 'See

him more than I do then. Quick pump on a Friday night's all I get and a cheerio as he heads out the door every bloody morning.

'Raeburn's got him—'

'Stop! Don't even say that word. It's banned in our house.'

McCoy grinned. 'Bet you wish he was back working for me.'

Mary sniffed. 'I wouldn't go that far. He's not that desperate.' She narrowed her eyes. 'What you doing here anyway, McCoy? Last I heard you were handing out parking tickets and telling wee kids about the Tufty Club.'

'It's no quite that bad,' said McCoy. 'But I'll be honest, it's no far off, hence the visit. You got a photo file on Bobby March?'

She nodded, looked suspicious. 'Might do. Why?'

'Need to see if you can find a photo of him carrying some sort of cloth bag. His father claims it's been stolen.'

Mary sat back. 'Now why would I want to spend my time with our esteemed picture editor – or, as I like to call him, the lech of the century – just to do a wee favour for you, McCoy?'

'Simple. Because apart from being charm itself I'm far less ethical than your man when it comes to discussing Alice Kelly and what's going on with her case.'

She was suddenly interested. 'You better not be mucking me about, McCoy.'

'When have I ever done that?' he asked.

'Far too bloody often.' Mary stood up. 'I'll be back in ten – and remember, this better be bloody worth it.'

McCoy sat in reception waiting for her to come back, watching the comings and goings. Mind started to drift back to Billy Weir. Would he really try and fuck Cooper over? And if so, was Cooper strong enough to do anything about it? Didn't seem like Billy, but you never knew. *Et tu, Brute* and all that.

'Here.'

He looked up. Mary was holding out a cardboard-backed photo. He held out his hand to take it and she snatched it away, held it out his reach.

'Alice Kelly,' she said. 'Good stuff, or this is going straight back upstairs.'

McCoy sighed. Knew he had to play ball. Also knew he had nothing real to trade. Decided to give it a go anyway.

'Two hundred and fifty police, uniforms and administrative staff, anyone they can press-gang into it, are doing a fingertip search of Ruchill Park right now. Dad arrives back from Ireland today. They're going to start the divers on the canal later. That enough?'

Mary handed over the photo, sat down beside him. Her face seemed to have gone a bit pale suddenly. Seemed distracted. Not that interested in his information.

'You okay?' asked McCoy.

She shook her head. 'Feel a bit sick all of a sudden.'

McCoy looked at the photo: a table outside a

cafe somewhere hot, sunshine giving the picture a whitish glow. He peered at the sign above the cafe door. 'L'AUBERGE'. France, then. Bobby March was laughing in the picture, head back. Keith Richards had never struck McCoy as much of a comedian, but who knew. He was leaning forward, cackling away. Must have told him a joke.

There were empty bottles of wine on the table, glasses, packets of Marlboro and, tucked in beside March's snakeskin-booted feet, was the bag. It was just as his dad had described. Beige, woven, long handle, couple of badges he couldn't make out pinned to it.

'Can I take this?' McCoy asked.

'Can you fuck!' said Mary. 'Needs to go back to the library or I'll be shot.'

She took it out his hand, just in case.

'What's up with you, anyway?' asked McCoy.

'What d'you mean?' she said, a little defensively.

'You usually know more about cases like Alice Kelly than I do. What happened to Mary Webster, intrepid girl reporter? Alice Kelly is right up your street. Wee girl missing, human interest, clock ticking. Why are you not out there, shaking and moving?'

She sat forward, put her head in her hands. 'Because I think I'm pregnant,' she said quietly.

Was the last thing McCoy was expecting. 'What?'

She sat back up, looked straight ahead. 'You heard me.'

'Well, that's good, eh?' said McCoy, not quite knowing what to say.

'Is it?' she asked, looking at him.

'Have you told Wattie?' he asked.

She shook her head. 'Nope. And I've no bloody idea why I just told you.' Old Mary back. 'And I swear, McCoy, if you tell a single living soul, especially and including Douglas Watson, I'll kill you, but not before I cut your dick off with a rusty penknife. Got me?'

McCoy nodded.

'What did you say when Angela told you about wee Bobby?' she asked. Then realised. 'Sorry, I shouldn't ask. Didn't think.'

'It's okay,' said McCoy, 'I like talking about him.' He was quiet for a moment, lost in thought. 'I can't remember really. I was pished. Had just come in from the Victoria. Think I asked her if she was sure.'

Mary rolled her eyes. 'Marginally better than asking if it was yours, I suppose.' She stood up.

'You should tell him,' said McCoy. 'He'll be over the moon.'

'I know he will,' she said. 'That's why I've not told him.'

'You want to wait until you're sure?' he asked.

She shook her head.

'What?' he asked. 'Scared he'll not want it?'

'No. He will. You know Wattie. It'll be a dream come true. It's me. I'm no so sure I want it.'

She turned and walked back to the lifts. The door opened and she got in. 'See you, McCoy. And thanks for the chat.'

CHAPTER 17

The cafe was just about closing when McCoy got there. Had walked from the *Daily Record*, taken him longer than he thought. The waitress was wiping down the tables, collecting the big plastic tomatoes from each table on a plastic tray. He checked his watch. Four twenty. He was late. Not many people left in the Golden Egg, just the stragglers. A young couple sitting at the front; a man with a sleeping toddler in his arms, kid's chubby hand still clutching a foil windmill. A girl sitting at the back. She was drawing something in a sketchbook: must have been a picture of Alfredo behind the counter, kept looking up at him. She finished, closed it over and looked up at McCoy.

'I was wondering if you'd turn up,' she said.

He wouldn't have recognised Laura Murray in a million years. She looked nothing like the girl in the photo he had in his wallet. The long brown hair was gone, was dyed blonde now, cut short. She was dressed in blue jeans and a man's white T-shirt. Duffel bag on the seat next to her.

She took a sip of her coffee. 'Iris said you wanted to see me.'

McCoy nodded, a bit taken aback that she seemed to be running the conversation. Felt like he was about to be interviewed.

'She found you, then?' he asked.

'She didn't have to try too hard. I know her from the shebeen. Donny liked it, liked to drink there with his cronies. I used to sit in the kitchen with her, help her count the stock and the money.'

'Playing shops with Iris?' said McCoy, sitting down. 'What, you two best pals now?'

'Why shouldn't we be?' Laura's posh West End voice carried across the cafe. 'She's had quite a life, Iris. More interesting than most people. You know she used to dance in Paris?'

McCoy snorted, tried not to laugh. 'Is that what she's calling it now? Dancing on her back, more like.'

Laura glared at him. 'Sorry, I forgot you were a policeman for a minute. Didn't mean to offend your bourgeois sensibilities.'

He'd never heard anyone say 'policeman' with so much contempt in his life. Or 'bourgeois', come to that, whatever it meant.

The waitress brought over a coffee, plonked down a Pyrex cup and saucer in front of McCoy. Turned to Laura. 'You want anything else, hen? We're closing soon.'

Laura shook her head. 'I'm fine, thank you.'

The waitress wandered back to the counter and started filling the plastic tomatoes from a big catering bottle of tomato sauce.

'Want to tell me what went on up at Whitehill Street?' McCoy asked, stirring two spoons of sugar into his coffee.

'Whitehill Street?' Laura repeated. 'I don't know what you're talking about. I thought you were here to persuade me to go home.' She fumbled in her bag, got out her cigarettes, lit up and stared at him.

McCoy sighed. Didn't have the energy for this. Needed to hurry things up.

'Let me remind you. Whitehill Street. Horrible street over by the Wills factory. It's where your boyfriend Donny lived. Top floor, single-end. Picture of the Rangers team on the wall. It's where he got stabbed, where he died, bled out onto the floor cloth. Remember it now, Laura? Coming back? Ringing any bells, is it?'

She looked at him, said nothing.

'C' mon, Laura. I've been doing this too long and you're too bright for this. Just tell me what happened.'

'I've never been to Whitehill Street. I don't even know where—'

The words died in her mouth as McCoy reached into his pocket and took out the paperback of *The Great Gatsby*. He put it on the table. Corner of it stained red with Donny MacRae's blood.

Laura looked at it. Looked at him, fear in her eyes. Fear that turned to tears soon enough.

'Come on, Laura, just tell me,' said McCoy. 'It's over now, it's done.'

She nodded, looked defeated. Got some paper serviettes out the silver dispenser, wiped at her eyes.

'We'd had a fight, a big fight. Donny was being an idiot, acting like a child. I stormed out the flat, left him to it, stayed at Iris's that night. She said I could stay on the bed in the kitchen, keep out the way of the party. I couldn't really sleep though, there was too much noise even back there, so I left early and walked back to the flat. Was going to be the bigger person and say sorry.'

She stubbed her cigarette out in the foil ashtray, wiped her eyes again. Carried on.

'When I got there the door was open and he was lying there, on the bed. There was blood everywhere. I didn't know what to do. So I just ran. I left him there. I know I shouldn't have but I . . .'

And that's when the real tears started. Big gulping sobs, snotty nose, the whole shebang. McCoy went up to the counter, got her another coffee and put it down in front of her. Found a clean cloth hanky in his jacket pocket and passed it over.

She smiled as she took it, started to calm down a bit. Then she began to fill him in about love's young dream. After a couple of minutes McCoy was having a hard time deciding what was worse, the crying or the pish she was telling him now.

'Donny could be a bit wild, but he was a good guy really, once you got past all the showing off and the tough guy stuff. He had a horrible child-hood, you know. He suffered a lot, but he was still really kind when he wanted to be.'

'Really?' said McCoy. 'He wasn't that kind to Alec Page. You know about that, do you, Laura? Know what happened to him?'

'That wasn't Donny,' she said quickly. Then looked like she wished she hadn't.

'Oh aye, who was it, then?' he asked.

She fumbled with her cigarettes, managed to get one lit. 'There was someone else there, they did it,' she said. 'Not Donny.'

'Did they now . . .' McCoy wasn't even trying to sound convinced.

'He never said who it was, never told me a name. Just told me someone had gone crazy, that it wasn't meant to happen like it did. The guy just took a Stanley knife out his jacket and went mad before Donny could stop him.'

'And Donny didn't say who this mystery guy was?' he asked. 'There's a surprise.'

'Windmill!'

The toddler had appeared by their table, foil windmill in hand, held up to show them. His mum arrived just behind him, scooped him up. 'Wee menace just runs,' she said. 'Doesnae care where.' Asked him who was a cheeky monkey as she carried him back to his dad counting out change at the counter.

Laura carried on. 'All he said was he didn't expect it, not from someone like him.'

'And what's that supposed to mean?'

She shrugged. 'Don't ask me. That's all he said.'

For some reason, he was inclined to believe her. When people were lying, they usually exaggerated a story, added details, thought that made it seem more convincing.

'Did you see anyone up at Whitehill Street?' he asked. 'Near the flat?'

She took a sip of coffee, too hot, blew on it. 'No, I just ran. Went over to Jean at the van.'

'So he was definitely dead when you got there?' McCoy asked.

'Yes, I tried to find a pulse but there was . . .'

Then she stopped. Something had dawned on her. 'You don't think it was me, do you?' Some of the attitude was starting to wear off. She sounded panicky. 'I didn't do it. Honestly.'

McCoy held up his hands. 'I never thought you did. Don't worry, I cleared the flat of all the stuff you left behind anyway. Only me and your uncle Hector are ever going to know you were there.'

The news didn't seem to make her that happy. 'Good old Uncle Hec,' she said. 'Always there to help in any situation. Whether you want him to or not.'

'Saw your dad today too,' said McCoy. 'Paid me a visit to tell me to get you home pronto.'

She looked him in the eye, sat forward, tone of her voice changed. 'You can tell my dad and uncle Hec that I'm fine, but if they think I'm going back they can forget it. I'm sixteen in a month and then they can't make me. All I've got to do is keep out their way for a bit and there's nothing they – or you – can do about it.'

McCoy sat back. Could see her father in her, the same entitled tone, the same superiority. Trouble was she wasn't wrong; he couldn't really bodily drag her into a car and drive her back. Wasn't going to tell her that, though.

'Okay. You tell me why you left, why you won't go back,' he said. 'You tell me a good reason and I'll think about it.'

She thought about it and then she shook her head. 'I just couldn't be there any more. I was suffocating.' She smiled and her face brightened. 'It was too bourgeois.'

McCoy grinned in spite of himself. Laura Murray certainly wasn't like most fifteen-year-olds he'd met. Now all he had to do was decide if that was a good or a bad thing.

'Where you have been staying?' McCoy asked her.

'In the storeroom at Iris's,' she said.

'What?'

She laughed. 'I was at the Co-op when you came, getting the messages.'

McCoy shook his head. 'She owes me five quid.'

'Two pound fifty actually. She gave me half.'

The waitress appeared again, bill in her hand. 'That's us closing now. Pound and ten.'

McCoy dug in his pocket, handed over the money. They stood up.

'Need to get you out of there,' said McCoy. 'It's not safe at that shebeen. Not for a young girl like you.'

'I can look after—'

'Spare me. It's no gonna happen,' said McCoy before she could finish. 'Weekends in there can get hairy. Believe me, I know.'

'Well, I'm not going home,' she said. 'I told you. Not in a million years. And you can't make me.'

He was about to tell her he could – but didn't. There was something about her that was bothering him. She was a bright, good-looking, capable kid. Why was a girl like that so determined to turn her back on her mum and dad? Needed time to find out.

'Cool your bloody jets. I've got somewhere else in mind. I think you'll like it.'

He nodded at her duffel bag. 'Is that all your stuff?'

'No, there's more back at Iris's, clothes and stuff like that. More sketchbooks.'

'Okay, you go to Iris's and get your stuff. She won't be there now, it'll be a big guy called Jumbo. He's a good lad, tell him I told you to come. I'll meet you at the Strathmore at quarter to ten. We'll go from there.'

McCoy dug in his pocket again, handed over a couple of quid. 'Get a taxi,' he said, looking over to the rank at the bus station.

She nodded, took his money. McCoy watched her go. Wondered what he was doing. Wondered

156

why he hadn't just taken her back to Bearsden like he was supposed to. Part of him knew. She wasn't just the sulky teenager intent on annoying her mum and dad that he'd imagined; he'd seen real fear in her eyes when he'd suggested it. He had a feeling Murray and his brother weren't telling him the whole story. Not by a long shot. And until they did he wasn't going to deliver her. No matter how much they asked.

CHAPTER 18

He knew something was up the minute he turned the corner into Stewart Street. There were four or five pandas outside the station, doors open, lights lazily spinning. He could see Larry Kerr from the *Evening Times*, Jamie Forsyth from *The Citizen*, a couple of other reporters he didn't recognise. All of them, jackets off, sleeves rolled up, fags in mouths, grim expressions. Billy the desk sergeant was outside too, standing talking to them, hat held in his hand, bald head already red from the sun.

McCoy's heart sank. Only one reason they'd all be there. Billy and the reporters nodded hello as he approached. Billy held out his packet of Regal and McCoy took one.

'Where'd they find her?' he asked.

'They didn't,' said Billy. 'Not yet anyway. But they arrested a guy a few hours ago.' He nodded back at the station. 'He's in there now. Seems like the fucker all right. Raeburn's got him in the interrogation room.'

'Anyone we know?' asked McCoy.

Billy shook his head. 'Young guy, can't be more

158

than sixteen, seventeen. Lives in the same close apparently.'

'Bloody nonce,' said Forsyth. 'Least he can do is hurry up and tell them where the body is.'

'How'd they get him?' asked McCoy, ignoring Forsyth as he always did.

'Seems one of the neighbours was away at her sister's for the weekend,' said Billy. 'Came back and read the paper.'

'*The Citizen*?' asked Forsyth hopefully.

Billy ignored him. 'So she goes into the Woodside and tells Raeburn she's seen the boy with Alice Kelly. Not for the first time either.' He flicked his cigarette into the gutter. 'Seems the dirty bugger's got a record as well. Indecent exposure. Wouldn't you know it.'

McCoy turned to go into the station and Forsyth called after him. 'By the way, Harry, anything on Bobby March? Editor's on my bloody back. Need an angle.'

McCoy shook his head. Whatever he thought about what had happened to Bobby March, the last person he'd tell would be Jamie bloody Forsyth. One step up from pond life, as far as he was concerned.

'Any sexy groupies hanging about?' He grinned. 'Anyone I could talk to?'

'Nope. Think his dad's still around. Try him.'

Forsyth nodded and McCoy walked into the station, hoped Forsyth would traipse over to the Tradewinds and experience the joys of Wullie

159

March. He pulled the double doors to the office open and walked in. The atmosphere was the same as it always was when a big case was breaking. Everyone standing around, leaning on desks, nobody doing any real work, eyes flicking to the corridor that led to the interrogation rooms every five seconds, waiting for a result. McCoy hung his jacket over his chair, went over to Thomson.

'Got someone, I hear,' he said.

Thomson nodded. 'Raeburn's in there with him now. Him and Wattie. Been at it for a few hours.'

'Wattie?' asked McCoy, surprised.

Thomson nodded. 'Thick as thieves those two these days.'

McCoy nodded. Felt even more out in the cold than usual. Knew he should be in there, not out here waiting, knowing nothing. He sat at his desk, tried to pretend he was interested in rearranging his files but he was just like all the rest of them. Glancing over every five seconds. Waiting.

An hour passed. Nothing happening, just the office getting hotter and hotter. McCoy looked at his watch for about the twentieth time. Decided he couldn't just sit here and wait. And yet that was exactly what he ended up doing, the same as everybody else.

He got up, yawned. 'How long's that now?' he asked.

Thomson looked up at the clock on the wall. 'Going on four hours.'

'Christ. Hope it's worth it.' He unbuttoned his

160

shirt and loosened his tie. 'It's bad enough out here; must be a hundred bloody degrees in that interrogation room.'

Thomson nodded. 'It's a bloody sweathole at the best of times.'

A cup of tea later McCoy had had enough. He was dying of the heat and needed some air. He stood up, told Thomson he'd be back in an hour or so. Thomson nodded, didn't pay much attention, knew that whatever McCoy was doing these days didn't matter much.

He stepped out the station, wondering what the noise was. Soon found out. The reporters had been joined by thirty or so assorted lunatics. Some of them had signs – 'BRING BACK HANGING' – some of them just had a look of blind hate in their eyes. They were milling about behind a rope cordon. One of them, a woman the size of a house, even had a picture of Alice from the paper pinned onto her dress. She was holding up a framed picture of the Sacred Heart, reciting the rosary.

A man with shorts and a vest got up to the front of the crowd, shouted at McCoy as he passed. 'Took you long enough!'

McCoy just ignored him.

'You one of the useless articles that let her die?' he shouted again.

The crowd started moving, pressing against the rope. He'd got them agitated.

McCoy left Billy trying to get them under control and started walking up the road. Was like a bloody

161

lynch mob in a cowboy film. God knows what would happen if they got a hold of the boy in the interrogation room.

Half an hour and a pint in the Eskimo later, McCoy was back at his desk. Crowd outside the station had got even bigger, more nutters, more press. Had to fight his way through them to get in. He looked over at Thomson and he just shook his head. No news. He couldn't believe it. They were still in the interrogation room.

'How long is that now?' he asked.

Thomson looked up at the electric clock on the wall. 'Five hours and nine minutes.'

'Fuck sake,' said McCoy.

He got out Wattie's robbery files, pretended to read them while he had a think. There was something about this whole Laura Murray thing that was beginning to bother him. Hadn't really noticed it at the time, but both Murray and his brother hadn't exactly seemed panic-stricken that Laura had run away, or even that surprised. Was more like they were expecting it somehow.

He got out his fags and realised he'd only a couple left. He lit up and just as he did the door to the corridor burst open and Raeburn was standing there. Everyone went silent, everyone turning to him in expectation. Raeburn's sleeves were rolled up, hair and shirt wet with sweat, looked exhausted. He waited a couple of seconds, slowly looked round the room at the waiting faces then grinned, raised his hands above his head.

'He's coughed,' he said. 'Full fucking confession!'

The change was immediate. All the tension went out the room and suddenly there were shouts, whistles. Thomson started clapping, uniforms and plainclothes gathered round Raeburn, slapping him on the back, congratulating him. Jacobs got a bottle of whisky out from the drawer in his desk, started splashing it into paper cups.

McCoy took one, drank it over, needed it if he was going to do the right thing. He went up to Raeburn, held his hand out to shake.

'Congratulations,' he said. 'Well done.'

Raeburn shook it. Nodded. A temporary truce.

'Got there in the end. Thank God that woman came back from her sister's!' he said, grinning.

'You did a good job, Raeburn. Case closed in three days. That takes some doing.'

Raeburn smiled. 'Just good police work, McCoy, that's what it always comes down to.'

And that was about as much as McCoy could take. He said congratulations again, then turned back to his seat before he said something he would regret. Was hard to believe, but Raeburn's false modesty was even worse than his usual blowhard attitude. He sat at his desk, took another cup of whisky when Jacobs brought the tray around, tried to look like he was happy.

The problem was that Raeburn really had done well, no doubt about it. So well they might give him the job permanently, move Murray up

163

the ladder to Pitt Street when he came back. McCoy could maybe manage another few months of Raeburn pissing on him from a great height but there was no way he could take it for much longer than that. He swallowed over the last of the whisky, crumpled the paper cup, threw it in the bin and went off to find Wattie.

Billy told him he'd seen him going round the back, so he took the long way round, couldn't face pasting a smile on and walking through Raeburn's celebrations again. He walked down by the garages and saw Wattie sitting on one of the kitchen chairs that had been dragged out into the sun.

'Congratulations are in order, I believe. You and the bold Raeburn did well.' He held out his hand to shake.

Wattie didn't take it. Didn't say anything. Just looked at him.

'What's up?' asked McCoy. 'Why the long face, as the farmer said to the horse. Shouldn't you be celebrating? It's no often that—'

'Not here,' Wattie said, standing up. 'Come on.'

18th July 1967

Fairmont Hotel, San Francisco

'He's coming down over from Berkeley, probably got stuck in traffic.'

Bobby nodded. Was probably true, but it wasn't helping his paranoia. 'You sure he's going to turn up?' he asked.

Cathy nodded. 'Just got to be patient.' Handed him a lit joint.

Bobby took a drag, hoped it would take the edge off. Wondered how long he'd spent in the past couple of months waiting for dealers to turn up. He walked over to the window. Could see the limo waiting outside, engine running. Could see Rusty the tour manager pacing up and down the street, hotel canopy obscuring him every now and then.

They were supposed to have left two hours ago. Headed to Monterey. Any minute now Rusty was going to get the lift upstairs, start knocking on the hotel room door telling him they had to go.

'You got works?' he asked Cathy.

She nodded absently, sat on the bed and flicked through a magazine, silent TV playing behind her. Helicopters and burning jungles.

'Owsley's going to be there. Sheri said he's bringing Grade A liquid acid for the musicians.'

Bobby nodded, had a feeling his days of acid were long gone.

'Bobby, he'll be here. I promise.'

He nodded, looked back out the window. Swore. Rusty was nowhere to be seen. He took another drag of the joint, pinched the end, put it in the pocket of his jacket. Didn't have to wait long, couple of minutes at most, then the knocking started.

Cathy looked up at him. 'Told you he'd be here,' she said, ran to the door.

Rusty was standing there. He took one look at Cathy in her underwear, Bobby's half-packed case on the floor, shook his head. 'For fuck sake, man, we should be on the road by now!'

Bobby mumbled, 'Sorry.' Started stuffing shirts into his case.

As Rusty stepped into the room, there he was, right behind him. Jackson. Standing in the doorway, big grin on his face.

'Traffic was a bitch, man.'

Bobby shut the door, locked it. Shouted through, 'Be five minutes, Rusty! Take the bags down!'

He turned to Jackson, grinned. Then he felt under the sink for his other washbag, opened it, took out a spoon and a length of rubber tube.

'Well, somebody's an eager beaver.' Jackson dug in his pocket, took out a small glassine bag, held it up.

Bobby grabbed it.

CHAPTER 19

McCoy had tried to get Wattie to stop, sit down, but he was having none of it. Kept striding on, wanted to get as far away from the station as he could. They were in Rose Street now, walking up the hill, McCoy trying to keep up, failing.

'You want to tell me what this is all about?' he asked, following two steps behind. 'Better do it quick before I pass out. This hill's killing me.'

Wattie didn't smile, didn't stop, just started talking.

'His name's Ronnie Elder, we brought him in this afternoon. That's what the uniformed lassie up at the park came and got me for. Raeburn wanted me back at the station pronto. I got there and he's lit up like a Christmas tree, full of it. All excited. "We've got him," he says. "You should be in on it." Was so happy you'd think he'd won the bloody pools. The neighbour that came back saw him and Alice Kelly together that afternoon. Last sighting of her by anyone. We'd even interviewed him. Thomson did it. Elder said he was playing football at the Blazes all afternoon with

168

his pals. No reason to disbelieve him. Now it turns out he hasn't got any pals and the pitches are closed for resurfacing.'

They were at the top of the hill now. McCoy stopped, hands on knees, breathing heavy.

'You're going to have to give me a minute,' he said. 'I'm no as young as I was.'

Wattie nodded, stopped. Kept talking, though, desperate to get it all out. 'Sent some uniforms up to his flat. They found a load of dirty mags, women dressed up as schoolgirls.'

'Christ,' said McCoy, finally managing to catch a breath.

'That's not the worst,' said Wattie. 'They also found a pair of the girl's knickers in his bedroom, dried spunk all over them. It all adds up. Guilty as sin.'

Wattie turned and looked at him. 'The trouble is, I don't think he did it.'

McCoy was leaning against the wall of St Aloysius Chapel, still wasn't quite right. He looked at Wattie, surprised. 'What?' he said. 'I thought he confessed.'

Wattie nodded. 'He did. Said he strangled her and chucked her body in the river. Just like Raeburn told him he did. Told him over and over for five fucking hours.'

Wattie turned, was about to walk down the hill.

'Wattie! I can't. I've got a bloody stitch. Give us a minute, eh?'

He bent over again, didn't help, still had the

pain in his side. Had an idea. Pointed over at St Aloysius. 'C'mon, we'll sit down on the steps.'

Water looked doubtful.

'It's the steps! I'm no asking you to convert. It's either that or I'm going to have to lie down on the pavement.'

Wattie had a quick look round, sat down, then started talking again. 'I don't think the boy's quite right, Harry. He's no real idea what's going on. Kept asking when he could see his mum.'

'What's his lawyer saying?' asked McCoy, finally getting his breath back.

'Hasn't got one. Raeburn told him he didn't need one. Said if he wasn't guilty, why would he need a lawyer? So he gave a personal statement.'

McCoy took a deep breath. Didn't really want to say what he was about to say.

'Look, Wattie. He might not be all there, but that doesn't mean—'

'Raeburn just kept on and on at him: "What did you do with Alice?" Kept asking over and over again. Boy was crying, kept asking for a drink of water and Raeburn wouldn't give him one. You know what that interview room is like, it's a bloody sweatbox. Just kept on at him: "Tell us what you did and you can go home and see your mum."'

'Christ.'

'He didn't even go to a normal school, went to the place up in Maryhill Road for, you know, kids with . . .'

McCoy nodded.

'Eventually he breaks down, starts bubbling and snottering, screaming for his mum. Raeburn grabs him, tells him to stop the bubbling, tells him he's never seeing his mum again if he doesn't tell us what he did with Alice. And then Raeburn started slapping him around. Really hitting the poor bastard, punches into the body, hitting him on the back of the head. Then he tells him that was nothing, things were going to get worse, much worse. That if he didn't tell us where Alice was he'd have to get a big polis to knock seven shades of shite out him until he did. Turns to me. Said I'd give him a doing if he didn't start cooperating. Then that was that. The boy was on the ceiling, wailing and crying for his mum, saying he would be a good boy and that he was sorry.'

He looked at McCoy.

'He would have said anything just to get Raeburn to stop, to get out of that room. So Raeburn walked him through it, bit by bit. "You took her up to Jaconelli's, didn't you? She didn't want to kiss you, did she? So you hurt her, taught her a lesson, didn't you?" The poor bugger just nodded, agreed to anything Raeburn told him. Raeburn wrote it all down for him, tells him if he signs it he can see his mum and go home.'

McCoy tried to get a word in, but Wattie kept going, needed to get it all out.

'You should see his signature, Harry, it's like a wee kid's writing. He signs it and then he says, "Can I see my mum now? Can I go home?" And

171

Raeburn says can you fuck. Gives him a couple of slaps. Tells him he's a nonce and that he's going to jail. Boy freaks out when he realises he's not going home, not going to see his mum. Starts banging his head on the table, screaming blue murder. So Raeburn puts him in handcuffs, shoves him down into the corner. Says to me, "That's how it's done, son." Was all proud of himself. "He did it all right, just needed a push to admit it." And then he boots him hard in the stomach a couple of times, tells him that's for Alice. And then . . .' Wattie stopped for a second, took a breath, managed to get it out. 'And then he gets his cock out and pisses on him. Tells him this is gonna happen to him every single day for the next twenty years.'

Wattie looked like he was going to cry.

McCoy was quiet for a minute, wondering how he was going to say it.

'Look, Wattie,' he said, trying to tread carefully. 'You've no worked on many cases like this one. One where everyone's wound up to high doh, a wee girl dead, public and Pitt Street on your back. They're different. The interrogations can be an ugly business, right enough, the gloves come off. Raeburn's no likely to do anything different, he's always been the heavy, it's his style. And he got a result.'

Wattie turned to him. Looked exasperated. 'No, he didn't! All he did was force a terrified boy to sign whatever he put in front of him. That's what he got!'

'Okay, let's look at it the other way.' McCoy took it slowly, counted it off on his fingers. 'One: he lives in the same close and he knows the girl, been seen with her before. The age gap isn't good, boy that age and a girl that age aren't just going to be pals, doesn't happen. Two: he had a pair of her knickers in her room. The fact he's wanked off on them shows clear and unlawful sexual interest. Three: he's got previous as a sex offender. He won't be the first one to start off flashing his dick and end up raping or killing some girl. Four: Raeburn's got a signed confession that he killed her. You think that was forced out of him. Probably was, but that doesn't necessarily mean it's not true. Sometimes these guys take a bit of pushing to get to the edge, to say what they've done.'

Wattie was looking straight ahead, not acknowledging anything McCoy was saying.

He kept trying. 'Look, Wattie, a crime like that is a hard thing to admit to. It's no a bank robbery or an assault that makes you a big man, that gets you points in the jail. It's just you having to admit to the world that you're the lowest of the low, the scum of the earth. It's saying you fucked a wee girl and then you killed her. Nobody is going to admit to something like that without some amount of persuasion. You admit it and you're signing your death warrant. Maybe Raeburn did go too far, but it won't be the first or the last time the polis have had to lean on someone like that to get a result.'

Wattie shook his head. 'No,' he said.

McCoy sighed, knew it wasn't going be that easy. 'Okay, look at it the other way. How come you're so sure he didn't?'

Wattie turned to him. 'Because he's a daft boy, maybe a pervert, I don't know, but he's not a murderer. He didn't really confess, he didn't even know what was going on, he just wanted to see his mum, thought if he said what Raeburn wanted then he'd let him.'

McCoy sat there, tried to think. He'd said what he was supposed to say, but there was something in what Wattie was saying that was bothering him. Wattie was inexperienced, but he wasn't daft. He was a good polis and if he was sure the boy was innocent then maybe he was right. Maybe.

'Where'd the knickers come from, then?' he asked, trying to ignore the fact that he was having this conversation outside a chapel.

'Said he got them off the washing line weeks ago. Mum can't remember what pair she had on when she went missing. He could be telling the truth, McCoy.'

McCoy nodded. He could. 'And how come Raeburn's so sure she's in the canal?'

'I don't think he is. It's just the most obvious place. Chances are that is where she is, no matter what happened to her. If she turns up somewhere else, he'll just say Elder was lying to put us off.'

'What did Raeburn actually charge him with?' asked McCoy.

'Murder,' said Wattie.

McCoy couldn't believe it. 'You're joking! Without a body? He's being a bit ambitious, isn't he? Could have just charged him with the theft of the knickers, been enough to keep him in until they find her.'

McCoy thought for a minute, then asked the real question. The one that they were going to have to answer if there was any hope of getting the boy off. 'Well, if Ronnie Elder didn't kill her, who did?'

Wattie shrugged. 'I don't know, but unless we do something whoever did do it is going to get away with it.'

'Look, Wattie, I know you're upset and you're angry, but I don't know what we can do. He's been charged with murder. It's out of our hands now.'

Wattie turned to him. Disappointment on his face. 'That it? That all you're going to say? Hard cheese, son. Barlinnie here you come? I thought better of you, McCoy. Thought you cared about what happened to people like that boy. Just shows how wrong you can be, eh?'

'Come on, Wattie, that's no fair!'

Wattie stood up, pushed past him. 'Neither's that boy being fitted up for something he didn't do. That's what really matters.'

McCoy called after him, but he didn't turn around, just kept going.

McCoy sat there on the steps, wondered if

Wattie was right. Maybe he had stopped caring about people like Ronnie Elder. Maybe he had become like every other polis. The kind of polis he swore he'd never become.

A man in a suit got out a cab opposite. Gave him an idea. An idea that might work. Just had to pick up Laura Murray first.

CHAPTER 20

Just like last time the Strathmore was rammed with young people, jukebox going, couple of drunk or stoned girls dancing to Mungo Jerry. Wee Tam put two pints on the table and sat down. Last time McCoy remembered talking to him was a couple of years ago. McCoy used to come in the Strathmore quite a lot round then, had a flat in Sandfield Street up the road.

Wee Tam had been picked up by the polis one night, had started hanging about with the Young Cumbie, got involved in some mass brawl in Ruchill. His dad wanted to try and put a stop to it before he got sucked in properly, asked McCoy to have a word. So he did. Told him all the horror stories about young guys with their faces slashed open, what really happened in Barlinnie to young guys like him, tried to put the fear of God into him.

He was about fifteen then, still not quite grown up, still Isa and Tam's boy. Not any more. He'd shot up, was broad too, over six foot. Like every other young bloke in the place, he had long hair, a T-shirt, jeans and sandshoes. Wee Tam's T-shirt in this case was long-sleeved, green scoop neck, Led Zeppelin's flying angel logo in bright yellow.

'Have to admit it, you've done well with this place,' said McCoy, looking round.

Wee Tam nodded. 'Wasnae too hard. Amazing what one jukebox will do. Just got to make sure it's got all the right tracks on it, they come flocking. Mind you, all the lassies do is put David Bowie on over and over again . . .'

'So I noticed,' said McCoy. 'The Jean Genie' had just come on for the third time.

Wee Tam took a sip of his pint. Grinned. 'No offence, and it's always nice to see you, Mr McCoy, but I'm not sure this is really your kind of pub any more.'

'You saying I'm too old for all this?' asked McCoy. Only half joking.

'Well . . .'

'Cheeky bugger. Don't worry, I won't cramp your style. I'm just here to meet someone. Girl called Laura Murray. You know her?'

Wee Tam nodded. 'She's been in a few times.'

'You talk to her?' asked McCoy.

'No really. She's no from round here. Bit too snobby for me, bit up herself.'

'You get a lot of snobby girls in here, do you?' asked McCoy, sipping his pint.

Wee Tam nodded. 'Loads of them. It's mental. They go for the boys from the teams. If they're bladed up, all the better. Seems to be their big thing, anything to annoy Mammy and Daddy. I steer clear, myself.'

'The teams come in here?' asked McCoy.

'Aye, a fair few. We're sort of in no-man's-land, neutral territory. Get the Gestapo mainly, the Shamrock. Depends if they're knocking lumps out each other that week or not. Mostly come in on Fridays and Saturdays.' He grinned again. 'All works out. The lassies come for the music. The teams come for the lassies. We're dead busy.'

'Much trouble?' asked McCoy.

He shrugged. 'No much. Most of it goes on later at the dancing. They're still no completely pissed when they leave here. Time they've drunk their half bottles on the bus into town they'd fight their own bloody shadows.'

'Donny MacRae come in a lot?' McCoy asked, raising his voice above some Roxy Music song blasting out the jukebox.

'You heard what happened to him?'

McCoy nodded. 'Nasty business.'

Wee Tam thought for a minute. 'He might have been in a few times. I didnae really know him, to be honest. Just another ned.'

'How about you? You keeping yourself out of trouble, Tam?'

'Yep. I keep away from the teams, I'm no daft. I'm a busy man, got a pub to run now. Speaking of which . . .' He nodded over at the bar. Tam was sweating, looking harassed, besieged by a crowd of young ones holding up notes.

'Off you go,' said McCoy. 'And Tam, just do

179

me a favour. Try and at least look like you're checking people's ages before you serve them.'

He saluted, said 'will do' and went off to rescue his dad.

McCoy watched him go, lit up and took another sip of his pint. Wee Tam was his father's son, right enough. He couldn't lie to save himself either. No way was he buying his 'I know nothing, I just run a pub' pish. He was sure Wee Tam knew a lot more about Donny MacRae than he was letting on, and if that was true the chances were he was lying about keeping away from the teams as well.

McCoy wasn't quite sure why he was playing everything close to his chest. He didn't think he was a bad lad. Just easily led, as they say. And sometimes that's the worst way to be. Gets you in even more trouble.

He sat for a while watching the dancers, sipping his pint, wondering what to do about Wattie. Still worrying that he was becoming the kind of polis he used to hate, the kind that took the easy road, didn't cause trouble. Wattie full of spit and fire reminded him of himself a few years ago. Maybe it was just time to pass the baton to people like Wattie, let them fight the good fight now. Maybe it was just part of getting old. Felt it tonight. He could still remember Wee Tam as a boy, running about the shut pub pretending to be an aeroplane, shouting on his dad to watch him. Old and tired. Had been a tough year. Maybe he just needed out from under Raeburn. Get a transfer to Southern maybe, start somewhere new.

It wasn't until both Tams started shouting last

orders that Laura Murray walked in. She dumped her bags on the bench beside him and sat down. Looked exhausted.

'My taxi broke down outside the Woodside Inn. I had to walk all the way up Maryhill Road. I was worried you'd be gone.'

Wee Tam came over and asked if McCoy wanted one for the road. He asked for a pint for himself and a Coke for Laura. Wee Tam said he'd bring it over, nodded hello at Laura and headed back to the bar.

'You know him?' McCoy asked, as they watched him pick up empty glasses from the tables.

'Unfortunately,' she sniffed.

'Why unfortunately?' asked McCoy.

She shrugged. 'He was always trying to hang around with Donny and his boys. Was like a wee dog running after them, wanting to be in on everything they were doing.'

'Did they let him?' asked McCoy.

'Occasionally. His dad owns a pub. I suppose they thought he had his uses. Donny didn't mind him, let him buy him drinks, hang around. I think he's a creep.'

'Oh aye. Why's that?' asked McCoy.

'Well, Donny wasn't a girl, put it that way. Didn't have tits to stare at, did he? Don't think Wee Tam's ever looked at my face when he was talking to me. Maybe he's just a bit immature.'

'So speaks the fifteen-year-old?' said McCoy.

She stuck two fingers up at him. Grinned. 'So where am I going to stay, then?'

181

CHAPTER 21

'Tell me you're kidding,' said Laura, as they got out the taxi in Great Western Road. Streetlights were on, but there was still light in the sky. Didn't really get properly dark this time of year. Just got dimmer for a few hours before dawn. 'Stevie Cooper?' She sounded shocked. '*That* Stevie Cooper?'

McCoy nodded. 'The one and only.'

He took one of her bags off her, seemed to be full of sketchpads, big notebooks and paint brushes. Weighed more than he thought.

Laura hoisted her duffel bag onto her shoulder. 'Stevie Cooper was the only guy Donny was really scared of. He told me he was an animal.'

'Did he now,' said McCoy, handing a couple of quid to the driver. 'He might well be an animal, but he's an animal with lots of spare rooms. Besides, your beloved Iris should be here. She can keep you company.'

'Iris?' said Laura, looking surprised.

McCoy rang the doorbell. 'Iris. The famous Parisian dancer.'

'Ha ha,' she said. 'What's Iris doing here?'

'You can ask her yourself. More strings to her bow than dancing at the Folies Bergère, old Iris.'

The door opened. Billy Weir was standing there, vest and pair of shorts on, looking a bit flustered.

'McCoy,' he said, looking Laura up and down. 'Come on in, more the merrier. It's like bloody Central Station in here. Who's your pal?'

'Laura,' said McCoy, handing him the bag. 'About to get even merrier. Laura, take your shoes off.'

Half an hour later McCoy and Billy were sitting at the kitchen table, open lager cans and two whiskies in front of them. French windows were open, bit of a breeze cooling the room down. Billy March's *Postcard from Muscle Shoals* softly playing in the background. McCoy looked around, still couldn't believe it. Six months ago, him and Billy would have been having this conversation at the stained kitchen table in that dump of a flat in Memen Road. Rats running wild in the back courts, tap dripping, no heating.

'She's whose niece again?' asked Billy, carefully licking along the edge of two cigarette papers he was using to roll a joint.

'Chief Inspector Murray's,' said McCoy. 'So keep your dirty paws off.'

Billy looked horrified. 'That fat bastard's got a niece like that? Cannae believe it. Anyway, don't worry, she's no my type.'

'No your type? Last time I noticed, anything with a pulse was your type.'

183

'Not any more. As befitting a posh West Ender, I've upped my standards.'

'What to? A pulse and the ability to form a sentence?'

'Ye of little faith,' said Billy, twisting the end of the joint, putting it in his mouth, pulling it out through pursed lips. 'Done!'

'Did you do what I said?' asked McCoy.

Billy nodded, put the joint behind his ear and reached under the table, pulled up a brown leather satchel. Put it on the table, took out a couple of official-looking letters. Held them up.

'Ta-dah! Purchased today. One betting shop in the Gallowgate and one pub in Royston. Pub actually makes money, apparently. Made sure I accidentally let slip who was buying them, the word should be out. Plus I told Jumbo to go visit Ronnie Drew in Barlinnie and tell him Cooper wasn't happy about the split he was getting from the Lindella and that Drew better not be messing him about.'

'Christ, Billy, you were taking a risk,' said McCoy. 'You asked Jumbo to do that?'

Billy nodded. 'Mind you, I had to go through it with him about twenty times before he went. Even phoned me from a box outside the prison to check again.'

McCoy started laughing, could imagine Jumbo panicking, desperate not to get it wrong. 'Poor bloke.'

'But he said it went okay. Even said Drew looked scared, said he'd sort it out.'

'Well done to Jumbo. Who'd have thought he had it in him? He over at the shebeen now?' asked McCoy.

'Yep. Holding the fort.' He lit up the joint, took a deep drag and handed it to McCoy. 'One of Iris's lassies is running it. He's just sitting in the kitchen doorway looking dangerous.'

'How's he getting on?' asked McCoy.

'Jumbo? Good. Can just about read properly now. Caught him with a *Broons* annual the other day, giggling away to himself.'

McCoy blew out a cloud of smoke, handed the joint back to Billy. Time to drop it in, try and catch Billy off guard, see what his reaction was.

'You been taking any photos, Billy?'

'What?' Billy looked up at him.

'Photos. With a camera. In this house.'

Billy shook his head, put the joint down in the ashtray. 'No idea what you're on about, Harry. Pictures of what? I couldn't, even if I wanted to. I havnae even got a camera.'

'Doesn't matter,' said McCoy. 'My mistake.' He stood up. Drank over the rest of his whisky. 'Suppose I better get this over with. Give us another drag before I go.'

'Good luck,' said Billy, handing him the joint. 'You might well need it. Let's just say Cooper wasnae that happy when he discovered his stash had been binned on your say-so.'

'Christ,' said McCoy. 'Just what I need. If I'm no down in twenty minutes, call an ambulance.'

McCoy climbed the stairs, was pretty sure Billy was telling the truth about the photos, hadn't seemed anxious to deny it or nervous. Just seemed like he genuinely had no idea what McCoy was talking about. Which was a relief, and a pain in the arse. If it wasn't Billy who'd taken the photos, then who the fuck was it?

He stepped onto the landing and walked towards the bedroom. Stopped. Could hear the sound of someone being violently sick, retching and retching. A moment later Iris emerged from the bedroom, bucket with a tea towel over it in her hand. Didn't look very pleased to see him.

'This your idea, was it, me as a bloody nursemaid!' she snarled at him. 'Bloody cheek.'

'Aye well, let's just say you owe him,' said McCoy.

'Owe him? For working for him for eight years for pennies? Lucky bloody me.'

'Come on, Iris. The shebeen stopped making money years ago, all of them did, that's why yours is the only one he's got left. He only keeps it on for you.'

'That's shite,' she said, looking less than certain.

McCoy shrugged. 'Believe what you want. You always do.'

Iris headed for the stairs, leaving the smell of acrid sick behind her. Muttered something about 'shitey polis acting smart' and disappeared.

McCoy stopped outside the door for a minute, trying to work out what he was going to say. Was just about to go back downstairs, maybe smoke some more of the joint, maybe just go home, when he heard a voice.

'I know you're out there, McCoy.'

Cooper. Sounded weak, but still like himself. Nothing for it. McCoy pushed the door open and went in.

The bedroom was dim, only light coming from candles dotted about. Cooper was sitting up in the bed, vest on, hair back in its usual quiff. He looked like he hadn't eaten for weeks. His muscles had faded away, vest looked too big for him now. His face was thinner too, drawn.

'Got you to thank for this, have I?' Cooper said.

'Looks like it.' McCoy sat down on an armchair by the bed. The room smelt stale, like sick and sweat. Like illness.

'Dr Purdie came by.' Cooper held up a small bottle of pills. 'Another bloody five hundred quid off his debt.'

'Worth it, though. How you feeling?' asked McCoy.

'Shite,' said Cooper. 'And all thanks to you, I hear.'

'Sorry about that, but I—'

Cooper held his hands up. 'You had to do it. I know, I know.'

'I was scared,' said McCoy quietly.

'So was I,' said Cooper. 'I didn't realise how quick it was. One day it was helping my back, I was feeling great, no pain for the first time in months, and then a couple of days later I'd forgotten all about Ellie. All I was doing was crawling up the walls waiting for Angela to turn up.'

'Angela?' said McCoy surprised. 'What? My Angela?'

Cooper nodded. 'Helped me out when Ellie wouldn't.'

'You're kidding me on,' said McCoy. 'What's it got to do with her? I thought she was working at the Maryland? Booking the bands or something.'

'She was,' said Cooper. 'Now she works for me. That okay with you, is it?'

It wasn't a question. A flash of the old Cooper.

McCoy shrugged. 'Up to her. I just hadn't heard. Why her, though?'

'Billy and I know all about the usual stuff, moneylending, protection, stuff like that, but I'm no expert when it comes to drugs.' Cooper smiled weakly. 'As you can see.'

He lifted his fags and lighter off the bedside table, went to light one and something seemed to hit him. He sat for a minute, sweat breaking out on his forehead. Put the fags back with a shaky hand.

'Maybe leave them for a bit,' said McCoy.

Cooper nodded, lay back against the headboard, shut his eyes. Looked exhausted. Carried on. 'After I set up the smack deal with Billy Chan it all went nuts. Like started coming to like. We're shifting it all now. Dope, speed, acid, pills, everything, so we needed someone who knows their way around that stuff.'

He opened his eyes, attempted a grin. 'And if

there's anyone who knows their way around that stuff it's your Angela. So she came to work for us. Been doing it for the past couple of months, bloody good at it too.'

'Can't believe it,' said McCoy shaking his head. 'Of all the bloody people.'

'Come on, McCoy, you split up a couple of years ago,' said Cooper.

'We did, but still.'

'You want me to fire her?' asked Cooper.

McCoy shook his head. Looked up at Cooper. 'Nope, don't want you to do that, but I want you to do me a favour.'

'What, besides putting up your waifs and strays?' asked Cooper. 'Give us a bloody break, McCoy!'

'Aye well, don't worry about that, hopefully that won't be for long. Archie Lomax still your lawyer?'

Copper nodded.

'Good. Need you to get Billy to call him. Tell him to take on a guy called Ronnie Elder. He's in the cells at Stewart Street. And I need you to pay for it.'

'Don't ask for much, do you? You know how much Lomax cost's a bloody hour? Who is this Elder anyway and why—'

Cooper stooped, suddenly gestured to the bucket in the corner.

McCoy got it quickly, held it under his chin as Cooper retched watery sick into it. Retched up nothing a few times then sat back on the pillows, looked so white he was almost transparent.

McCoy put the bucket under the bed, poured

him a glass of Lucozade from the yellow cellophane-covered bottle by his fags. Cooper got one of Purdie's pills out, swallowed it over, handed the glass back.

'Elder's a sixteen-year-old boy,' said McCoy. 'They're saying he killed that wee girl Alice Kelly.'

Cooper looked blank. Wasn't surprising he wasn't up to speed, given his past couple of days.

'Anyway, I don't think he did. And he's no got a lawyer,' said McCoy.

'So you want me to pay for Lomax, take in some waif and stray . . .' Cooper shook his head. 'Anything else I can do for you?'

McCoy grinned. 'That'll do for now, but I'll let you know.'

He stood up.

'Where are you going?' asked Cooper, already looking sleepy.

'Leaving before Angela gets here,' said McCoy. 'Last thing I bloody need. I'll come back tomorrow, tell Laura to stay put, not to go out of the house until I get back.'

Cooper nodded.

McCoy headed for the door.

'McCoy.'

He turned and Cooper was looking at him.

'Thanks for . . .'

Didn't have to say it.

'Anytime,' said McCoy.

Cooper nodded, lay back on the pillows. Went out like a light.

CHAPTER 22

McCoy stepped out the house, started walking up towards Great Western Road. Looked at his watch. He was tired, ready to go home. Last thing he wanted to do was to try and get a hold of Liam and tell him about Mila, but Phyllis had left a message reminding him he'd promised to help Mila, so he whistled at a passing taxi, got in. Took a bit of persuading to get the driver to take him to Orton Street. He didn't want to go anywhere near it. McCoy took out his police card, told him to get on with it. The driver mumbled something under his breath, pulled the wee glass screen over. Suited McCoy fine. He had no great desire to engage the moaning-faced bastard in conversation.

Twenty minutes later the driver turned off Broomland Road and into the land of no return. McCoy got out, slammed the door shut and didn't give him a tip. Driver leant out the window, shouted at him as he drove off: 'Wanker!' McCoy didn't entirely blame him. He wouldn't go down into Wine Alley unless he had to either. It wasn't big, Wine Alley. Just five or six blocks of pebble-dashed three-storey flats. But it was like nowhere else in Govan. Like nowhere else in Glasgow.

Wine Alley had started off as Moore Park, a scheme they'd built to house people from the Gorbals whose tenements had been knocked down. Started off okay, but within a couple of years it was notorious. Shebeens, alkies, problem families, beggars, knives, and an awful lot of drink. Had become infamous. Forever in the papers. Got its nickname. The worst scheme in Western Europe, some said.

'You!'

McCoy turned and a man in his fifties, in a pair of suit trousers and nothing else – no shirt, no shoes – was standing in the middle of the street. He was trying to walk towards him, wasn't having much luck, swaying back and forward, looked well gone. Yellow streetlight reflecting off the long kitchen knife in his left hand. He raised it up.

'Money. Gies your money,' he said.

'Fuck off before I chase you,' said McCoy.

The man stepped forward, swayed a bit more, lost his balance. He fell forward, horrible crack as his head hit the pavement, knife skittering off into the gutter. A tiny woman in her nightie appeared from nowhere, ran over and knelt down beside him.

'He okay?' asked McCoy.

She nodded. The man had managed to sit himself up, was cursing, spitting blood out his mouth. McCoy walked over, held out a quid. The wee woman looked at him suspiciously. Hand stretched out and grabbed it.

'Tell him not to be such an arse. He'll get himself damaged,' said McCoy.

She nodded. Looked up and down the street. 'Shouldn't be walking around here at this time of night, son. It's too dangerous.'

McCoy nodded and walked off, the man already starting to ask how much he'd given her and how half of it was rightfully his.

McCoy found number 43, walked up what was left of the garden and climbed the stairs to the second floor. Knocked on the door and it fell open. Looked down, the lock was broken, hanging off by a screw.

'Liam, you there?' McCoy asked.

He stepped into the flat just as the bedroom door opened and Liam appeared. Paisley pattern pyjama bottoms, hair everywhere, rubbing the sleep out his eyes.

'Harry? Jesus Christ. You gave me a fright. What are you doing here?'

'Need a favour,' said McCoy. 'Got a minute?'

Liam closed the bedroom door behind him and pointed towards the living room. McCoy went to put on the light, pressed the switch and nothing happened.

'Need money for the meter?' he asked, digging in his pocket.

Liam shook his head. 'Been shut off for weeks.'

McCoy sat down on a kitchen chair in the middle of the room, light from the street outside giving the room a dim yellow glow. He looked round. A miserable sight. There were the remnants of some bamboo-patterned wallpaper on one wall, a bare hardboard floor and a couple of dirty cushions in the corner that looked like they had come from an old couch.

Liam leant on the windowsill. Now McCoy could see him properly, the light illuminated an angry and fresh-looking scar dotted with stitches running from his ear along his left jaw to his chin.

'Liam, Christ, what happened?'

Liam shook his head. 'Was sleeping rough the other night, passed out with the biddy, woke up and this was here. Blood everywhere. Fella told me there were young ones going about, doing it for a laugh. Slashing the jakeys. I wasn't the only one.'

'Christ,' said McCoy. He looked round again. 'This your place, is it?'

Liam shook his head. 'Shelia's. Got it off the council a year ago. It's a dump, but it's somewhere. Now, nice as it is to see you, Harry, I can't believe you're waking me up in the middle of the night just to enquire after my welfare. What's up?'

McCoy told him about Mila, how she needed a guide and protector to take her round.

Liam smiled. 'What? Give her the Grand Tour of Glasgow's Shitholes, you mean?'

McCoy nodded 'Exactly. Worth a bob or two to you. You in?'

Liam nodded. 'Sure now, what else have I got to do?'

McCoy stood up. 'One o'clock tomorrow, by the bullet in Central Station. I'll introduce you, then leave you to it.'

Liam nodded. 'I'll walk you up to Broomlaw Road. You'll get a taxi there, no chance getting one round here, and we wouldn't want a delicate flower like yourself walking Wine Alley at this time of night.'

McCoy shook his head. 'I'm a big boy, Liam. I'll be okay.'

'Aye, and you're the only polis that gives a shit for people like us. Don't need you removed from the picture. Selfish reasons, that's all it is.'

McCoy gave up. Liam was coming, no matter what he said.

'Give us a minute to get me breeks on,' he said and disappeared into the bedroom.

McCoy caught a glimpse of a mattress on the floor and a sleeping figure through the closing door. And just before it shut he caught a glimpse of something else.

He pushed the bedroom door open.

Liam was naked, stepping into a pair of jeans. Looked surprised. 'Christ, McCoy, can you no give a man a minute?' he said, pulling them up.

McCoy walked over to a pile of clothes and shoes in the corner. Picked up a bag. A hippy-looking bag. Long handles, beige, woven cloth.

'Where'd this come from?' he asked.

Liam was looking at him like he was mad.

'God only knows. It's Shelia's. She collects all sorts of shite, tries to find stuff to sell at Paddy's.'

McCoy walked over to the window to get some light and opened the bag wide. It was empty, just

195

a tiny balled-up bit of paper in the very corner. He dug in, got it out, unrolled it. It was a receipt. Some place called Max's Kansas City, 213 Park Avenue South, New York NY 10003. Fourteen dollars and twenty cents. He looked at Liam.

'Need to know where this came from, Liam. Can you wake her up?'

Liam was still looking at him like he was mad, but he bent over, shook the sleeping form in the bed.

'Shelia, love. Need to wake up.'

A moan.

Liam kept shaking and eventually Shelia sat up. McCoy was surprised at how young she was, could only be early twenties. She had a port wine stain birthmark covering half her chin and neck, long hair. She looked around the room, scared.

'Liam? What's going on?' she asked.

'This is Mr McCoy. He's a polis. Needs to ask you about a bag.'

McCoy held it up. 'You're no in trouble, Shelia. I just need to know where this came from.'

She looked at the bag, looked at him, looked at Liam. He nodded at her.

'I got it in the bins behind that hotel, the Royal something,' she said.

'Royal Stuart,' said McCoy.

She nodded. 'I go through the bins behind the big hotels, looking for the wee bottles of shampoo and bath stuff. I pour the dregs into one big bottle, then sell it at Paddy's.'

McCoy nodded. 'When was this?'

She thought. 'Be early Friday morning, I think. Lorries come at half nine to pick up the big bins, so it'd be before that.'

'Where was the bag?' McCoy asked.

'It was just lying there on top of one of the bins. Looked like someone had left it there.' She was starting to look a bit panicked. Glanced over at Liam for reassurance. 'I only took it because no one wanted it any more, it was just—'

'Don't worry,' said McCoy. 'You're no in trouble, honest. Was there anything in it?'

'No, just a wee jotter, full of writing. Blue ball-point pen.'

'Lyrics? That sort of thing?' asked McCoy.

Shelia didn't answer. Looked over at Liam.

'Shelia can't read,' he said.

'Don't worry, it'll be long gone now anyway.' She looked embarrassed. 'I just put it back in the bin with the rest of the stuff and took the bag. I thought it might be worth a couple of bob. You sure I'm no in trouble?'

McCoy shook his head. 'No, no trouble.' He dug in his pocket, found a quid, gave it to her. 'Need to buy it off you. That okay?'

She looked down at the pound note. Nodded.

'Go back to sleep, love. I'll be back in a while,' said Liam.

Outside it was still warm. Moths battering themselves off the streetlights, distant sound of music and shouting coming from some party. There was a group of lads waiting by the corner, all of them dressed in white jeans and bovver boots, black braces over their bare chests. One even had a bowler hat on. They started to walk towards them, one of them pulled a long screwdriver from inside his jeans.

'Shite,' said McCoy under his breath.

'All right, boys?' said Liam. 'He's with me.'

They nodded, screwdriver went back and they retreated to their corner.

'Glad you came after all,' said McCoy.

Liam nodded down at the bag. 'What was all that about?'

'Long story,' said McCoy. 'Probably nothing. Think it belonged to Bobby March.'

Liam looked blank.

McCoy mimed playing a guitar. 'Bobby March, rock star?'

Liam shook his head. 'I like the showbands myself, proper music.'

'Aye, if you're deaf as a post, that is.'

Liam grinned. 'Watch it, McCoy. Don't insult the greats. I saw the Miami Showband one night in Sligo. Bloody brilliant, they were.'

A taxi appeared at the top of the street and McCoy waved at it. The light went off and it drove towards them.

'One,' he said, getting in the cab. 'Central.'

'I heard you the first time,' said Liam. 'See you there.'

McCoy got in the cab, said he was going to Gardner Street. Half listened as the driver started a rant about how many taxi licences they were giving out these days. He nodded, said 'That's terrible' in the right places, but he had other things on his mind. Wattie, Ronnie Elder, some photographs of Stevie Cooper, and most of all Bobby March's bag sitting on the seat beside him.

He leant on the cab window, tried to think. Watched the city go past. He'd always liked Glasgow at night, even when he was on the beat. Liked the empty streets, occasional drunken straggler making his way home. Just him wandering through the empty city, seeing the things most people never did. The starlings covering Sauchiehall Street, flour-covered men through the windows of the baker's, working girls sitting on a wall passing cigarettes and a half bottle. Liked coming home when everyone was still asleep. Liked sliding under the covers beside Angela's warm body, trying not to wake her up.

The cab turned into Dumbarton Road. Almost home. He yawned, sat up. And now Angela was working for Stevie. Wasn't quite sure what he thought about that. There was nothing he could do about it anyway. She'd walked out on him years ago. No note, no wave goodbye. Just came in from the beat one night and she wasn't there and neither was her stuff.

Cab stopped outside his close and he got out and paid the man. Looked up at his empty flat, realised he still missed her.

30th December 1968

Gulfstream Park, Florida

Terry was nervous. Terry was always nervous before a show. Strumming his guitar, standing up, sitting down, pacing round the motorhome. Fiddling with his hair, the necklaces round his neck. Bobby took a drag, handed him the joint. Terry took a drag, handed it back, sat down on the kitchen counter, swig of Dr Pepper.

'What should we start with?' he asked. '"Tinker Tailor"?'

Bobby nodded. 'Great idea,' he said.

Truth was he didn't much care what they started with or even what they ended with. He just wanted this tour to be over and after tonight it would be. Three months of shit hotels, shit food, shit drugs, watching the headliners from the edge of the stage. Three months of trying to warm up bored audiences waiting for the main attraction. He'd had enough.

One thing he did know, this was the last tour he was going to do as a member of somebody else's band. He was going to do something of his own. Was sick of being a gun for hire, even if the pay was good. It wasn't Terry's fault. Terry was a nice guy, one of the good ones. He was just ready to jump. Had been working on his songs for a year. Hadn't told anyone, hadn't played them in the dressing rooms or the jam sessions after the shows. He was keeping them. Keeping them for himself. When he got back to London he was going to go and see Kit Lambert, maybe Peter Grant, someone who could make things happen.

He'd been out of it one night, rehearsals for the Rock and Roll Circus mess. Been so stoned and coked and fuck knows what else he had told Keith what he was going to do. Only person he'd told. Keith told him to get going, get it started. Time waited for no one. Wished him luck, told him anything he could do to help he would.

Wasn't sure Keith even remembered the conversation. He'd run into him a couple of days later in the Speak. Hadn't said anything, just dug into the pouch round his neck with a key, held it out. Bobby sniffed, wiped his nose. Good stuff.

'Maybe "When You Get Home"? Faster tempo . . .'

He looked up and Terry was standing over him. 'What?' he asked, still back in London.

'Start with "When You Get Home"?' Terry said again.

Bobby nodded, took another pull of the joint. 'Great idea.'

Terry nodded. 'Think it'll work.'

Bobby stepped out the motorhome into the noise and wet heat of Gulfstream Park. Tried to work out whether to tell Terry tonight or on the plane home tomorrow. Didn't matter much, he supposed. Wasn't going to be happy either way.

16TH JULY 1973

CHAPTER 23

McCoy took a sip of his tea and looked at his watch again. Ten past eight. Maybe Wattie wasn't going to turn up after all. Had sounded grumpy on the phone this morning. McCoy thought it was because he'd woken him up, but maybe it was more than that. Still smarting about Ronnie Elder probably. Or maybe Mary had told him the news. Still wasn't quite sure why she'd told him; maybe she'd just needed to tell someone. Now that he thought about it, he'd never heard her mention any family, a sister, mother, anything like that. God help her if he was the only person she had to turn to for advice.

The Golden Egg felt different. Was usually mobbed at this time. Serving breakfasts like nobody's business. Not today – today it was just him and the guy that always sat in the corner, coat and bunnet, woollen fingerless gloves even in this heat. He yawned again. Didn't get to his bed until after one, head whirring with Alice Kelly and Bobby March. Was thinking he should have ordered a coffee instead, wake himself up when there was a thud and a pile of the morning's papers landed on the table in front of him followed by Wattie sitting down opposite.

'Aye, good morning to you,' said McCoy. 'You nearly spilt my bloody tea.'

Wattie wasn't bothered. He fanned the papers out. Front page headlines all much the same, just variations of.

'BEAST ARRESTED!'

'HE KNEW HER!'

'"HE MUST HANG!" SAYS ALICE MUM.'

'What chance have we got now?' asked Wattie, staring at him.

'You want to order anything?' asked McCoy. 'Before you start giving me the third bloody degree.'

'Sorry,' he said, pushing his still wet hair off his forehead. 'These bloody papers just got me wound up.'

The waitress – desperate to serve them for once, nothing else to do – was hovering over them. 'What can I get you?' she asked, pencil ready.

'Tea,' said Wattie.

'A black coffee and some toast,' said McCoy.

She nodded, didn't bother writing it down, wandered off, smell of stale sweat and some kind of sickly perfume thankfully leaving with her.

'You don't like coffee,' said Wattie. 'Late night?' He grinned. 'Who was the lucky lady?'

'Liam,' said McCoy. 'Had to go to bloody Wine Alley.'

Wattie let out a low whistle. 'Surprised you got out alive. Eat coppers for breakfast there, I heard.'

McCoy piled the papers up, put them on the floor and sat back in his chair. 'Well, ye of little bloody faith. Wine Alley's not all I've been doing. I've been busy.'

'Doing what?' asked Wattie.

'Helping your bloody pal. So, due to my many connections and level of influence in this fair city, in about twenty minutes Archie Lomax is going turn up at the desk at Stewart Street and demand a meeting with his new client, Ronnie Elder.'

'No!' said Wattie, looking surprised.

'Yes,' said McCoy, smiling as the waitress put down the order.

Wattie waited until she'd wandered back to her post by the door. 'How'd that happen?' he asked.

McCoy tapped the side of his nose.

'Wanker,' said Wattie, grinning.

'Watch it, Watson. You may be Raeburn's bum chum but I'm still your superior officer. Probably be a good idea if you're there when Lomax arrives, don't want Raeburn trying any funny business.'

'You can come too,' said Wattie.

'Don't think that's a good idea. He's going to be pissed off enough with Lomax turning up without seeing my handsome face.'

Wattie shook his head. 'Don't think he'll be anything this morning. Apparently he was in the Eskimo all night celebrating, ordering whiskies for all the bar. He'll still be in his bed. We'll go to

Stewart Street, see Lomax, then I need to go up to the canal. Divers started again this morning. If she's in the canal, they'll find her today.'

McCoy looked down at the pictures of Alice Kelly on all the front pages. 'Poor wee bugger,' he said. 'Wasn't much of a life, was it?'

'Nope,' said Wattie. 'And neither will Ronnie Elder's be, not unless Lomax pulls something out the bag. You know something?'

'What?' McCoy sipped his coffee. Rotten.

'You may be a wanker, but you're a good guy.'

'Great guy, you mean,' said McCoy. 'Now away and pay the woman and make sure you give her a tip. With any luck, she'll spend it on some deodorant.'

The shop was firmly in 'morning after' mode. Hardly anyone in and those who were, were sitting at their desks, head in hands. The desks, the filing cabinets, the drawers were littered with the remnants of last night's celebrations: pint pots, cans, ashtrays full of butts and the occasional whisky bottle. Whole place stank of sweat, cigarettes and stale beer.

Wattie tipped a balled-up fish and chip wrapper off his chair and sat down. McCoy tiptoed over to the sleeping Thomson, bent down and shouted in his ear. 'Morning!!'

Thomson jumped, swore, then put his head back in his hands. Looked a right state. No tie, shirt half undone, exposing a yellowy-looking vest.

'You stay the night here?' asked McCoy.

He nodded. 'Fell asleep under the desk about three.' He scratched his head. 'Christ, I feel shocking. You got any fags?'

McCoy gave him one, watched as Thomson lit up, drew deep and the coughing fit started. Spat a lump of phlegm into the bin, seemed to be back to normal.

'Where's Raeburn?' asked McCoy, looking round.

'Fuck knows. In his bed hopefully.' Thomson yawned, exposing a mouth full of dark metal fillings. 'Him and Jacobs left here about two, talking about going for another drink in some shebeen.' He stood up, swayed a bit. 'And now I am going to the bogs to spew up and then fall asleep for another half an hour.'

He bowed theatrically, then wandered off.

'McCoy!' A shout from Billy at the front desk. 'Mr Lomax to see you.'

Lomax appeared a second later. He was dressed, as always, in immaculate chalk-stripe suit, snow-white shirt, navy-blue tie, shiny black brogues. He took a look around at the mess of the office, raised his eyebrows. 'Is it me or are standards within the Glasgow Constabulary declining dramatically?'

McCoy was about to explain when Lomax started again. 'Mr McCoy, I believe you are aware I have a new client?' he asked.

McCoy nodded.

'I would like to interview him, if that's not too much trouble?' Looked at his watch. 'Some of us are busy.'

McCoy pointed the way towards the cells. Hoped Brian the turnkey was in some sort of acceptable state. They walked down the corridor and the smell of bleach hit them. They turned the corner and Brian was swabbing the floor with a mop, bucket beside him. He looked up.

'As if my job's no bad enough with they mucky bastards in the cells, never mind bloody Thomson spewing up in my corridor. The stupid bugger didn't make it to the bogs. Who are you wanting?'

'Ronnie Elder,' said McCoy. 'Lawyer to see him.'

Brian reached for the keys around his waist. 'Least the wee bastard's stopped crying.' He nodded at cell number 4. 'He's in here.'

McCoy and Lomax waited as he fumbled with the lock, swore under his breath, eventually got it to turn, pushed the thick iron door open.

'That bloody lock needs replaced, don't know how many . . .'

He stopped. Just stood there, staring into the cell.

McCoy pushed past him into the doorway. Knew what he was going to see.

Ronnie Elder was hanging from the bars on the window, face contorted, a twisted sheet around his neck.

He heard Lomax say 'Jesus Christ' behind him, heard Brian running down the corridor and hitting the alarm. He ran into the cell and tried to push Elder's body back up, release the tension.

Knew as soon as he touched him there was no point. His body was lifeless, heavy like a sack of potatoes. But he put his fingers on the boy's neck. No pulse. Held his hand up at his mouth. Couldn't feel any breath. He managed to untie the sheet from the bar on the window, half carried and half pushed Elder onto the foam mattress on the floor.

McCoy sat down beside him. Looked at Ronnie Elder's swollen face, his sock half hanging off his foot, his bitten-down nails, and he swore he was going to get Raeburn for this. He didn't care if it cost him his job. Some stupid, pathetic boy was dead, had hanged himself in despair because of Bernie Raeburn, so he was going to pay for it.

And then Wattie was there behind him and Thomson was there and Lomax was shouting and the alarm was going and he realised there was a bit of paper on the floor beside him. A blank page ripped out the Bible sitting on the other mattress. He picked it up. Note written on it in pencil in what looked like a child's writing.

'Tell my mum I'm sorry.'

He looked up, handed it to Wattie. 'What a mess,' he said. 'What a bloody mess.'

Half an hour later they were watching the ambulance men carry a covered stretcher through the office. Wattie hadn't said much, just sat there watching, look on his face that was half anger and half fear. Raeburn was still nowhere to be found.

Thomson had tried everywhere they could think of, had even sent a uniform to his flat. No answer. He could hear Billy on the front desk telling the ambulance men they'd be better taking him out the back door, through the garage. There were still reporters milling about outside.

McCoy stood up. He'd had enough. Didn't want to be there any more. Needed air. Needed away.

'No point in me sitting here,' he said. 'When Raeburn turns up, he'll just tell me to fuck off and the mood I'm in I'll lamp the bastard.'

Wattie nodded, face was pale. He was fiddling with a paper clip, straightening it and bending it again.

'Come on, Wattie, it's not your fault,' said McCoy.

'Aye, it is. Why do you think he did it?' he asked. 'For the fun of it? Because of what Raeburn and I put him through, that's why.'

McCoy sat back down, sighed. 'Look, we still don't know if he was innocent or not. Doesn't matter how many times he said it. Or that you believed him. The evidence is strong. Maybe he just couldn't live with the guilt.'

Wattie went to protest and McCoy held his hand up, silenced him. 'You reported your concerns to a senior officer immediately after the interview. If anyone drove him towards it, it wasn't you, it was Raeburn. Okay?'

Nothing.

'I said okay?'

Wattie nodded, looked about as far from okay as any man could be.

McCoy stood up again. 'I'll be back in a couple of hours. They'll have to bring in another team to look at this. Gilroy'll have to do a post-mortem. Raeburn'll have to turn up from wherever the fuck he is. Nothing's going to happen for a while yet.'

He left Wattie sitting there. Heard Thomson say to someone on the way out, 'At least the wee bastard has saved us the trouble.' Supposed that would be the opinion of most of the polis.

Still wasn't sure whether it was his or not.

CHAPTER 24

McCoy decided he needed a walk. Needed the air and the time to think. Most of all he needed to be away from the shop and the thought of Ronnie Elder hanging in his cell.

He found himself walking along Great Western Road. Thought he may as well head for Cooper's. The lights changed and he crossed Park Road. A gaggle of student types passed him. Long-haired boys in cut-off denims and T-shirts, girls with cheesecloth shirts open over bikini tops. They were carrying a couple of bottles of rosé, no doubt heading for Kelvingrove Park. Looked like they didn't have a care in the world. Wondered what they thought when they passed him. Just another sad old guy in a suit probably. Depressing, but they weren't far wrong.

Couldn't get the image of Elder hanging there out his head. Raeburn should have put the poor bugger on suicide watch. Too busy celebrating to think of it, and even if he hadn't Wattie should have. Too busy burning with injustice to pay attention to his job. Supposed it was what the young did. Tried to fight the big fights while forgetting the people they were supposed to be fighting for. There'd be an inquiry, automatic with any death in custody. Had the feeling no one was going to come out of it very well.

He crossed the road at the lights, stopped. There was another one on the wall by the subway station. Same red spray paint, same big letters.

'BOBBY MARCH WILL LIVE FOREVER!!'

Shook his head, was regretting giving that boy the money. He had March's bag now, not that it was doing him any good. Nobody seemed to care much about what had happened to Bobby March, not his dad certainly. Papers had moved on. Alice Kelly was all they cared about. Was beginning to think it might be better to just let Bobby and his overdose fade away into the background.

He turned into Hamilton Park Avenue, could see Cooper's ugly big house at the end of the road. He noticed his lace was undone, bent down to tie it and saw what looked like spots of Ribena or something on the pavement. Looked closer. It wasn't Ribena, it was blood. The street was empty but for a wean sitting in a big Silver Cross pram on the pavement opposite. The baby looked at him, smiled. He smiled back, waved and then he heard a moan.

Then another.

He looked round. Saw a leg coming out from under Cooper's neighbour's hedge, black baseball boot on the end. He bent down, pushed the hedge aside and suddenly he was looking at Laura

215

Murray. She was pale, breathing shallow, blood running down her face and a pool of it between her legs, skirt stained red.

'Fuck sake! Laura!'

She opened her eyes, tried to smile at him.

'McCoy,' she said. 'Thank God. I couldn't make it to the house.'

Then her eyes closed and she sank back into the leaves.

An hour later McCoy was sitting at the kitchen table, watching the stairs. Dr Purdie had turned up half an hour ago, muttering something about 'having a proper job, you know'. Soon shut it when McCoy told him he could take another five hundred off his debts. Since then he had been in and out Laura's room, sending Iris for water, towels, all sorts. When Iris came out the bedroom carrying a dripping blood-soaked towel that was more than enough for McCoy. He'd retreated downstairs, sat at the table, smoked and waited.

Laura had come round when he was carrying her into the house. Made him promise he wouldn't phone the police. They'd tell her parents where she was. McCoy told her he wouldn't to shut her up, but he was waiting on Purdie to tell him how bad she was; if it was anything serious he would have to call Murray, didn't have a choice.

He heard footsteps on the stairs and Purdie appeared, shirt sleeves rolled up, tie over his shoulder. He dumped his leather bag on the table, pushed his fair hair back off his face, undid the top button of his shirt and pointed at the sink.

'May I?' he asked.

McCoy nodded and Purdie poured a big glass of water and sat down, lit up.

'Is she okay?' McCoy asked.

Purdie nodded, blew out a cloud of smoke from his nostrils, waved it away.

'She's a bit battered and bruised. She's had a fright more than anything else, but she'll live.' He hesitated. 'I know Mr Cooper is being helpful with my debts, but when it comes to getting involved in assaults on young girls I could honestly do without it. I don't want to get involved in any sort of crime scenario that—'

'Maybe when you're back to owing nothing, you can pick and choose,' said McCoy. 'Until then, you do what you're told. Got it?'

Purdie nodded, looked resigned to his fate. 'Sorry. Who is she anyway?'

'A friend's niece. I'm looking after her,' said McCoy.

'What age is she?' he asked.

'Fifteen,' said McCoy.

'That might go some way to explain it,' said Purdie.

'Explain what?'

'She's had an abortion.'

'She's what?' asked McCoy.

'An illegal abortion,' said Purdie. 'Not the best idea, but it happens.'

'Christ.'

'Exactly. Isn't the worst I've seen, but it's far from the best. She's got heavy bleeding, clots. Beginnings of an infection. So I've injected her with a big dose of antibiotics, which will hopefully see it off.'

'Will she be okay?' asked McCoy.

Purdie shrugged. 'She's young and in good health, she should be. Anything else happens, any change in her condition, you'll need to take her to the hospital immediately, regardless of the consequences.'

McCoy nodded, was still trying to take it all in.

'Why would someone attack her?' asked Purdie. 'By the looks of it she's been given a fair few kicks in the stomach as well as the bump on her head.'

'I've no idea,' said McCoy. Realised he really hadn't. Wasn't much chance it was a random attack, not in broad daylight. But why would someone be after Laura Murray? 'Is that why she's, you know, bleeding?' he asked.

'Certainly wouldn't help,' said Purdie. 'Kicks seemed to be aimed there, probably knew she'd had the procedure.'

Purdie fiddled with his Dunhill lighter, turned it over and over in his hands. 'If I was really doing my job, I'd be calling an ambulance now,' he said.

McCoy got up and took glasses and a bottle of whisky from the shelf, poured them two belts.

'You know that I am supposed to report this kind of thing?' said Purdie.

'Which you aren't going to,' said McCoy.

'Which I'm not going to,' repeated Purdie. He

smiled, looked a bit sad. 'Just like I don't report the various slashings and knife wounds I come here to stitch up.' He took a sip of the whisky. 'You know, the day I graduated from medical school I told my parents I was going to be a surgeon, specialising in coronary care.' Smiled again. 'Was all on track until the gee-gees got me and now I do anything for the money. Fix up dirty abortions, inject Mr Cooper with Seconal to let him ride out his withdrawal symptoms.' He held up his glass. 'Cheers, here's to my brilliant career!'

He swallowed the whisky over and stood up. 'Time to go back to the practice, back to the important stuff, reassuring middle-aged men with flu that they're not about to die.' He dug in his pocket, handed McCoy a small bottle. 'Forgot to give these to Iris. There's six in there. Two a day for your friend Cooper. Should be fine when they're finished.' Pretended to tip his hat and left.

McCoy watched him go, took another sip of his whisky. Wasn't sure if he should tell Murray what had happened or not. If he did, he was pretty sure he'd take her back to Bearsden, come hell or high water, and maybe he was right to. If someone had beaten her up, there was a reason and it might happen again. Chances were she'd be a lot safer at home with her mum and dad, no matter what Laura wanted.

McCoy was just about to go up and see how Cooper was doing when Iris appeared, big ball of bloody bedclothes held out in front of her. She

219

stuffed them into the washing machine and sat down. Poured a shot of whisky into Purdie's glass and swallowed it in one.

'Christ, I needed a drink after all that.' She glanced upwards. 'She's sleeping,' she said. 'Out like a light. Purdie gave her something. So's Cooper. It's like night of the living bloody dead up there.'

'Did she say what happened?' asked McCoy.

'No really, says someone came up behind her. She was walking back from getting the messages, heard a shuffle behind her and then something hit her on the head. She falls down, gets kicked a good few times and shoved into next door's bloody hedge.'

'Did she see who it was?' asked McCoy.

'Naw, he was behind her the whole time. Cowardly bastard that he was. Why'd someone attack her?'

McCoy shrugged. 'You know about the . . .' he started.

Iris looked at him like he was mad. 'What do you think all those bloody sheets were from? The wee bump on her head? Christ, McCoy.'

'Sorry.' He poured them another drink. 'Suppose we know why she didn't want to go home. Wonder if Donny MacRae knew.'

Iris snorted. 'What? You think if he hadnae got killed they'd be getting married, painting the nursery? Wise up. She's young but she's no stupid. She'd have done it anyway.' She looked at him. 'And why are you so bloody sure it was Donny MacRae anyway?'

'Who else would it be? She have another boyfriend on the go?'

Iris rolled her eyes. 'Christ, but men are stupid. It won't be the first bloody time. Fathers, brothers, uncles. A pregnant girl runs away from home. You're supposed to be a polis, must have crossed your mind.'

And the terrible thing was that until that moment it hadn't. McCoy suddenly felt like the ice was cracking under his feet. Suddenly it all seemed so obvious. Her dad not wanting the police involved. Murray telling him not to dig too deep. Laura telling him, 'Even good old uncle Hec couldn't fix it this time.' It had been there all along and he'd missed it. No wonder nothing was going to make her go back home.

'You all right?' Iris was peering at him. 'Look like you've seen a ghost.'

McCoy sat up in his chair. 'I'm fine, fine.' He dragged himself to his feet. 'I'll just go up and see how she's doing.'

Iris narrowed her eyes. 'Purdie told you, no questions. She needs rest.'

He held his hands up. 'Couple of questions, that's all, I promise.'

She shook her head. 'On your own head be it.'

McCoy stopped at the doorway. Turned.

Iris looked at him. 'What?'

'Just in case you think I'm that daft, Iris, I know you either did it or you sorted it out. How else is a nice teenager from Bearsden going to get in touch with a back-street abortionist?'

221

The blood drained from her face. 'Don't know what you're bloody talking about.'

'Let's hope you just put her in touch. Because if something happens to her, if this gets worse, it won't be me that's after who did it, it'll be Chief Inspector Murray.'

Iris stood up, walked towards him, put her face right into his. He could smell her perfume, the whisky on her breath.

'What is that, McCoy? Some kind of threat? You think I'm scared of you or that fat arsehole Murray? You must be joking. And if you think I'm going to stop helping women in trouble you're very much mistaken. Because I'm sick of men like you. Stick it anywhere you want, then fuck off when she gets up the duff. You're all the bloody same, leaving some lassie's life ruined all because you wanted your hole and she was stupid enough to believe your shite.'

She was getting angrier as she went on. Spitting it out now, face screwed up with contempt.

'I'm fifty-three. I work in a shitty shebeen. Do you think I give a fuck if you try and send me to jail? I don't care. I'm proud of the women I've helped and given my time again I'd do the bloody same. So before you start issuing threats, why don't you try and find out who really gave her the baby. Happens all the time. Even in leafy bloody Bearsden.'

She was furious now, hands in fists. McCoy wasn't sure if she was going to hit him. But she sat back down, screwed the top off the whisky and poured herself another, hands shaking so much she spilt most of it.

McCoy stood there, feeling like a wee boy who'd been given a row. The worst thing was most of what she'd said was true. She looked up at him, took a swig of the drink.

'Beat it, McCoy,' she said, sounding tired. 'Just get out my sight.'

Laura was awake when he went in. The bedroom was dim, warm, light coming through a crack in the closed curtains. Laura looked tired and very, very pale.

McCoy sat on the side of the bed. 'You okay?' he asked.

She nodded.

'Dr Purdie told me to leave you to rest, but I need to know a couple of things, Laura. It's all getting too serious for me to be polite, okay?'

She nodded again and pulled herself up on the pillows, effort making her grimace.

'Whose baby was it?' he asked

She looked at him, surprised. 'Donny's,' she said. 'Who else's would it be?'

'Are you sure?'

She looked at him puzzled. 'Of course I'm sure. I've only had one boyfriend. What are you asking me that for?'

McCoy took a deep breath. 'You ran away from home, you were fifteen and pregnant. Things happen in families, Laura. Things that aren't right.'

She was looking at him with shock. 'You thought it was my dad?'

'I had to ask,' said McCoy

'No, you didn't, but it wasn't him, I swear on my life. You happy now?'

She turned away and looked at the wall. McCoy felt like a bastard doing it, but he had to keep pressing, he needed some answers.

'So are you going to tell me why you really won't go back?'

She didn't turn round. Was almost a whisper when she said it. 'It's not my dad. It's my mum.'

'Your mum?' he asked. Was the last thing he expected.

She took her arm out from beneath the covers and pulled up the sleeve of her nightie. There were burns all up her arm, some faded, some still angry red welts. Scars too. Deeps slashes across her forearm.

'Burns are from the poker,' she said. 'It's one of her favourites. Cuts are from anything that comes to hand, bread knives are what she usually uses. You want to see my leg too?'

McCoy shook his head. 'I'm sorry, I didn't think . . .'

'I'm not going home,' she said. 'Not now, not ever.'

She kept her face to the wall but McCoy could hear her sobbing. He left her, shut the door behind him and stood on the landing. Seemed leafy Bearsden could be just as dangerous and brutal as anywhere else in Glasgow.

CHAPTER 25

McCoy walked out Cooper's house, shut the door behind him. Still didn't really know what had happened to Laura. Why would her mother do something like that? Whatever it was she was doing looked like it had been going on for years. Some of the scars and burns had almost faded away. No wonder she didn't want to go home, couldn't blame her.

He stopped at the corner of Great Western Road and lit up. As far as he was concerned Murray had some explaining to do. What was happening to her couldn't have gone unnoticed, he must have known. A taxi pulled up just along the road. He was about to run and try and catch it when the door opened and Angela got out. Couldn't help it, heart skipped a bit when he saw her. She paid the driver, walked down the road and saw him, smiled. She was wearing jeans, suede boots, a little leather jacket, a T-shirt with a Superman symbol on it. Looked fantastic.

'Harry? What are you doing here?' she said. 'Long time no see.'

'Was in seeing Cooper,' he said, pointing back

at the house. Seemed easier than explaining about Laura.

'Me too,' she said. 'I've been summoned, must be on his feet again. About time.' She looked at her watch. 'I'm early for his majesty and it's a lovely day. You fancy a walk?'

'Perfect,' said McCoy. 'Need to talk to you anyway.'

'That sounds ominous,' she said, smiling. 'Come on, I'll buy you a cone. I'm boiling.'

They wandered up Great Western Road, vaguely heading for the Botanic Gardens. Sun was high in the sky, must have been nearly eighty. McCoy took his jacket off, slung it over his shoulder. Angela took a pair of huge sunglasses out her pocket, put them on. Hanging about bands must be getting to her; she was starting to look like a rock star these days.

'So, where were you?' asked McCoy. 'Cooper said you were away.'

'Liverpool,' she said, lighting up. 'You ever been there? Makes Glasgow look like bloody Paris. Total dump.'

McCoy shook his head. Then realised. 'Actually, I have. Forgot. Uncle Tommy's funeral.'

Angela stopped. 'Tommy died?'

'Aye, in June. Cancer. Diagnosed and then he was dead a month later.'

'You should have told me. I liked the old bugger.'

'Would you have come?' he asked.

She smiled. 'Probably not.'

'What were you doing there?' he asked.

226

Realised he suddenly sounded like he was interviewing her like a policeman. She must have felt the same.

'That would be my business,' she replied coldly.

'Sorry,' said McCoy. 'Force of habit.'

They walked on. Had to step aside to let a group of women pushing prams get past, then a man walking three big Alsatians, none of whom looked friendly.

'I was thinking about you last night,' said McCoy.

'Were you now. Why's that?'

'Don't know, just remembering when we lived in Vulcan Street, when I was on the beat.'

'Christ . . . That was a while ago.'

'And I used to come in and get into bed while you were still asleep.'

Angela stopped. 'What's up with you, Harry? What's with the trip down memory lane?'

And for a second he was going to say it. Tell her he missed her. But he didn't. He just shrugged. 'Life's a bit shit at the minute,' he said. 'Work. I've been better.'

'And Cooper?' she asked.

'Didn't help,' said McCoy, glumly. 'Did you know what was going on?'

'Not really. I knew Ellie was one for the occasional dabble in heroin, but I thought that was it, then Cooper just sort of disappeared, never out his room. I started dealing with Billy. Should have been obvious, but I just thought he was being the Big Man, delegating, you know?'

227

He nodded. Wasn't quite sure whether he did or not, mind still half on the sight of Ronnie Elder hanging in his cell. They were at the crossroads now, entrance to the park across the road obscured by an ice-cream van. They waited for the light to change.

'You all right, though, Harry?' she asked.

He smiled. 'You know me, bounce back in no time.'

'Not so sure about that. You always were a bit of a miserable bugger. So what was it you wanted to ask me about?' she asked.

'Heroin,' said McCoy.

'Why? Thinking of giving it a go? Don't think that'd cheer you up much. Well, would for a bit, maybe.'

'I've got enough bad habits without starting any more,' said McCoy.

'That's true. So, what do you want to know?'

The lights changed, the green man appeared and they started walking across the street.

'Bobby March. Came into town from New York, and unless he was more stupid than anyone thought he wouldn't be carrying any smack. Then he was dead of an overdose twenty-four hours later. Where'd he get it from?'

'Me,' said Angela, as they stepped up onto the pavement.

McCoy stopped. 'You?'

'Me,' she said, stepping in behind two wee girls in the queue for the Mr Whippy van. 'You want a ninety-nine?'

228

McCoy nodded, walked up the park path a bit, found an empty bench outside the Kibble Palace and sat down. The huge greenhouse was boiling at the best of times, hated to imagine what it was like today, had no intention of going inside to find out. Was better off out here with the breeze and the smell of flowers from the big beds cut into the lawns. A group of boys were playing football just past the beds, shirts vs skins, shouts, insults and laughter drifting over.

Angela appeared, ninety-nine in each hand, can of Coke poking out her jacket pocket. She held one out. 'Take this before it melts all over me,' she said.

McCoy took it and she sat down beside him, started licking the melted ice cream off her fingers.

'This is between you and me, Harry. I don't want any trouble with the law and I really don't want any trouble with Stevie.'

McCoy nodded, pulled the flake out his ice cream and stuffed it into his mouth.

Angela had managed to stem the flow of melted ice cream, started talking. 'We have a, how shall we say, an understanding with the venues in town. Greene's, Electric Garden, Burns Howff, places like that. We—'

'The Burns Howff?' said McCoy. 'That dump? Worst place to see a band in Glasgow.'

She ignored him. 'We do good business in them. The bands coming through every week get what they need easy, are happy to come back, and we supply the lower-grade stuff to the bouncers on the door to sell to the punters.'

He smiled. 'It's funny hearing you talking like some drug dealer.'

'Aye well, needs must. Stevie offered me the job. Was either that or keep working in the Maryland for bugger all.'

'You not feel funny about it? Being on the wrong side of the law and all that?'

She looked at him. 'I'm not you, Harry. I don't have a career, a proper job. Never did have. What was I doing when I met you? Working in a pub. Pubs, shops, cafes . . . that's my brilliant career. Least this way I'm making money for once. That all right with you, is it?'

'Would you care if it wasn't?'

She grinned. 'Nope. Do you want to hear the story or not?'

He nodded. 'Sorry.'

'So I don't normally bother going myself. Billy goes if it's a big order or he sends Jumbo. But this was Bobby March. And as we know Bobby March played with the Stones.'

McCoy had forgotten Angela's devotion to The Rolling Stones, them and The Faces and a bit of Rod Stewart, depending on how she was feeling about him leaving them. They were all she had ever played on the record player in the old flat in Vulcan Street. Must have almost worn out the copy of *Let It Bleed*. Remembered them both stoned, drunk, singing along to 'You Can't Always

Get What You Want', her in tune, him way off. Good times.

'You remember that record we had, *Olympic Silver*?' she asked.

McCoy shook his head.

'You must do! The bootleg that cost me four bloody quid! The one with "Jiving Sister Fanny" on it? Black cover? "Blood Red Wine" on it as well?'

'Oh, that one. Aye, I remember it now,' said McCoy. Still didn't really remember it, but it was easier to just agree.

Angela was shaking her head in disappointment.

'Sorry,' said McCoy. 'Remember I wasn't a bloody fanatic, unlike you.'

'You bloody should have been, if you'd had any taste. Anyway, that's Bobby March playing on it, that record. That was his audition,' she said. 'When they asked him to join.'

'"The best version of the Stones there ever was", according to Keith Richards,' said McCoy. 'I read it in the paper.'

She nodded. 'Exactly. So when the call came in from the Maryland I said I'd go. See him, see the people I used to work with. I really wanted to meet him, talk to him about it.'

'Ya big groupie,' said McCoy, grinning.

She sighed. 'Do you want to hear this bloody story or not?'

'Sorry, aye. Crack on,' he said, crunching the cone, safe now all the ice cream was gone.

'So I goes to the sound check, delivers the goods to the guitar tech. He gives me passes, says come to the show, come backstage afterwards. No way was I going to the show but I came down about eleven. Figured it would be over by then.'

'You were smarter than me. I went. Apart from "Sunday Morning Symphony" it was bloody awful.'

'There's a surprise. Anyways, I go to Bobby's—'

'Bobby's, is it?' McCoy was grinning again. 'Sorry.'

She ignored him, got the can out her pocket, opened it and took a drink.

'So I go to the dressing-room and we start chatting, about Glasgow, bands we'd seen. He was nice, bit spaced out but funny. Then I ask him about the Stones and I can tell right away he's sick of talking about it, but I don't care. I keep asking. So eventually he gives in, starts talking about Villa Nellcôte, about all the drugs and the dealers and the hangers-on and Bianca and Mick, how him and Keith are big buddies, and how he's all over *Exile* without a credit. I'm lapping all this up. So I tell him I've got the *Olympic Silver* bootleg and how great it is.'

She lit up, took another sip of her drink.

'And he smiles and he says, "You've no idea!" By this point, whatever he's taken is kicking in. Looked like mandies, but fuck knows. He's a bit all over the place, slurring, spilling his drink. And then he says, "That was only day one. No one's ever heard day two." Taps the side of his nose. "Day two is really why they asked me to join." Then has a sleep and the tech comes in and says, "Do you want to go back to the hotel?" I'm thinking, is there any point? But I goes anyway and we get back to his room and we do some coke he's got from somewhere and he perks up a bit and starts acting like a dick, telling me he's going to be bigger than the Stones ever were and then he starts pawing at me and I tell him to fuck off and he says what the fuck are you here for then and I leave.'

'That it?' asked McCoy.

She nodded.

'You didn't shoot him up in the hotel room?' he asked.

'No, I bloody didn't!' she said. 'I was only there for about ten minutes. Whatever happened to him happened long after I was gone.'

'Did you see a bag when you were there? Shoulder bag thing with a long handle, brownish?'

She nodded. 'Had it with him when we left the venue.'

'And it was still there when you left?' McCoy asked.

She nodded again. 'Yes, officer. Far as I remember, that is. I was a bit gone myself.'

'So you left and he must have injected himself and had an overdose, that the story?'

'I don't know! I wasn't there, as I keep bloody telling you. He was a junkie, junkies overdose. Not the first or the last time that's going to happen,' she said, pushing her hair behind her ear. Just like she always did when she was nervous. She looked at her watch.

'Fuck, I better get going or Cooper'll go spare.' She stood up, finished her can and dropped it in the wire bin next to the bench. Leant over to him. 'Remember, Harry, between you and me. You promised.'

'Sure, don't worry,' he said. 'Take care of yourself, Angela.'

He watched her walk down the path, waited until she disappeared out the park gates, then he got his hanky out his pocket, went over to the bin and wrapped it carefully around the Coke can and put it into his jacket pocket.

CHAPTER 26

McCoy scanned the morning papers piled up on the big wooden John Menzies counter. All of them much the same. All about Ronnie Elder or 'The Beast' or 'The Teenage Killer' and what he'd done. The news about his death wasn't out when they'd gone to print, definitely would be by the afternoon editions. Wondered if Raeburn had surfaced yet, must have done. Had the feeling Wattie and Raeburn would be in Pitt Street by now, giving a statement about exactly how Ronnie Elder managed to kill himself in custody.

He could feel the wrapped-up Coke can in his jacket pocket. Needed to get Angela's fingerprints taken off it, compared to the ones on the syringe. Might be a job for PC Walker. She was bright enough, just wasn't sure if he could trust her to do it on the fly. Wasn't quite sure why he kept coming back to what had happened to Bobby March, but he did. Didn't think that Angela would have deliberately given Bobby March enough smack to kill him. Why would she? Chances were he's been bumming his chat about how he and

235

Keith Richards were such big-time users that she'd thought he'd need more than normal. Probably scarpered when he keeled over. Couldn't really blame her. Couldn't really call it much of a crime either. So why was he trying to prove Angela was involved? Wasn't sure he even knew himself.

He was early, was only quarter to, so he had a wander round the station. It was busy, people still setting off on their holidays as well as the usual everyday punters. The wooden destination boards above the shops rattled and clacked every few minutes as trains came and went. He bought some fags, stood under the clock and lit up, let the crowds pass him either side and hoped Liam hadn't gone on a bender after he'd left him and wouldn't turn up.

'McCoy!'

He turned and Mila was standing behind him. Faded army jacket, two cameras around her neck and a bag over her shoulder, big smile on her face. He'd forgotten how good-looking she was: tall, blonde, blue eyes. Not your usual Glasgow girl.

'Mila, how are you doing?' he asked.

'Good! It's another lovely day. Are you coming with us?' she asked.

He shook his head. 'Liam'll show you around, though. He's had a bit of an accident with his face, so don't worry when you see him.'

'That's a shame,' she said, smiling. 'The party was fun. Those girls were crazy, had me drinking Boofast?'

'Buckfast,' said McCoy.

'That's it! Evil stuff. Why didn't you come? I asked the boy at the next table to give you the address.'

'Ah,' he said. Not entirely sure whether to believe her or not. 'Think there was a bit of a mix-up.'

'I think tonight we would like to do something a bit more exciting, to thank you for this. Do you want to?'

He nodded. 'Definitely.' And then he stumbled forward. Had no idea what had happened, then realised Liam had clapped him on the back. Forgotten his strength, as usual.

'McCoy! I'm here! Reporting for duty.'

And he was. Dressed for the weather in a pair of jeans and a red T-shirt with 'Property of Alcatraz' written on it, sandshoes completing the look, big scar and big smile on his face. He looked Mila up and down and the smile got even wider.

McCoy went to speak but the tannoy started to blare out, announcing the arrival of the 1.06 from Ayr, and suddenly the station was full of returning holidaymakers. Kids, red-faced dads carrying luggage, harassed mums and aunties. McCoy tried to talk above the hubbub but there was no point, neither of them could hear him. Eventually, the crowd thinned out, the noise went down a bit and he tried again.

'Mila, Liam. Liam, Mila. Mila here wants to take photographs of the worst kind of living conditions. That right?'

Mila nodded. 'The charity I am working for wants to shock people, let them see how people are really living in 1973.'

'Okay,' said McCoy, turning to Liam. 'Maybe try what's left of the Gorbals? Woodside? Blackhill?'

Liam nodded. Still smiling. Still looking at Mila.

'Then maybe take her down by the Clyde, the people living rough, then along to the Great Eastern?'

No response.

'Liam?'

Liam seemed to come back, nodded, stopped staring at Mila. 'No bother. We can do that. You all set, Mila? You want to get a piece or a bottle of ginger?'

Mila was nodding, plainly didn't understand a word of Liam's broad Irish accent. He tried again, talking slower, somehow only made his accent broader. She nodded again, not quite understanding it was a question and she was supposed to answer.

The board rattled and announced the 1.14 to London was leaving from platform three. Another rush of people. McCoy could hear some kid crying, a woman shouting on her friend to hurry up or they wouldn't get seats, inspector at the gate shouting 'Tickets ready, please!'

'We're gonna go, Harry,' said Liam.

'Okay. Hope it all goes well,' said McCoy. 'See you later.'

He watched them head off, Mila turning back

238

with a comedy look of fear on her face as they walked towards the Hope Street exit. The crowd had settled down, formed a line at platform three, but he could still hear the kid crying. Maybe he'd lost his mum. McCoy looked around, couldn't see where the noise was coming from. Eventually spotted a little boy crouching by the toilets. He looked about nine or ten, short blond hair, a Scotland strip, white training shoes.

McCoy waited in the hope someone else would deal with it. No luck. No railway police to be seen, everyone else hurrying for their trains. He sighed. Just about his level these days, rescuing lost weans.

He walked over, the crying getting louder as he got a bit closer. The boy's face was all scrunched up, fists in his eyes, wailing away. An elderly woman in a pair of huge white sunglasses, a straw hat and tartan dress had appeared beside him.

'I think he's lost,' she said. 'Maybe he got left behind when his family got on the train. Poor wee bugger.'

McCoy tried to sound friendly, knelt down in front of the boy. 'Come on, son. It can't be that bad. What's your name, eh? You lost your maw, eh? Don't worry, we'll find her soon enough.'

The boy stopped crying for a second, raised his head, looked up at him and McCoy realised he wasn't looking at a boy at all. What he was looking at was a girl with her hair cut short.

'Do you want me to get him an ice cream or a bottle of juice?' asked the woman. 'I could go across to the shops. Would maybe cheer him up a bit?'

She kept talking, but McCoy wasn't listening, just trying to understand what he was looking at.

'Alice? he said. 'Is that you?'

The girl nodded.

McCoy couldn't believe it, but it was true. He was kneeling down in Central Station looking into the dirty, tear-stained face of a very alive Alice Kelly.

CHAPTER 27

Billy looked up from his desk when McCoy walked into the station, put the phone down.

'Is it true? She's alive?' he asked.

McCoy nodded. 'He here?'

Billy didn't have to ask who he was talking about.

'Came in about an hour ago, looks bloody shocking. Must have—'

McCoy didn't wait to listen to the rest, pushed the door of the office open and walked in. A few faces looked up. Could see Raeburn sitting on his desk at the back. If he doubted what he was going to do, the sight of him had made his mind up. Felt the anger growing in him, was all he could think about. Knew it was one of the few times in his life he was about to surrender to it. Knew he was getting out of control and he wasn't sorry about it. Not this time. He walked straight across the office floor towards him, could hear Wattie shouting 'Harry!' behind him.

Raeburn looked up, saw him and stood up as he got closer. 'Better call your pal off, Watson,' he said. 'Before he does something he shouldn't.'

McCoy felt Wattie grab him, arms around his shoulders, but he managed to shrug him off and ran at Raeburn. Raeburn went to duck but not quick enough. McCoy managed to punch him in the side of the head. Hard. Raeburn went down and McCoy straddled him, knees on his shoulders and punched in at his face. Again and again and again. Didn't even stop when Raeburn's nose gave way under his fist and spurted blood all over the carpet and all over him.

He could hear shouts, Raeburn crying out, people scrambling, and then Wattie was on him, hands round his neck, trying to pull him off. He struggled, managed to get a few more punches in at Raeburn's bloody face before Wattie dragged him off and rolled him onto the floor.

He lay there for a second, chaos around him, tried to get his breathing back to normal. His knuckles were killing him, felt like he'd broken something. He sat up, rubbed at them and looked over at Raeburn. Thomson was helping him up. He managed to get him to his chair and Raeburn sat down heavily. He looked over at McCoy and McCoy realised he was smiling through the blood. Looking at him in triumph.

'That's assault of a superior officer,' he said, wiping the blood from his nose. 'You're gone, McCoy. Out the fucking door.'

McCoy got up to go at him again, stopped dead, heard a voice boom out behind him.

'What the bloody hell is going on here?'

Everyone turned, looked at the doorway. Detective Inspector Murray was standing there. He was pointing at him, fury on his face. 'You! McCoy! Away out my sight. I'll deal with you later.'

Murray's face got even angrier. He pointed again. 'And you, Raeburn, you useless prick of a man. In my office. Now!'

He walked past them and slammed his office door behind him. Raeburn stood up, walked towards the closed door. Wasn't grinning any more.

McCoy was leaning on the edge of a sink in the toilets, running cold water over his right hand, trying to stop the swelling. Was pretty sure he'd just chucked what was left of his career in the bin, but he didn't much care at this point. If his career was going to be working for people like Raeburn they could shove it. Looked up into the mirror and Wattie was standing there.

'Not sure that was the best idea in the world,' he said. 'Glad you did it, though. The arsehole deserved it and more.'

'Done now,' said McCoy. 'Can't take it back. What's Murray doing back?'

'Dealing with Raeburn, I suppose. Even by Murray's standards he looked furious.'

'Great. Just what I need. Murray on a bloody rampage,' said McCoy.

'Where is she now?' asked Wattie. 'Is she okay?'

McCoy nodded, inspected his knuckles, red and swollen, and put them back under the tap. 'Took her up to the Royal. She's alive, but she's all over the place. They think she's been drugged. Doesn't really know where she is or what's happened.'

'Christ,' said Wattie.

'Going to go back up there, see what's going on. Assuming Murray doesn't murder me. They tell the mum and dad?'

Wattie nodded. 'Doing it now.'

McCoy decided his knuckles were as good as they were going to get, pulled some paper towels out the holder, dried his hand. 'Think we can get out of here without Murray knowing?'

'Don't think so,' said Wattie, grinning. 'He sent me in here to get you.'

McCoy knocked on the doorframe. 'You wanted to see me?'

'Come in. Shut the door behind you,' said Murray without looking up.

He did, sat down in the chair in front of Murray's desk. He wasn't wearing his usual tweed suit, must have been pulled in from leave. Wondered if he'd come from Perth or Phyllis Gilroy's. He had cords on, tattersall shirt with the sleeves rolled up. Top of his head red from the sun. McCoy watched as he finished writing whatever he was writing and screwed the top back on his fountain pen. Hands were dirty, must have been gardening. Murray put the pen on the desk and sat back, looked at him.

'How did this mess happen?' he asked calmly.

McCoy decided he had nothing to lose. 'Raeburn wanted a quick resolution. Got the boy in.

Kept him in. Terrified him, threatened him, battered him until he signed the confession.'

'And why didn't you stop him?' asked Murray.

'What?' asked McCoy, couldn't believe what he was hearing. 'I wasn't there. I've been doing suspicious deaths, house calls, any old shite Raeburn could find, anything but the Alice Kelly case. Wouldn't let me anywhere near it.'

Murray looked genuinely surprised. 'What? You're a senior officer. You should have been on it. Don't tell me Raeburn was still pulling that shite, was he?'

McCoy was beginning to get exasperated. 'I told you this at Phyllis Gilroy's! I tried to get on the case but Raeburn wouldn't have it. He hates me, has done since I requested out Eastern and away from him. So he had the opportunity to chuck his weight about, make sure everyone knows he was the boss and I was a piece of shit beneath his shoe. It was Wattie that was in the interview, came and told me after.'

'Well, why didn't he do something?' asked Murray, looking increasingly frustrated.

'Come on, Murray, he's no in a position to stop an interview. He did what could, he told me,' said McCoy.

'And how did that boy manage to kill himself in our bloody custody? How did that happen?'

McCoy wasn't having anything to do with that one. 'You'll have to ask Raeburn and Brian about that. Ask them why he wasn't on suicide watch.'

Murray stuck his hand in his pocket, came out

with a pipe, opened the desk drawer, started rifling through it looking for matches. Couldn't find any, slammed it shut in frustration. 'Three months! That's all! Three bloody months I'm away and this happens! It's a disgrace. An absolute bloody disgrace!'

McCoy held his hands up. 'You don't have to tell me.'

'Stop acting so bloody innocent, McCoy! You, my boy, aren't getting away scot-free either. Not by a long shot. You should have told me what was going on.'

'What?' said McCoy. 'It's my fault now, is it? I did tell you! Jesus Christ, Murray!'

'Where was your common sense? Raeburn's an idiot. I only let his promotion go through because I knew you were here. I thought you could stop him doing too much damage until I got back.'

McCoy was starting to get annoyed now. Was happy to take responsibility for what he'd done, not for what Murray thought he should have done. 'Well, maybe you shouldn't have bloody promoted him in the first place!'

'I didn't! He's brown-nosed Pitt Street for years. I couldn't stop it.'

'Well, stop blaming me, then!' shouted McCoy. 'Blame Raeburn and his lodge pals!'

Thought Murray would explode but he didn't, just sat there looking a bit defeated. There was silence for a few moments.

'Is she okay?' he asked. 'The girl?'

McCoy nodded. 'She's alive. But that daft boy is lying in the morgue because of Raeburn and his bloody glory-hunting.'

Murray had finally found some matches, lit up his stinking pipe. Waved the smoke away. 'Leave that with me.'

'What are you going to do about him?' asked McCoy.

'As I said, Detective McCoy. Leave it with me,' said Murray.

Knew by his tone that he couldn't push any harder. He nodded.

Murray looked pained. 'So, who took her? Do we have any idea? Has she been, you know . . .'

'They don't think so,' said McCoy.

Murray ruffled through a pile of assignment forms. 'What else have you got on just now?'

'Nothing,' said McCoy. No way was he mentioning the robberies, not if he could help it.

'Give me a few minutes,' said Murray. 'Away and sit down.'

McCoy stepped outside Murray's office and looked up. Realised everyone in the office was staring at him. He sat down at his desk, felt the Coke can in his pocket, slipped it into his drawer without anyone noticing. Could feel Raeburn's eyes on his back, hear him muttering away to Thomson. Pretended to look at the papers in front of him but, like everyone else, he was just waiting for Murray's door to open.

Ten minutes later it did and Murray stepped out his office, stood in front of the blackboard, papers in hand. Office gradually went quiet. He looked round at them, looked disappointed, like a headmaster in front of a class who had been misbehaving for a new teacher.

'I'm supposed to be off today. I'm supposed to be working in Perth next week. That's not going to happen because of the shitshow here. And to top it off I walked into this station, my station, to see two senior officers brawling on the floor. Not acceptable. A boy hanged himself yesterday down that corridor. Not acceptable. And worst of all we had charged him with the murder of Alice Kelly. The same Alice Kelly that is sitting in the Royal right now, very much alive and kicking.'

He looked round them again, caught every face, even if they were trying to look at the floor.

'Do you clowns have any idea what that makes us look like to the public? Incompetent, glory-hunting idiots. That's what. And I'm not going to disagree with them. I'm ashamed that this is my station. I'm ashamed that officers that were under my watch acted the way they did. So . . .' He looked round again. 'As of now, Detective McCoy will be in charge of the investigation into Alice Kelly.'

'You're joking!' Everyone turned. Raeburn had got off his seat, pulled the bloody hanky away from his nose. 'That bugger just attacked me for no reason and you're taking me off the case?'

Murray looked at him with contempt. 'And Acting Detective Inspector Raeburn will be relieved of his duties pending an investigation into his handling of the Alice Kelly case and the death of Ronnie Elder.'

'Fuck sake, Murray! McCoy?' Raeburn was shouting now, ranting, blood down his shirt, hair everywhere. Fury on his face. 'He's a liability, drunk half the time. Oh, but I forgot, he's your wee pet project, isn't he, wee teacher's pet? Well, fuck that, and fuck you! I'm no gonna forget this.'

He kicked his chair over, headed for the door.

Murray didn't even bat an eyelid, pointed at Wattie. 'Watson? Brief me and McCoy on everything to do with Alice. Soon as.'

An hour later McCoy was standing in front of the assembled station. They were all looking at him, waiting for him to start, some of Raeburn's cronies looking down their noses, others with notebooks ready. He took a breath.

'This investigation has been a shambles so far.' A few mutters, intakes of breath. 'But that stops now. As of now we work together to find out who took Alice and why, and to make sure he's caught before he does something like it again. Ronnie Elder was never our man. Too young, too stupid. The person that took Alice managed to make her disappear in broad daylight a couple of hundred yards from her home. That takes planning and intelligence.' He looked round at them. 'And that's what worries me. Because someone like that might well do it again and this time he might be planning to do something worse with whoever he takes.'

He stopped for a minute, pointed to the blown-up picture of Alice taped to the blackboard.

'For all we know, Alice might be able to tell us what happened to her. We don't know that yet. If she can't, it's back to us. She must have been kept somewhere. A cellar, a garage, a coal bunker. I want all of these in a quarter-mile radius searched. I want any known nonces rolled. Talk to her pals. Do they know if she was talking to anyone she shouldn't have been? She'd a Scotland strip on, a new one. Who sells them and who've they sold them to? Fact they cut her hair and put her in that strip to make her look like a boy means she must have been somewhere at some time when she could be seen. So we're looking for any sightings of a boy in a football strip.'

He nodded over to Wattie.

'Wattie here is your man. He's been on this since the very beginning. He knows what has and hasn't been done. Use him. If in doubt about something, ask him. I don't want anything done twice or missed out. As soon as we're back from interviewing Alice he'll be sitting here helping to organise everything, as will I.'

He held up a sheet of paper. 'Assignments have already been divvied up. Get on them as soon as possible.' Looked round again. 'This station has made an arse of itself. Now's the time for us to redeem ourselves. To show people we are real polis by getting this wrapped up as soon as. For Alice's sake. Thank you.'

A collective letting out of breath. People lit up, started talking.

Wattie walked up to McCoy and grinned. 'You actually sounded like a boss. Well done.'

'C'mon,' said McCoy to Wattie. 'You can tell me how great I am in the car.'

CHAPTER 28

McCoy stood out front, waiting for Wattie to bring the car round. He realised in all the drama he'd forgotten to speak to Murray about Laura. Supposed it could wait. Needed to get his head around the Kelly case and quick. Sun was still high in the sky. Seemed to be getting more humid, hotter, maybe the weather would break soon. Felt like it needed to. Everyone needed a change. A honk on the horn and Wattie was there in a blue Viva. He leant over and opened the passenger door.

'What's going to happen to Raeburn?' asked Wattie, as they pulled out the station yard.

McCoy shrugged. 'No idea. Not my problem.'

'Not sure he sees it that way,' said Wattie.

'Probably not, but the minute I start giving a shit what that incompetent bastard thinks it'll be a minute too soon.'

'He's a right vindictive swine, you know,' said Wattie. 'And he's got pals. He won't forget it.'

'Aye well, so am I, and I won't forget the sight of Ronnie Elder hanging from the bars of that window. So whatever he wants to do, he can go ahead. As I said, not my problem.'

Wattie nodded, drove on.

Wasn't much else they could do but wait. Wait until the blood tests came through. Wait until the doctors said they could talk to her. Wait for Murray to turn up. So that's what they did. Drank cups of tea in the hospital cafe surrounded by men in pyjamas, women in wheelchairs, relatives trying to think of something to say to each other. They'd opened all the windows in an effort to get the temperature down, wasn't doing much good. Breeze hardly moved the net curtains. Heat was making McCoy tired. He yawned for about the third time in five minutes. Was just about to stand up, go for a walk to try and wake himself up, when the last person either of them expected to see was standing in the doorway of the cafe looking round.

Wattie waved and Mary Webster made her way through the tables towards them. She leant down, kissed Wattie on the cheek.

'Well, well,' she said, wiping some crumbs off the orange plastic chair and sitting down. 'Can't wait to see how the Glasgow polis is gonna try and talk its way out of this one. I'm thinking of calling her "The Lazarus Girl". Like it?'

She took out her cigarettes and put them on the table, found a lighter in her handbag.

'Why the silence, boys?' she said, looking at the both of them. 'Cat got your tongues. Fire ahead. I'm all ears.'

McCoy shook his head. 'Not us you need to talk to. It was nothing to do with me. Wasn't even on the case, as you well know, and Wattie here was convinced the boy was innocent, made sure he told me. So might need to take your enquiries elsewhere. Ask a certain arse called Bernie Raeburn. And, by the way, what are you doing here anyway?'

Mary looked very pleased with herself. Lit up, leant over to another table and grabbed their ashtray, put it in front of her.

'If you must know, Mr McCoy, I am here accompanying the delighted and vastly relieved parents of Alice Kelly, who' – she looked at her Mickey Mouse watch for effect – 'as of half an hour ago, contracted to tell their story to yours truly and only yours truly. On three double-page spreads with exclusive photos, of course. And yes, you may congratulate me on beating out Ian Gourlay from the *Express* and that wee snotter McGinlay from the *Mail* to the exclusive.'

'They upstairs?' asked Wattie.

'You mean my exclusive parents? Yes, they are. And at this very moment they are behind closed doors being tearfully reunited with Alice herself right in front of Tam Renfrew's clicking Nikon.'

'Told you it was your kind of story,' said McCoy.

'Let's just say I took your advice for once and once only.'

'You want anything?' asked Wattie.

'Cup of tea, doll, thanks.'

'Me, too,' said McCoy. 'One sugar.'

They watched Wattie lumber over to the counter, start telling the smiling woman behind what they wanted.

'You'd think he'd be happy, wouldn't you?' Mary asked. 'He always said that boy was innocent.'

'Not as simple as that,' said McCoy. 'The trouble is Wattie was present at the interview. Even if he thought what was going on was wrong, he was in the room and he didn't stop it. There'll be an inquiry, death in custody, always is. The only way he can save himself is to drop Raeburn in it. Tell them exactly what he did.'

'Good,' said Mary. 'The prick deserves it.'

'You won't find me arguing about that, but, much as Raeburn is a prick and was completely in the wrong, he's also a polis and the polis aren't too keen on other polis telling tales. Especially ones that are telling tales on a twenty-year veteran with pals in the lodge.'

'Fuck,' said Mary. 'I hadn't thought of that. No wonder he looks like he's got the weight of the world on his shoulders.'

'One way to cheer him up,' said McCoy. 'Tell him he's going to be a daddy.'

'Very funny. And I told you to never mention that again. Besides, I'm still no sure whether he's going to be or not.' She turned to him. 'Any idea where she's been?'

'Nope,' said McCoy. 'But seems she's okay.'

'Did they . . . you know.' She let it lie there.

'Not as far as we know,' said McCoy.

'Here,' said Wattie, putting the tray down.

'Thanks,' said Mary. 'You okay?'

'Nope,' he said, sitting down. 'Chances are I'm going to get my jotters and if I don't I'm going to get a disciplinary and every polis in Glasgow is going to hate me. Might be looking for another job soon.'

'That's shite,' said McCoy, with more conviction than he felt. 'You're a good polis. People know that.'

Mary took his hand. 'Stop being so bloody hard on yourself, you've not done anything wrong. Raeburn has, not you.'

Wattie nodded, couldn't have look glummer if he'd tried.

'Mr Watson? Is there a Mr Watson here?'

The woman behind the counter was holding the receiver of the phone attached to the wall in her hand. 'Mr Watson? Call for you.'

Wattie stood up. 'Who's that?'

'Only one way to find out,' said McCoy.

Wattie walked over to the counter.

'You think he'll be okay?' asked Mary. 'At work, I mean.'

'I don't know,' said McCoy. 'I really don't know.'

'Fuck sake,' said Mary. 'It's that bad?'

McCoy shrugged. 'Maybe. Tell you something, it's not going to be a pleasant few months, that's for sure. Depends what Raeburn does, really. If he falls on his sword, it should be okay. If he tries to fight it? Chances are he'll take Wattie down with him.'

'Christ,' said Mary.

Wattie came back. 'Doctor says we can go up now.'

The doctor looked like more like some sort of woodland creature. McCoy had never seen so much hair on a man in his life. Auburn it was, too. It was poking out from under his shirt cuffs, his collar, one big eyebrow right across his brow. He scratched his nose and McCoy noticed it was all over his hands too. The man looked like a ginger werewolf.

He held out his hand to shake. 'Mr McCoy? I'm Adrian Potter.' North of England accent. 'Why don't you come in here and I'll run you through things.'

He held the door open to a meeting room, three orange-cushioned chairs, a table with a plastic pot plant and a box of hankies on it.

'Wattie, go and make sure that your better half's behaving herself. Don't want her finding out anything we need to know before we do.'

Wattie nodded, set off down the corridor and McCoy stepped into the werewolf's lair.

They sat down and Potter took out his file, skimmed through it. Looked up and smiled. Seemed to have a five o'clock shadow already. The poor guy must have to shave three times a day.

'Alice Kelly. 12/02/61,' he said. 'Poor girl seems to be okay. The blood tests came back: she's got traces of Valium, some other tranquilliser, possibly Seconal, and alcohol in her bloodstream. A potent combination in someone of her age and weight. She's undernourished, dehydrated, doesn't seem to have been fed. Not quite my area of expertise but I assume the idea was to keep her docile and disorientated. And by the amount they have given her they would certainly have succeeded.'

'Will she remember anything?' asked McCoy.

Potter scratched his nose again. 'I wouldn't think so, not anything concrete anyway. May have some hazy impressions. Combination of those kinds of drugs and alcohol tends to wipe out the short-term memory. I'd be surprised if she remembered anything helpful. However, I would appreciate it if she was left alone until tomorrow morning. Whatever has happened to her, she has undergone an ordeal. She's still got the drugs swirling round in her bloodstream and she's on a drip to try and get some fluids into her. Maybe in the morning she'll be fit to speak. Until then she needs to rest.'

'Great,' said McCoy glumly.

Potter looked at his notes again. 'No evidence of assault, sexual or otherwise. The idea seemed to be to simply contain her rather than harm her.' He looked up. 'Did they ask for a ransom?'

McCoy laughed. 'No, they're no that stupid. She lives in a council flat in Maryhill.'

'Ah,' said Potter, smiling. 'I see. Sorry.' He closed his file. 'Over to you, then.'

'Anything else you can tell me?' asked McCoy.

'She's had a haircut, amateur by the look of it, and was dressed in boy's clothing, as you no doubt noticed. Other than that, not much. You found her in Central Station?'

McCoy nodded.

'Very odd. Can only assume she was dumped there somehow.'

'Christ,' said McCoy. 'So we don't know why she was taken, where she was taken, who took her or why they let her go.'

Potter stood up. 'Bit of a mystery all round, I'd say. Thought that's what you detectives liked. Agatha Christie and all that. Good luck.'

McCoy walked along the hospital corridor, the familiar smell of bleach and something underneath that. Started climbing the stairs to the next floor. Felt like he'd lost a pound and found a penny. Never get what you wish for, as someone said. He had been desperate to get on the case and now he was, big time. Had to find out what had happened to Alice Kelly and why and do it pronto.

A thought crossed his mind, wasn't a happy one. What if Alice Kelly wasn't going to be the only one? What if there was some madman who got his kicks out of kidnapping kids? Didn't want to think about that. Not until he had to anyway. Spotted what he was looking for just along the corridor. A row of phones under curved silver

259

awnings. Put his money in and called the shop.

'Billy, can you put me through to PC Walker?'

A click, a wait, sound of a phone ringing. Knew he was chancing his arm, but didn't know who else to ask.

'PC Walker speaking.'

'Tracey. It's McCoy.'

'Ah, hello, sir.' She sounded a bit surprised and a bit scared. 'Can I help you?'

'That depends,' he said. 'Know anyone in finger-prints that knows how to keep their mouth shut?'

Wattie was standing outside Alice Kelly's room, her door flanked by two uniforms.

'What did the doctor say? he asked as McCoy walked up.

'Drugged but unharmed. Can't speak to her until tomorrow. Even then, he doubts she'll remember anything.'

'Shite,' said Wattie.

'Exactly. Where's the mum and dad?' he asked.

'In there with her now. With the photographer and Mary. Couldn't really stop them.'

'Suppose not,' said McCoy. 'You and Raeburn's files and notes back at the shop?'

Wattie nodded.

'We'll go back and plough through them again, see if I can see anything we've missed. Get Thomson to go back to Maryhill, to the neighbours, the ones who said she was more of a teenager than a wee girl. See if they remember anyone older hanging around, ask them if they saw her hanging round somewhere she shouldn't be.'

Wattie nodded, hesitated. 'You really think Raeburn'll try and take me down with him?' he asked, worry written on his face in capital letters.

McCoy shook his head. Lied. 'He'll be too busy looking after his own skin to bother about you.' Trouble was, the first thing someone like Raeburn would do was flail about trying to find someone to blame for what happened, and there was only one obvious candidate: Wattie.

The door opened and Mary appeared, followed by Alice's mum and dad. The mum was red-eyed, hands shaking, wiping at her face with a hanky. She was in a blue sleeveless dress, white crocheted cardigan thing, looked like she'd had her hair done for the photos. The dad was dressed in a suit and tie, looked about forty odds, seemed quiet, sandy hair in a side shed. Looked like he wasn't quite sure what was going on.

'Mr McCoy,' said Mary. 'These are Alice's parents.'

McCoy shook their hands, told them he would be taking over the case. They nodded, didn't really seem to be taking much in.

'I'd like to come and talk to you tonight, if that's okay?' he asked.

They nodded.

'I'm sorry to say I'll be asking you a lot of questions you'll have been asked before, but hopefully we'll find something we've missed. That'll let us know what happened to Alice and why. That okay?'

They nodded again, then the mum started crying properly. Dad put his arms round her.

'They won't be at home, McCoy,' interrupted Mary. 'We're taking them to the Loch Lomond Hotel, a bit of pampering to help get over their ordeal. The gran's going to stay with Alice. She's out for the count, will be for hours, needs the sleep.'

And the best way to keep them out the way of any other reporters, thought McCoy.

'Okay, no problem. I'll see you out there. You heading there now?'

Mary nodded. 'Got a car and a driver downstairs.'

'Tell you what. I'll come with you. Have a chat when we get there. Save time,' said McCoy. 'All good?' he asked the parents, who nodded before Mary could object.

She looked daggers at him. 'No problem at all.' Expression saying the exact opposite. 'We all want to get this solved as soon as possible. Let's go.'

They walked towards the lift.

'I'll go back to the shop and get started,' said Wattie.

McCoy nodded as Mary sidled up beside them. 'Thanks a bloody lot,' she said. 'That's my interview back two hours.'

'Happy to be of service,' said McCoy and pressed the button.

CHAPTER 29

The car was waiting outside, big black Daimler shining in the afternoon sunlight. McCoy tried not to look impressed.

'The *Record* splashing out?' he asked Mary.

'Biggest story of the year, told them to up it a bit. Mind you, they seem to have taken the ball and run with it. Looks like we're going to a bloody funeral.'

She got in the passenger seat and McCoy got in the back with the mum and dad. The driver was an amicable middle-aged bloke in a chauffeur's uniform with a buzz-cut and a beer belly.

'Name's Peter Lawson, call me Pete. Sit back, enjoy the ride and I'll have you there in no time.'

McCoy decided to take him at his word, relaxed back into the leather seat, stretched his feet out and looked through the window as they turned onto the motorway and headed west. Realised too late he should have called Murray too, told him Laura was safe. Too late now, he'd have to phone him from the hotel.

They weren't far out of Glasgow before the mum and dad were asleep. He couldn't blame them:

the combination of sleepless nights and the sun beating down on the car was enough to send anyone off. Mary and Pete were engaged in some long conversation about growing up in Govan. What school they went to, what street they lived in, what people they knew.

'Thought you grew up in Wine Alley?' said McCoy, grinning.

'Did I chooky,' said Mary, glowering at him in the rear-view mirror.

'I did, though!' said Pete and they both laughed. McCoy sat back in the seat, let his mind drift in and out of the conversation, let his eyes feel heavy, and he drifted off.

When he woke up he could see the flash of the blue loch through the trees on his right. The road snaked round and there it was in all its glory: Loch Lomond. On a day like this, it looked like all the postcards of it he'd seen. Blue water. Green hills. Blue sky without a cloud. He was about to roll down the window when the car swerved as a navy-blue Rover overtook them on the inside. Must have been doing fifty or sixty.

'Stupid bugger,' said Pete.

'Arsehole,' Mary muttered.

McCoy looked over but the mum and dad were still out for the count.

'How much further? he asked, trying to stifle a yawn.

'Ten minutes or so,' said Pete. 'No far.'

'Should I wake the Babes in the Wood?' asked McCoy.

Mary leant over the seat, had a look. 'Just leave them,' she said. 'They look like they need it.'

McCoy nodded, leant his head against the window and watched the scenery go by. Wasn't long until he saw a big wooden sign by the side of the road.

THE LOCH LOMOND HOTEL TWO MILES ON RIGHT.

Then it suddenly occurred to him.

'You staying the night, Mary?' he asked.

'Me? Too bloody right. Looking forward to running up the *Record*'s bill in the bar. Why?'

'How am I going to get home?' he asked.

She laughed. 'That's your problem, McCoy. Serves you right for hitching a bloody ride.'

'I can wait an hour or so before I head back,' said Pete. 'That long enough?'

'Gonnae have to be. Thanks, pal. Nice to see some people from Govan have manners.'

Mary stuck her tongue out at him in the mirror, gave him the V-sign.

They slowed down and turned the corner into the long driveway up to the Loch Lomond Hotel. They could see the big castle-style building up ahead, had to be half a mile of driveway before they got there. It was lined with old trees, some of them touching each other, making a kind of tunnel.

'Is that the mad bugger that overtook us? asked

McCoy. A navy-blue Rover had stopped in the middle of the driveway up ahead.

'Looks like it,' said Pete.

'Good. I'm going to give him a piece of my mind,' said Mary and started to roll down her window. And then she stopped, looked puzzled. 'What the fuck?'

The Rover had started up and was reversing towards them. Fast.

'Get your head down!' shouted Pete.

His voice cut off as the Rover hit them full tilt. A bang and a grinding and everyone was thrown forwards. The mum and dad ended up on the floor, Mary hit her head on the windscreen and McCoy's face hit the back of the seat in front. He sat up, held his head, felt warm blood on his fingers. Just had time to see the doors of the Rover open before he caught movement in the rear-view mirror. He turned around, looked out the back window in time to see another Rover accelerating towards them.

He tried to get down, but there wasn't enough time. He was thrown against the side window, head hitting it hard. Then the mum was screaming, Mary wailing. There were men in balaclavas all around the car, the door he was leaning on was opened and he half fell, was half pulled out and dumped on the driveway.

He tried to get up. Heard someone say 'Not him! The other one!' before a boot hit him in the stomach, followed by another one in the face. He tried to roll over to get away and saw two men pulling the dad out the other side of the car. They got him on the ground; he was trying to crawl away, screaming and shouting on his wife as they kicked in at him. One of the men got behind him, sat on his back, hit him on the head with the grip of a gun. The screaming stopped immediately and he collapsed. Two of them grabbed his arms, dragged his inert body towards one of the Rovers.

McCoy tried to stand up, wobbled, thought he was going to fall, heard Mary shout: 'McCoy! Behind you!'

Then an explosion of pain at the back of his head and he fell forward onto the driveway. He felt the gravel in his mouth, blood down his face. Heard the cars accelerate away and then nothing.

CHAPTER 30

McCoy woke up with Wattie peering at him.

'You okay?' he asked. 'Mary phoned me.'

McCoy tried to sit up and winced, head really hurt. He put his hand up to it, felt a big bandage.

'Woman in the kitchens was a nurse during the war. Must have been the Indian Mutiny. Looks like a bloody turban sitting on your head.'

McCoy tried to smile, tried to work out where he was. A hotel bedroom, big old-fashioned bed, tartan wallpaper, a portrait of some guy in a kilt on the wall above the fireplace. Could see the loch through the window, shining in the evening sunlight.

'I feel shite,' he said.

'Not surprised,' said Wattie. 'There was blood everywhere. Must have given you some whack.'

It all came back: the cars, the guys in balaclavas pulling the dad out the car, bundling him into the other one. 'What was that all about?' he asked.

'You tell me,' said Wattie. 'Why would anyone want to kidnap her dad? This some sort of weird vendetta against the family? I don't get it.'

'Me neither,' said McCoy, swinging his legs over the side of the bed. 'Mary okay?'

Wattie nodded. 'The mum was hysterical. She took her back to Glasgow in a taxi. She said she needed to make sure Alice was safe. Driver's in worse shape than you. Took him to the hospital in Luss. Broken nose and jaw.'

McCoy stood up, wobbled. Wattie held a hand out to steady him. 'Plus the local polis want to have a word with you. Keeps saying it happened on his patch, so he should be investigating.'

'Bugger that,' said McCoy. 'Need to get back and talk to Murray. Let's get going before PC Plod appears.'

Wattie radioed ahead from the car, spoke to Murray. Said they'd meet him in the Victoria near McCoy's flat. Didn't sound too happy about going to a pub, but Wattie told him McCoy might not last that long, should be in his bed soon.

McCoy lay on the back seat listening to the two of them on the radio. Kept getting waves of nausea, sparkles at the edge of his vision, but he felt happy. Something about being in the back of a car at night, lying down, listening to adults talking, reminded him of being a wee boy. Not that his dad could ever afford a car. Must have been his uncle Terry's he was thinking about. A Hillman something, couldn't remember.

Wattie turned the radio on and the sound of T. Rex filled the car. He closed his eyes. Tried to think why anyone would want to take the dad. Wasn't a small operation. Two cars, must have been five or six of them. Guns. All well prepared. More like a military operation than anything else. Wondered how they knew they were going to the hotel. Wondered how Jackie was getting on with the fingerprints. Wondered why anyone would kidnap a daughter, then her dad.

One good thing, though. The idea of him investigating the robberies seemed to have gone away. Wondered how Auntie Margery really was. Seemed more shook up than she was letting on. Wondered what Angela was really up to. And then he remembered the dad had been in Belfast doing God knows what, so maybe the attack wasn't military, maybe it was paramilitary. Maybe the dad had – he winced as a sharp pain spread inside all of his head at once. Waited for it to pass, but it didn't.

Said to Wattie he didn't feel very well. Threw up onto the floor of the car before he could help himself. Tried to sit up. Saw the lights on the Erskine Bridge. Told Wattie his head really hurt. Felt the car decelerate and then he passed out.

11th August 1970

Sunset Sound Studios, Los Angeles

'I can't hear the backing track.'

The engineer pressed a button on the desk, let his voice be heard in the booth. 'You want me to turn it up?' he asked.

Bobby nodded. Adjusted his headphones, took a quick drag of the joint burning in the ashtray on the little table beside him.

'Rolling.'

The engineer looked at the clock on the wall. Coming up for six p.m. and they had been at it since twelve. Trying to nail the solo on the 'Symphony' track. If anyone had asked him, which they wouldn't, they got it on the fourth pass. That was the trouble with artists producing themselves. No one to tell them to stop.

Through the glass he could see Bobby listening intently, hands on his Les Paul, waiting for the moment. Suddenly his face screwed up, fingers started moving and he was in. The engineer sat back, only took a few seconds to realise something different was happening this time. He sat forward, listened intently.

In the booth, Bobby had gone somewhere else. Eyes closed, foot tapping, hands moving up and down the neck of his guitar. The engineer double-checked the levels, moment of panic that he had missed this but he hadn't. Tape was safely turning. Out the corner of his eye he could see his assistant standing by the machine, dumbstruck look on his face, just watching Bobby, listening to him play like no one had played before.

Forty seconds later Bobby stopped, dropped his hands, looked at them through the glass of the booth. He was grinning. The engineer was grinning, the assistant was grinning, none of them quite believing what they had just heard.

The engineer leant forward, pressed the button on the desk so Bobby could hear him. 'I think that's a keeper.'

All of them started laughing.

In the booth, Bobby leant into the mic. 'Time to celebrate, I think.'

18TH JULY 1973

CHAPTER 31

Light was streaming through the windows of the dayroom. Twenty or so armchairs, a few coffee tables with worn magazines on them, a wasp buzzing on the windowsill. McCoy looked at his watch. Quarter to nine. Wattie was supposed to be there at nine. Said they wouldn't let him go home unless someone came to collect him. Didn't have the energy to argue. Hoped Wattie had brought a shirt. One he had on smelt of sweat and still had a sick stain down the front, no matter how many times he'd tried to dab it off.

Concussion. He didn't feel too bad, really, a bit of a headache but he'd had worse hangovers. Didn't remember coming to the hospital. Apparently he'd been a bit confused, thought he was checking into a hotel, tried to pay the doctor. Had slept most of yesterday. Woke up at teatime, wolfed down some mince and tatties, and immediately fell back asleep.

The door opened. He looked round, expecting Wattie, but it wasn't him. Was a big guy with a proper Ted's quiff, pyjamas and a stripy dressing gown, packet of Regal and a box of Swan Vestas in his hand. He nodded over at him and sat down.

'How's ye?' he said. Broad Northern Irish accent. He held up the cigarettes. 'Dying for a bloody fag. Won't let you smoke in the bed in case you set yourself on bloody fire.' He nodded at McCoy's bandage. 'Looks like you've been in the wars.'

'Something like that,' said McCoy. 'You from Belfast?'

The man nodded, lit up. Looked blissful as he dragged in a lungful of Regal smoke. Held it and let it out. 'Born and bred. Been over here for a couple of years, though. Wife's from here. Couldn't stand it there any more. Can't say I blame her.'

'Lot of construction over there, is there?' asked McCoy. 'They need workers?'

The man shrugged. 'Fair bit. A fair bit of work cleaning up bomb sites as well.'

'Enough that they need workers from over here?' asked McCoy.

The man sucked air through his teeth. 'Don't think so. Maybe if you've got some specialty, a spark or something, but not if you're just an ordinary joe with a shovel. Got more than enough of those at home.' He smiled. 'Why? Thinking of moving over there? I wouldn't if I was you. The place is a bloody nightmare at the moment. Breaks my heart.'

McCoy nodded. Had started to wonder what the hell Finn Kelly was really doing over in Ireland.

Didn't look like he was labouring like he said he was, that was for sure.

'McCoy!'

He turned and Wattie was standing there. He bowed. 'Your chauffeur's arrived.'

McCoy stood up, wave of dizziness hit and he held onto the back of the chair.

'You okay?' asked Wattie.

He nodded. Wasn't. Sat back down. 'Might need a minute or so,' he said.

Wattie nodded at the man in the dressing gown as he got up to leave.

'Be better one day,' he said. 'God willing. Then I'll go back. Good luck.'

Wattie sat down opposite McCoy. 'What's that about?'

'Belfast,' said McCoy. 'How's Mary?'

Wattie smiled. 'How do you think? Delighted. Front page of the *Record*. "MY KIDNAP HELL BY STAFF WRITER MARY WEBSTER". Haven't seen much of her. Think she's sleeping at the office. You see Murray?'

McCoy shook his head.

'He was in last night. You must have been sleeping.' Looked a bit guilty. 'He spoke to the doctor.'

'Did he now,' said McCoy, uneasily. 'And what did the doctor say?'

'Told him you needed to be off for a week. I'm not here to take you to the shop. I'm here to take you home.'

McCoy argued, shouted and swore, but it didn't do any good. Wattie just kept saying that Murray had said McCoy was off for a week on doctor's orders; if he turned up at the shop, he was being sent straight home. No arguments.

'And what about Alice Kelly and her dad?'

'Murray's taken it over,' said Wattie. 'He's moved back from Perth for a while.' Looked guilty again. 'I'm helping him.'

'Great,' said McCoy. 'So I have to sit on my arse in the house while all this is going on?'

'Not my idea,' he said. 'Don't blame me.'

'I don't. It's that arse of a doctor I blame. Was it that werewolf?'

Wattie looked taken aback. 'Eh? What you on about?'

Didn't get an answer.

'Where is Murray anyway? I need to talk to him,' McCoy said.

'Harry, he won't—'

'Not police business. Personal.'

Wattie looked doubtful. 'Working from home this morning.'

McCoy stood up. Another rush of dizziness, but this time he managed to disguise it. 'Good. Let's go. We'll drop in on him on the way home.'

CHAPTER 32

He made it out of the hospital without stumbling, got into the car and rolled down the window. Was still boiling, no sign of the weather breaking yet. Seemed to have got worse, if anything. Really humid now as well.

McCoy pulled the sun visor down, looked at himself in the wee mirror. 'I don't look that bad,' he said.

'Not from the front,' said Wattie. 'But that's because you can't see the baldy bit at the back with the line of stitches. You look like a spayed dog.'

'Christ, thanks a lot,' said McCoy. 'Don't hold back or anything.'

'You asked,' said Wattie, grinning.

McCoy twisted his head in the mirror, but it was no use, couldn't see anything. 'Twelve stitches,' he said. 'Least someone'll be happy I got a doing. How is your ex-boss anyway?'

Wattie's face clouded. 'Not good,' he said.

McCoy pushed the sun visor back up. 'Neither would I be if I was parked and waiting for the big boys to nail me to the wall.'

'And me with him,' said Wattie glumly.

'You'll be fine,' said McCoy. 'Got any fags?'

Wattie nodded at the glove compartment. 'Try there.'

McCoy did. No luck.

'He was waiting outside the station yesterday when I got out, Raeburn was. Said he wanted a word.'

'Did he now,' said McCoy, a fair idea why.

'He said we needed to get our stories straight,' said Wattie. 'Needed me to back him up.'

'What a surprise,' said McCoy. Pointed out the windscreen. 'Take Great Western Road. What did you say?'

Wattie indicated, took a left turn. 'I told him I'd be telling the truth.'

'That go down well, did it?'

'What do you think? That wasn't even the worst bit. Then he started in on you.'

McCoy looked at him. 'Me? What did he say?'

'Load of shite. How you were to blame for what Murray had done, how you were out to get him, always had been.'

'Arsehole,' said McCoy

'He sounded serious, Harry. Said he was going to get his own back. Said you needed a doing. You should watch out.'

'Like fuck I will. Raeburn's just a blowhard, all mouth and no trousers.'

'You sure?' asked Wattie.

'Yep,' said McCoy, with more conviction than he felt. What was it they said about a trapped rat?

Nothing as dangerous. Would need to worry about that later. Had to get through the chat with Murray first.

'I thought Murray lived in Jordanhill?' said Wattie, as they turned into Hyndland Road and pulled over where McCoy had pointed.

'Not any more,' he said, opening the passenger door. 'You okay to wait in the car for five minutes?'

Wattie nodded. Looked puzzled. Was about to ask why Murray had moved, but McCoy slammed the door before he could get any questions in. Managed to make it up the path without feeling dizzy and pushed the doorbell. The big polished door opened and Murray was standing there, suit trousers, white shirt open to reveal a string vest, navy tie hanging around his neck.

'No,' he said. 'The doctor was very clear. No work. Rest.'

'That's not why I'm here,' said McCoy. 'Laura's why I'm here.

They ended up in the garden. There was a table and some chairs in the shade of the trees by the wall. McCoy shoved a not happy tabby cat off one and sat down, head spinning a bit.

Murray sat down opposite, peered at him. 'You look bloody terrible,' he said.

'Should see the other guy.' McCoy smiled. 'He looks fine.'

He moved his chair further into the shade. Sunlight was hurting his head. 'Any sign of the dad?' he asked.

Murray shook his head. 'Disappeared into thin air. Any idea why they took him?'

'Thought I wasn't supposed to be at work?' said McCoy.

'Aye well, you're here now, smart arse,' said Murray.

'Not a bloody clue. He's got no money. They gave the daughter back and took him instead. Two kidnaps in one family? Something's going on with the Kellys. They're not the bloody Gettys. Only thing I can think of is it's to do with his being in Belfast.'

'What do you mean?' asked Murray.

'Grabbing him was set up to go like clockwork, military-style. Maybe it was paramilitary?'

Murray groaned. 'Oh Christ, don't say that. You think they're mixed up in the bloody IRA or something?'

McCoy shrugged. 'Maybe.'

'Well, we're going to go down every road before that one. The last thing I need is bloody Special Branch involved. Besides, I did a bit of digging. The wife's brother lives in Dundee. Was arrested a couple of years ago when he still lived here. Sex with a fifteen-year-old. Claimed he thought she was seventeen. Got a suspended sentence. Being brought in today.'

Sounded like clutching at straws to McCoy, but he wasn't going to say. Supposed any lead had to be worth following up at this point. And by the look on Murray's face and the dark circles round his eyes, that's what they were down to.

'I found Laura,' he said.

Murray's face brightened. 'Well done, Harry, that's one bloody bright spot. Did you take her back to Bearsden?'

McCoy shook his head. 'She's not going back.'

Murray looked at him incredulously. 'What do you mean? She's bloody fifteen, it's not up to her what she does. Where is she?'

McCoy took a breath, wished his head was clearer. 'I'm not telling you.'

Murray looked at him, face starting to go red, usual warning of an explosion, but he spoke quietly and slowly. 'What do you mean you're not telling me? It's not up to you what—'

'She's got burns and cuts all up her arm, burns her mother gave her.' McCoy spoke quietly. 'I'm not sending her back to get more.'

He looked over at Murray. He was staring down the garden, wouldn't look him in the eye.

'You knew, didn't you?' said McCoy. 'You knew all along.'

Murray sighed, rubbed at the stubble on his chin. 'It's not that simple, Harry. I don't . . .'

McCoy stared at him, couldn't believe what he was hearing. 'You tell me why it's not that simple, Murray. Because the scars up her arm make it look pretty simple to me.'

Murray pulled his pipe and his tobacco out his trouser pocket, lit it up, blew out a cloud of smoke and started talking.

'Laura's mother has always been highly strung,

skittish. She's been in and out of Gartnavel since her and John got married. Her nerves, as John calls it. The past couple of years she's been better, she's got religion now. Some church in Shettleston, evangelical nutters, seemed harmless enough.'

'But . . .'

'But as Laura got older, she convinced herself that Laura's bad behaviour wasn't the usual teenage stuff. She got it into her head that it was a manifestation of some inner evil.'

Murray hesitated. McCoy wasn't sure he was going to go on, but he did. 'Laura woke up in the middle of the night, her mother was standing over her with a hot poker, said she needed to cleanse her through suffering, release the spirit.'

'Jesus.'

Murray smiled weakly. 'The very man.'

'What happened?' asked McCoy.

'Her mother got packed off to Gartnavel for a month, had some electricity treatment or suchlike, supposed to be foolproof.'

'Wasn't foolproof enough, Murray. You should see her arm.'

He looked pained. 'I didn't know, Harry. I swear to you. John said she was fine, that the treatment had worked. Said her and Laura were getting on fine. He said he'd no idea why Laura was running away.'

McCoy leant back in his chair, head settled a bit. 'Is your brother such a bastard that he'd drag his daughter back to that just to play happy families for the voters?'

Murray didn't answer, didn't have to. Answer to McCoy's question was written all over his face.

'Is she safe where she is?' he asked.

McCoy nodded. No way was he telling Murray she was at Stevie Cooper's.

'Tell her I'm sorry,' Murray said, then stood up.

'You off to Stewart Street?' McCoy asked.

He nodded. 'Yep. Then I'm going to take a trip out to Bearsden. Pay my brother a little visit. He must have known more than he told me. Thought I might take him out to the garden and teach him a lesson.' He smiled grimly.

McCoy nodded, wouldn't want to be his brother for all the tea in China.

'And you,' said Murray. 'Home. Now.'

CHAPTER 33

McCoy thanked Wattie for the lift and told him he was fine to get up the stairs. He walked halfway up the close, leant against the wall and lit up. Smoked half his cigarette, decided that would be long enough for Wattie to be gone. Dropped it on the ground, stamped on it and walked back out into the sunshine.

Talking to Murray about Laura had got him thinking. If Laura had managed to keep what had happened with her mother a secret, he had a feeling that she was keeping something else secret too. He needed a word.

He walked down the hill, waited outside the phone box until a fat bloke with a Rangers top and denim shorts finished his conversation, then went in. Called Cooper's house to make sure she was there. She wasn't, but Billy told him where she was. He sighed. Nothing was ever easy. Came out the phone box, walked down to Dumbarton Road and hailed a cab.

There had to be a reason they had let Alice go, then taken the dad. She hadn't been harmed, sexually or otherwise. Family had no money for a ransom. Couldn't even come up with a reason for taking her, never mind her father. Whole thing made less sense the more it went on.

The taxi stopped outside Trerons and he got out. Looked up at the big department store. Windows were full of summer dresses, displays of china, bolts of fabric. Wasn't a place McCoy often visited. He opened the door, let two ladies out and stepped into the store. Looked at the directory on the wall by the lifts. Second floor.

'Ladies,' said McCoy cheerily, pulling up a gilt-backed chair and sitting down.

Laura looked surprised to see him, Iris just looked.

'Harry, what are you doing here?' asked Laura, putting down her teacup.

'I phoned the house and Billy told me you were here,' he said.

He looked round the elegant department store tearoom. Windows over Sauchiehall Street letting the light stream in, pale carpet, waitresses in stiff black uniforms and wee lace caps busying around. Customers were all of a type: women from the expensive suburbs, doctors' wives, lawyers' wives. All dressed to the nines. He'd never seen so many hats in his life.

'Not exactly either of your styles, is it?' he said.

Laura smiled. 'Actually, I really like it. I used to come here with my gran when I was wee.'

'Oh aye. And what's your excuse, Iris? Getting some tips on silver service for the shebeen?'

'Get it right up ye, McCoy,' Iris said brightly.

She'd got all dressed up for her lunch with the Glasgow smart set. No matter what the weather was. Hat, fur stole over the chair, pink dress with a deep neckline showing off her assets. One thing he could say about Iris, she still scrubbed up well.

'So, what's this meeting of the minds in aid of?' asked McCoy, taking a wee orange cake off the top layer of the china plate tower.

Laura smiled. 'Simple. It's called friendship, Harry.' She smiled at Iris. 'Maybe if you had any friends, you'd know how it works.'

'Very funny. But now we're talking about friends, when was it you were going to tell me who it was that attacked you?'

'What?' Laura said quickly, but not quite quick enough.

'You're a clever girl, Laura, but you didn't get it quite right.' He brushed the cake crumbs off the front of his shirt. 'You never said anything about the attack. Never asked me where the guy might be or why he'd done it. Never even wondered why it had happened. Only one explanation for that, as far as I can see. You know fine well who did it and why.'

No reply. Around them the sound of polite chatter, cups clinking and tea being poured suddenly seemed very loud.

McCoy shifted round in his seat. Smiled. 'How about you, Iris? You got anything to add?'

Silence from both of them. McCoy was getting a

wee bit tired of Laura and her selective memory. Tired of getting the run around from her and her family. Tired of being fed wee bits of information rather than the whole picture. Time to poke the fire.

'I tell you what, girls, let me make this simple for you. Unless one of you starts talking I'm going to go over to that phone by the toilets, put a tanner in and call Maitland Street and get Iris here's shebeen shut down. And then every single time Cooper pays Archie Lomax his exorbitant fee and it gets opened up again, I'll get it raided again. And again, and again.'

He leant back and lit up a cigarette.

'Stevie Cooper is many things, but he ain't stupid. Won't take him long to realise it's Iris that's the real problem and, bearing in mind he's only keeping the place open to shut you up, he'll count the cost of Lomax, and show how much he really cares about you by booting you out on your arse.'

He leant forward, picked up a bit of shortbread. 'Nobody want this last one?'

No response, so he bit into the biscuit. Iris and Laura staring at him as he chewed it over. 'Good shortbread,' he said.

'Now, Iris, let's be realistic about what'll happen next. You're a good-looking woman but you're a bit long in the tooth to be working the hotels now, so unless you want to end up standing on the corner of Blythswood Street doing hand jobs for five bob I'd persuade your wee pal here to start talking.'

Popped the rest of the shortbread in his mouth.

'That's not fair, Harry!' Laura hissed at him. 'It's nothing to do with Iris, leave her out of it.'

He shrugged. 'You wanted to be away from the bourgeois suburbs, Laura, making your way in the big bad world. First thing you've got to learn is that life isn't fair. Is that not right, Iris?'

Laura looked at him and then she looked at Iris, at the too-red lipstick, the creases around her eyes and the out-of-date fur stole. She gave McCoy a look that would curdle milk and started talking. 'Alec Page was selling pills. Sold them in pubs like the Strathmore and at the dance halls. The Maryland. Places young people go. He was making a fair bit of money.'

'Who was supplying him?' asked McCoy.

She shook her head. 'I don't know. Honestly. But whoever it was worked out that Alec was skimming him. He was selling the pills for more than he was meant to, keeping the extra money back for himself.' She hesitated, chewing the side of her lip. 'When they found out they came to see Donny, asked him to take care of it. Said they'd hand the business over to him if he took care of Alec.'

'What does that mean?'

'Scare him off. Beat him up.'

McCoy didn't say anything, didn't have to. Laura looked ashamed enough. Not only was her boyfriend not the good guy she'd tried to persuade him he was, he was happy to batter his pal for the sake of a few quid.

'You sure you've no idea who this person was that asked him?'

She shook her head emphatically.

'So Donny MacRae got to Page?'

'No,' she said. 'Not Donny.'

'Who, then?' said McCoy, voice rising. 'Who was with him when it happened? Who was it tortured him first?'

The ladies at adjoining tables were looking over. Iris reached out and held Laura's hand. 'Come on, hen, just tell him, get it over with.'

Laura straightened herself up, dabbed her face with the hanky. 'It was Wee Tam,' she said. 'Wee Tam was with him.'

'Wee Tam?' McCoy wasn't expecting that. 'Why didn't you tell me before?'

'I was too scared. After I found Donny lying there in the flat I just wanted to get away, so I went to Iris's. I didn't know what to do. I didn't know whether Wee Tam knew if Donny had told me about what he'd done. When you said to meet you in the Strathmore I thought if I went in there with you he'd think I was protected. And when he spoke to me he was just normal, just annoying Wee Tam looking at my tits again. So I thought everything must be okay, that he didn't know Donny had told me.'

'Until Cooper's?'

She nodded. 'He was waiting for me in the street. He punched me, hit my head off the pavement when I fell. Then he kicked me in the . . .' She

291

faltered, couldn't think of the best word to use. 'He kicked me down there. He said he knew where I'd been, what I'd had done. He must have been following me. He told me if I ever said a word about him or Donny or Alec he'd follow me again and this time he'd do to me what he did to Alec.'

Laura was wringing the napkin in her hands, tears running down her face. She looked lost and terrified, fifteen again. Iris leant over, put her arms around her, pulled Laura into her, patting her back, telling her everything was going to be all right. McCoy hoped it was. Wasn't sure it ever would be.

'Will you keep an eye on her?' he asked.

Iris nodded.

'Take her back to Cooper's. She'll be safe there. Don't let her out on her own.'

Iris nodded again. 'Is that it, McCoy? You finished?'

He nodded, about to go but Iris put her hand on his arm.

'Two things, McCoy,' she said. 'First of all, never ever threaten me again. And second, don't ever use me to do your dirty work.' Then she stood up, picked up her cup of tea and threw it in his face. The women at the next table gasped and the head waitress hurried over.

McCoy stood up, wiping the cold tea from his eyes with a napkin. 'I suppose I deserved that,' he said.

'You did. Just think yourself lucky I waited till it was cold.'

CHAPTER 34

McCoy pushed open the doors of the Strathmore, looked round the empty pub.

'We're shut!'

A shout from behind the bar, then Big Tam appeared from the cellar steps, wooden crate of beer bottles in his hands.

'Don't worry,' said McCoy. 'I'm not here for a drink.'

Big Tam didn't even say hello, just nodded when McCoy approached the bar. Almost as if he'd been expecting him.

'Need a word, Tam,' said McCoy. 'With you and your boy.'

Tam reluctantly opened the bar counter and led him through to the back room.

Been a while since he'd seen Tam's wife May, not that he was complaining. She didn't seem pleased to see him either. She was sitting on the couch knitting, didn't get up when he walked in, hardly even looked up. Obviously, she hadn't been expecting company. Her hair was in curlers and she was wearing a floral housecoat, feet in slippers.

'Evening, May. How's Wee Tam?' asked McCoy.

No reply or invitation to sit down was forthcoming, so he made himself comfy on the couch right beside her. If they wanted to play silly buggers, so be it. They'd come to the right man.

McCoy leant in close and peered into her lap. 'What's that your knitting, May?'

She drew her eyes off him and stuffed the knitting down the side of the couch.

Big Tam was hovering by the fireplace, looking like thunder. 'Remember you're a guest here, McCoy.'

McCoy held up his hands. 'Spare me the lecture, Tam. Just go and get the wee fucker. I want a word.'

Big Tam looked down at May. She nodded imperceptibly and he went off to fetch him. After two long and silent minutes marked off by the ticking of the sunburst clock above the mantelpiece the door opened and Wee Tam shuffled in, his dad behind him.

McCoy let out a low whistle. Wee Tam was a changed man.

He sat down on the armchair and pulled his flannel dressing gown around him. Didn't look very happy. McCoy could hardly blame him. He was eighteen years old and stuck with a face like Frankenstein for the rest of his life. A long scar stretched across the bottom of his chin and almost up to his ear.

'Who did that to you, son?' McCoy asked.

May suddenly sparked into life. 'He's no idea, he spoke—'

McCoy held his hand up. 'Button it, May. It's the razor king I'm here to talk to, no his mammy.' He turned back round to the boy.

Wee Tam shrugged. 'No idea.'

'Is that right?' McCoy said. 'So you've no idea why someone would want to run a razor up your face?'

He shrugged again. 'Haven't a clue.'

McCoy leant back in the settee, stretching his arms along the top of it. His left hand brushed the back of May's head. She tutted and sat forward.

'All right, son,' said McCoy. 'Let me try and help you, then, how's about that? Somebody messing with somebody's girlfriend maybe, that the story?'

May couldn't manage to keep it shut any longer. 'He's no got a girlfriend. All those drunken wee whoors in the bar chasing after him. He's no interested. Are you, son?'

Wee Tam shrugged again.

McCoy turned back to May. 'That what they are, then, May, your customers? Drunken wee whoors?'

'Painted up like whoors, no even sixteen some of them.' She spat the words out, face full of contempt.

'Not all the girls that come in here are wee whoors, are they, Tam? Some of them are smart girls from the posh end of town. That the ones you like? Even if they don't like you?'

Wee Tam said nothing.

McCoy decided he'd had enough of sitting there being treated like an arse. 'Okay, I'll make it crystal clear for you, Tam. You come anywhere near Laura Murray again and you are fucked. If I hear you're even in the same fucking pub, I'm going to march her into the station and make her repeat what she told me about you under oath. You understand me?'

'He wouldnae hit a lassie,' said May defiantly.

'You know what's funny, May? I didn't say anything about hitting lassies. Why are you talking about that?'

May scowled. Realised she'd been caught out.

'Come on, McCoy, you cannae make accusations like that without any evidence. When was this supposed to have happened?' asked Big Tam.

'Frankenstein here did it two days ago.'

Soon as McCoy said it, he realised he'd fallen into a trap.

May smiled triumphantly. 'Two days ago was Thursday. He was with me all day, went to see my mother in the hospital in Perth. Took us all bloody day to get there and back, didn't it, son?'

Wee Tam nodded. Smiled.

McCoy knew he was about to lose his temper but he didn't care. 'I always knew you were a stupid cow, May. I just hadn't realised how truly bloody stupid you were. False alibi for a lad that beats up wee girls, kicks them in the stomach. Christ, but you must be proud of yourself.'

Big Tam jumped to his feet. 'That's enough, you. Out!'

McCoy looked at him. 'Sit down and shut the fuck up before you do yourself an injury,' he said. 'If you think I'm scared of you, better think again.'

Big Tam reluctantly sat down, seethed in his armchair.

McCoy took the cigarettes out his pocket and offered Wee Tam one. He reached out and took it. As McCoy was lighting it for him, he asked, 'Who were you selling the pills for, son?'

And that was the step too far.

Big Tam jumped up again and went to take a swing. May started screaming, telling McCoy to get the fuck out of her house. He stood up. Done what he'd come to do. May was shooing him out and he was walking towards the door, then he caught a glimpse of Wee Tam reflected in the mirror above the fireplace. Sitting back in the armchair, blowing smoke rings into the air above him, not a care in the world.

McCoy left the pub, started walking down Maryhill Road. Wasn't happy about Wee Tam, wasn't happy at all. There was something about him that wasn't right. Something that made McCoy think he'd only just started what he planned to do and there was fuck all he could do about it. All he had on him was what Laura had said and there was no way her parents or Murray were going to let that come out. If it did, then so did Donny MacRae and what had happened to him. Papers would be all over it. Prospective MP's runaway daughter and her slain gangland boyfriend.

Was glad he'd told Iris to keep her inside. Knew that if she was under Cooper's wing there was no way Wee Tam would dare go anywhere near her. And then it struck him. What Cooper had said. *We get everything. Like comes to like. Speed, acid, pills.*

Pills.

He saw a cab coming down the street, held his hand out.

CHAPTER 35

It was Jumbo that answered the door. Big smile broke on his face when he saw McCoy.

'How's things, Jumbo? Thought you'd be out in the garden in this weather.'

'I wanted to be, but I had to help Mr Cooper. He's having a bath now.'

He stood there smiling.

'Can I come in?' asked McCoy

It looked like the idea had only just occurred to him. 'Oh aye! Come in!' He held the door wide and McCoy stepped into the hall. Jumbo closed it behind him, carefully locked it. Glanced up the stairs.

'Billy's down in the kitchen, if you want to go and see him. I better go up and see how Mr Cooper's getting on.'

'How is he?' asked McCoy.

Jumbo looked guilty. 'He's a wee bit wobbly, but he's started swearing at me again so I think he's getting better.'

Billy was sitting at the kitchen table in a pair of football shorts and nothing else, counting out piles of twenties, fag burning away in the ashtray beside him. He looked up when McCoy appeared, held his hand up. 'Hang on.'

Started a new pile, his lips moving as he counted.

McCoy wasn't surprised he was down here. Kitchen was a good few degrees cooler than the rest of the house.

'Four eighty. Five hundred.'

Billy put the last note down, looked relieved. 'Finished. I always lose my bloody place and have to start all over again.' He nodded over. 'Beers are in the fridge, if you fancy.'

McCoy got one out, found the opener, sat down. He nodded at the piles of notes. 'Speaking of ill-gotten gains, is Wee Tam from the Strathmore one of yours?'

Billy shook his head. 'Funny you should ask that. Not any more, he isn't. Thieving wee bastard that he is. Kept dipping his hand into the profits, thinking he was big-time. Had to go.'

McCoy drew his finger across his chin. 'That you, was it?'

Billy grinned. 'Not me. That kind of stuff's beneath me now. It was Percy Thrower up there. Training him up.'

'Jumbo?' asked McCoy, surprised.

Billy nodded. 'Has to earn his living like everyone else.'

'You need to watch Wee Tam, Billy. I just left him. Tried to rattle his cage but he was having none of it. Stayed ice cold like he didn't have a care in the world. He did Alec Page over, took great pleasure in it. And he's the one that attacked Laura. Could be more dangerous than you think.'

Billy sat back. 'Duly noted. I thought he was just a wee toerag. That's why I sent Jumbo.'

'He's more than that. Make sure he doesn't get anywhere near Laura, eh?'

Billy nodded. Went and got them another pair of cans. Sat back down.

'How's Cooper?' asked McCoy.

'Getting there. Been on the phone all afternoon, then got Jumbo to go into town, get him some gear, his old stuff's too big now.'

'What's he up to?'

Billy shrugged. 'Don't ask me. He must be feeling better. Isn't telling me a bloody thing.'

'Christ, you here now?' Iris was standing in the doorway, a pile of underpants and vests in her hands. 'Hoped I'd seen the last of you for a while. His bloody lordship wants his skivvies ironed. Give me bloody strength.'

Billy pointed over her shoulder. 'Utility room is down the corridor.'

Iris looked at him, shook her head. 'Utility room? It's far from a bloody utility room you and Stevie Cooper were raised, I'll tell you that.'

She disappeared.

'It's getting like bloody *Upstairs Downstairs* in here,' said McCoy. 'Never thought I'd be pining after Memen Road.'

'I know,' said Billy. 'Things are moving fast, it's nuts. He'll have a bloody butler next. Hudson!'

They laughed.

'God help us,' said McCoy. 'You think he'll start drinking with a china cup? Pinky in the air?'

'Will I fuck.'

They looked up and Cooper was standing in the doorway, naked but for a towel around his waist. He still wasn't what he had been, but he looked a heck of a lot better. He had some colour; body didn't look quite so thin and weak. Freshly shaved, hair in its proper quiff. He walked over to the sink, poured himself a pint glass of water and drank it over. Wiped his mouth.

'Billy, that's too much money to be in here. Get it over to the accountant. Send Jumbo in a cab. There's a couple of grand in my bedside drawer. Get him to take that as well.'

Billy nodded, stood up. Bundled the notes into a Galbraith's carrier bag and headed for the stairs.

'Somebody's feeling better,' said McCoy.

'What happened to your head?' asked Cooper, pointing to McCoy's bald patch and the line of stitches.

'I got in the way of a kidnap.'

'Arse,' said Cooper. 'Probably deserved it.'

'Aye well. They think I've got concussion, so I'm signed off for a week.'

'Have you?' asked Cooper, peering at him.

McCoy shook his head. 'I feel fine.'

'You've got nothing to do, then?' asked Cooper.

'Not really. Got a few things I could be—'

'Good. You can come with me. Hold me up if I get wobbly. Do you good.'

'Where? Come where?' asked McCoy, not quite sure what was going on.

'My uncle Seamus died. Need to go to the funeral.'

McCoy hated funerals – was just about to launch into an excuse about his concussion maybe coming back when Cooper told him where the funeral was.

'Okay,' said McCoy. 'I'll go and pack a bag. Pick me up in half an hour?'

Cooper nodded. 'Remember a black tie.'

25th August 1970

1004 Wonderland Avenue, Los Angeles

Bobby sniffed, sat back on the leather couch and let the coke run down his throat. Hit him immediately, the familiar burn, the rush of blood. Stuff was good all right. The dealer looked up at him, waiting. Bobby nodded, and he grinned.

'Told you it was good. I told you, man!' The dealer started emptying the wrap onto the mirror on the coffee table.

'This guy – I don't know what he is, Colombian, Brazilian, I don't know, somewhere down there – anyway, he comes up from Mexico in a little plane. Lands out by Bakersfield, some avocado farm or something. Insane! The guy's in and out in two hours, and you know what?'

Bobby wasn't really listening, just watching the dealer's hand go up and down, the chop, chop, chop of the credit card on the mirror.

Suddenly realised the dealer was looking at him. 'What?' he said.

'He's the straightest guy you've ever seen. I mean totally straight, like blue leisure pants, white short-sleeve shirt, looks like he sells TVs! Can you believe it?'

Bobby shook his head. Didn't much care either way. Leant down and snorted another two lines. A car horn sounded outside. He wiped his nostrils, rubbed his finger on his gums.

'Car's here,' he said. 'Need to go.'

The dealer nodded. 'Sure, man, anything you need. Where you off to?'

'Troubadour. Some English guy. Meant to be good. The whole town's going.'

The dealer nodded, handed him two wraps and pocketed the hundred-dollar bill Bobby held out.

'What's the guy's name?' he asked.

Bobby shook his head. 'Can't remember. John somebody, I think.'

19TH JULY 1973

CHAPTER 36

Milltown Cemetery. Even in the bright sunlight it was a miserable place. Seemed to go on forever, rows and rows of graves and statues and neglected family mausoleums. McCoy stood at the side of the grave, dark suit and black tie like the rest of the mourners, hands clasped in front of him. Even with their suits on, they looked a rough lot. Big men, most of them. Face and hands bearing the wear and tear and scars of a working life in the margins. Bouncers, labourers, hired muscle. The women were small, worn down by cleaning jobs and kids and never having enough money to make ends meet.

McCoy looked past them up to the hills in the distance as the priest began. He'd never been to Northern Ireland, didn't know what to expect, but it looked strangely familiar. Belfast was a lot like Glasgow. The city centre was another Victorian grid of sandstone buildings built to reinforce civic pride and to celebrate the money made from ship-building. Libraries, town halls, churches – all of them looked the same. The only difference being Belfast was at war.

He'd stared out the taxi window on the way in from the docks. Couldn't quite believe it. Army patrols walking through the town, rifles pointing down in front of them. Roadblocks, some official, some just burnt-out buses and old sofas. Blown-out buildings everywhere. The Troubles had always been something distant, on the news or in the paper. He only realised now how close they were, only forty-odd miles away. The people looked tired, beaten by it all. Friendly enough but wary, no one quite sure where they were on the shifting sands of suspicion.

'Ashes to ashes . . .'

McCoy looked back at the grave and Uncle Seamus's coffin lying in it. Cooper's dad's brother. Remembered him a bit, met him in Glasgow a few times. A big man in a suit and brown suede shoes, grin on his face, pint in his hand. Smelt of fags, beer and a shirt that needed changing. Supposed he might have been the closest thing Cooper had had to a father. Even if he was just another drunk, same as the real one.

A few women came forwards, dropped some flowers into the grave. The priest crossed himself and that was that. Uncle Seamus was gone. Despite himself, McCoy crossed himself as the gravediggers moved forward and the group of twenty or so mourners started walking back up to the gates.

McCoy, like everyone else, waited until he was outside before he lit up – wasn't quite sure why, just didn't seem respectful to smoke in a graveyard.

Cooper appeared beside him. Got a light. 'Anyone asks, I had pneumonia,' he said as he blew out the smoke from his Regal.

McCoy nodded. Wasn't sure anyone would really notice Cooper's condition. He was looking better every day, more colour, more weight on.

'You coming to the Rock?' he asked.

McCoy nodded. 'I'll come for one,' he said. Felt it was the least he could do.

'One?' said Cooper. 'What's up with you? It's an Irish wake, for fuck sake!'

'Yep, and it's an Irish wake in West Belfast for a man who was maybe part of the IRA and I'm a British polis. Not sure I'll be too welcome when the rebel songs start.'

Cooper grinned. 'Might be right. You going back to the hotel after?

McCoy nodded. 'Going to have a lie down this afternoon. Still feel a bit dizzy.'

'All right. C'mon, we'll get a lift from Sean.'

They hurried over to Sean, his young nephew, who was getting into a battered Cortina. Squeezed in the back next to a granny with a wee boy in a suit on her lap. The wee boy looked at him. 'My uncle Seamus is dead,' he said.

'Johnny! Behave!' said the granny, slapping his legs. Immediate tears.

Cooper turned round, rubbed the wee boy's head. 'Och, you're all right, Johnny. Here . . .' He dug in his pocket, found a new fifty pence and gave it to him.

Tears immediately replaced with a broad grin. 'Granny, can I get sweets?'

McCoy listened to the two of them argue. He'd need to wait until after his dinner was the gist of it. He wasn't quite sure why he'd lied to Cooper, but he had. He had plans for the day. And they didn't include having a lie down in the hotel.

He ended up having two pints, was just about to have another when Cooper's auntie started singing 'The Men Behind The Wire'. Decided discretion was the better part of valour. He'd shown his face, laughed at the 'you better watch yourself round here' jokes, done his time. He said cheerio to Cooper and headed for the door. Realised Sean was following him.

'I'll give you a lift into town,' he said. 'Be safer.'

McCoy started to tell him he was fine, but Sean cut him off. 'Uncle Stevie says I was to give you a lift.'

McCoy nodded, no real point arguing.

The road into town down the Falls Road took a while. They had to keep turning off and going round, army patrols rumbling past, half the streets blocked off.

'Always like this?' McCoy asked.

Sean grinned. 'This is a good day. Should see it when a bomb's gone off.'

McCoy nodded, wondered what a young guy like Sean's future looked like here. Only two options, as far as he could see. Get out. Go to London, Liverpool, anywhere. Or stay here and get sucked into it all, whether you liked it or not.

They stopped at the lights, Sean telling him all about his trying to get an apprenticeship, McCoy nodding, not really listening. Was still trying to take it all in. There was a group of four or five soldiers standing at the corner outside a small park, five, ten feet away, guns pointing down in front of them, constantly scanning left and right. Oldest one looked about nineteen. Couldn't be easy for them either, he supposed. Just another way out of a shitty town in the Midlands or the North East or Glasgow. Places where things had closed down, jobs were difficult to come by.

'Where are you staying?' asked Sean.

'The Europa,' said McCoy.

Sean whistled. 'Fancy.'

'Aye well, it's not me paying or we'd be in some boarding house, believe me.'

'Drop you in Donegal Square?' asked Sean.

'Sounds good,' said McCoy.

Five minutes later he watched Sean drive off into the traffic, tried to work out where he was. Asked a woman the way to Victoria Street. She told him in an accent he could almost follow. Assured him it was ten minutes away at the most. He set off in the direction she told him.

The town centre took a bit of negotiating. There were checkpoints and barriers everywhere, mesh bomb screens over the shops, hardly any people on the streets. He didn't blame them. Who would go through all the trouble to get into town and then spend the time worrying you were going to get bombed as you wandered round Woolworths?

He turned into Victoria Street. Was about to ask someone where it was when he saw it. Couldn't miss it, really. A hugely fortified Victorian building surrounded by fences and cameras and concrete blocks. Had to be Musgrave police station. He walked down the wire tunnel to the door and pressed the buzzer. A camera spun round to film him, a voice barked at him through the speaker, he said he was here to see Hugh Faulds.

Nothing much seemed to happen, then he heard a buzzer and click and Hughie Faulds was standing in the open doorway, hand out to shake. 'Harry bloody McCoy!' he said, pumping his hand up and down. 'Great to see you. C'mon, let's get out of this bloody place.'

Faulds had come up with McCoy, been a pal. He was a huge guy, six foot four, broad as a house. Good polis, too. Couldn't believe it when he'd told him he was going back to Northern Ireland. Troubles had already started, bombs on the TV every night. McCoy had told him he was mad. Faulds happily admitted he was right, but he said he was still going. Home was home.

'How was the funeral?' he asked as they walked around the building.

'Usual,' said McCoy. 'Get the body in the ground quick as you can, then start drinking.'

Faulds laughed. 'Not much bloody changes.' He

314

pointed at a light-blue Viva sitting amongst the other cars in the yard at the back of the station.

'Shite car, but it's safe parked in here.'

McCoy nodded.

'Need to go to the mortuary. Don't worry, I remember what you're like, just need to pick up a report, no blood and guts, and there's a cafe beside it does a great Ulster fry. We can have a chat while we stuff ourselves. Hungry?'

McCoy nodded, realised he was. Had left the Rock before the sandwiches and soup had come out.

They got in the car, Faulds managing to squash himself into the driver's seat. McCoy found a space on the passenger side after he'd transferred all the sweetie wrappers and files into the back. Faulds wasn't joking: it was a shite car, made clunking noises every time they got above twenty miles an hour. Clunking noises accompanied by a litany of swearing from Faulds.

McCoy had no real clue where they were going, but the town seemed to get more normal the further they got away from the centre. Faulds chatted away, asked after Murray and the others they knew and had in common. Took out his wallet when they stopped at the lights, showed him a picture of a fat toddler sitting on a swing. Stuart. The wife was pregnant again, too.

Twenty minutes or so later he pulled in the gates of what looked like a hospital and they got out. Faulds told him he'd be back in five minutes and headed for a low building with a big sign saying 'CITY MORTUARY' on the front. McCoy was going nowhere near that so leant on the car, lit up and waited. Wondered what being a polis here must be like. Bloody awful, he decided. Looking over your shoulder all the time, mirror on a stick under your car, scared to go into the wrong street. Scared of being kidnapped and shot or, even worse, being tortured. Being a polis was bad enough, never mind all that on top. Having said that, Faulds seemed happy enough. Wife and family, a normal life. Maybe.

He appeared out the building door, buff file in his hand.

'You sure you're hungry?' he asked.

McCoy nodded. 'Starving.'

Faulds grinned. 'You better be.'

Three rashers, two fried eggs, three sausages, two kinds of fried bread, black pudding, half a tomato, a potato scone and what looked like white pudding stared up at him from a plate. No wonder Faulds was the size of a bloody house. Looked tasty, though. Like it would fell an elephant, too, but McCoy did well, almost cleared it. Sat back, took a sip of rotten tea and burped.

''Scuse me,' he said.

'No worries,' said Faulds, wiping the last of the egg yolk off his plate with a bit of toast.

'Now the important stuff is out the way, what was it you wanted to ask me about?' he said.

McCoy sat back, lit up. 'How much traffic is

there between Glasgow and Belfast? Paramilitaries, I mean.'

'Quite a bit,' said Faulds. 'Mostly Glasgow this way. People bringing money for the boys, that sort of thing. Plus Glasgow's full of bloody Territorial Army bases. And they have armouries, and those bloody armouries aren't that secure, so we get the weapons for break-ins there, occasional Semtex from mining concerns. For every shipment we stop there's probably another twenty that get through.'

'And the other way?' asked McCoy.

'Mostly that's people on the run, either from the police or the Boys. Or guys in the brigades that need to disappear for a while, let the heat die down.' Faulds took a sip of his tea. 'I'm assuming this isn't hypothetical?'

'No. Just trying to get some background. A guy we're looking for in Glasgow has gone missing, looks like he was abducted, might be mixed up in it. The kidnap was pretty professional stuff, maybe paramilitary. Would be on the Catholic side.'

'That case you're probably asking the wrong guy. RUC intelligence isn't great on the Provos, better on the UDA.' Faulds grinned, sat back. 'You might have been better asking your pals at the funeral.'

'How'd you know about them?' asked McCoy, surprised.

Faulds tapped the side of his nose. 'Belfast's a small town. Seamus Cooper was a kent face. Maybe in, maybe not, but he definitely had connections. You not see the photographers at the graveyard?'

McCoy shook his head.

'Must have been doing a good job for once.' He looked serious for a minute. 'You should be careful, Harry. No matter what your pal Cooper is, or who his pals are, you're a police. An instrument of the British State, as they say. And now, thanks to the funeral, the IRA know you're here. You need to watch yourself.'

McCoy nodded. Hadn't really thought about it before. Hadn't been worried. Was starting to be now. Tried to make light. 'Going back tomorrow. They'd have to be quick.'

'They are,' said Faulds. 'So watch yourself. I mean it.' He looked up at the clock on the wall.

'You need to go?' asked McCoy.

Faulds nodded. 'Meeting back at Musgrave at three, need to go see someone on the way. You fit?'

'Not sure I can stand up after that. Think I've eaten enough for a few days.'

'Puts hair on your chest,' said Faulds, grinning. 'And meat on your bones. Breakfast of champions.'

They hadn't gone far, couple of miles, when Faulds turned into what looked like a new housing estate. Pulled up outside a house with its curtains closed.

'You okay here for five minutes?'

McCoy nodded and Faulds got out. Obviously didn't intend to tell him what he was doing and McCoy wasn't going to ask. He lit up, looked round the estate. Same as all the ones in Scotland.

Houses all much the same, few kids about on bikes. He rolled the window down, tried to lower the temperature in the car. Belfast wasn't as hot as Glasgow, but it was still stifling. He looked at his watch. That was ten minutes already. Was obviously going to be longer than Faulds thought.

For want of something to do, he picked up the file from the mortuary. Opened it gingerly – if there were any photos, it was getting shut again straight away. Luckily it seemed to just be printed sheets. He skimmed them. Usual blood results, stomach contents. There was a drawing at the back, outline of a man with the wounds marked. Crosses across the kneecaps. Usual paramilitary punishment stuff.

'Solving my cases for me, are you?'

He looked up and Faulds was at the window. 'Sorry, was just bored.'

'No worries,' said Faulds, getting in.

'What happened?' asked McCoy, putting the file back on the seat.

'Guy found dead in the park off Falls Road. No ID, no clothes, just his underpants on. Been tortured, kneecaps blown off before they killed him.' He started the car.

'Hate to say it,' said McCoy, 'but isn't that kind of thing par for the course here?'

Faulds indicated and they set off. 'Would be, but a couple of things don't make much sense if he was dumped there with that done to him.

319

Would be the UDA or the UVF that would have done it, but there's no claim from either and those boys like to crow when they've killed someone.'

They turned back out onto the main road and the clunking started again.

'Bloody thing!' said Faulds, slapping the steering wheel. 'And another funny thing. Torture wasn't just the usual kind.'

'What do you mean?' asked McCoy.

'He's only one finger left on his left hand. Looked like they had been cut off with bolt cutters, something like that. Whatever they wanted to know, looks like it took them three fingers to get it out of him. More like something we used to see over your way, eh? Remember that guy – who was he again? Wee Cammy? Got half his toes cut off for nicking two hundred quid from Ronnie Naismith. You'd have thought it was the crime . . .'

Faulds kept talking but McCoy had stopped listening. He reached over, got the file, started flicking through it.

'What's up?' asked Faulds.

McCoy was skimming it. Reading it to himself. *Five foot ten. Approx. age forty. Sandy hair.*

He looked at Faulds. 'Can we go look at the body?'

Faulds did a double-take. 'You want to see a body? You?'

McCoy nodded.

CHAPTER 37

It was him all right. Finn Kelly. Alice Kelly's dad. Recognised him from the hospital and the trip in the car. Same fair hair swept to the side, same long nose. He tried not to look at his hands. Seeing his ruined face was bad enough.

McCoy took his mask off and Faulds pushed the big body drawer back in.

'You know him?' asked Faulds.

McCoy shook his head. 'My mistake. Can we get out of here?'

Faulds nodded, already looked preoccupied. 'I'll drop you off at the hotel. Need to get into Musgrave quick.'

McCoy got back in the car, wondering if he'd done the right thing. He'd said he didn't recognise the body before he'd had a chance to think. Maybe he just didn't want to get Faulds and the RUC involved. Maybe he just needed time to work out why Finn Kelly was lying in a mortuary drawer back in Belfast. Knew if he said anything that would be it. Special Branch would be all over it.

Supposed he should call Murray, let him know what he'd found. Whole case was going to get an awful lot more complicated if the paramilitaries were involved. Special Branch were involved. God knows how much paperwork. Meant they'd probably be bumped off it as well. After they'd done the donkey work, that is. Might just leave it until tomorrow. Go and see Murray in person. After all, he was still off sick and Kelly wasn't going anywhere. He decided to give himself the day to try and find out more. If he couldn't, he'd go see Murray and tell him he'd seen a body, tell him he wasn't sure if it was Kelly or not.

McCoy stood outside the Europa and watched Faulds drive off, gave him a wave. The driveway in front of the hotel was a row of expensive cars, drivers in them, waiting. He'd promised Faulds again that he'd be careful. The Crown Bar across the road from the hotel was as far as he was to go. He agreed, told Faulds he was going to go to his bed, have a rest, spend some of Cooper's money on room service. All of which was true, but he had something else to do before that: try and find out what on earth Kelly was really doing in Belfast when Alice went missing.

Finn had told his wife he was working on a building site. Seemed a logical place to start. They hadn't been able to turn up the mysterious mate he was supposed to be working for. His wife had said he was called Colm, that was all she knew. McCoy crossed Victoria Street, headed for the noise and dust of the construction going on behind the Crown Bar.

The site was a half-built office block, picture of what it was going to be like on a big board on the fence round it. Was a huge thing, had to be twenty or so storeys. WINDSOR HOUSE. Wasn't sure that was the best name for something in Belfast, but what did he know. He showed the photo of Kelly around, got a lot of shaking heads and can't help you's. A guy with a clipboard and a suit tucked into wellies told him there was another big building project going on down by the Laggan. McCoy got directions and started walking. He knew he was clutching at straws, but it gave him something to do and it was definitely better than sitting in the Rock waiting for the wrong person to ask him what he did for a living.

Turned out it was a big post office they were building and it turned out no one recognised Finn there either. Another tip. Some bomb clearance site on Donegall Street had been taking on casual labour. He wanted to stop for a drink, but Faulds had made him wary, scared of going in the wrong place. He was sure it was all rubbish, but something about the city, the army, the checkpoints was getting to him, making him nervous. Started to wonder if he was being followed. Decided he was just getting paranoid. Who'd be following him? He wasn't bloody James Bond.

He got a bit lost on the way, was about to forget it, turn back and go to the hotel bar, when he saw the site up ahead. A red sandstone building had been surrounded by a temporary fence, one side of it half collapsed. The buildings leading up to it were scarred and pitted, windows blown out. He called over one of the guys behind the fence, a middle-aged man spraying a pile of rubble with a hosepipe, trying to keep the dust down. The worker unwrapped the cloth around his mouth and nose and approached the fence.

'Looking for someone,' said McCoy. 'Was working on a site.'

He held out the photo and the man squinted at it. Shook his head.

'No recognise him?' asked McCoy.

'Not that, son. I don't have my bloody specs on. Couldn't even tell you if it was a picture of me.' He turned, shouted 'Paul!' and a young guy with a skinhead put down his shovel and wandered over. McCoy showed him the picture.

'Guy was working on a site. You recognise him?' he asked without much hope.

Paul shook his head.

McCoy went to put the picture back in his pocket.

'He wasn't working on any site, believe me. Not that guy.'

'What?' asked McCoy. 'You know him?'

Paul shook his head, took a ginger bottle full of water out his back pocket and had a long slug. 'Sorry,' he said, 'but this bloody dust dries up your throat so much you can't speak. Couple of days ago was my sister's engagement party. Me and my brother jumped ship. He was back from the navy, hadn't seen him for ages. We ended up in the Crown.' He tapped the picture. 'This guy was propping up the bar, half pissed. Started talking to us, a load of shite but he was buying so we didn't mind. Had a wallet bulging with twenties.'

'What did he say?' asked McCoy.

'Said he'd come into money, was going to go to Spain. Was staying across the road at the Europa – a suite, no less – until he got going.'

'He say what the deal was?' asked McCoy.

Paul shook his head. 'Said it was hush-hush. Tapped his nose, all that shite. Kept wanting to drink 'to the Boys'. Just another arsehole in town pretending he was a bigger man than he was. We waited until he went to the jacks and we fucked off. Had had enough.'

He started coughing, got his bottle out again, had another slug. 'He a pal of yours?'

McCoy shook his head.

'Good,' said Paul. 'He's the last kind of guy you want to hang about with in this city. Drunk and talking shite too loud and in the wrong place about "the cause". You get them here, Americans mostly, think that because their great-grandfather came from the back arse of Limerick they're in the bloody provos. The kind of stupid bugger that says shite like that in front of the wrong person and ends up killed.'

McCoy thanked him, walked away. According to all they knew, Kelly didn't have a pot to piss in, never mind the money to stay in the Europa and go out on the town acting like Daddy Warbucks. What was he bringing from Glasgow that was worth that much? He was a casual labourer, no way was he going to get a hold of guns to sell. Information, maybe? Semtex from some destruction job? The whole thing just didn't make sense. Maybe he was just a courier, taking stuff back and forward? Would it pay that much? Didn't think so.

About ten minutes later McCoy realised he was lost. He looked up and down the street for someone to ask, but there was no one around. Hughie Faulds' warning started echoing in his head.

Be careful. Don't go anywhere but the Crown. The IRA know you are here.

He turned a corner and saw a black Granada with two guys sitting in it at the end of the street, engine running. Started to get a bit scared, told himself not to be so stupid. No one was interested in him. Just an everyday guy over for a funeral. He started walking. Tried not to hurry. Granada started up, moving his way.

He turned into another street, could see the concrete tower of the Europa in the distance, immediately felt better. Wasn't that far now. Be in the room soon, club sandwich and a few beers on Cooper's tab. Had a smile to himself about how easily he'd got spooked. Heard a rush of feet coming towards him, tried to turn and a bag went over his head.

CHAPTER 38

It came in waves, the panic. Your hands are tied, there's a hood over your head, you're in the boot of a car in Belfast. Just think about that. You're fucked. Best you can get away with is a beating or a kneecapping and we all know what the worst is. Dragged out the car, forced to kneel, feel of a gun barrel at the back of your head and then nothing.

The car turned sharply and he hit the side of the boot. Shifted, tried to get in a less painful position. Wasn't easy. Had no idea how long he'd been in there, just knew he wanted out, wanted to be in Glasgow buying a drink at the Victoria, talking shite to Wullie the barman. Wanted to be anywhere but where he was.

The car turned again, seemed to drive off the road, started lurching from side to side. A huge wave of fear and nausea as he realised they were driving across a rutted field. Only one reason to be in a field. And that was the worst reason he could think of. The car slowed, stopped. He could hear two doors opening, then being banged shut. Then nothing. His heart was racing. Felt like it was thumping in his chest. Felt like he was going to start crying or to piss himself.

He could hear voices – not what they were saying, just the noise and rhythm. And then he heard a gunshot and he thought he was going to be sick. Started praying to his mum, God, anyone to get him out of there. He tried to separate his hands, but they were tied tight at the wrist. Bag over his head smelt of sweat and hair oil, realised it must have been used before. Another lurch of terror. Heard someone laughing. Heard crows or some sort of birds squawking.

Wondered if this was it. Where he was going to die. Crying for his life in a field outside Belfast. Another lurch of fear. What if they thought he was something more than just a Glasgow polis? What if they thought he was Special Branch or Intelligence? That he knew something. Something that they would torture him to find out? That was it. Fear broke him and he was sick into the bag, felt it run down his chin. Had never felt as scared or as lonely in his life. Realised he was sobbing too.

And then the boot opened, hands pulled him out and he was dropped onto the ground. The bag was pulled off his head. He blinked a few times in the dim evening light, looked up. Realised he was looking up into the face of William Norton.

'What did I tell you, McCoy?' he said. 'Don't ever try and take the piss out of me.' He smiled, wiped some cigarette ash off the sleeve of his blazer. 'And what did you go and do?'

He pulled his foot back and kicked McCoy straight in the face. McCoy's nose burst and blood added to the sick and the tears. He tried to sit up, couldn't. All he could do was lie there and look at Norton and Duncan Stewart his driver, and the fact that Duncan Stewart was holding a gun.

'How did you know I was here?' he managed to get out.

'I didn't,' said Norton. 'Not until Duncan saw you outside the Europa, was waiting to pick me up, take me to the ferry, and there you were. Asked the boys at the site across the road what you had been asking them. So we thought we should have a chat and get the later ferry.'

He laughed, Duncan laughing along with him.

McCoy's mind was going full tilt. Adrenaline pumping into his brain. Realised he had to keep them talking, play for time.

'I'm a polis, Norton. You better watch yourself.'

Norton laughed. Duncan joining in like the good yes man he was.

'This is Bandit Country, McCoy. The Wild West. Anything can happen here. All bets are off.' He grinned. 'And in case you haven't noticed, you're the one tied to a tree.'

'I should have known,' said McCoy. 'Realised what was going on.'

'And what would that be, McCoy?' asked Norton.

'You even told me, didn't you?'

'What?'

'In the back of your car in Bilsland Drive,' said McCoy. 'One of them will always think he can fuck the others over.'

Norton hacked up, spat on the ground. Looked at McCoy, didn't look happy.

'Kelly fucked you over, didn't he? Took the money from the Gartnavel job and ran. Took his chance to change his life. Came here to lie low until he could move on. Driver, was he?'

Norton smiled, not an ounce of humour in it. 'Clever boy.'

'What happened to the usual one? He get pulled in?'

'Measles,' said Norton. 'Got it off his daughter.'

'Thirty grand or so. Must have buried it somewhere near Belfast.'

'That right?' said Norton.

'And you took his fingers off one by one until he told you where,' said McCoy.

Norton smiled, shook his head. 'Great imagination you've got, McCoy. Wasted being a polis. Imagination like that you should write a book something.'

Norton squatted down in front of him, pointed over to the left.

'Over there, Belfast, lovely city but a dangerous place. People get murdered all the time. Wander into the wrong district, say the wrong thing, meet the wrong people. Think that's what happened to poor Finn Kelly. Wrong place at the wrong time.'

He smiled again.

'Nothing to do with me. Stupid bugger must have had an argument with some of the Boys. It's obvious. Why else would he be lying dead just off the Falls Road with both his kneecaps gone? Just another casualty of these terrible troubles. That right, Duncan?'

His driver nodded, didn't take his eye or his gun off McCoy for a second.

'Same thing could happen to anyone, any stranger in town. Maybe even a Glasgow polis wandering round Belfast asking questions. Wouldn't be a surprise if the Boys took him for a ride in their car. Maybe bring him to a field like this one. After all, a man like that must have a reason for being here, eh? Can't just be an ordinary copper. Must be up to something. Maybe that's why they tortured him before they killed him. Find out who he really was.'

McCoy couldn't think for the fear. Kept rising up, filling his mind, images of kneecapping and bolt cutters. He tried to breathe, tried to think clearly, just hoping that something, anything, would happen. His mind was racing. Needed to do something quick.

'Not your style, I didn't think,' he said.

'What's that?' asked Norton, lighting his cigarette with a gold Dunhill lighter.

'Well, I can see the theory. Makes sense. You kidnap Alice to flush the dad out. Get him to appear back in Scotland so you can pick him up. What father wouldn't?' He stopped, shook his head. 'But things go wrong, don't they. The wee girl's not so wee, she's almost a teenager, a pain in the arse, so you start drugging her to shut her up, force whisky down her throat. Christ knows, doing that to a kid was bad enough, but then to do something like that to a wee girl . . .'

Norton snapped the lighter shut, walked over and kicked McCoy in the stomach. Hard.

'Don't know what you think you're implying, McCoy, but nothing like that happened.'

'You sure?' asked McCoy, still wincing from the pain.

Slight flicker on Norton's face.

McCoy pressed on. His only hope.

'I was at the hospital when they examined her. She'd been raped. Repeatedly. That the kind of people you run with these days, Norton? Nonces like that?' How are you going to keep wandering around Milton like the bloody Godfather when people find that out? They'll be fucking spitting on you in the—'

Didn't manage to get 'street' out. Boot in the face from Stewart.

McCoy rolled back in the grass, tried to deal with the pain. Lay there. Could hear Norton hissing at Stewart, voice low but angry, very angry. McCoy opened his eyes a bit, took a look. Stewart was holding his hands up, shaking his head. McCoy shut his eyes again. He'd bought himself a couple of minutes anyway. Not sure how much good it would do him. His mind was starting to drift. Wasn't sure if it was the last of the concussion or just his mind shutting down so it wouldn't have to deal with what was happening, but he felt calm, even a bit sleepy. Could hear Norton and Stewart arguing. Could feel the dry grass beneath him, watched the sun starting to fall behind the hills in the distance.

Suddenly he was pulled up, set against a fence. Norton was standing in front of him.

'Without you,' he said, 'no one is going to connect the body with Glasgow, me or any bank robberies. So you tell me why I shouldn't just let Stewart here shoot you?'

'No reason. Tell him to go ahead,' said McCoy, trying to sound calm.

Norton raised his eyebrows.

'But if you do, all that gentleman bank robber stuff is gone, no matter how much money you've got. All that will happen is you'll be remembered for kidnapping a wee girl who got raped over and over again on your watch. Soon enough people will just think it was you. It's a better story that way.'

Norton looked white. 'It was nothing to do with me!'

'Maybe so,' said McCoy. 'Pity that.'

Stewart advanced towards him, pulled his boot back again.

'If that clown touches me again,' hissed McCoy, 'I'm going to stop talking.'

Norton put his hand out and Stewart stepped back.

'I can fix it,' said McCoy. 'Make sure the assault disappears off the report. Persuade the mum that it's better for the girl if nobody knows about it and she doesn't try and prosecute. You let me go and I'll do it. If the truth comes out and people find out what really happened to her, you can shoot me in the street.'

Norton looked at him. McCoy could see his mind working behind his eyes. He held out his hand to the driver, nodded at the gun.

'Give us that. Away and get me more fags from the car. I've none left.'

Stewart nodded, handed the gun over and walked off.

Norton knelt down in front of McCoy, pushed the gun into his mouth, pushed it as far as he could. McCoy gagging on the metal and the oily taste. Norton primed the trigger.

'You try any funny stuff and this is what will happen to you. Except you'll be in so much pain you'll be praying for me to pull this trigger. Deal?'

McCoy tried to nod.

'Who?' asked Norton. 'Who was it?'

Norton pulled the gun out his mouth and McCoy spat on the ground, gagged. Was his last chance but he could hardly get the words out. 'She said he had red hair. The man that did it. He said call me Daddy Duncan.'

Stewart walked back from the car, a new packet of Rothmans in his hand. He held it out and

Norton took it, put it in his pocket, then he turned, held the gun up and shot him in the face.

McCoy felt the hot blood splatter across his chest, saw Stewart fall, blood pumping out of what was left of his head. He leant over and retched. Nothing came out, just saliva, felt Stewart's hot blood running down his face, retched again. He looked up to see Norton aim at the driver's kneecap. He shot the left one, then the right. Shot him again in the chest. Air was full of smoke, the smell of bullets and blood, noise ringing in McCoy's ears.

Norton walked back to him. 'Fucking nonce deserved it.'

McCoy nodded.

Norton turned, started walking towards the car and McCoy realised he was going to leave him there, bound hands and feet, covered in blood and lying next to a dead body.

He shouted after him. 'Norton! Norton!'

Norton didn't turn back. He walked towards the car and got in, started the engine. The headlights cast white beams over the rutted field.

'Norton!' he shouted again, tried to make himself heard over the car engine. 'Come back!'

McCoy watched as the car did a slow circle, headed for the gate and the dirt road back to the main road. Watched the lights until they disappeared round a hill. Sat there in the gathering darkness, Stewart's blood drying on his face.

CHAPTER 39

The fox came back again, tentatively circling Stewart's body. McCoy shouted and it walked away, but it didn't go as far this time, sat a couple yards away from the body, watching. Wouldn't take it long to work out all that McCoy could do was shout, then it would start on the body and he would be ten foot away, hearing the whole thing.

He pulled at the ropes behind his back. No use. Tried to stand up, but he couldn't balance with his feet tied so close together so he fell, face hitting the soft earth. He lay there wondering what would happen. Supposed he'd lie there all night until a farmer appeared and called the police and he'd have to explain what he was doing tied up next to a dead body.

Had no idea what he was going to say. Tried to think of something, but his mind was either in a panic or slow and sluggish. Maybe he was suffering from shock, he had no idea. Wasn't that sorry about what had happened to Stewart. He was an evil bastard. Wasn't going to shed any tears over what he'd done. It was either Stewart or him. He'd made the right choice.

The fox started to advance towards the body again. He was about to shout when it looked up startled, then ran away into the darkness.

McCoy heard a few seconds later the noise of a car engine. He could see the headlights now, expected it to go past on the main road, but it stopped, turned into the dirt road, heading for the field.

Another lurch of fear. Maybe Norton had changed his mind, decided to come back and finish the job. The car advanced, headlights dazzling him now, came nearer, stopped a few yards away. McCoy shut his eyes; headlights were pointing right at him. The engine stopped and the lights went off. He opened his eyes.

At first he couldn't see anything, just a white flash burned on his eyes. Heard the doors open and slam shut. Sound of someone coming towards him.

'Fuck sake, McCoy. What's going on here?'

He looked up at a grinning Stevie Cooper. He'd never been so happy to see anyone in his life, thought he was going to start crying. Cousin Sean stepped out behind him, eyes wide as he took in the scene.

'Sean,' said Cooper. 'Untie the man, I'm too pissed.'

He realised Cooper was swaying from side to

side, big daft grin on his face. Sean knelt down beside him, got a penknife out and started sawing at the ropes round his wrists.

Cooper was still grinning, took out his cigarettes, dropped them, muttered 'fuck sake', picked them up. 'You ruined a bloody good night, you know,' he said. 'It was just getting going.'

Sean managed to cut the ropes and he was free. He rubbed at his wrists, winced at the pain as the blood flowed back into them.

'What are you doing here, Stevie? How did you know I was here?'

Cooper had managed to light his cigarette, pointed at Sean, now trying to hack through the ropes around McCoy's legs. 'He's been following you since you left the wake. Told him to keep an eye on you. Came back and got me when you ended up here.' He pointed at the body. 'Who the fuck is that?'

'William Norton's driver,' said McCoy.

Cooper looked surprised. Moved closer and peered down.

'You're right. Duncan Stewart, nasty shite that he is. Well, was.' He laughed. 'What was that old bastard Norton doing here?'

Sean managed to get through the ropes and the pain hit McCoy's ankles.

'It's a long story. You got anything to drink?'

Cooper nodded, went into the car, came back with a can of Harp. Opened it, drank half and handed it over. McCoy swilled the warm lager round his mouth, spat it out, swallowed back the rest.

'Can we get out of here?' asked McCoy.

Cooper nodded 'Too right. Wake'll still be going. I need to get back. My cousin Anne's brought a pal. She was all over me like a cheap rash.' He nodded over at the body. 'What do you want to do about that?'

McCoy leant on Sean, managed to stand up. 'I don't give a fuck. Let's just go. Please.'

3rd August 1971

Villa Nellcôte, South of France

Quarter to three in the morning and the basement was still like a sauna. He wasn't quite sure why it was so hot down there. Never really asked. Thought it was all the amps and the tape machines, all plugged in, all giving off heat. Whatever it was, he actually liked it, was sort of like going down a mine to work.

Heat was terrible but it served a purpose – only people that could face going down there were the musicians. No dealers, no girlfriends, no hangers-on. They were all upstairs, sprawled across the couches they'd dragged out onto the lawn, talking about restaurants in New York and what the best air service was to the Hamptons.

Nicky had fallen asleep on his chair, Longhorns cap on his head, saxophone lying by his side. Lately everyone seemed to be falling asleep, or not appearing for days, or spending the time they should have been recording looking out the window, waiting for the big

340

Citroën to arrive. He wasn't innocent himself, but at least he was still a musician who occasionally took smack rather than a smack addict that occasionally played.

He got up, took his headphones off, stretched. He was down to a pair of Scotland football shorts; everything else – T-shirt, shoes, socks – shed as the heat got worse. Fingers were sore doing overdubs all night on 'Good Time Women', or whatever it was called now.

Nicky suddenly sat up straight, rubbed his eyes. 'What time is it, man?' he asked.

'About three,' said Bobby.

'Jesus, we done?' he asked, adjusting his cap.

'Think so,' said Bobby. 'If Keith was coming, he'd be here by now.'

Nicky nodded, stood up. Grinned. 'How's about we go upstairs and see what the candyman done brought the children?'

Bobby smiled, put his guitar on its stand.

'After you, my dear Alphonse.'

20TH JULY 1973

CHAPTER 40

McCoy was leaning on the rail of the ferry looking down the dock, seagulls circling overhead, last of the cars on board now and still no sign of Cooper. Hadn't been in his room at the hotel this morning either. Bed not even slept in. McCoy'd had his breakfast, eye on the door of the dining room, waiting for him to turn up but he hadn't.

He looked up at the sky: clear blue, another blistering hot day on the way. Although he wasn't that keen on boats, he was looking forward to the trip, planned to spend most of it on deck, letting the fresh air clear the cobwebs out his head. He looked at his watch. Fifteen minutes until they were meant to depart. The cranes along the dock were unloading a big cargo ship, distant sound of instructions being shouted.

Cooper and Sean had dropped him off at the hotel last night, sped off into the night, determined to get back to the wake. McCoy hadn't said much in the car, was still trying to come to terms with what had happened, still felt scared, like he wasn't safe yet. Cooper and Sean didn't seem to care.

Cooper had spent most of the journey pumping Sean for information about his cousin's friend. In a way he was glad. The last thing he wanted to do was go over it all again.

He checked his watch again. Ten minutes. Was about to give up the ghost, go and get a cup of tea, when a blue Viva rounded the warehouses and sped towards the ferry. It pulled over and Cooper, looking like he'd just woken up, funeral suit still on and without any luggage, got out, slammed the door and ran for the gangway. Blokes were about to pull it up, shaking their heads as he ran up it. He'd made it with seconds to spare. He looked up, saw McCoy, pumped his fist.

'Ya dancer!' Cooper shouted and hurried up the gangplank.

Ten minutes later they were nursing mugs of tea, watching the port of Belfast slowly getting smaller through the windows of the cafe.

'Don't suppose I need to ask where you got to last night?' asked McCoy.

'Nope,' said Cooper, grinning. 'I couldn't tell you anyway. Anne's house, wherever the fuck that is. Woke up with Sean battering at the door, didn't have a clue where I was. I thought it was the bloody peelers!'

'How you feeling?' asked McCoy.

'I've got a hangover, a fuck of a hangover to be exact, but for the first time in months I feel like me. Think all that shite is finally out my system.'

'That's good,' said McCoy. 'Back to normal.'

'Will be after I drink this,' he said, taking a half bottle of Bushmills out his pocket and splashing it into their mugs of tea. He took a slug, grimaced as it went down. 'Now, do you want to tell me what the fuck was going on last night?'

So McCoy did. The whole story. The robberies, Alice Kelly, Norton's advice, Finn Kelly's death, and what he'd told Norton about Alice Kelly.

Cooper listened, sat back. 'So what happens now?'

'Hopefully nothing,' said McCoy. 'They don't identify the body as Kelly. I don't tell them it was him. And Norton leaves me alone and goes back to being the big man handing out fivers to the good people of Milton.'

'And what about the money?'

'Norton's got it back. Polis weren't getting anywhere with the robberies before. Don't think that's going to change.'

Cooper looked thoughtful.

'So you're telling me that Norton's sitting on almost thirty grand and nobody's looking for it?'

McCoy's alarm bells started ringing. 'Stevie . . .'

'What?' he asked, sounding defensive.

'You don't want to take on Norton. He may be old, but he's still all that. It's not worth it.'

'That right?' said Cooper. 'So, who made you the boss all of a sudden?'

'I just meant that—'

'I know what you meant, don't worry. And yet a few days ago you were telling Billy I had to make a splash, show people I was still in the game. Seems to me Norton is a good way to do it.'

McCoy was going to argue, but he knew there was no point. The old Cooper was back and the old Cooper would do exactly what he wanted, no matter what McCoy said.

'Just be careful, eh?'

Cooper nodded, but McCoy could see he was miles away. Already thinking about how he could get his hands on Norton's money.

When he came back with two more teas and two bacon rolls, Cooper was asleep, looked like he needed it, lying flat along three seats, shoes on the floor, snoring away. McCoy ate both rolls, then made his way back up to the deck. Could see the coast of Scotland in the distance, wouldn't be long now until he was home.

After a few tries, he managed to light up in the wind, took a deep drag. What was he going back to? Another few days holiday. Raeburn on the warpath. Laura Murray needing somewhere to stay. Almost forgotten he'd given the Coke can to Tracey, would soon see what that would bring, see if Angela was lying or not. Almost felt like staying on the ferry and going back to Ireland, wasn't much he was looking forward to in Glasgow. He flicked his cigarette butt into the sea. Went back downstairs to wake Cooper. They were due to land in twenty minutes.

CHAPTER 41

There was a big brown envelope pinned to his door when he got home. MR MCCOY was written on it in black felt pen. He pulled it off, opened the door. The flat was boiling, full of stale air. He wandered around, opening all the windows, put his bag down, sat at the kitchen table and opened the envelope.

There was a black and white photograph in it – big, ten by twelve maybe. It was of a wee boy, six or seven. He was filthy, clothes worn and tattered. He was standing in a backcourt full of rubbish and washing hung out on lines. He was holding up a toy fire engine, showing it to the camera, biggest smile on his face. McCoy turned it over.

Thank you for Liam. Got some amazing photographs. Dinner to say thank you? Mila

He put the photograph on the table, looked at it again. The wee boy shining out. No matter how shitty his life was he had a fire engine and he was happy. For now. Decided he would get it framed, put it up in the flat somewhere. He looked around, trying to decide where he would put it. Now that he was looking at it for the first time in a while, he realised his flat looked bloody miserable.

Ironing that he hadn't done piled on a chair. Worn armchair by the fire with a rip in the arm. Wallpaper he'd meant to change and still hadn't. Thought back. Wasn't like this when Angela was here. Then it seemed like home. Comfortable. Somewhere you would want to be. He looked around again. Not now. Maybe he'd have a go at a bit of decorating next weekend.

Half an hour later he was bathed, shaved, dressed in a short-sleeve shirt and a pair of Levi's and sitting in a cab heading for Stewart Street. Been five days: no way was Murray going to object to him popping in to say hello. Besides, the fingerprint results might be in by now.

'Well, if it isn't the Merry bloody Wanderer,' said Billy the desk sergeant as he walked in. 'You back?'

'No yet,' said McCoy. 'Murray in?'

Billy nodded. 'Unluckily for us. He's been like a bloody bear with a sore head since he came back. Right pain in the arse. Ask Wattie. He's had to deal with him.'

McCoy nodded, walked through to the office. Could see Wattie's big blond head bent over a typewriter, occasional plonk as one finger hit a key.

He sneaked up behind him. Shouted 'WATSON!' Watched him jump.

'For fuck sake!' he said. 'You could have given

me a heart attack.' He looked him up and down. 'What are you doing here anyway? You should be in Rothesay or Blackpool, shouldn't you?'

McCoy sat on the edge of his desk. 'Came to check up on you, see how you were getting on.'

Wattie looked glum. 'I'm not. No bloody sign of Finn Kelly anywhere. Alice came round eventually. I went with Murray to question her and, as predicted, she couldn't remember a bloody thing. We're as fucked as we were when you left.'

'I didn't leave,' said McCoy 'I was forced to step away for a few days because of my horrific injuries sustained in the line of duty.'

'How you feeling?' asked Wattie, rolling his eyes.

'Fine, but unless Murray changes his mind I've got another two days of purgatory. Speaking of which . . .' He stood up. 'Let's see what he's got to say.'

'Rather you than me,' said Wattie. 'Watch yourself.'

McCoy nodded, walked towards Murray's door and knocked. Waited. Knocked again.

'What?' came a voice from behind the door.

McCoy pushed it open and stepped in. Murray was bent over his desk, writing something on a typed letter. He looked up. Didn't exactly seem happy to see him.

'McCoy. You've got another two sick days. What are you doing here?'

'I was just passing, thought I'd come in and say hello.'

'Shite you were.' He pointed at the chair in front of his desk. 'Sit down.' He looked over McCoy's shoulder and bellowed out the open door, 'Tracey! Two teas!'

'How are you getting on?' asked McCoy innocently. 'Any news on the Kelly stuff?'

'Bugger all,' said Murray. 'He's disappeared into bloody thin air. Touts know nothing either. Whoever did it was keeping their cards close to their chests.'

'I hate to ask this,' said McCoy, 'but what about Wattie and Ronnie Elder?'

Murray shook his head. 'Not much to report there either. Inquiry into Elder's death is still going on. Wee birdie tells me Raeburn's telling them him and Wattie were in it together. Saying he had to hold Wattie back, kept punching the boy, shouting at him. Overeager young officer stepping out of line.'

'Christ,' said McCoy.

'Raeburn is fighting for his life, he's going to say anything he thinks makes him look better. It'll come down to who they believe: a two-year rookie or a twenty-year veteran.' He looked serious. 'I don't think the boy will come out of this unscathed.'

'But it wasn't him!' argued McCoy. 'It was Raeburn! He was the one—'

Murray held his hand up. 'I know that, and you know that, but a boy is dead. Dead in police custody. Blame has to be assigned and Raeburn is determined it's not all going to be on him.'

Tracey appeared with a tray and put it down on the desk. Murray thanked her. She stopped on the way out. 'Mr McCoy, nice to see you back,' she said.

'Thanks, Tracey. I'll come and say hello on the way out.'

He turned and Murray was looking at him, eyebrows raised.

'What?' said McCoy, then realised. 'Jesus, Murray, it's nothing like that. She's a smart girl, be good to see her get ahead, that's all.'

'Bloody better be,' said Murray, shoving a digestive into his mouth.

McCoy picked up his tea, sipped it. Rotten.

Seemed the Kelly case was safely parked. Now it was time to ask about the other one. He picked up a biscuit, tried to sound nonchalant. 'What about those robberies? How's that going?'

'It isn't,' said Murray. 'At least they seem to have ground to a halt. You know what it's like. First days of a case are the important ones, when the work really gets done. The robberies and Kelly happened when that clown Raeburn was at the helm. Think we're fucked before we even start.'

So far so good.

'Speaking of Raeburn, you seen him?' asked McCoy.

Murray shook his head. 'Still suspended. Spending his days in pubs, drinking in coppers' bars and telling anyone that listens how you ruined his life.' He reached for another digestive, munched it down. 'He's a vindictive bastard, Raeburn, so you watch yourself. Wouldn't put it past him to try something stupid.'

He drank over the last of his tea, licked his finger and picked up some biscuit crumbs from the plate. 'Now, if you're happy enough with my report, away you go and let me do some work. I'll see you in two days.'

McCoy stepped out of the office to see Tracey looking at him. She stood up. 'I'm away to the shop – anyone want anything?' she asked the office.

No response.

'Don't say I didn't ask,' she said and picked up her purse, headed for the door.

McCoy said goodbye to Wattie, said he'd see him on Tuesday, and followed her out.

Tracey was standing in the shadow of the awning of the newsagent's down the road, waiting for him. Smiled as she saw him walking towards her. 'You okay?' she asked. 'I heard you got hurt when they took Kelly.'

'A bump on the head. I'm fine. The doctor and Murray are conspiring to keep me off.'

'Lucky you. I could do with a few days off while the weather holds.'

She took out an envelope she'd slid down the back of her skirt and handed it to him.

'Flatmate gave me this. It's got the name of the fingerprints on the Coke can.'

She handed it to him.

He took it. Realised it was still sealed. 'You didn't have a look?'

She shook her head. 'Not my business. Better get back. Take care of yourself, eh?'

McCoy nodded. 'Thanks for this, Tracey.'

She smiled again. 'Just remember it when I ask you for a reference for the sergeants' exam.'

He watched her cross the street and disappear through the double doors of the station. Now that he had the result, he didn't really want to know it. Was only going to cause more trouble. Bobby March was dead. What did it matter now?

He slipped his finger under the flap and tore the envelope open, took out the folded paper inside and unfolded it. Read the name.

He was right. More trouble and he only had himself to blame.

He screwed up the paper and the envelope and dropped them in a bin attached to the bus stop. Started walking.

CHAPTER 42

He had the address written on a bit of paper, but it wasn't doing him much good. He was walking up and down London Road not finding what he was looking for.

'It's between the Braemar and the sweetie shop,' Billy Weir had told him. 'Cannae miss it. There's a card by the bell.'

So here he was, pacing between the Braemar and Glickman's, paper in hand. Was just about to give up when a guy walked out the Braemar, guitar case in his hand. McCoy ran over Charlotte Street, stopped him.

'All right, pal, you know a rehearsal place about here? Mason Studios?'

The man nodded, ran his hand through his long, long beard, shaping it. He pointed up past Glickman's. 'One six five. Need to keep ringing, though, they never bloody hear you.'

McCoy thanked him, cursed Billy Weir and his useless directions, and walked up to 165. Pressed the bell. Was surprised when it was opened immediately. Was even more surprised by who opened it.

The wee guy – the Bobby March fan he'd given money to – was standing there. Looked as surprised as he was.

'You the one that's been spray painting everywhere? McCoy asked.

'No,' he said too quickly. 'What you doing here?'

'Same as you,' said McCoy, stepping into the damp-smelling hallway. 'Waiting for Angela.'

'This way,' said the boy. 'You can wait with us.' He walked up the hall, opened a heavy door like the sort you get in a submarine, an instant noise of guitars. He stood aside to let McCoy in. The room was tiny, boiling hot, walls seemed to be lined with underfelt, floor was a mess of different worn carpets. Three other guys about the same age as the boy were leaning on a big speaker thing, reading an article in *Melody Maker*. Looked up in surprise.

'This guy—'

'McCoy,' said McCoy.

'McCoy,' he continued, 'is waiting for Angela too.'

One of the boys, lanky, hair to his waist, purple vest and cords, looked him up and down. 'You a manager, too?' he asked.

'Nope,' said McCoy. Couldn't think what else to say, so he said, 'You're a band, then?'

The lanky boy nodded. 'Holy Fire.'

'Are you the singer?' McCoy asked the spray paint boy.

He nodded. 'Jake Scott.'

They stood for a minute, neither of them quite sure what to do.

'If you want to rehearse, go ahead. I'll just stand over here,' said McCoy.

Jake nodded and McCoy lit up as they fiddled with the knobs on the guitars and the pedals on the floor, tuned up. A low hum started coming from the speakers. Jake held onto the mic. 'Ready? he asked.

The band seemed to be.

He leant into the mic. 'This is "Introducing Mr Crowley".' He nodded, the drummer counted them in, and they were off.

McCoy was prepared for the usual amateur rehash of whoever was popular that week. What he wasn't prepared for was what he heard. The band sounded tight as a drum, bit like the Spiders from Mars, but it was Jake who was the real surprise.

Looked nervous until he started to sing and then suddenly he was all swagger, twists and twirls. Voice sounded like a cross between Rod Stewart and someone he couldn't put his finger on, the guy from Free maybe? The song was great too, repeated squealing riff, stop-start drums and a soaring vocal over it all.

He felt the door open behind him and Angela stepped in, smiled at him, leant against the wall. The band powered through an instrumental middle eight, repeated the last chorus, a screaming ending from Jake, and then it was over.

'Good, aren't they?' said Angela.

'They really are,' said McCoy, trying not to sound too surprised.

Angela smiled. 'Sounding good, boys, but Ewan?' The drummer looked round from behind his cymbals. 'You were late coming in on the third chorus. Again. Thought you were going to practise?'

The drummer looked guilty. Mumbled something about having to do shifts, said he'd get it next time.

Angela nodded. Got a fiver out her pocket, handed it to Jake. 'Away you go and get some cans and some fish and chips. Be back in twenty minutes. Need to go through the whole set for tonight, okay? Think the blokes from London are going to be there, so make sure we are tight.'

The boys nodded, shuffled out one by one.

'Manager?' asked McCoy, looking at Angela. 'When did that happen?'

'When I saw Jake fronting a shitty band third on the bill at the Maryland. Been hard work to get them to this stage. Found the guitarist in some covers band, from Wishaw of all places.'

She stopped, looked at him. 'What are you grinning at?'

'You!' said McCoy. 'Mrs bloody showbiz.'

'Why not?' Angela asked.

'Couldn't agree more. You'll be a great manager. Know music inside out, good organiser, don't take any shit and the band are great.'

'Well, thanks for your approval,' said Angela.

'Where they playing tonight?' McCoy asked.

'Electric Garden. Supporting some shit band called The Mob. Just needed a gig.'

'Makes sense. Need to speak to you about something, that's why I'm here.'

'Sounds ominous,' said Angela.

He didn't say anything.

She looked at him. 'Christ, it must be. Fine, but let's get out of here. Whole place stinks of sweat and teenage boys.'

They ended up sitting on the grass on Glasgow Green. McCoy went over to the ice-cream van and came back with two cans of Coke. Handed one to Angela, sat down beside her.

'Uh-oh,' she said, opening the can. 'You've got that look on your face.'

'What look?' said McCoy.

'The "I'm sad that you've let me down again, Angela" look. Used to see it a lot when we were together.'

They watched as a toddler in a nappy escaped the clutches of his mum and started running, laughing all the way.

'So, what have I done now?' she asked.

Wasn't an easy way to say it, so he just came out with it. 'Bobby March,' said McCoy. 'Your fingerprints are on the syringe that killed him.'

Angela reached forward and picked up the packet of cigarettes and lighter she'd put down on the grass. Lit one.

'I told you already, McCoy. He was fine when I left. I didn't shoot him up.'

'I don't believe you,' said McCoy quietly.

'That was the trouble, McCoy, you never did. Even when I was telling the truth. Always thought you knew better.'

She sighed, took off her leather jacket and rolled the left sleeve of her blouse up, held out her arm. Turned it so he could see the inside of it. The inside that was covered in puncture marks and bruises.

'It was my works. I shot myself up, then left them for him to use. He had to leave his in America.'

She rolled her sleeve down, put her jacket back on. Looked out over the Green.

'That wee guy's off again,' she said, as the toddler made another bid for freedom.

McCoy looked at her. 'You want to tell me about it?' he asked.

She turned to him, smiled, wiped the tear running down her cheek. 'Not really,' she said

'Okay,' said McCoy. 'Up to you.'

'Fuck it!' She blew out a stream of smoke. 'It's hardly worth the telling. It's just the same sad stupid story as everyone else's. Ends with needle punctures in their arm.' She smiled. 'Was all fun until someone lost an eye. That not what they say? Well, I lost my eye around the same time as Stevie.'

'How?' asked McCoy. 'You've been around more drugs than I have . . .'

'Because I liked it.' She picked a blade of grass, started fiddling with it. 'When Ellie got together with Cooper, she didn't know anyone here so we started hanging out. I like her, has life about her and she liked smack.' She shrugged. 'So I ended up giving it a go. Saw what the attraction was and that was that. Once a week became twice a week became every day and then it wasn't that much fun any more.'

'She got you hooked?' asked McCoy.

Angela shook her head. Smiled. 'No, I managed to do that all by myself. She kept warning me. Said she was one of the rare people who could take it or leave it and that it wasn't like that for most people and I should be careful. Went in one ear and out the other.'

'What are you going to do?' asked McCoy.

She shrugged. 'She phoned last night. Apparently there's some place in Upstate New York, a farm with therapists, doctors, gets you off it. She wants me to go.'

'Are you?' asked McCoy.

'Don't know. It's expensive. Besides, I'm here. My job is here. That band are here. Might just have to wean myself off.'

'Not that easy when you're dealing it,' said McCoy.

'Nope. But nothing is, eh, Harry?' She stubbed out her cigarette in the grass. 'But you know me,' she said, 'not much holds me back.'

'This might, though. It's felled better men and women than you.'

She rolled her eyes. 'Always did believe in me, I'll say that for you.'

'I didn't mean it that way,' he said. 'I just meant it'll be difficult.'

She stood up. 'As is life, Harry, as is life. And just so we're clear, I really didn't shoot up Bobby March. I didn't care that much about him. Once I'd done my hit out his supply, I was out of there. Past it. Rock stars trying to feel me up aren't my idea of fun. I'll see you around.'

She walked back towards London Road. He watched her cross the road, disappear into the entrance of the rehearsal place. He lay back in the grass, looked up at the clouds.

Had no reason to disbelieve Angela and that made it all the more puzzling. If she didn't shoot up Bobby March, then who did? Had the feeling he wasn't ever going to find out. Wasn't too sure if he really cared any more either.

CHAPTER 43

Whatever McCoy had been expecting from his night out with Mila, it wasn't this. Wasn't even quite sure what this was. They were standing in a large room with windows over Blythswood Square watching a fat man in dungarees sitting on the floor playing the harmonium and singing some songs that sounded to McCoy like he was making them up on the spot. Two guitarists were sat either side, trying to play along, both looking equally puzzled.

He knew it was going to be something arty by the look of the crowd in the Scottish Arts Council building – half young hippies and half rich-looking middle-aged couples – but this was pushing it.

Apparently, the man they were watching was a famous poet, Allen Ginsberg, and they were supposed to be honoured by his presence. McCoy'd never heard of him – tried to look like he had when Mila told them where they were going. Now, to McCoy's horror, the musicians had been dismissed and he was reciting one of his poems.

Mila turned to him and smiled. He smiled back, tried to look interested.

She leant into his ear. 'You want to go, I think?' she said.

He nodded and they wove their way through the crowd and headed for the door. Outside, it was a beautiful summer night, still light at nine o'clock, heat had died down, was pleasant now.

'Mr Ginsberg not to your taste?' asked Mila.

'Not exactly. You like him?'

'A bit, but it gets too male for me, you know?' she said.

McCoy nodded, no real idea what she was talking about. Had been a bit off kilter all evening, wasn't sure if this was a date or just a thank you for Liam. She was hard to read, Mila, didn't give much away, and her broken English didn't help that much either.

'You fancy a drink?' he asked.

She nodded. Hit her hand off her forehead. 'I've left my bag in the cloakroom,' she said. 'Back in a minute.'

McCoy lit up and sat down on the steps, waiting for her to come back. Tried to think about what pub to go to, then inspiration struck. The Electric Garden. Holy Fire. And it was just round the corner. He heard the door opening behind him and stood up, turned to tell Mila they were going to see a band, but it wasn't Mila. It was Raeburn. And he didn't look good.

Didn't think he'd ever seen Raeburn not suited and booted, Brylcreem hair swept back. Not this time, though. He'd a pair of trousers that looked like he'd slept in them, an un-ironed shirt, five o'clock shadow and half his hair was hanging over his forehead. Stank of drink, too.

'What you doing here, Raeburn?' McCoy asked, then it struck him. 'Are you following me?'

'Need to speak to you,' he said.

'Need to be quick then,' said McCoy. 'I'm waiting for someone.'

Raeburn nodded. 'Saw her. A wee blonde bird. Tasty.'

'Fuck off, Raeburn. What do you want?'

'I need you to talk to your wee pal,' he said.

'Who? Wattie?' asked McCoy.

He nodded. 'Need you to persuade him to tell the inquiry that he came down heavy on Elder, knocked him around, got out of control. Him, not me.'

'Why the fuck would I want to do that?' asked McCoy.

Raeburn was looking up and down the square. 'Want to go for a drink?'

'No,' said McCoy.

Raeburn sighed, got a half-full bottle of Bell's out his trouser pocket, unscrewed the cap, slugged down a good mouthful. Held it out to McCoy. He shook his head and another mouthful went down Raeburn's gullet.

'I'm twenty-three years in. Wife and three kids. If they do me, I lose everything. The pension'll go. I'll be sacked or demoted to bloody traffic duty. I can't afford for that to happen. Wattie's

366

young, inexperienced, he made a mistake. He'll get a warning, a suspension maybe, he's got nobody to support, he'll get by.'

McCoy shook his head. 'You don't get it, do you, Raeburn? A boy killed himself because of you. An innocent boy that you scared the shit out of and bullied and took great pleasure in doing it. That's different from looking the other way when a landlord puts a twenty in your pocket or when you get a few free drinks and fucks at the shebeen because you're a cop.'

'McCoy, don't be a bastard, just tell him to—'

'I'm no telling him anything but to tell the truth.'

Raeburn stared at him, took another swig of the bottle. Eyes narrowed. 'Don't know why I even asked. Should have known better. You always did have it in for me, McCoy. Ever since Eastern, when you used to turn your nose up at the Friday backhanders. Holier than thou, you were. Better than anyone else. Bet you were waiting for this to happen, rubbing your bloody hands together, running back to Murray to tell him what a bad polis I am and try and get your nose as far up his arse as you can.'

'Finished?' said McCoy.

'I've just started,' said Raeburn, stepping forward. 'This has been coming a long time, McCoy, so you watch yourself. Next time you're in trouble and look round for a hand it won't be there. I'll make sure of that. I'll make sure that every polis in this city knows what a pair of backstabbing bastards you and Watson are.'

'You need to fuck off, Raeburn,' said McCoy. 'Before I start taking your shite personally.'

'Too late,' said Raeburn. 'I've taken your shite personally, really personally. If it wasn't for you, I wouldn't be in this mess. You sniping about behind my back while I was trying to run a station, telling tales, watching me, reporting back . . .'

'You're wrong, Raeburn. You're mad if you think I was wasting my time spying on you. I don't care that much about you, never have, you're just another shite cop on the take and in over his head. Wasn't me that stopped you running that station, it was you and the stupid bloody things you did. Leave me out of it.'

Raeburn smiled at him, took another slug from his bottle. 'Oh, but I can't leave you out of it, McCoy, because it's your fault, and you're going to pay for that. Unless you persuade Watson, I'm going to come after you. Because I'll have nothing to lose, will I? May as well be hung for a pound than a penny.'

He moved into McCoy, the stink of whisky on his breath. 'Get Watson to change his mind or watch your back. The choice is yours, McCoy. The choice is yours.'

McCoy watched him walk down the pavement towards West Regent Street. He'd been right. He was a trapped rat. A very dangerous trapped rat indeed.

'Got it!'

He turned and Mila was standing there, holding up her bag.

'Where are we off to?' she asked.

McCoy paid for two tickets and they went in. Almost wished they hadn't bothered. The Electric Garden was pretty much empty. Obviously The Mob's career was on a downturn. There was something depressing about empty venues, McCoy always thought. Without the people filling them up, you could see what they were really like. The sticky floor, the peeling wallpaper, the mirrorball missing half its tiles. Apart from him and Mila, there were about thirty people there. Most looked like friends and family of The Mob. Ten or so younger glam rock-looking kids who were maybe there for Holy Fire.

They got some drinks and sat down at a table near the back. McCoy could see Angela hurrying about, looking busy, talking to the guy working the lights, ushering two guys with London accents to a table near the front, setting them up with drinks and a wee wrap dropped into one of their jacket pockets.

Mila seemed happy enough, though, was wandering around taking photos, talking to people, getting them to pose or just to let her photograph them. McCoy sipped his pint and thought about Raeburn. Wasn't much he could do about him. Wattie was going to tell the truth and chances were Raeburn was right, that was him fucked. Wasn't quite sure why Raeburn was so determined to blame all his troubles on him, supposed it was easier to blame someone else rather than admitting you'd got yourself in the shit by your own doing.

Mila appeared back, sat down. 'You sure this band is good?' she asked, grinning.

'Sure,' he said. 'Years from now you'll be boasting you were here.'

She looked around the miserable venue. Didn't look like she believed him. 'If you say so.'

Angela looked up from the two guys and he waved. She stood up and came over. 'You came,' she said. 'Thanks for making up the numbers, and remember, clap loud when they come on, okay?'

McCoy nodded. 'Angela, Mila. Mila, Angela.'

Angela nodded at Mila. 'Nice to meet you.' A squeal of feedback and she winced. 'Better go,' she said and hurried off towards the stage. Turned and came back. 'Harry, you look after yourself, eh?'

He nodded, slightly puzzled, and she walked back to the stage.

'You used to sleep with her, I think,' said Mila.

'I did,' said McCoy.

'I could tell. The way you looked at each other.' McCoy nodded.

'And now you want to sleep with me,' she said.

He almost spat out his pint. 'I wouldn't put it like that!' he said.

She grinned. 'Why not? It's true, isn't it?'

'Yes,' he said.

'Good. Me too.'

A rumble and the lights went down. Band made their way onstage. Started in darkness, Jake reciting through the distorted mike.

'And lo, a Holy Fire came upon the land and cleansed it. Burning the unbelievers, leaving them in ashes in its wake. And those that survived came together in a joyous celebration, a dance of joy, a dance of sex, a dance of now.'

And then the spotlight hit him and he grinned. Silver make-up on his eyes. 'Hit it,' he said. And they did.

A guitar like a motorbike starting, pounding drums, Jake singing for his life. Mila turned to him and grinned, held her thumb up. Couldn't do much more over the deafening noise. She edged closer, put her hand on his thigh.

By the end of the third number, it was on his crotch.

McCoy leant into her. 'We need to go,' he said. 'Or I'm not going to be able to stand up in a minute.'

13th July 1973

Room 514, Royal Stuart Hotel

He thought it was the woman coming back – Annie? Angie? – when he heard the knocking. Must have changed her mind. He made his way to the door, still felt a bit woozy. Coke and mandies – not the best combination, but he was in that kind of mood. Hated coming back to Glasgow, just wanted to be somewhere else, to feel nothing.

He walked through to the hall, bumping off the walls, and saw his bag lying on the floor. He picked it up, weight was all wrong. He knew already, but he looked anyway. All that was in it was a blue jotter, a pen, some receipts. No tape. He sank onto the floor. Knew it was pointless but he did it anyway: looked in the bag again, and again, but it still wasn't there. She must have taken it. Sudden thought. A ray of hope. Maybe that was her back, going to return it.

He got himself up, opened the door. Found himself looking at a teenage boy, one of the group that had been camping outside. He seemed terrified, had a Bobby March T-shirt on, looked like he'd made it himself, half the glitter had fallen off.

'You're not her,' he said.

The boy looked at him blankly. 'Sorry,' he said, 'I just wanted to talk to you, sneaked up the fire exit stairs. I think you're the best—'

Bobby stopped him, walked back through to the living-room area, sat down on the couch. The tape was gone. Day two of the Rolling Stones audition. The only copy. His get out of jail card. The thing that was going to make people realise how great a guitarist he was again. This album was fucked. He knew it. The record company knew it, everyone knew it. Needed something to make up for it.

He searched amongst the mess on the coffee table for a cigarette, found a packet with a couple in it. Lit up.

He was going to ride this album out, then get the tape released. Get a new deal. Start again. Not any more. He put his head in his hands. Wished he'd never come back to Glasgow. Was still his father's city. Still the place he had to escape from. The man he had to escape from.

He looked up and the boy was standing there. He had almost forgotten him.

'What's your name, son?' he asked.

'Jake,' said the boy.

'Well, Jake, now that you're here, maybe you can make yourself useful. I'm too fucked to do it myself. Be a good story to tell your pals.'

The boy nodded. 'What do you want me to do?'

Bobby smiled to himself, remembered him and Kit Lambert. So naive, he'd asked the same question. Different answer this time.

'What I want you to do is find a blue washing bag in the toilet somewhere. I've probably tried to hide it.'

The boy nodded, disappeared.

Kit Lambert. Hadn't thought of him for ages. Despite it all, he'd liked him. Had life about him, an energy. He dropped the cigarette on the floor, cursed, picked it up. Was more out of it than he thought.

'This it?'

March looked up, nodded. 'Now, Jake, you need to listen to me carefully, eh? Do exactly what I say. That okay?'

The boy nodded enthusiastically.

He talked him through it.

Put the powder in the spoon.

Put a teaspoon of water in with it.

Hold the lighter under it until it bubbles.

Put half a cigarette filter in it.

Put the needle in, suck it up into the syringe.

Tie the rubber tube round the top of my arm.

Wait for a vein.

'You sure you can do this?' he asked.

The boy nodded, syringe in hand. Looked like there was a lot in it, wasn't sure, vision was a bit fuzzy. Didn't care. All he wanted was to be somewhere else, somewhere safe with no Glasgow, no Dad, no lost tape.

'Okay.' He held out his arm. 'Stick it into a vein.'

The boy nodded, leant over him, pushed the needle in.

'Not too hard! Jesus!'

'Sorry,' said the boy, looking mortified.

'It's okay, we're okay now. Okay, now push the plunger down, slowly!'

The boy nodded, slowly pushed the plastic stopper down.

Felt it hit almost immediately, smiled to himself, decent stuff. Not what you'd expect in Glasgow. Heard the boy say 'That okay?' He tried to nod but his head felt too heavy. He lay back on the couch as the warmth spread through his body. Thought about that day in Sunset Sound, 'Sunday Morning Symphony', how he'd nailed it in one. Those were good days, days when he thought everything was going to go his way. That it would alw —

21ST JULY 1973

CHAPTER 44

He woke up, stretched his arm out to the other side of the bed, but she wasn't there. He sat up, blinking at the morning light coming through the gap in the bedroom curtains.

'Morning,' said Mila. She was sitting on the chair at the end of the bed, camera pointed at him. She clicked the shutter a few times.

'You're dressed,' he said.

'I am. I said I'd meet Liam at ten in town.'

McCoy shook his head. 'You're telling me you'd rather wander around the shiteholes of Glasgow with that big waster than come back to bed with me?'

'Yep,' she said. 'And I'm late.'

She came over, kissed him.

'McCoy, I don't want you to think that this is more than it is.'

'What? You're telling me that I'm just another notch in your bedpost?' he said.

She smiled. 'Precisely.'

'Don't worry. I'll get over it.'

She kissed him again. 'Ciao!'

He lay back in the bed, listened to her footsteps, then the door slamming. That was him told.

McCoy spent the rest of the morning doing all the stuff he never did. The laundry, tidying up, buying lightbulbs at Woolworths. Had quite enjoyed it, pottering about, not worrying about work for a change. He was coming back from Galbraith's, two bags of messages in his hands, when he noticed it. The weather was changing. Had been stuffy all morning – still, heavy air – and now there were black clouds gathering in the distance over the hills. Looked like the heatwave might be about to break.

He'd just finished his Heinz tomato soup when there was a knock on the door. For a second he thought it might be Raeburn, but no way was he going to knock so politely. He opened the front door and Jumbo was standing there.

'Mr Cooper would like to see you,' he said.

Jumbo seemed to have acquired a new set of duds. A light-blue shirt, new jeans, white sandshoes.

'Looking very spiffy,' said McCoy.

Jumbo looked embarrassed. 'Billy bought them for me, said I needed to stop looking like someone's mental wee brother.'

'Well, thought that counts, eh?' said McCoy. 'Give us a minute.'

They walked up the hill and over into Hyndland Road, heading for Cooper's.

Jumbo looked up at the sky. 'Storm coming,' he said.

McCoy nodded. 'You slash that Wee Tam lad, Jumbo?' he asked.

Jumbo looked flustered. 'Billy said I had to, need to start earning my keep, he said.'

'And how'd you feel about that?' asked McCoy.

'I didn't like it,' he said. 'I didn't want to do it.'

'He's right, though, Jumbo. That's the business they're in, it's not nice.'

Was obvious Jumbo didn't want to talk about it. Walked on in silence for a few minutes.

'I've been doing the garden,' he said. 'I like that.'

'So I hear. Good at it, too.'

'Angela told me I could get a job with the council, in the Parks. Do you think that's right?' asked Jumbo.

'I'm not sure, Jumbo. You'd need to apply, fill out a form. Maybe have an interview. Don't think you'd need exams, but you never know.'

'What would Mr Cooper say?' he asked. 'Would he be angry?'

McCoy didn't answer him. Far as he knew, no one left Cooper voluntarily. He took that sort of thing as an insult, had an idea he wouldn't be happy if Jumbo tried it.

'Tell you what, the summer's almost over, Jumbo. Why don't we leave it until next spring? That's when they'll really be wanting people, when all the planting goes on. And it'll give you a chance to get better at your reading and writing, eh?'

Jumbo nodded. Seemed happy enough with that idea. They turned into Hamilton Park Road. If

Jumbo made it to spring in one piece and out of jail, McCoy swore to himself he'd talk to Cooper, make it all right. The least he could do. Jumbo got a key out his pocket, carefully placed it in the lock, tongue out, opened the big front door.

McCoy walked through the house: seemed a bit empty and quiet now, no moaning Iris to fill it up.

'Don't think you'll be sitting out here much longer,' said McCoy, walking into the garden.

Cooper was sitting at the table, ashtray and a brown envelope in front of him. He looked up. 'Eh?'

McCoy pointed up to the sky. Grey clouds sitting low in the sky.

'Oh, right. Sit down,' said Cooper. He was back to the usual look, short-sleeve shirt, denims, hair in a James Dean-style quiff.

'What's up with you?' asked McCoy, pulling out a chair and sitting down. 'You've got a face like a wet Wednesday.'

'Angela's gone,' said Cooper.

'She's what?' asked McCoy. 'I saw her last night.'

'Aye well, she's gone now. Vamoosed. Disappeared. Fucked off. And she's taken fifteen fucking grand of my money with her.'

McCoy tried to take it in. 'She's what?' he asked. 'Gone where?'

'America, I think,' said Cooper. 'She's with that cow Ellie, no doubt.'

'You sure,' asked McCoy. 'It doesn't seem like—'

Cooper slammed his fist on the table. 'Of course I'm sure. Left me a nice wee note telling me, and telling me not to try and find her because if I did, these' – he pushed the brown envelope towards McCoy – 'would be going to half the bloody bosses in Glasgow.'

McCoy picked up the envelope, opened it. Took out two eight by ten photographs. One of Cooper shooting up and one of him passed out on the bed. The photos Ally had developed. The photos he said he'd no copies of.

'Fuck,' he said.

'Fuck is right,' said Cooper. 'She's fucked me right over.'

McCoy picked up Cooper's packet of Embassy. Lit up. 'I didn't think she had it in her.'

'Didn't you? You lived with her, had a kid with her. Love is blind, eh?'

'Did you?' asked McCoy.

'Yep,' said Cooper. 'That's why I employed her. Better her pissing out that pissing in. Didn't think she'd do this, though.'

'Would she leave Glasgow, burn her bridges, all for fifteen grand? I know I shouldn't be saying this, but is it worth it for that?' asked McCoy.

'She say anything to you?' asked Cooper.

'Me?' said McCoy. 'No! Come on, Stevie.'

Decided to leave the story about the expensive place in New York out of it.

'Can you afford to lose it?' he asked. 'The money, I mean?'

Cooper shook his head. 'I'm doing well, but not that well. She's cleared most of me out.'

'What are you going to do?'

He shrugged. 'I can always make more money. I can't fix my reputation if these photos get out. Just have to do what she says. Leave her alone. And wait, bide my time. No fucking way she's getting away scot-free.' He looked straight at McCoy. 'No matter how long it takes, I'm going to get her,' he said. 'No one does something like this to me and gets away with it.'

McCoy had no reason to disbelieve him. Only hoped Angela was safely on a jumbo jet, miles away from the reach of Stevie Cooper.

He left him there, brooding, and walked back through the house. Said goodbye to Jumbo, head deep in his *Broons* annual, and walked up the path. Just as he shut the gate behind him a green Daimler turned into the road, pulled up outside Cooper's. The passenger door opened and William Norton stepped out. Blazer, slacks and shiny shoes as usual.

He looked up at the sky. 'Looks like this fine weather is going to break,' he said. Turned to McCoy. 'Thought you'd still be making your way out that bloody field.'

'Nope,' said McCoy. 'Back here. No thanks to you.'

A young guy, looked like a heavyweight boxer, stepped out the driver seat. 'Everything okay, Mr Norton?'

'Fine, Jackie,' he said. 'Away for a birl in the motor, twenty minutes.'

The guy stepped back into the car, drove off.

'That the new one, is it?' asked McCoy. 'Didn't take long. You got a production line somewhere?'

Norton smiled. 'Lots of young lads desperate to join my organisation, get ahead in life.'

'Well, let's just hope that this one isn't a nonce, eh?' said McCoy.

The smile disappeared from Norton's face.

'Don't worry,' said McCoy. 'I don't go back on my promises. What are you doing here anyway?'

'Didn't realise you were Cooper's gatekeeper,' he said. 'Mind you, dirty cops seem to get everywhere.'

'Just for the record, I'm not his gatekeeper and I'm not dirty. I'll ask you again: what are you doing here?'

Norton moved into McCoy, pushed his face into his. 'That's my business, son. Now get out of the way before I decide to take offence.'

McCoy stood for a couple of seconds, both of them eye to eye, then he stepped aside, let Norton up the garden path.

He walked down the street, heading for Great Western Road. Whatever it was Norton and Cooper were cooking up, he didn't want to know.

CHAPTER 45

'Lucky you're still signed off,' Murray growled, staring at McCoy, or more accurately McCoy's outfit.

'What's up?' McCoy looked down at his clothes. 'No like it?'

'No, I bloody don't. A man your age shouldn't be wearing bloody denim jeans,' said Murray.

McCoy sat down. 'I'm thirty, Murray, no bloody fifty. Give us a break.'

Murray sat back in his chair. 'Still too old for jeans, you're not a bloody teenager. Anyway, to what do I owe this early visit?'

'You know me,' said McCoy. 'Couldn't keep away. You seen Raeburn?'

Murray shook his head. 'The clown's suspended. Why would I?'

'He's been following me around, talking shite, threatening all sorts.'

Murray looked exasperated. 'Christ, if that man's not in enough of a hole. Does he not know?'

'Oh, he knows all right. That's why he's doing it. Thinks he's going to get bounced out, no pension.'

Murray looked down at his papers, rearranged them.

'That's what's going to happen, isn't it?' asked McCoy.

No response.

'Murray?'

Murray started the search for his pipe. 'Not exactly.'

'So what exactly?' asked McCoy, beginning to suspect. 'What's going to happen to him?'

Murray found the pipe under a copy of *The Herald*. Started going at the bowl with a penknife, old tobacco falling into the ashtray. 'There are certain people who don't want Raeburn treated too harshly.'

'His bloody Masonic mates?' asked McCoy.

Murray nodded. 'He's pulling in every favour he can. And unfortunately I think it's going to work.'

'For fuck sake, Murray! He hounded a sixteen-year-old boy to his death. That not count for anything? Charged him with murder while the girl was still alive. If he hadn't done that, the boy'd still be here today.'

'Watch it, McCoy. Remember who I bloody am.'

McCoy nodded, just wanted to hear how lightly Raeburn was going to be treated.

'Now, before you start shouting, this isn't me talking. Right?'

McCoy just looked at him. Couldn't bring himself to answer.

'Right?' asked Murray.

McCoy nodded again.

'Raeburn is twenty-three years in. Has friends in high places in the force and the lodge – and before you start, that isn't always the same thing – who don't care that much that a nonce hanged himself in the cells. One less of them on the streets, that's how they look at it. Raeburn didn't cover himself in glory in the investigation, but it was a difficult case on inexperienced shoulders. He did his best and they don't think that one mistake in a long career is enough to send him to the lions. So they won't.'

'Does he know?' asked McCoy wearily.

'He will do tomorrow,' said Murray. 'He'll be suspended without pay for a month or so, told to keep his head down, retire the minute he can.'

'With a full pension?' asked McCoy.

Murray nodded.

'And what about Wattie?' asked McCoy. 'What happens to him?'

'A slap on the wrist. Written warning. Nothing to worry about.'

Murray sat back, waited for McCoy to explode. 'Go on, say your bit, get it out your system.'

He didn't. He just shrugged, looked past Murray at his framed citations on the wall, his awards, the picture of him and the Queen at the Garden Party. The framed back page of a newspaper with a younger Murray holding up a cup: 'HAWICK TAKE TITLE!'

'Why do you want me to care when no one else does? What's the point?' he asked.

'Come on, McCoy, you can't take it personally.'

'Can't I? Why not? You going to tell his maw that? Sorry, love, we killed your boy but don't take it personally. It's just that one of our boys got out of hand, not going to do anything about it, though, because, you know what? He's in the Super's lodge, drinks in the same pubs as us. He's one of our own.'

'Come on, McCoy, that's not—'

McCoy shook his head and Murray fell silent. 'I'm not going to make you feel better because I rant and rave. You're as responsible for this as they are, Murray. Look at all that stuff on the wall behind you. You can't have it both ways. You know what's happening and you're going to wring your hands for a day or two and then, you know what? You're going to do fuck all about it. That boy's blood is on your hands as much as it's on Raeburn's. Don't use me to wash it off.'

'You listen to me, Detective—'

'No,' said McCoy quietly. 'Not this time. I'm done listening to you. I just don't have the fight in me any more.' He smiled. 'Looks like the City of Glasgow Police have finally managed to knock it out of me.'

He stood up and walked out of the office.

'McCoy!' shouted Murray. 'You get back in here now!'

He didn't turn around.

CHAPTER 46

His hands had stopped shaking after the second pint. He ordered another one, tried to work out if he'd just resigned from his job. Trouble was he didn't much care if he had. Far as he was concerned the one man he trusted had crossed the line. And if he'd crossed the line, then the battle was lost. May as well just give up. If Murray had crossed the line, then soon enough the police would just be all Raeburns. Ignorant arseholes, chucking their weight about, lining their own pockets, bending the law whichever way suited them. And if that was the case he didn't want to be part of it.

Ronnie Elder was just another nonce, so why bother? Not worth a jot compared to the fine Raeburn. He could hear them now, all those bastards in the lodge deciding what was right and what was wrong. He was fed up fighting them. He'd given it his best shot but – what was it they said? – 'You can't fight City Hall.' The ones in power will always win in the end. Even if that included washing their hands of poor, dumb Ronnie Elder. Could still see the boy's face – blue, swollen, dead.

He swallowed over the rest of his pint, decided it was time to go. Two pints in the Eskimo was as much as he could stand, the last place he wanted to be was a polis pub. Was time to head for the Victoria, sit in the corner, drink himself to sleep or not caring, whatever came first. He'd just stood up when the pub door opened and Wattie was standing there, big grin on his face, packet of cigars in his hand.

He saw McCoy, hurried over. Handed him a cigar. 'Guess what?' he shouted, and half the pub turned to look at him, grin was so broad it looked like it was about to split his face.

'You're going to be a daddy,' said McCoy, smiling despite himself.

Wattie grabbed him, hugged him, started jumping up and down. Wouldn't let McCoy go. Suddenly all the punters in the pub were smiling, couple at the back shouted, 'Congratulations!'

'Can you believe it?' he asked. 'Me, a dad?'

McCoy managed to extricate himself, slapped him on the back. 'Congratulations. Can't think of a better man to be somebody's dad.'

Wattie looked at him, a bit tearful suddenly. 'Do you mean that?' he asked. 'That's the nicest thing anyone has ever said to me.'

'Course I don't,' said McCoy, grinning. 'Just thought I better say something nice. Now have a seat and calm the fuck down and I'll get you a drink.'

McCoy walked over to the bar, ordered the

drinks. The last thing he needed was a jolly chat and drink with Wattie, but he was going to do it if it killed him. The boy deserved it, deserved to celebrate without McCoy's mood hanging over him like a wet weekend. The barman gave him two pints and two whiskies on the house and McCoy carried the drinks back, set them down on the table.

Wattie looked a bit dazed. 'I still can't believe it. Nearly bloody fell over when she told me.'

'Who?' asked McCoy.

'Mary, who else . . .' Realised. 'Very funny, McCoy. Very funny. Need to ask you something. We had a chat, Mary and me.'

'Oh aye, sounds worrying.'

'Will you be the godfather?' he asked.

Now it was McCoy's turn to feel a bit tearful. Disguised it by trying to light up one of the cigars. Coughed as he inhaled, tried to recover. 'I'd be honoured,' he said. 'Thank you. Thank you very much.'

Wattie beamed, took another packet of cigars out his pocket and started handing them round the pub.

McCoy sank his whisky, had another go at the cigar, coughed some more, then gave up. 'Enough of this nicey-nicey pish,' he said. 'Drink up and let's go somewhere that isn't this shithole. Get pissed, properly pissed.'

Wattie went for a pee and McCoy walked towards the door, thought he heard a rumble of thunder outside. He went to pull the handle and the door almost opened in his face. He stepped back and Big Tam was standing there, dark circles under his eyes, the stink of stale alcohol and sweat coming off him.

'You all right, Tam?' McCoy asked.

Tam didn't even pretend, just shook his head and stood there looking like a whipped dog. 'Bloke on the desk said you might be here,' he said

Wattie appeared beside them, buttoning up his flies.

Tam looked over at him nervously. 'Can I have a word with you in private, Harry?' he asked quietly.

McCoy wasn't in the mood for accommodating Tam, not by a long shot. 'Anything you've got to say, you can say it to Wattie as well. Up to you.'

Tam looked at him, nodded.

They walked back to the table and what was left of their drinks. McCoy pulled out a chair for him and Tam sat down wearily.

'Looks like we're staying. I'll go to the bar,' said Wattie.

'What's the matter, Tam?' asked McCoy. 'What d'you want to see me for?'

Had a feeling that whatever Tam was about to say he didn't want to hear it. Someone had put money in the jukebox. Frank Sinatra came on. 'New York, New York'.

'It's Wee Tam,' he said, staring at the floor. 'I think he's going to do himself in.'

McCoy sat back in his chair. Wasn't what he'd expected to hear. 'And what makes you think that?' he asked.

Tam took a half bottle of Laing's out his jacket and took a slug. He put the cap back on, slowly twisting it round.

'May made it up,' he said quietly. 'She lied. She wasn't with him on the day the girl got beat up. Wasn't with him when that Page boy got done.'

'Don't tell me you're only realising that now, Tam? For fuck sake!'

Tam was shaking his head. Looked up at him. 'I swear, Harry, on my life, I didn't know, I didn't fucking know. I believed her.'

McCoy looked at him. Realised he was probably telling the truth. May had always been the boss. Had always made his decisions for him, told him what to do, what was what.

McCoy sighed. As if his day hadn't been bad enough.

'Just start at the beginning, Tam,' he said. 'Just tell me why you think he's going to do himself in.'

Wattie appeared with three pints, put them down. Tam slugged down half of his, looked at McCoy nervously. 'He's no been home for a few days. May's been going up the wall, sending me out to look for him. She got a message this after-noon to go and meet him in a cafe. He told her he wanted to see her to say goodbye.'

'Look, he's not had an easy time this past couple of days,' said McCoy. 'I probably didn't help either. Maybe he just wants a change of scene, getting the train down to London, something like that.'

Tam shook his head. 'He told her he was finished here, said it was over. Wanted to see her one last time.'

'You sure he was serious, not just looking for sympathy?'

He shook his head. 'May said she'd never seen him so serious, she was terrified, sent me to find you. She was too scared to come herself, says she knows what he's done is wrong but she just wants him found before he can do something to himself.'

'Very charitable of her,' said McCoy. 'Pity she didn't extend the same courtesy to the girl he battered.'

Tam looked at him with tears in his eyes. 'Please, Harry. I'm begging you. Help me find him before he does it. No matter what he's done, he's still my son.' He wiped at his cheeks. 'He's no well, it's no his fault.'

'Let's make one thing clear, Tam. I'm going to help you find the wee shite, not because I care if he tops himself or if May dies of a broken heart. I'm going find him because he's guilty of killing Alec Page and Donny MacRae—'

'You saying Wee Tam killed Donny MacRae?' Tam looked surprised. 'I don't think so, McCoy.'

'Well, he did. May no tell you about that one? Would you have come running here if she had?'

Tam was sobbing now, wiping his eyes with the sleeve of his shirt. 'I didn't know, I didn't know . . .'

'Aye well, you do now, and I'm going to make sure May gets done as well. Accessory to murder, whatever I can get the evil cow on.'

'Harry,' Wattie said, 'calm it, come on.'

Tam got his bottle out his pocket with his shaky hands and took a swig.

Before McCoy could stop himself he'd knocked the bottle out Tam's hand. It smashed off the wall of the pub, glass flying everywhere, stink of gut-rot whisky filling the air.

'You need to fucking sober up and stop feeling so sorry for yourself if we're going to find him. You hear me?'

Tam nodded, tried to get himself together.

'Where did May last see him?' McCoy asked.

'In the cafe this afternoon,' he said.

'What cafe was it?' asked Wattie.

Tam thought for a minute. 'Benassi's she said it was.'

'Where's that?' asked Wattie.

'Great Western Road, just across from—' McCoy stopped. As soon as he'd said it he'd realised why Wee Tam had picked that cafe. 'From Cooper's house.'

McCoy looked over at Wattie. 'He's not going to kill himself at all. He's going after Laura.'

CHAPTER 47

McCoy was right. He had heard thunder. The weather finally broke as they came out of the pub. Another distant rumble and then the heavy clouds above them burst. The rain was sudden and total, pounding down like a monsoon. They started running, made it to the car just before they got totally soaked.

'Christ,' said Wattie, wiping the rain off his face and turning the key. 'All we fucking need.'

They turned off Stewart Street, windscreen wipers at full tilt, heading for Hamilton Park Street.

'Why are you so sure he's after Laura?' asked Wattie.

'He's had a go at her before,' said McCoy. 'Kicked her around a bit. He's got a thing about her.' He sat forward and rubbed at the condensation on the windscreen. 'And besides, what else is the wee bastard going to be doing hanging around Cooper's?'

What he didn't say was the feeling it was his fault. He'd threatened Wee Tam, told him what Laura knew. Maybe in trying to warn him off he'd really just pushed him into a corner, made him think he had to shut Laura up once and for all.

Nothing he could do about it now but find her and find her quick.

Wattie turned the car into Great Western Road and they fell in behind an old Albion Van.

'Can you no go any faster?' asked McCoy.

'Not if you want to get there in one piece,' said Wattie, sounding exasperated. 'You should try driving in this, it's bloody murder. Cannae see two feet in front of my face.'

Another clap of thunder and a sudden flash of light illuminated the inside of the car.

'And it's getting bloody nearer,' said Wattie. 'God help us.'

Two minutes later they turned into Hamilton Park Road, the car skidding to a halt outside Cooper's house. McCoy opened the car door and stepped out into the downpour, ran for the door. He hammered on it, heard Billy say 'Hang on' and the door opened.

'Christ, McCoy, what is this weather like. I thought—'

'Is Laura here?' he asked urgently.

Billy shook his head. 'Gone with Iris to her sister's. Left a couple of hours ago.'

'Fuck! If she comes back, you keep her in here, Billy. Hear me? Don't let her out of your sight.'

Billy nodded. 'What's going on, McCoy?' But he was already talking to his back; McCoy was running to the car, pulling the door open and getting in.

'We need to get up to Haghill,' he said to Wattie. 'Now!'

Wattie turned the car, bumped it up on the opposite pavement and headed back up the road.

'Can we radio in, get a couple of uniforms up there?' asked McCoy.

Wattie shook his head. 'The radio's kaput. I just tried it. Think the weather's taken the whole system down.' He turned to McCoy. 'Where is it we're going exactly?'

'Kennyhill Square, just off Alexandra Parade.'

Wattie nodded, started speeding down Great Western Road towards town. The road was running with water, overflow pipes gushing streams of it off the side of the tenements. Everyone that had been out in the street was sheltering in doorways, looking up at the sky. Really was biblical. McCoy'd only been out the car two minutes but was complete soaked, could feel his shirt and jeans clinging to him.

'Ten minutes at the most,' said Wattie. 'As long as we don't crash, that is.'

It took less. Wattie gunned the car the whole way, skidding and sliding on the wet roads. He turned in Kennyhill Square, pulled in behind a butcher's van and they ran for the close. Tulip lived in number 5, up on the top floor. They could hear the noise of an accordion and people dancing as they started climbing the stairs. Wattie knocked as McCoy put hands on his knees, tried to get his breath back, water dripping off them both, staining the stone floor like blood.

Tulip pulled the door open; she was a little woman, always neat and tidy. She wasn't tonight, though; she'd obviously had a drink and a couple of turns on the floor. Her face was bright red, hair all undone, heat coming off her in waves.

'Harry!' she exclaimed. 'I wasnae expecting you! Come in, son, come in.' She flapped the front door back and forward, trying to get some air into the house. 'It's like a bloody oven in here. This rain couldnae come soon enough. I said to Aidan it's about time that—'

'Iris here?' McCoy interrupted.

'No,' she said. 'She phoned from a pub, said they were on their way, her and that wee lassie Laura. Joined at the hip these days, they two. They havenae turned up yet. Maybe they cannae get a cab in this weather.'

McCoy looked at Wattie. It wasn't what either of them wanted to hear. Tulip must have seen it on their faces.

'What's up with you two?' she asked.

'Anybody been up here looking for them, Tulip?' asked McCoy. 'Anyone hanging about?'

She shook her head; she was starting to look worried. 'No. Nobody. Why?'

'Probably nothing,' he said, trying to smile.

A door in the hall opened behind her and an old man with a tartan bunnet stuck on his head looked round. 'Tulip! Wee Benny's looking for you, says you'd sausage rolls.'

She looked at them. 'Are you coming in?'

McCoy nodded, couldn't think what else to do. Needed time to think. And a drink. He walked through the hall, past all the pictures of the Queen, into the living room, Wattie trailing behind, looking at the pictures in surprise.

'Born the same day,' said Tulip. 'Always loved her.'

Tulip was right about the living room; it was boiling. There were about twenty people in there; few kids running round daft, record player going, glasses and dishes of nuts and crisps dotted about everywhere.

Everyone nodded hello. Wee Benny shouted, 'Look at the two drowned rats!' and everybody laughed. McCoy took the whisky he was offered, found an empty space next to a display cabinet full of plates and crockery with the Queen on them.

'What are we doing here, Harry?' asked Wattie, sliding in beside him. 'They're no here.'

'I know,' said McCoy. 'I'm just trying to think. Have you got any better ideas?'

Wattie shook his head. 'No, but I don't think standing here getting pissed is going to help.'

It was a fair point. McCoy knocked back the whisky, put his glass down on top of the display cabinet. 'Do you want to trace their route, see if they're standing somewhere trying to get a cab?'

Wattie nodded. 'It's better than nothing.'

McCoy looked round, trying to find Tulip to say cheerio. She was on the other side of the room now, standing by the windows. She'd a fan out with pictures of flamenco dancers on it, was waving it in front of her face. McCoy edged his way through the crowd towards her. Normally you could see all the way across Alexandra Park from Tulip's living room. Not today. Was hard to see anything through the driving rain streaming down the windows. Was why Tulip had bought the flat, she always said. Loved the view of the park and the trees.

McCoy took a look out. Didn't remember ever being in Alexandra Park, but he knew it was huge, even had a golf course in it. The rain was drumming hard on the windows, could just make out the wee pond surrounded by trees just over the iron railings. Some Alsatian dog was running about in the rain, barking and jumping, poor thing terrified of the lightning and thunder. Another rumble and the dog howled, tried to get under a bush. Seconds later the park was illuminated with light, three or four flashes.

And that's when he saw it. The shoe lying on the concrete path by the pond. A platform shoe, the kind Iris had worn since they were fashionable the first time round.

'Fuck,' he said under his breath. 'Fuck!'

He turned and made for the door, barging past the partygoers, grabbed Wattie. 'C'mon,' he said. 'We need to go. I think I know where she is.'

CHAPTER 48

McCoy raced down the stairs, Wattie clattering behind him, and out into the square.

'What's going on?' Wattie asked, standing in the close doorway. He was breathing hard, steam coming off his back. 'What's the bloody hurry all of a sudden?'

'I think I saw a shoe, in the park,' said McCoy, realising how weird it sounded. 'From Tulip's window.'

Wattie looked sceptical. 'A shoe? Whose shoe? I don't . . .'

McCoy pointed down the square to the iron fence surrounding the park.

'Just come on!' He started running. He could hear Wattie cursing behind him, splashes as he followed him through the puddles on the pavement.

There was a railing missing in the fence, looked like the gap was just wide enough to squeeze through. McCoy tried to push himself into it, just made it. Turned and Wattie was standing there, looking at the gap.

'It's too small,' he said. 'I'll never make it.'

He started to climb the fence, no use. The railings were wet, no grip. He kept trying, finally managed to haul himself up, got his weight above the top and half jumped, half dropped to the ground on the other side. There was a loud rip as he fell and half his shirt was left on the spikes at the top of the railings.

'For fuck sake!' he said, standing up, knees and hands covered in mud. He pulled off what was left of his shirt and threw it under a tree. 'You owe me a bloody new shirt after this,' he grumbled.

'Not my fault you're a big bastard' said McCoy. 'Come on.'

They hurried up the path as another rumble of thunder rolled in. Had to keep wiping the rain from their faces, trying to see. Few seconds later there were another couple of flashes and McCoy pointed up the path.

'There!' he said.

They ran up and stopped in front of a woman's platform shoe. It was red suede, worn, looked second-hand.

'That's Iris's,' said McCoy. 'I'm sure it is.'

They looked round, hard to see much in the driving rain. It was cascading off the trees, hitting the ground, splashing back up again. The paths were an inch or so deep in it already, level of the pond was rising, lapping over the top, flooding the grass.

'What now?' asked Wattie.

'I don't know,' said McCoy, looking round. 'She can't be far, maybe try—'

'You hear that?' asked Wattie.

'Hear what?' said McCoy. 'I didn't hear—'

Wattie shushed him. 'Listen!'

They stood in silence: the only noise was the drumming of the rain. McCoy was just about to tell Wattie he was imagining things when he thought he heard a moan. The hair on the back of his neck stood up and he turned around, scanned the park, trying to work out where it was coming from.

'See?' said Wattie. 'I told you.'

'Laura? Iris? You there?' shouted McCoy, trying to be heard over the rain.

There was a rustle in the bushes to the left. Wattie spun round and the bushes rustled again. McCoy picked up a stick from the ground, held it up, stood there, waiting. Started to walk towards the noise.

'Iris? That you?' he shouted. 'You—'

Suddenly there was a howl and the Alsatian dog jumped out from the bushes and tore up the path, barking and howling.

McCoy breathed out in relief, heart pumping, lowered the stick. Then he heard the moan again. Looked at Wattie. He nodded. He'd heard it, too.

'Iris, that you?' he shouted again. 'Laura?'

He moved along the row of bushes, trying to work out where the sound was coming from. He stopped, stood still, holding his breath, eyes getting accustomed to the darkness, and that's when he saw it. There was a woman's hand poking out from under one of the bushes. He jumped back before he could stop himself, swore under his breath.

'Wattie! Here!'

The moan came again and the hand moved. McCoy knelt down, pushed the bushes out the way and there was Iris; she was lying on the ground, face turned away from him.

'Iris?' he asked. 'You okay?'

Wattie knelt down beside her, picked her up, carried her out to the path and laid her down. There was blood coming from a big gash across the back of Iris's head, her eyes were closed. She was moaning, trying to say something. McCoy knelt down beside her. Put his head next to hers.

'Iris, it's Harry, are you okay?'

Her eyes flickered, opened, seemed to focus for a second, recognising him. 'Harry?' she whispered.

McCoy pushed the wet, blood-soaked hair back from her face. 'Just lie there, Iris. You're going to be all right, you're going to be all right.'

She was trying to talk; her lips were moving but there was nothing coming out. McCoy leant forward, trying to hear what she was saying. He could smell the gin on her breath and the perfume she always wore. Realised that as much as they squabbled with each other he liked her; last thing he wanted was for her to come to any harm. He held her hand. She squeezed his weakly.

'Again, Iris. Try again. I didnae hear you, what are you saying?'

He leant in even closer, his ear touching her lips.

'Laura,' said Iris. 'He's got Laura.'

McCoy's stomach dropped. 'What do you mean? Iris? Iris?'

He was cradling her head in his hands, fingers wet with blood. 'Where is he? Can you tell me?'

Her lips moved, no sound coming out, her eyes flickered for a second and they shut.

'Iris, hold on. Hold on, hen,' McCoy said, panicking.

He took his shirt off, folded it up and put it under her head. She lay there, taking small, shallow breaths, eyes flicking from side to side under the lids. McCoy looked around the park, worried someone was watching them.

'Anyone there?' he shouted.

Another rumble of thunder, and as it died down they heard a muffled scream, seemed to come from somewhere over by the left of the pond. They both looked up.

'Go!' said Wattie, 'I'll stay with Iris. Quick!'

CHAPTER 49

McCoy left Wattie cradling Iris and started running. He skirted around the side of the pond, trying to see where he was going in the driving rain. Kept battering off the bushes round the sides, sliding in the water on the path. Another lightning strike and suddenly he could see across the whole of the park. There were formal flower beds in front of him and then another wide path, almost like a road. Beyond that he couldn't see much, just some shapes and outlines in the darkness.

He ran past the flower beds, slipped and cursed, was hard to keep on his feet; the grass was mostly mud now, sodden and sticky. He stayed down for a second, tried to get his bearings. There was a shape in the distance, just at the edge of his vision, down at the bottom of the hill. He tried to wipe the water from his face to see better. Narrowed his eyes, tried to focus. It looked like a big tree or some kind of tall, thin building. Whatever it was, something was moving beside it.

He stood up, started walking in that direction. The shape seemed to move again. He strained his eyes, cursed the rain. He thought it was a man, but it was hard to tell if it was real or just the shifting of the shadows across the rain. Only one way to find out. He started running. Was about fifty yards away when he suddenly worked out what it was. It was a fountain, a huge fountain about the height of a double-decker bus.

He could hear shouting now, and it was coming from there. Someone screamed 'No!' in a terrified voice, and then there was the noise of splashing, a scream.

He started running faster, got down to the bottom of the hill, ran onto the concrete surrounding the fountain, tried to stop and skidded in a puddle. He went down hard, banging his head on the ground. He lay there for a minute, head feeling like someone had got a good kick into it. Got up on his hands and knees, then pulled himself upright using the low wall.

There was someone on the central tower, between the columns. Looked like he was on something, a rug or a pile of clothes. A rumble, another flash illuminated the park in a silvery light and he saw who it was.

Wee Tam was standing there. Grinning. It wasn't a rug he was standing on, it was a body. Laura Murray's body.

McCoy stepped into the pool.

'Stop there, McCoy,' said Wee Tam, drawing back his leg and stamping on the body beneath him. There was a moan and Laura doubled up.

'She's no dead yet, but she will be if you come any closer.'

McCoy stopped, could make out the glint of a blade in Wee Tam's left hand.

'So why don't you stay exactly where you are.'

McCoy stood there, knee deep in the water, looking up at him, unsure what to do next.

'You've interrupted me, McCoy. I was busy.' Wee Tam grinned again. 'Was almost done, in fact.'

He held the knife up to the light, then used it to scratch at the line of stitches running down his face. Blood ran down, red path on his wet shirt.

'Thought it was about time I finished what I started.' He giggled.

Laura started to moan again, tried to get out from under Wee Tam's foot. She looked over at McCoy, pale face terrified in the moonlight. 'Harry, help me, please.'

'Let her go, Tam, come on,' said McCoy. 'Just do it, son.'

Wee Tam looked down at Laura. 'Everybody thinks they can tell me what to do. Always have. You, my mum, Alec Page. All of you think I'm just some wee prick who can't run with the big boys. Even she thought that.'

He stamped on Laura and she moaned.

'Made it clear I wasn't good enough for someone like her.' He crouched down, pulled Laura's head up by her hair. 'Not so stuck up now, though, are you?'

Laura looked up at him with terror.

'Bet you've changed your tune now, bet you'd be happy to fuck me now, bet you'd do anything I asked, eh?'

He looked up at the sky, rain and blood pouring down his face.

'Tam, don't do this,' said McCoy. 'Please, I'm begging you, it's not . . .'

Tam bent over, wrapped his arm around Laura's neck and pulled her up, holding her into him. Held the knife to her stomach.

McCoy was panicking now, didn't know what he could do, how he could stop him. Shouted at him. 'Tam, Jesus Christ, she's just a wee girl!'

Laura was putting up a struggle, looking over at McCoy with wild eyes.

Tam tightened the arm around her neck and the fight gradually went out of her. She slumped against him, head back against his body, just trying to breathe through the choke hold.

'Chit chat's over, McCoy.' Wee Tam held the sharpened blade to her neck. 'Time for you to fuck off.'

McCoy started wading through the water towards him. 'I'm not going anywhere, Tam,' he said. 'Not a fucking chance. Put her down.'

'I don't think so, McCoy,' said Wee Tam and slowly pushed the blade into Laura's shoulder. She screamed, tried to struggle, realised that was making it worse and started sobbing. Wee Tam pulled the stiletto out and held it up, blood running down the blade onto his hand.

'One more step, McCoy, and I'll put it in her fucking neck while you watch. Now, fuck off. I mean it.'

McCoy started to back away, careful not to fall over in the water. Was going to try to keep him talking. 'Just leave her, Tam, you've done enough. Just leave her now. You can get away.'

Wee Tam held the blade up at her neck again and Laura screamed.

'I mean it, Harry, get tae fuck, I've work to do.'

McCoy held his hands up and climbed out the bowl of the fountain. Started backing up the path, water pouring off him, keeping his eyes on Tam, trying to buy time. Wondered what was going on with Wattie. If he was here, maybe the two of them could rush him. Chances were he'd manage to stab Laura before they got within ten yards of him.

'Stay calm, Tam. There's still a way out of this,' he shouted.

Wee Tam looked at him. Said it slowly and clearly. Like he meant it. 'Not for me, there's not.'

And then he pushed Laura off the base of the column and she plunged six feet into the water below. She landed with a cry, stood up and tried to run, but it was no use. Tam jumped down after her and was on her in a second. He punched her in the back of the head and she fell head first into the water. He reached down, pulled her head and shoulders out the water and she spluttered, coughing up water. Another lightning strike. Wee

Tam standing there, grin on his face, knee deep in the water, holding Laura by the hair in his right hand, the blade in his left.

'Tam, for fuck sake!' shouted McCoy.

And that's when he saw a figure coming down the path behind the fountain, weaving, sticking to the shadows, making its way towards them. Wattie at last. He felt a surge of hope. If he could keep Tam talking for a couple of minutes, Wattie could maybe grab him from behind.

'Tam, I can get you out of this, you just need to—'

Another booming thunderclap and then a lightning flash. And in that flash he saw it wasn't Wattie at all. It was Raeburn. His heart sank. Must be still following him, waiting for his moment to have a go at him.

'Can you fuck, Harry! You think I'm fucking stupid?' shouted Wee Tam, face contorted in fury. 'Get going! Now! Or I swear I'll fucking carve her up!'

That's when Raeburn appeared from behind the central post of the fountain and grabbed him.

McCoy started running. Tam dropped Laura and spun around, batted Raeburn aside and drew the blade down and across his chest. Raeburn stopped, looked down as his white shirt split and the blood started flowing. He put his hand to the cut and collapsed into the water. Tam turned back just as McCoy jumped off the edge of the fountain and threw himself at him.

He felt the knife go through his shoulder first, didn't feel spiky or like a cut, it felt like someone hitting him with a sledgehammer. Then he felt his head collide with Tam's and they both went down into the water.

Both struggled up at the same time, coughing and spluttering, and McCoy brought his hands up, tried to get them round Tam's neck. Just as he did he slipped on the slimy floor of the fountain and fell backwards, pulling Tam down on top of him. He screamed as Tam fell onto the knife sticking out his shoulder, pushed it in another few inches. A wave of white-hot pain hit McCoy. Felt like he was going to pass out. He opened his mouth to scream and took in a mouthful of water.

Wee Tam was properly on top of him now, hands around his neck. McCoy tried to get his up, tried to pull Tam's hands off, knock them aside, anything, but it was useless. Tam had the weight advantage. He kept trying, but he didn't seem to have any real strength in his arms any more. He was beginning to see stars, starting to feel pleasantly warm instead of cold. He could make out Tam's face above him – grimacing, neck all cords, straining to hold him down, to strangle the life out of him.

McCoy inched his hand along his shoulder, feeling for the knife. He touched it and the vibration sent another wave of pain through his body. He couldn't hear anything now, just rushing in his ears, vision getting blurry. One last chance.

He had to take it before it was too late. He said a prayer to a god he didn't believe in, gripped the knife handle and pulled as hard as he could.

The pain was unbelievable, twice as bad as it was going in. He felt the blade come out, felt the rush of hot blood against his cold skin. He moved his hand down his body to stomach level, twisted the knife up and pushed up with all his might.

There was another gush of warmth and the pressure on his neck slowly released. Tam fell down on top of him, face falling into his neck. McCoy managed to roll out from under him and sat up, trying to get some air into his lungs.

He looked up. Raeburn was standing on the path, Laura laid out at his feet.

'Is she dead?' McCoy said, trying to get up.

Raeburn looked up at him and shook his head. 'She's alive. I think she's unconscious.'

McCoy nodded, sat down in the water, let the rain fall on him, tried to get his breath back. He looked round and saw Tam floating beside him, red cloud around him.

'Never thought I'd say this, but thank Christ you were here, Raeburn,' he said.

Raeburn walked towards the fountain, climbed over the side and dropped into the knee-deep water.

'I think I'm okay,' said McCoy. He touched the skin around his wound, groaned as more blood flowed out. 'It hurts like fuck, though.'

He looked up and Raeburn was standing over

Tam. He knelt down, put his hands round the knife sticking out his stomach and pulled.

McCoy winced again. 'Christ, Raeburn, you should leave that in. It's evidence.'

Raeburn held the knife up, looked at it. Then he looked over at McCoy and smiled. 'Knew if I bided my time something would come up,' he said. 'Just didn't think it would be this easy.'

McCoy's stomach suddenly dropped. 'What do you mean? What you on about?' Tried to stand up but he was too weak.

Raeburn waded towards him through the water. 'You and Wee Tam. A fight to the death. He stabbed you, you stabbed him, then he came at you again, managed to stab you in the lung just before he died.'

'Raeburn . . .'

'Both of you dead. I live to tell the tale. How I discovered the bodies, gave poor Laura the kiss of life. Looks like I'm going to be back in the good books, eh?'

Raeburn advanced towards him, blade out in front. McCoy tried to stand up again but he'd lost too much blood, was too weak, couldn't even kneel. He slumped down again.

'You're getting off anyway, Raeburn,' he said. 'Murray told me. You don't have to do this.' And then he laughed. Even though it was true, it sounded like the lamest excuse to get him to back off.

Raeburn was getting closer now. All McCoy

could do was watch. He closed his eyes, held his face up to the sky, let the rain pelt down on him. Was definitely feeling warmer now. Thought about his son, how happy he'd been when he was born, how he'd have liked to see Angela again, hold her hand.

'Raeburn! Get the fuck away!'

He opened his eyes and Wattie was climbing over the fountain edge. Raeburn turned just in time for Wattie to punch him in the face. He went down and Wattie was on top of him.

McCoy tried to stand up, to say something but he couldn't. He couldn't hear anything any more. All he could see were the shadowy outlines of two figures fighting, rolling round in the water, then he fell back and felt the cold water close over him . . .

22ND SEPTEMBER 1973

TWO MONTHS LATER

McCoy walked out the kitchen and into the garden. Cooper was sitting on a chair by the wooden table, *Daily Record* folded at the sports pages in front of him. He looked up.

'You're out, then?' he said.

McCoy nodded, eased himself down into the other chair, tried not to grimace too much.

'You're like a bloody old man,' said Cooper.

'I feel like one,' said McCoy. 'Still bloody hurts.'

He nodded over to the hulking figure at the back of the garden. 'What's Jumbo doing?'

'Topping the hydrangeas,' said Cooper.

'What's that?' asked McCoy, getting his fags out.

'No idea,' said Cooper. 'But he's been at it all day.'

They watched Jumbo for a while, scissors in hand, tongue out in concentration. There was the first hint of autumn in the air, a sharpness, a warning of the cold air to come. Might be the last time they would be sitting out in the garden this year.

'I still can't believe you've got a garden,' said McCoy, lighting up. 'Not very gangland boss, is it?'

'Aye well, it's not all I've got,' said Cooper. 'That came this morning.'

He nodded at an envelope on the table.

McCoy peered at it. American stamp.

'From Angela,' said Cooper.

'My Angela?' asked McCoy, surprised.

'No,' said Cooper, 'some other bloody Angela we know who fucked off to America. Who'd you think?'

'Sorry,' said McCoy. 'What does it say?'

'Have a look for yourself,' said Cooper.

McCoy picked up the letter, grimaced again. Knife wound from Wee Tam was still bothering him; would do for another couple of months, according to the hospital. He slipped the letter out the envelope, started to read.

> *Hi Stevie,*
>
> *Bet I'm the last person you expected to hear from!!*
>
> *I'm sorry I took the money but I needed it for a few weeks. I've paid it back into the slush account the accountant has. Should be with you any day. Destroy the photos, they were the only copies, I promise. Sorry I messed you about. Hope we're okay.*
>
> *Angela*

McCoy put it down on the table.

'Is she?' he asked.

Cooper shrugged. 'Maybe. She's in America, probably never see her again.'

McCoy nodded. Had no real idea whether Cooper meant it or not. What Angela had done couldn't be undone, even if she had paid the money back. People like Cooper lived by their reputations. Angela's only real hope was that just he and Cooper knew she'd taken the money; any more public than that and justice would have to be seen to be done.

Cooper stood up. 'You know what's really good for the pain of being stabbed?' he said.

'Smack?' asked McCoy.

Cooper grinned. 'Smart arse. Getting pished. Come on, I'm feeling generous, I'll even go to that shithole of yours, the Victoria.'

'Not my shithole,' said McCoy, struggling to get up. 'Everybody in Partick's shithole. You buying?'

Cooper nodded. 'Why not? Looks like I'm in the money.'